"You are lost, s

In Italian, his voice wa_____
she'd ever heard, but hi_____
English sent a shiver rippling down her spine that had
nothing to do with the snow dripping from her hair.
That was trickling between her breasts and turning to
steam.

"I know exactly where I am, *signor*," she said, looking
into those lusciously dark eyes. To emphasize the
point, she eased off the fine leather glove and tapped
the piazza on the map with the tip of a crimson nail.

"No," he repeated, and this time it wasn't a question
as, never taking his eyes from hers, he wrapped long
fingers around her hand and moved her finger two
inches to the right. "You are here."

His hand was warm against her cold skin. On the
surface everything was deceptively still, but inside,
like a volcano on the point of blowing, she was liquid
heat.

She fought the urge to swallow. "I am?"

Breathe, breathe…

Hoping she sounded a lot more in control than she was,
she said, "One piazza looks very much like another on
a map. Unfortunately, neither of them is where I was
going."

"And yet here you are."

Ar_____as the
esp_____

VETTORI'S DAMSEL
IN DISTRESS

BY
LIZ FIELDING

Published in Great Britain 2015
by Mills & Boon, an imprint of Harlequin (UK) Limited,
Eton House, 18-24 Paradise Road, Richmond, Surrey, TW9 1SR

© 2015 Liz Fielding

ISBN: 978-0-263-25151-7

23-0715

Harlequin (UK) Limited's policy is to use papers that are natural, renewable and recyclable products and made from wood grown in sustainable forests. The logging and manufacturing processes conform to the legal environmental regulations of the country of origin.

Printed and bound in Spain
by CPI, Barcelona

Liz Fielding was born with itchy feet. She made it to Zambia before her twenty-first birthday and, gathering her own special hero and a couple of children on the way, lived in Botswana, Kenya and Bahrain—with pauses for sightseeing pretty much everywhere in between. She now lives in the west of England, close to the Regency grandeur of Bath and the ancient mystery of Stonehenge, and these days leaves her pen to do the traveling.

For news of upcoming books, visit Liz's website, www.lizfielding.com.

This book is dedicated to the authors I hang out with online. They are the best support group in the world— always up for a brainstorming session when the plot wobbles, ready to celebrate the good stuff and reach out through cyberspace with comfort when fate lobs lemons.

They know who they are.

CHAPTER ONE

'Life is like ice cream on a hot day. Enjoy it before it melts.'
—from *Rosie's Little Book of Ice Cream*

IT WAS LATE and throwing down a sleety rain when Geli emerged from the Metro at Porta Garibaldi into the Milan night. Her plan had been to take a taxi for the last short leg of her journey but it was par for the course, on a day when everything had conspired to keep her from her destination, that there wasn't one in sight.

Terrific.

The weather had been mild with a promise of spring in the air when she'd left Longbourne and, optimistically, she'd assumed Italy would be warmer; something to do with all those sun-soaked travel programmes on the television, no doubt. If she'd had the sense to check the local weather she'd have been wearing thermals instead of lace beneath her dress, leggings over her ultra-sheer black tights and a lot more than a lace choker around her neck.

Not the most practical outfit for travelling but she was going to Milan, style capital of Europe, where the inhabitants didn't wear joggers unless they were jogging and policewomen wore high heels.

In her determination to make a fashionable impression

she had overlooked the fact that Milan was in the north of Italy. Where there were mountains. And, apparently, sleet.

Okaaay...

According to the details she'd downloaded from the Internet, her apartment was no more than a ten-minute stroll from the Metro. She could handle a bit of sleet. In style.

She checked her map and, having orientated herself, she pulled the wide hood of her coat over ears that were beginning to tingle, shouldered her roomy leather tote and, hauling her suitcase behind her, set off.

New country, new start, new life.

Unlike her sisters, who were married, raising families and, with their rapidly expanding ice cream events business, had life all sewn up and sorted, she was throwing herself into the dark—literally.

With little more than an Italian phrasebook and a head full of ideas, she was setting out to grab every experience that life offered her. If, as she crossed the railway bridge into the unknown, the thrill of nervous excitement that shot through her was edged with a ripple of apprehension, a shiver of fear—well, that was perfectly natural. She was the baby of the family.

She might be the one with the weird clothes, the 'attitude', but they knew it was all front; that this was her first time out in the world. Okay, she'd been to Italy before, but that was on a student study trip and she'd been with a group of people she knew. This time she was on her own, without the family safety net of loving hands reaching out to steady her if she stumbled. To catch her if she fell. Testing herself...

'Scusi!'

'Sorry...um...*scusi*...' She steered her case to one side to let someone in a hurry pass her and then, as she looked up, she saw the colourful street art gleaming under the street lights—bright tropical scenes that lit up dull concrete—and caught her breath.

Despite the icy stuff stinging her face, excitement won out as she remembered why she had chosen Italy, Milan... Isola.

The minute she'd opened a magazine, seen the photographs, read about this enclave of artists, musicians, designers all doing their own thing, she'd been hooked. This was a place where she could spread her wings, explore her love of fashion, seek new ways of making art and maybe, just maybe fall in love. Nothing serious, not for keeps, but for fun.

Twenty minutes later, her face stiff with cold, the freezing stuff finding its way into a hood designed more for glamour than protection, and totally lost, the bounce had left her step.

She could almost see her oldest sister, Elle, shaking her head and saying, *You're so impatient, Geli! Why didn't you wait for a taxi?*

Because it was an *adventure*! And the directions had been simple enough. She'd counted the turnings, checked the name of the street, turned right and her apartment should be there, right in front of her, on the corner.

Except it wasn't.

Instead of the pink-painted five-storey house on the corner of a street of equally pretty houses that overlooked the twice-weekly market, she was faced with eight-feet-high wooden barriers surrounding a construction site.

No need to panic. Obviously she'd missed a turning. There had been a couple of narrow openings—more alleys than streets—that she'd thought were too small to be the turnings on her map. Obviously she was wrong.

She backtracked, recounted and headed down one just about wide enough to take a Fiat 500. It ended in a tiny courtyard piled up with crates and lit by a dim lamp over what looked like the back entrance to a shop. In the dark something moved, a box fell, and she beat a hasty retreat.

The few people about had their heads down and her, *'Scusi...'* was blown away on wind that was driving the sleet, thicker now, into her face.

It was time to take another look at the map.

Ducking into the shelter of the doorway of a shuttered shop, she searched her tote for the powerful mini torch given to her by her explorer brother-in-law as a parting gift.

She'd reminded him that she was going to one of the world's great cities rather than venturing into the jungle. His response was that in his experience there was little difference and as something wet and hairy brushed against her leg she let out a nervous shriek.

Make that one for the explorer.

A plaintive mew reassured her and the bright beam of her torch picked out a tiny kitten, wet fur sticking to its skin, cowering in the doorway.

'Hey, sweetie,' she said softly, reaching out to it, but it backed away nervously. She knew how it felt. 'You're much too little to be out by yourself on a night like this.'

The poor creature, wetter and certainly colder than she was, mewed pitifully in agreement. She'd bought a cheese sandwich on the plane but had been too churned up with nerves and excitement to eat it and she opened it up, broke a piece off and offered it to the kitten. Hunger beat fear and it snatched the food from her fingers, desperately licking at the butter.

Geli broke off another piece and then turned her attention to the simple street map. Clearly she'd taken a wrong turn and wandered into the commercial district, now closed for the night, but for the life of her couldn't see where she'd gone wrong.

Phoning Signora Franco, her landlady, was not an option. The *signora*'s English was about on a par with her own Italian—enthusiastic, but short on delivery. What she needed was one of Isola's famous cafés or bars, somewhere warm and dry with people who would know the area and, bracing herself to face to what was now whiter, more solid than mere sleet, she peered along the street.

Behind her, the kitten mewed and she sighed. There were a few lights on in upper floors but down here everything was shut up. The tiny creature was on its own and was too small to survive the night without shelter. The location might be new, but some things never changed.

Inevitably, having begged for help, the kitten panicked when she bent and scooped it up but she eased it into one of the concealed seam pockets hidden amongst the full layers of her coat.

She'd come back tomorrow and see if she could find someone who'd take responsibility for it but right now it was time to put her Italian to the test. She'd memorised the question and could rattle off '*Dov'è* Via Pepone?' without a second thought. Understanding the answers might be more of a problem.

She stuffed her torch, along with the useless map, in her bag and began to retrace her steps back to the road from the station, this time carrying straight on instead of turning off.

In the photographs she'd seen it had been summer; there were open-air jazz concerts, the communal garden and collective 'bring a dish' lunches where every Tuesday the local people gathered to share food and reinforce the community ties. People sitting outside trendy cafés. Perfect.

This was the wrong time of day, the wrong time of year. Even the famous Milan 'promenade' was on hold but, encouraged by a sudden snatch of music—as if someone had opened a door very briefly—she hurried to the corner and there, on the far side of a piazza, lights shone through a steamy window.

It was Café Rosa, famous for jazz, cocktails and being a hangout of local artists who used the walls as a gallery. More relieved than she cared to admit, she slithered across the cobbles and pushed open the door.

She was immediately swathed in warmth, the rich scent of luscious food and cool music from a combo on a tiny stage in the corner mingling with bursts of steam from the expresso machine. Tables of all shapes and sizes were filled with people eating, drinking, gossiping, and a tall dark-haired man was leaning against the counter talking to the barista.

If the scene had been posed by the Italian Tourist Board it couldn't have been more perfect and, despite the cold, she felt a happy little rush of anticipation.

A few people had turned when the door opened and the chatter died away until the only sound was the low thrum of a double bass.

The man standing at the bar, curious about what had caught everyone's attention, half turned and anticipation whooshed off the scale in an atavistic charge of raw desire; instant, bone-deep need for a man before you heard his voice, felt his touch, knew his name.

For a moment, while she remembered how to breathe, it felt as if someone had pressed the pause button on the scene, freezing the moment in soft focus. Muted colours reflected in polished steel, lights shimmering off the bottles and glasses behind the bar, her face reflected, ghostlike, behind the advertisement on a mirror. And Mr Italy with his kiss-me mouth and come-to-bed eyes.

Forget the thick dark hair and cheekbones sharp enough to write their own modelling contract, it was those chocolate-dark eyes that held her transfixed. If they had been looking out of a tourist poster there would be a stampede to book holidays in Italy.

He straightened, drawing attention to the way his hair

curled onto his neck, a pair of scandalously broad shoulders, strong wrists emerging from folded-back cuffs.

'*Signora...*' he murmured as he moved back a little to make room for her at the counter and, oh, joy, his voice matched the face, the body.

She might have passed out for lack of oxygen at that moment but a tall, athletic-looking blonde placed a tiny cup of espresso in front of him before—apparently unaware that she was serving a god—turning to her.

'*Sta nevicando? E brutto tempo.*'

What?

Oh...

Flustered at being confronted with phrases that hadn't featured so far on the Italian course she'd downloaded onto her iPod, she took the safe option and, having sucked in a snowflake that was clinging to her lip, she lowered her hood. The chatter gradually resumed and, finally getting a *move it* message through to her legs, she parked her suitcase and crossed to the bar.

'*Cosa prendi, signora?*'

Oh, whew, something she understood. 'Um...*Vorrai un espresso...s'il vous plait...*' Her answer emerged in a mangled mixture of English, Italian and French. 'No...I mean...' *Oh, heck.*

The blonde grinned. 'Don't worry. I got the gist,' she replied, her English spiced with an Australian accent.

'Oh, thank goodness you're English. No! Sorry, Australian—' Achingly conscious of the man leaning against the counter, an impressive thigh stretching the cloth of his jeans just inches from her hip, she attempted to recover the cool, sophisticated woman of the world image with which she'd intended to storm Milan. 'Shall I go out, walk around the block and try that again?'

The woman grinned. 'Stay right where you are. I'll get

that espresso. You've just arrived in Isola?' she asked as she measured the coffee.

'In Isola, in Milan, in Italy. I've been working on my Italian—I picked some up when I spent a month in Tuscany as a student—but I learned French at school and it seems to be my brain's foreign language default setting when I panic.'

Her brain was too busy drooling over Mr Italy to give a toot.

'Give it a week,' the woman said. 'Can I get you anything else?'

'A side order of directions?' she asked hopefully, doing her best to ignore the fact that it wasn't just her brain; her entire body was responding on a visceral level to the overdose of pheromones wafting in her direction. It was like being bombarded by butterflies. Naked...

She was doing her level best not to stare at him.

Was he looking at her?

'You are lost, *signora*?' he asked.

In Italian, his voice was just about the sexiest thing she'd ever heard, but his perfect, lusciously accented English sent a shiver rippling down her spine that had nothing to do with the snow dripping from her hair. That was trickling between her breasts and turning to steam.

She took a breath and, doing her best to remember why she was there, said, 'Not lost exactly...' Retrieving the apartment details from her tote, she placed it, map side up, on the counter and turned to him, intending to explain what had happened. He was definitely looking and, confronted with those eyes, the questioning kink of his brow, language of any description deserted her.

'No?' he prompted.

Clearly he was used to women losing the power of speech in his presence. From the relaxed way he was leaning against the bar, to eyes that, with one look made her feel as if he owned her, everything about him screamed danger.

First day in Isola and she could imagine having a lot of fun with Mr Italy and, from the way he was looking at her, he was thinking much the same thing about her.

Was that how it had been for her mother that first time? One look from some brawny roustabout at the annual village fair and she'd been toast?

'I know exactly where I am, *signor*,' she said, looking into those lusciously dark eyes. To emphasise the point she eased off the fine leather glove that had done little to keep her hand warm and tapped the piazza with the tip of a crimson nail.

'No,' he repeated, and this time it wasn't a question as, never taking his eyes from hers, he wrapped long fingers around her hand and moved her finger two inches to the right. 'You are here.'

His hand was warm against her cold skin. On the surface everything was deceptively still but inside, like a volcano on the point of blowing, she was liquid heat.

She fought the urge to swallow. 'I am?'

She was used to people staring at her. From the age of nine she had been the focus of raised eyebrows and she'd revelled in it.

This man's look was different. It sizzled through her and, afraid that the puddle of snow melting at her feet was about to turn to steam, she turned to the map.

It didn't help. Not one bit. His hand was still covering hers, long ringless fingers darkly masculine against her own pale skin, and she found herself wondering how they would look against her breast. How they would feel…

Under the layers of black—coat, dress, the lace of her bra—her nipples hardened in response to her imagination, sending touch-me messages to all parts south and she bit on her lower lip to stop herself from whimpering.

Breathe, breathe…

She cleared the cobwebs from her throat and, hoping she sounded a lot more in control than she was, said, 'One piazza looks very much like another on a map. Unfortunately, neither of them is where I was going.'

'And yet here you are.'

And yet here she was, falling into eyes as dark as the espresso in his cup.

The café retreated. The bright labels on bottles behind the bar, the clatter of cutlery, the low thrum of a double bass became no more than a blur of colour, sound. All her senses were focused on the touch of his fingers curling about her hand, his molten eyes reflecting back her own image. For a moment nothing moved until, abruptly, he turned away and used the hand that had been covering hers to pick up his espresso and drain it in one swallow.

He'd looked away first and she waited for the rush of power that always gave her but it didn't come. For the first time in her life it didn't feel like a victory.

Toast…

'Where are you going, *signora*?' He carefully replaced the tiny cup on its saucer.

'Here…' She looked down but the ink had run, leaving a dirty splodge where the name of the street had been.

'Tell him the address and Dante will point you in the right direction,' the barista said, putting an espresso in front of her. 'He knows every inch of Isola.'

'Dante?' Geli repeated. 'As in the *Inferno*?' No wonder he was so hot… Catching the barista's knowing grin, she quickly added, 'Or perhaps your mother is an admirer of the Pre-Raphaelites?'

'Are you visiting someone?' he asked, ignoring the question.

'No.' Mentally kicking herself for speaking before her brain was in gear—he must have heard that one a thousand times—she shook her head. 'I'm here to work. I've leased an apartment for a year. Geli Amery,' she added, offering him her hand without a thought for the consequences.

He wrapped his hand around hers and held it.

'Dante Vettori.' Rolled out in that sexy Italian accent, his name was a symphony of seduction. 'Your name is Jelly?' He lifted an eyebrow, but not like the disapproving old biddies in the village shop. Not at all. 'Like the wobbly stuff the British inflict on small children at birthday parties?'

Okay, so she'd probably asked for that with her stupid *'Inferno'* remark, but he wasn't the only one to have heard it all before.

'Or add to peanut butter in a sandwich if you're American?' She lifted an eyebrow right back at him, which was asking for trouble but who knew if he'd ever lift his eyebrow at her like that again? This was definitely one of those 'live for the day' moments she had vowed to grab with both hands and she was going for it.

'é possibile,' he said, the lines bracketing his mouth deepening into a smile. 'But I suspect not.'

He could call her what he liked as long as he kept smiling like that…

'You suspect right. Geli is short for Angelica—as in *angelica archangelica*, which I'm told is a very handsome plant.' And she smiled back. 'You may be more familiar with its crystallised stem. The British use it to decorate the cakes and trifles that they inflict on small children at birthday parties.'

His laugh was rich and warm, creating a fan of creases around his eyes, emphasising those amazing cheekbones, widening his mouth and drawing attention to a lower lip that she wanted to lick…

Make that burnt toast…

In an attempt to regain control of her vital organs, Geli

picked up her espresso and downed it in a single swallow, Italian style. It was hotter than she expected, shocking her out of the lusty mist.

'I had intended to take a taxi—' Her vocal cords were still screaming from the hot coffee and the words came out as little more than a squeak. She cleared her throat and tried again. 'Unfortunately, there were none at the Porta Garibaldi and on the apartment details it said that Via Pepone was only a ten-minute walk.'

'Taxis are always in short supply when the weather's bad,' the barista said, as Dante, frowning now, turned the details over to look at the picture of the pretty pink house where she'd be living for the next year. 'Welcome to Isola, Geli. Lisa Vettori—I'm from the Australian branch of the family. Dante's my cousin and, although you wouldn't know it from the way he's lounging around on the wrong side of the counter, Café Rosa is his bar.'

'I pay you handsomely so that I can stay on this side of the bar,' he reminded her, without looking up.

'Make the most of it, mate. I have a fitting for a brides-maid dress in Melbourne on Tuesday. Unless you get your backside in gear and find a temp to take my place, come Sunday you'll be the one getting up close and personal with the Gaggia.' She took a swipe at the marble counter top with a cloth to remove an invisible mark. 'Have you got a job lined up, Geli?' she asked.

'A job?'

'You said you were here to work. Have you ever worked in a bar? Only there's a temporary—'

'If you've been travelling all day you must be hungry,' Dante said, cutting his cousin off in mid-sentence. 'We'll have the risotto, Lisa.' And, holding onto the details of her apartment and, more importantly, the map, he headed for a table for two that was tucked away in a quiet corner.

CHAPTER TWO

'There's nothing more cheering than a good friend when you're in trouble—except a good friend with ice cream.'

—from *Rosie's Little Book of Ice Cream*

TOO SURPRISED TO REACT, Geli didn't move. Okay, so there had been some fairly heavy-duty flirting going on, but that was a bit arrogant—

Dante pulled out a chair and waited for her to join him.

Make that quite a lot arrogant. Did he really think she would simply follow him?

'Angelica?'

No one used her full name, but he said it with a 'g' so soft that it felt like chocolate melting on her tongue and while her head was still saying, *Oh, please...*her body went to him as if he'd tugged a chain.

'Give me your coat,' he said, 'and I'll hang it up to dry.'

She swallowed.

It was late. She should be on her way but for that she needed directions, which was a good, practical reason to do as he said. Then again, nothing that had happened since she'd walked through the door of Café Rosa had been about the practicalities and, letting her tote slide from her shoulder onto the chair, she dropped her glove on the table and began to tug at its pair.

Warm now, the fine leather clung to her skin and as she removed her glove, one finger at a time, Geli discovered that there was more than one way of being in control.

A chain had two ends and now Dante was the one being hauled in as she slowly revealed her hand with each unintentionally provocative tug.

She dropped the glove beside its pair and everything— the heartbeat pounding in her ears, her breathing—slowed right down as, never taking her eyes off his, she lowered her hand and, one by one, began to slip the small jet buttons that nipped her coat into her waist.

There were a dozen of them and, taking her time, she started at the bottom. One, two, three... His gaze never wavered for a second until the bias cut swathes of velvet, cashmere and butter-soft suede—flaring out in layers that curved from just below her knees at the front to her heels at the back—fell open to reveal the black scoop-necked mini-dress that stopped four inches above her knees.

She waited a heartbeat and then turned and let the coat slip from her shoulders, leaving him to catch it.

An arch *got you* lift of an eyebrow as she thanked him should leave him in no doubt that the next move was up to him and she was more than ready for anything he had to offer, but as she glanced over her shoulder, fell into the velvet softness of his eyes, she forgot the plot.

He was so close. His breath was warm on her cheek, his mouth was inches away and her eyebrow stayed put as she imagined closing the gap and taking his delicious lower lip between hers.

Make that burned to a crisp toast. Toast about to burst into flames...

She blinked as a clatter of cutlery shattered the moment and Dante looked down at her coat as if wondering where it had come from.

'I'll hang this by the heater to dry,' he said.

'Are you mad?' Lisa, the table swiftly laid, took it from him. 'You don't hang something like this over a radiator as if it's any old chain store raincoat. This kind of quality costs a fortune and it needs tender loving care.' She checked the label. 'Dark Angel.' She looked up. 'Angel?' she repeated and then, with a look of open admiration, 'Is that you, Geli?'

'What? Oh, yes,' she said, grateful for the distraction. Falling into bed for fun with a man was one thing. Falling into anything else was definitely off the agenda... 'Dark Angel is my label.'

'You're a fashion designer?'

'Not exactly. I make one-off pieces. I studied art but I've been making clothes all my life and somehow I've ended up combining the two.'

'Clothes as art?' She grinned. 'I like it.'

'Let's hope you're not the only one.'

'Not a chance. This is absolutely lush. Did you make the choker, too?' she asked. 'Or is that an original?'

'If only...' Geli touched the ornate Victorian-style lace and jet band at her throat. 'It's recycled from stuff in my odds and ends box. I cut my dress from something I found on the "worn once" rack at the church jumble sale and—' if she kept talking she wouldn't grab Dante Vettori '—my coat was made from stuff I've collected over the years.'

'Well...wow. You are so going to fit in here. Upcycling is really big in Isola.'

'It's one of the reasons I'm here. I want to work with people who are doing the same kind of thing.'

'And I suggested you might want a job behind the bar.' She rolled her eyes. 'If you've got something you want to exhibit I'm sure Dan will find space for it.' She glanced at him, but he offered no encouragement. 'Right, well, I'll go and find a hanger for this,' she said, holding the coat up so that it didn't touch the floor. She'd only gone a couple of steps when she stopped. 'Geli, there's something moving... Omigod!' She screamed and, forgetting all about its lushness, dropped the coat and leapt back. 'It's a rat!'

The musicians stopped playing mid-note. The patrons of the café, who had resumed chatting, laughing, eating, turned as one.

Then the kitten, confused, frightened, bolted across the floor and pandemonium broke out as men leapt to their feet and women leapt on chairs.

'It's all right!' Geli yelled as she dived under a table to grab the kitten before some heavy-footed male stamped on the poor creature. Terrified, it scratched and sank its little needle teeth deep into the soft pad of her thumb before she emerged with it grasped in her hand. 'It's a kitten!' Then, in desperation when that didn't have any effect, *'Uno kitty!'*

She held it up so that everyone could see. It had dried a little in the shelter of her pocket but it was a scrawny grey scrap, not much bigger than her hand. No one looked convinced and, when a woman let loose a nervous scream, Dante hooked his arm around her waist and swept her and the kitten through the café to a door that led to the rear.

As it swung shut behind him the sudden silence was brutal.

'Uno kitty?' Dante demanded, looming over her. Much too close.

'I don't know the Italian for kitten,' she said, shaken by the speed at which events had overtaken her.

'It's *gattino*, but Lisa is right, that wretched creature looks more like a drowned rat.'

And the one word you didn't want to hear if you were in the catering business was *rat*.

'I'm sorry but I found it shivering in a doorway. It was soaking wet. Freezing. I couldn't leave it there.'

'Maybe not—' he didn't look convinced '—but rats, cats, it's all the same to the health police.'

'I understand. My sisters are in the catering business.' And in similar circumstances they would have killed her. 'I only stopped to ask for directions. I didn't mean to stay for more than a minute or two.'

Epic distraction…

She was about to repeat her apology when the door opened behind them. Dante dropped his arm from her waist as Lisa appeared with her coat and bag over one arm and trailing her suitcase, leaving a cold space.

'Have you calmed them down?' he asked.

'Nothing like free drinks all round to lighten the mood. Bruno is dealing with it.'

Geli groaned. 'It's my fault. I'll pay for them.'

'No…' Lisa and Dante spoke as one then Lisa added, 'The first rule of catering is that if you see a rat, you don't scream. The second is that you don't shout, *It's a rat*… Unfortunately, when I felt something move and that something was grey and furry I totally— Omigod, Geli, you're bleeding!'

Geli glanced at the trickle of blood running down her palm. 'It's nothing. The poor thing panicked.'

'A poor thing that's been who knows where,' Lisa replied, 'eating who knows what filth. Come on, we'll go upstairs and I'll clean it up for you.'

'It's okay, honestly,' Geli protested, now seriously embarrassed. 'It's late and Signora Franco, the woman who owns the apartment I've rented, will be waiting for me with the key. I would have called her to let her know my plane had been delayed but her English is even worse than my Italian.'

Geli glanced at her watch. She'd promised to let her sisters know when she was safely in her apartment and it was well past ten o'clock. She'd warned them that her plane had been delayed but if she didn't text them soon they'd be imagining all sorts.

'There's no need to worry about Signora Franco,' Dante said.

'Oh, but—'

'Via Pepone has been demolished to make way for an office block,' he said, his expression grim. 'I hoped to break it to you rather more gently, but I'm afraid the apartment you have rented no longer exists.'

It took a moment for what Dante had said to sink in. There was no Via Pepone? No apartment? 'But I spoke to Signora Franco…'

'Find a box for Rattino, Lis, before he does any more damage.' Dante took her coat and bag from his cousin and ushered her towards the stairs.

Geli didn't move. This had to be a mistake. 'Maybe I have the name of the street wrong?' she said, trying not to think about how the directions on the map she'd been sent had taken her to a construction site. 'Maybe it's a typo—'

'Let's get your hand cleaned up. Are your tetanus shots up to date?' he asked.

'What? Oh, yes…' She stood her ground for another ten seconds but she couldn't go back into the restaurant with the kitten and if there was a problem with the apartment she had to know. And Lisa was right—the last thing she needed was an infected hand.

Concentrate on that. And repeating her apology wouldn't hurt.

'I really am sorry about the rat thing,' she said as she began to climb the stairs. 'The kitten really would have died if I'd left it out there.'

'So you picked it up and put it in the pocket of your beautiful coat?' He liked her coat… 'Do you do that often?'

'All the time,' she admitted. 'Coat pockets, bags, the basket of my bicycle. My sisters did their best to discourage me, but eventually they gave it up as a lost cause.'

'And are they always this ungrateful? Your little strays?'

As they reached the landing he took her hand in his to check the damage and Geli forgot about the kitten, her apartment, pretty much everything as the warmth of his fingers seeped beneath her skin and into the bone.

When she didn't answer, he looked up and the temperature rose to the point where she was blushing to her toes.

Toast in flames. Smoke alarm hurting her eardrums...

'Frightened animals lash out,' she said quickly, waiting for him to open one of the doors, but he kept her hand in his and headed up a second flight of stairs.

There was only one door at the top. He let go of her hand, took a key from his pocket, unlocked it and pushed it open, standing back so that she could go ahead of him.

Geli wasn't sure what she'd expected; she hadn't actually been doing a lot of thinking since he'd turned and looked at her. Her brain had been working overtime dealing with the bombardment of her senses—new sights, new scents, a whole new level of physical response to a man.

Maybe a staff restroom...

Or maybe not.

There was a small entrance hall with hooks for coats, a rack for boots. Dante hung her coat beside a worn waxed jacket then opened an inner door to a distinctly masculine apartment.

There were tribal rugs from North Africa on the broad planks of a timber floor gleaming with the patina of age, splashes of brilliantly coloured modern art on the walls, shelves crammed with books. There was the warm glow and welcoming scent of logs burning in a wood stove and an enormous old leather sofa pulled up invitingly in front of it. The kind with big rounded arms—perfect for curling up against—and thick squashy cushions.

'You live here,' she said stupidly.

'Yes.' His face was expressionless as he tossed her bag

onto the sofa. 'I'm told that it's very lower middle class to live over the shop but it suits me.'

'Well, that's just a load of tosh.'

'Tosh?' he repeated, as if he'd never heard the word before. Maybe he hadn't but it hardly needed explaining. It was all there in the sound.

'Total tosh. One day I'm going to live in a house exactly like this,' she said, turning around so that she could take in every detail. 'The top floor for me, workshops on the floor below me and a showroom on the ground floor—' she came to halt, facing him '—and my great-grandfather was the younger son of an earl.'

'An earl?'

Realising just how pompous that must have sounded, Geli said, 'Of course my grandmother defied her father and married beneath her, so we're not on His Lordship's Christmas card list, which may very well prove the point. Not that they're on ours,' she added.

'They disowned her?'

She shrugged. 'Apparently they had other, more obedient children.'

And that was more personal information than she'd shared with anyone, ever, but she didn't want him to think any of them gave a fig for their aristocratic relations. Even *in extremis* they'd never turned to them for help.

'The family, narrow-minded and full of secrets, is the source of all our discontents,' Dante replied, clearly quoting someone.

'Who said that?' she asked.

'I just did.'

'No, I meant…' She shook her head. He knew exactly what she meant. 'I have a great family.' For years it had just been the four of them. Her sisters, Elle and Sorrel, and their grandmother. They'd been solid. A tight-knit unit standing against the world. That had all changed the day a stranger had arrived on the doorstep with an ice cream van. Now her sisters were not only successful business-women, but married and producing babies as if they were going out of fashion, while Great-Uncle Basil—who'd sent the van—and Grandma were warming their old bones in the south of France.

'You are very fortunate.'

'Yes…' If you ignored the empty space left by her mother. By an unknown father. By the legions of aunts, uncles, cousins that she didn't know. Who didn't know her.

'The bathroom is through here,' Dante said, opening a door to an inner hall.

'Il bagno…' she said brightly, making an effort to think in Italian as she followed him. Making an effort to think.

His *bagno* would, in estate agent speak, have been de-scribed as a 'roomy vintage-style' bathroom. In this case she was pretty certain the fittings—a stately roll-top bath with claw feet and gleaming brass taps, a loo with a high tank and a wide, deep washbasin—were the real deal.

'I'll shut the door so that you can put the kitten down,' he said, and the roominess shrank in direct proportion to the width of his shoulders as he shut the door. 'He can't escape.'

'I wouldn't bank on it,' she said as, carefully unhook-ing the creature's claws from the front of her dress, she set it down in the bath. 'And if it went under the *bagno*…' She left him to imagine what fun it would be trying to tempt him out.

Dante glanced down as the kitten, a tiny front paw rest-ing against the steep side of the bath, protested at this in-dignity. 'Smart thinking.'

'When you've taken a room apart looking for a kitten that's managed to squeeze through a crack in the skirting board,' she told him, 'you learn to keep them confined.'

'You live an interesting life, Angelica Amery,' he said,

watching as she attempted to slip the buttons at her wrist without getting blood on her dress.

'Isn't that a curse in China?' she asked.

'I believe that would be "May you live in interesting times",' he said, 'but you'll forgive me if I say that you don't dress like a woman in search of a quiet life.'

'Well, you know what they say,' she replied. 'Life is short. Eat ice cream every day.'

A smile deepened the lines bracketing his mouth, fanned out from his eyes. 'What "they" would that be?'

'More of an "it", actually. It's Rosie, our vintage ice cream van. In her *Little Book of Ice Cream*.' He looked confused—who wouldn't? 'Of course she has a vested interest.'

'Right...'

'It's the sentiment that matters, Dante. You can substitute whatever lifts your spirits. Chocolate? Cherries?' No response. 'Cheese?' she offered, hoping to make him laugh. Or at least smile.

'*Permesso?*' He indicated her continuing struggle with shaky fingers and fiddly buttons.

Okay, it wasn't that funny and, giving up on the buttons, she surrendered her hand. '*Prego.*'

He carefully unfastened the loops holding the cuff together, folded the sleeve back out of the way, then, taking hold of her wrist, he pumped a little liquid soap into her palm.

Her heart rate, which was already going well over the speed limit, accelerated and, on the point of telling him that she could handle it from here, she took her own advice. Okay, it wasn't ice cream or even chocolate, but how often was a seriously scrumptious man going to take her hand between his and—?

'*Coraggio,*' he murmured as his thumb brushed her palm and a tiny whimper escaped her lips.

'Mmm…'

He turned to look at her, the edge of his faintly stub-bled jaw an enticing whisper away from her lips. 'Does that sting?'

'No…' She shook her head. 'That's not…stinging.'

She was feeling no pain as he gently massaged the soap between her fingers, around her thumb, wrist and into her palm. All sensation was centred much lower as he rinsed off the soap, pulled a thick white towel from a pile and carefully dried her hand.

'Va bene?' he asked.

'Va bene,' she repeated. Very, very *bene* indeed. He was so deliciously gentle. So very *thorough*.

'Hold on. This *will* sting,' he warned as he took a box of antiseptic wipes from the cupboard over the sink and opened a pouch.

'I'll try not to scream,' she said but, taking no chances— her knees were in a pitifully weak state—she did as she was told and, putting her other hand on his shoulder, hung on.

She'd feel such a fool if she collapsed at his feet.
Really.

His shoulder felt wonderfully solid beneath the soft wool shirt. He was so close that she was breathing in the scent of coffee, warm male skin and, as his hair slid in a thick silky wedge over his forehead, she took a hit of the herby shampoo he used. It completely obliterated the sharp smell of antiseptic.

He opened a dressing and applied it carefully to the soft mound of flesh beneath her thumb.

'All done.'

'No…'

Dante looked up, a silent query buckling the space be-tween his brows and her mouth dried. He'd been right about the need to hang on. The word had slipped through her lips while her brain was fully occupied in keeping her vertical.

'There's something else?' he asked.

'Yes… No…' She hadn't been criticising his first aid skills; she just hadn't wanted him to stop. 'It's nothing.'

'Tell me,' he pressed her, all concern.

What on earth could she say? The answer that instantly popped into her mind was totally outrageous but Dante was waiting and she managed a careless little shrug and waited for him to catch on.

Nothing…

For heaven's sake, everyone knew what you did when someone hurt themselves. Did she have to spell it out for him?

'Un bacio?' she prompted.

'A kiss?' he repeated, no doubt wondering if she had the least clue what she was saying.

'Sì…' It was in an Italian phrasebook that her middle sister, Sorrel, had bought her. Under 'People', sub-section 'Getting Intimate', which she'd found far more engrossing than the section on buying a train ticket.

Posso baciarti?—Can I kiss you?—was there, along with other such useful phrases as *Can I buy you a drink?*, *Let's go somewhere quieter* and *Stop bothering me!*

There hadn't been a phrase for kissing it better. Perhaps it was in the 'Health' section.

'This is considered beneficial?' Dante asked.

He was regarding her with such earnestness that Geli wished the floor would just open up and swallow her. Then the flicker of a muscle at the corner of his mouth betrayed him and she knew that Dante Vettori had been teasing her. That he'd known exactly what she meant. That it was going to be all right. Better than all right—the man wasn't just fabulous to look at; he had a sense of humour.

'Not just beneficial,' she assured him. 'It's absolutely essential.'

'Forgive me. I couldn't have been paying attention when this was covered in first aid,' he said, the muscle working overtime to contain the smile fighting to break out. 'You may have to show me.'

Show him? Excitement rippled through her at the thought. It was outrageous but a woman in search of an interesting life had to seize the day. Lick the ice cream—

Coraggio, Geli—

'It's very simple, Dante. You just put your lips together—'

'Like this?'

She caught her breath as he raised her hand and, never taking his eyes from hers, touched his lips to the soft mound of her palm, just below the dressing he'd applied with such care.

'Exactly like that,' she managed through a throat that felt as if it had been stuffed with silk chiffon. 'I'm not sure why it works—'

'I imagine it's to do with the application of heat,' he said, his voice as soft as the second warm kiss he breathed into her palm. Her knees turned to water and her hand slid from his shoulder to clutch a handful of shirt. Beneath it, she could feel the thud of his heartbeat—a slow, steady counterpoint to her own racing pulse. 'Is that hot enough?'

Was he still teasing? The threatened smile had never appeared but his mouth was closer. Much closer.

'The more heat,' she murmured, her words little more than a whisper, 'the more effective the cure.'

'How hot do you want it to be, Angelica?' His voice trickled over her skin like warm honey and his eyes were asking the question that had been there since he'd turned and looked at her. Since he'd put his hand on hers and moved it across the map.

His hand was at her back now, supporting her, his breath soft against her lips and her answer was to lift the hand he'd kissed, slide her fingers through his dark silky hair. This close, she could see that the velvet dark of his irises was shot through with tiny gold sparks, sparks that arced between them, igniting some primitive part of her brain.

'Hot,' she murmured. *'Molto, molto caldo...'* And she touched his luscious lower lip with her mouth, her tongue, sucking in the taste of rich dark coffee that lingered there. Maybe it was the caffeine—on her tongue on his—but, as she closed her eyes and he angled his mouth to deepen the kiss, cradled her head, she felt a zingy hyper-tingle of heat lick through her veins, seep into her skin, warming her, giving her life.

'Hello?' Lisa's voice filtered through the golden mist. 'Everything okay?' she called, just feet from the bathroom door and, from the urgency with which she said it, Geli suspected that it wasn't the first time she'd asked.

Geli opened her eyes as Dante raised his head, took a step back, steadying her as a cold space opened up between them where before there had been closeness, heat.

'Don't open the door or the kitten will escape,' he warned sharply.

'Right... I just meant to tell you that there are antiseptic wipes in the cabinet.'

'I found them.' His hand slid from her shoulder and he reached for the door handle. 'We're all done.'

Noooo... But he'd already opened the door and stepped through it, closing it behind him. Leaving her alone to catch her breath, put some stiffeners in her knees and recover what little dignity remained after she'd flung herself at a total stranger.

Okay, there had been some heavy-duty flirting going on, but most of it had been on her side. Dante, realising that she was in a mess, had tried to sit her down and quietly explain about the apartment while she had put on a display that wouldn't have disgraced a burlesque dancer. One minute she'd been struggling with her glove and the next…

Where on earth had that performance come from? She wasn't that woman.

Bad enough, but when he'd told her that she'd been the victim of some Internet con she'd practically thrown herself at him.

What on earth had she been *thinking*?

What on earth must *he* be thinking?

Well, that was easy. He had to be thinking that she'd do anything in return for a bed for the night and who could blame him?

As for her, she hadn't been thinking at all. She might have been telling herself that she was going to grab every moment, live her mother's 'seize the day' philosophy, but it was like learning how to parachute: you had to make practice jumps first—learn how to fall before you leapt out of a plane or the landing was going to be painful.

Cheeks burning, her mouth throbbing with heat, she dampened the corner of the towel he'd used to dry her hand and laid it against her hot face before, legs shaking, she sank down onto the side of the bath.

'Mum,' she whispered, her head on her knees. 'Help…'

CHAPTER THREE

*'Ice cream is cheaper than therapy and you don't
need an appointment.'*
—from *Rosie's Little Book of Ice Cream*

DANTE WALKED INTO the kitchen, filled a glass with ice-cold
water from the fridge and downed it in one. The only effect was to make him feel as if he had steam coming out
of his ears and, from the way Lisa was looking at him, he
very well might have.

Angelica...

Her name suggested something white and gold in a
Renaissance painting, but no Renaissance angel ever had
a body, legs like that. A mouth that felt like a kiss from
across the room. A kiss that obliterated every thought but
to possess her.

He hadn't looked at a woman in that way, touched a
woman in that way for over a year but when he'd turned,
seen her crimson mouth, the one jolt of colour against the
unrelieved black of her clothes, her hair, against skin that
looked as if it had never seen the sun, every cell in his
body had sat up and begged to go to hell.

Someone must have been listening...

Dark Angel was right.

Aware that Lisa was regarding him with undisguised
amusement, brows raised a fraction, he stared right back

at her, daring her to say a word. She grinned knowingly then turned away as Angelica finally joined them.

'How did he do?' Lisa asked. 'Has he earned his first aid badge?'

'Gold star,' Angelica replied, holding out her hand for inspection. She was doing a good job of matching Lisa's jokey tone but she wasn't looking at him and there was a betraying pink flush across her cheekbones.

'Did you find a box, Lis?' he asked sharply.

'I have *this* box,' she said, 'thoroughly lined with newspaper.' She looked down at the deep box she was holding and then up at him, her brows a *got you* millimetre higher and he could have kicked himself. So much for attempting to distract her. 'Chef gave me some minced chicken for Rattino. I assumed you'd have milk up here.'

'I have, but it'll be cold,' he said, grabbing the excuse to escape. 'I'll put a drop in the microwave to take the chill off.'

'Thank you. That's very kind,' Angelica replied quietly as she took the box from Lisa and retreated to the bathroom. He watched her walk away, trying not to think about what her legs were doing to him. What he wanted to do to her legs…

He turned abruptly, opened the fridge door, poured some milk into a saucer and put it in the microwave for a few seconds.

'Haven't you got something to do downstairs?' he asked as, feeling like an idiot with Lisa watching, he put a finger in to test the temperature.

'It's snowing hard now. Everyone's making a move and I've told the staff to go home.' She leaned against the door frame. 'What are you going to do about Geli?'

'Do?'

'If it's true about her apartment.'

'It's true about Via Pepone,' he said. 'My father demolished it last year. He's about to put a glass box in its place.'

'That's the place—?'

'Yes,' he said, cutting her off before she said any more.

'Right.' She waited a moment and then glanced towards the bathroom. 'So?'

'So what?' he snapped.

'So what are you going to do about Geli?'

'Why should I do anything?' he demanded. 'My father may have demolished the street but he didn't con her out of rent for an apartment that no longer exists.' Lisa didn't say anything but her body language was very loud. 'What do you expect me to do, Lis? Pick her up and put her in my pocket like one of her strays? Have we got a cardboard box big enough?'

'No,' she said. 'But she's been travelling all day, it's late and, in case you hadn't noticed, it's snowing out there.'

'I'd noticed.' Snowflakes had been clinging to Angelica's hair and face when she'd arrived. She'd licked one off her upper lip as she'd walked towards him.

'That's it?' Lisa asked. 'That's all you've got?'

'Lis…'

'It's okay; don't worry about it.' She raised a hand in a gesture that was pure Italian. 'I've got a room she can have.'

'A room?'

'Four walls, ceiling, bed—'

'I wasn't asking for a definition,' he said, 'I was questioning the reality. You and Baldacci live in a one-bedroom flat and Angelica's legs would hang over the end of your sofa.' He could picture them. Long legs, short skirt, sexy boots—

'The sofa is a non-starter,' she agreed, 'but the room is here, just along the corridor. Right next to yours.'

That jolted him out of his fantasy. 'That's not your room!'

'No? Whose clothes are hanging in the wardrobe? Whose book is on the bedside table? Nonnina Rosa believes that it's my room and that, my dear cousin, makes it a fact.'

'Nonnina Rosa is on the other side of the world.'

'She's just a second away in cyber space. You wouldn't want her to discover that when I selflessly volunteered—'

'Selflessly? *Madonna!*'

'—when I selflessly volunteered to come halfway across the world to pick up the pieces and glue you back together, you did nothing to stop me from moving in with a Baldacci?' She mimed her grandmother spitting at the mention of the hated name. 'Would you?'

'The only reason you're here is because Vanni Baldacci's father sent him to his Milan office to keep him out of the scheming clutches of a Vettori.'

'Epic fail. The darling man has just texted me to say he's on his way with my gumboots and a brolly.'

'Lisa, please…'

'Nonnina was desperately worried about you, Dan. She felt responsible—'

'What happened had nothing to do with her. It was my choice. And you were about as much use as a chocolate teapot,' he added before she could rerun what had happened. It was over, done with. 'The only reason I keep you on is because no one else will employ you.'

She lifted her shoulders in a theatrical shrug. 'Whatever,' she said, not bothering to challenge him. 'Of course, if you object so strongly to Geli having my room you could always invite her to share yours.'

'Go away, Lisa, or I swear I'll call Nonnina myself. Or maybe I should speak to Nicolo Baldacci.'

'How long is it, exactly, since you got laid, Dan?' she asked, not in the least bothered by a threat that they both knew he would never carry out. 'It's time to forget Valentina. You need to get back on the horse.'

He picked up the saucer of milk and waited for her to move.

'I mean it. You've been looking at Geli like a starving man who's been offered hot food ever since she walked through the door,' she said, staying right where she was. 'In fact, if I were a betting woman I'd be offering straight odds that you were taking the first mouthful when I interrupted you.'

'I met her less than an hour ago,' he reminded her, trying not to think about the feel of Angelica's tongue on his lip even as he sucked it in to taste her. Coffee, honey, life…

'An hour can be a lifetime when lightning strikes. I wanted to rip Vanni's clothes off the minute I set eyes on him,' she said with the kind of smile that suggested it hadn't been much longer than that.

'I'm not about to take advantage of a damsel in distress.'

'Not even if she wants you to take advantage of her? She looked…interested.'

'Not even then,' he said, trying not to think about her crimson lips whispering *'caldo…'*, her breath against his mouth, the way she'd leaned into him, how her body fitted against his.

'You are so damned English under that Italian exterior,' she said. 'Always the perfect gentleman. Never betraying so much as a quiver of emotion, even when the damsel in question is stomping all over you in her designer stilettos.'

'Valentina knew what she wanted. I was the one who moved the goalposts.'

'Don't be so damned noble. You fall in love with the man, Dan, not some fancy penthouse, the villa at Lake Como, the A-list lifestyle. I'd live in a cave with Vanni.'

'Then talk to your parents before your secret blows up

in your faces.' Dante had experienced that pain at first-hand… 'It won't go away, Lis.'

'No.' She pulled a face, muttered, 'Stupid feud…' Then she reached out and touched his arm. 'I'll leave you to it. Good luck with finding a hotel that'll take Rattino,' she said, heading towards the door. She didn't get more than a couple of steps before she stopped, turned round. 'I suppose Geli could put him back in her coat pocket and sneak him in—'

'Are you done?' he asked, losing patience.

'—but it will only be a temporary solution. Tonight's scene in the bar will be the talk of the market tomorrow.'

'The snow will be the talk of the market tomorrow.'

She shook her head. 'It snows every year but the combination of a head-turning woman, the rare sound of Dante Vettori laughing and a rat? Now that is something worth talking about.'

'Lis,' he warned.

'Never mind. I'm sure you'll think of something.'

'You don't want to know what I'm thinking.'

She grinned. 'I know exactly what you're thinking. You and every man in the bar when she arrived in a flurry of snowflakes. How to make an entrance! Tra-la-la…' Lisa blew on her fingers and then shook them. 'Seriously, Dan, I don't know if Geli needs a job but she will need space to show her stuff and having her around will be very good for business.'

'Are you done now?'

'As for the other thing, my advice is to get in quickly or you're going to be at the back of a very long queue.' She almost made it to the door before she said, 'You won't forget that you offered her supper? Have you got anything up here or do you want me to look in the fridge?'

'Just lock up and go home.'

'Okay.' She opened the door, looked back over her

shoulder. 'I've brought up Geli's suitcase, by the way. It's in her room.'

'*Basta! Andare!*'

'And you have lipstick—' she pointed to the corner of her own mouth '—just here.'

Geli's hands were shaking as she scooped out a tiny portion of chicken for the kitten, her whole body trembling as she sank to her knees beside the bath, resting her chin on her arms as she watched him practically inhale it. Trying to decide which was most disturbing—kissing a man she'd only just met or being told that the flat she'd paid good money to rent did not exist.

It should be the flat. Obviously.

Elle was going to be furious with her for being so careless. Her grandmother had lost everything but the roof over their heads to a con man not long after their mother died. Without their big sister putting her own life on hold to take care of them all, she and Sorrel would have ended up in care.

Fortunately, there was the width of France and Switzerland between them. Unless she told them what had happened they would never know that she'd messed up.

Which left the kiss. Which was ridiculous. It wasn't as if it was her first kiss—her first anything—but for a moment she'd felt as if she'd been on the brink of something rare, something life-changing.

As she leaned against the edge of the bath watching the kitten, she remembered the moment when she'd caught her sister on the point of kissing Sean McElroy. Their closeness, the intensity of their focus on each other, had terrified her. Elle was hers—surrogate mother, surrogate father, big sister, carer—but suddenly there was someone else, this man, a total stranger, getting all her attention.

For a moment, with Dante's arm around her waist, his

lips a millimetre from her own, she'd known how Elle had felt, had wanted it for herself. That was why she was shaking. For a moment she had been utterly defenceless…

'I'm sorry I took so long to bring the milk. I was arranging with Lisa to lock up for me.' Dante placed the saucer in the bath but, instead of joining her, he stood back, keeping his distance.

Which was a very good thing, she told herself. Just because she wanted him here, kneeling beside her, didn't make it a good idea…

'We're putting you to a lot of trouble,' she said, keeping her eyes fixed on the kitten as he stepped in the saucer and lapped clumsily at the milk.

'He's looking better already,' he said, his voice as distant as his body.

'He's fluffed up a bit now he's dry but he hasn't learned to wash.' Keep it impersonal. Talk about the cat… 'He's much too young to be separated from his mother. I'll take him back to where I found him tomorrow and see if I can reunite them.'

'How do you think that will work out?' he asked.

'About as well as it usually does.' She reached out and ran a finger over the kitten's tiny domed head. 'About as well as my escape to Isola is working out.'

'Escape? What are you running away from?'

She looked up. He was frowning, evidently concerned. 'Just life in a small village,' she said quickly before he began wondering which asylum she'd broken out of. 'Conformity. I very nearly succumbed to the temptation to buckle down to reality and become the design director for my sisters' ice cream parlour franchise.' She did a little mock shiver. 'Can you *imagine*? All that *pink*!'

He snorted with laughter.

'You see? You only met me half an hour ago but even you can see that's ridiculous.'

'Let's just say that I find it unlikely.'

'Thank you, Dante. You couldn't have paid me a nicer compliment.' She hooked her hair behind her ear, stood up and faced him. *Forget the kiss...* 'And thank you for trying to break the news about my apartment gently over supper.'

He shrugged. 'I wanted more information before I leapt in with the bad news,' he said, turning away to reach for a towel. 'You could have made a mistake with the address.'

'But you didn't believe I had.'

'No.' He stopped looking down at the towel and looked at her. 'The map you had was out of date. If you had followed the directions you were given, you would have ended up at a construction site.'

'Which I did,' she admitted. 'Lisa was right when she said you know Isola like the back of your hand.'

'I spent a lot of my childhood here but it's changing fast. We're struggling to hang on to what's left.'

'You'll forgive me if I say that I wish you'd struggled a little harder.' He didn't exactly flinch but clearly she'd said the wrong thing. 'I'm sorry. It's not your fault.'

'Here, Rattino will be more comfortable on this,' he said. 'Bring the box through to the fire when he's settled.'

She looked down at the towel he'd thrust into her hand and then at the space where, a moment before, Dante Vettori had been standing.

What had she said?

Everything about Dante was still except the hand holding the wooden spoon as he stirred something in a saucepan. The light glinting off the heavy steel band of his wristwatch was mesmerising and Geli could have stood in the doorway and watched him for ever.

'Is he settled?' he asked without looking up.

'Asleep and dreaming he's in heaven,' she said. 'Life

is so simple when you're a cat.' She held up the lease that was currently severely complicating hers.

He turned down the heat and took it from her. 'There's no mistake about the address,' he said.

'No. I have Signora Franco's number,' she said, clutching the phone she'd used to tell her sisters that she'd arrived safely. Well, she'd arrived... 'If I call her will you talk to her?'

'Of course.'

The wait to connect seemed endless but, in the end, was nowhere near long enough.

'No reply?' he asked when she let the phone drop to her side.

She shook her head. 'The message was in Italian, but "number unavailable" sounds the same in any language.'

He shook his head. 'Tell me, Angelica, how did you learn such impressive self-control?'

She held her breath momentarily. Let it out slowly. 'Self-control?'

'Few women I know—few men, come to that—would have taken the news about the apartment without throwing something, even if it was just a tantrum.'

'Oh...' Momentarily thrown, she said, 'I don't do tantrums.'

'Is there a secret to that? Anything you're prepared to share with Lisa?' he asked.

'Yoga?' she offered. 'It's all in the breathing.'

He turned back to the sauce without a word, stirring it very slowly.

Damn it, she didn't know him... He might regret kissing her but he'd been kind when he didn't have to be. He hadn't yelled at her, or thrown her or the kitten out when they'd caused a near riot in his café.

She took one of those yoga breaths.

'I cried a lot when my mother died. It made things difficult at school and my sisters sad because there was nothing they could do to make things better.' This was something she never talked about and the words escaped in a soft rush of breath. 'I wanted to stop but I didn't know how.'

'How old were you?' He continued to stir the sauce, not looking at her.

'Eight.' Two days short of her ninth birthday.

'Eight?' He swung round. *'Madre de Dio...'*

'It was cancer,' she said before he asked. 'The aggressive kind, where the diagnosis comes with weeks to live.'

'Non c'è niente che posso dire,' he said. And then, in English, 'There are no words…'

'No.' She shook her head. 'There's nothing anyone can say. No words, not an entire river of tears… Nothing can change what happened.'

'Is that when you stopped crying?' he asked. 'When you realised it made no difference?'

'I was eight, Dante!' So much for her self-control…

'So?' he prompted, 'you were too young for philosophy but clearly something happened.'

'What? Oh, yes… My grandmother found an old black hat in the attic. With a floppy brim,' she said, describing in with a wavy gesture. 'Crocheted. Very Sixties. My grandmother was something of a style icon in her day.'

'And that helped?' he asked, ignoring the fashion note that was meant to draw a thick black line under the subject.

'She said that when I was sad I could hide behind the brim.' She still remembered the moment she'd put it on. The feeling of a great burden being lifted from her shoulders. 'It showed the world what I was feeling without the red eyes and snot and was a lot easier for everyone to live with. I wore that hat until it fell apart.'

'And then what did you do?'

'I found a black cloche in a charity shop. And a black

dress. It was too big for me but my grandmother helped me cut it down. Then, when I was twelve, I dyed my hair.'

'Let me guess. Black.'

'Actually, it was nearer green but my grandmother took me to the hairdressers' and had it sorted out and dyed properly.' The memory of the moment when she'd looked in the mirror and seen herself still made her smile. 'My sisters were furious.'

'Because of the colour or because they hadn't had the same treat?'

'Because Grandma had blown all the housekeeping money on rescuing me from the nightmare of going to school with green hair. They thought eating was more important.'

'Hunger has a tendency to shorten the temper,' he agreed, turning the sauce down to minimum and pouring two glasses of wine from a bottle, dewed with moisture, that stood on the china-laden dresser that took up most of one wall.

'Where was your father in all this?' he asked as he handed a glass to her.

'I don't have one. None of us do.'

His eyebrows rose a fraction. 'Unless there's been a major leap forward in evolution that passed me by,' he said, leaning back against the dresser, 'that's not possible.'

'Biologically perhaps, but while my mother loved babies, she didn't want a man underfoot, being moody when his dinner wasn't ready.' She turned and, glass in hand, leaned back against the dresser. It was easier being beside him than looking at him. 'My grandparents' marriage was not a happy one.' She took a mouthful of the rich, fruity wine. 'I imagine the first time she got pregnant it was an accident, but after that, whenever she was broody, she helped herself to a sperm donation from some man she took a fancy to. A travelling fair visits the village every year for the Late Spring Bank Holiday,' she said. 'Our fathers were setting up in the next county before the egg divided.'

'She lived dangerously.'

'She lived for the moment.'

'"Take what you want," says God, "take it and pay for it…"' He glanced sideways at her. 'It's an old Spanish proverb. So? What colour is your hair?'

She picked up a strand, looked at it, then up at him. 'Black.'

He grinned and it wasn't just the wine that was warming her.

'How did you find it?' he asked. 'The apartment.'

'What? Oh…' Well, that was short-lived… 'On the internet.' He didn't have to say what he thought about that. A muscle tightening at the corner of his mouth wrote an entire essay on the subject. 'It was an international agency,' she protested, 'affiliated to goodness knows how many associations.' Not that she'd checked on any of them. Who did? 'There were comments from previous tenants. Some who'd enjoyed their stay in the apartment and couldn't wait to come back, and a few disgruntled remarks about the heat and the lack of air conditioning. Exactly what you'd expect. Look, I'll show you,' she said, clicking the link on her smartphone.

Like the phone line, the web link was no longer available.

Until that moment she hadn't believed that she'd been conned, had been sure that it was all a mistake, but now the air was sucked right out of her and Dante caught her as her knees buckled, rescued her glass, turned her into his chest.

His arm was around her, her head against his shoulder and the temptation to stay there and allow him to hold her, comfort her, almost overwhelmed her. It felt so right, he was such a perfect fit, but she'd already made a fool of herself once today. She dragged in a deep breath, straightened her shoulders and stepped away.

'Are you okay?' he said, his hand still outstretched to steady her.

'Fine. Really.'

He didn't look convinced. 'When did you last have something to eat?'

'I don't know. I had a sandwich at the airport when they announced that my flight had been delayed.'

'Nothing since then?' He looked horrified. 'No wonder you're trembling. Sit down while the pasta cooks.' He tested it. 'Another minute or two. It's nothing fancy—*pasta al funghi*. Pasta with mushroom sauce,' he added in case her Italian wasn't up to it.

She shook her head. 'I'm sure it's wonderful but, honestly, I couldn't eat a thing.' He didn't argue but reached for a couple of dishes. 'The apartment looked so perfect and the rent was so reasonable...' *Stupid, stupid, stupid!* 'I assumed it was because it was the middle of winter, off-season, but it was a trap for the gullible. No, make that the cheap.' She'd had it hammered into her by Elle that if something looked too good... But she'd been enchanted.

'Did you give them details of your bank account?' Dante asked.

'What? No... At least...I set up a direct debit for the rent...' As she realised what he was getting at, she blinked, looked down at her phone and then swiftly keyed in her password.

As she saw the balance she felt the blood leave her head.

CHAPTER FOUR

'When things are bad, send ice cream. With hot fudge sauce, sprinkles and mini-marshmallows.'
—from *Rosie's Little Book of Ice Cream*

'MADONNA...'

Dante caught her before she hit the floor and carried her through to the living room. He placed her gently on the sofa, her head flat and her feet propped up on the arm, and knelt beside her until she opened her eyes.

For a moment they were blank as she tried to work out what had happened, where she was.

'Angelica...' She blinked, focused, saw him, tried to sit up but he put a hand on her shoulder. 'Lie still for a moment. Breathe...'

He'd thought she was pale before but now she was white, emphasising the size of those extraordinary silver fox eyes, the splendour of her luscious crimson mouth.

'What happened?'

'You fainted.'

She groaned. 'How unutterably pathetic.'

'The combination of shock and a lack of food,' he suggested. Then, as she made an effort to sit up, 'No. Stay there. I'll get you some water.'

'Dante—' For a moment she challenged him, but then

sank back against the cushion. 'Why do you call me Angelica?'

'Geli is not a name for a grown woman.'

'Oh…' She thought about it for a moment. 'Right.'

Once he was sure that she was going to stay put, he fetched a glass of water from the kitchen. Angelica had dropped her phone and, as he bent to pick it up, he saw why she'd fainted. The con artists had cleaned her out.

He half expected her to be sitting up, fretting when he returned but she was exactly where he'd left her, flat on her back but with one arm thrown across her eyes. The gesture had pulled up her dress, exposing even more of her thighs, and it was a toss-up whether he gave her the water or threw it over himself.

'Here,' he said, 'take a sip of this.'

She removed her arm, turned her head to look up at him. 'Your first aid skills are being thoroughly tested this evening.'

'I may have been a bit slow on the kissing-it-better cure,' he assured her, 'but I remembered the head down, feet up recovery position for a faint.'

'Gold star. I said so…' She made a move to sit up and take the glass.

'Don't sit up too quickly,' he said, slipping his arm beneath her shoulders to support her while he held it to her lips.

'*Sì, dottore…*' She managed a smile which, under the circumstances, was pretty brave but drew unnecessary attention to her mouth. The temptation to see just how much kissing it would take to make this better was almost irresistible. So much for his declaration to Lisa about not taking advantage…

Putting the glass down on the end table, he moved to the safety of her feet.

'What are you doing?' she asked when he slid a hand beneath her ankle and reached for the zip of her boot.

'Taking off your boots. Didn't they teach you that at your very comprehensive first aid course?'

'Absolutely. It came right after kissing it better, but I thought you were absent that day.'

'It's just common sense. Everyone feels better with their boots off.'

'That's true,' she said, stretching her foot and wiggling her long toes. Apparently there was no 'safe end' when it came to Angelica Amery, and he quickly dispensed with the second boot and took a step away.

'Okay. You can sit up when you feel up to it,' he said, 'but slowly. Take your time.'

She eased herself up into the corner of the sofa, smoothing her skirt down and tucking her feet beneath her. 'What happened to my phone, Dante? I have to call the bank.'

He took it from his pocket and handed it to her.

'You saw?' she asked.

'When I picked it up. Will they refund you?'

She sighed. 'Not the first month's rent and deposit, that's for sure. I created the direct debit so that was a legitimate withdrawal as far as they're concerned. The rest would appear to be straightforward fraud so I should get that back. Eventually.' She found the number in her contact list and hit call. 'After they've done everything in their power to imply that it's my fault.' She looked up at him. 'Dante...'

'Angelica?'

'Thank you. For catching me.'

'Any time.'

The jet brooch at her throat moved as she swallowed down her emotions. 'You rate a gold star while I'm a triple chocolate idiot. With fudge topping. And sprinkles.'

'You won't be the only one who's been caught.'

'That doesn't make me feel any less stupid.' She shook

her head then winced, clearly wishing she hadn't, and he had a hand out to comfort her before he could stop himself. Fortunately, she was listening to the prompts and didn't see. 'I should have run some checks, but we'd found a short-term tenant for the house and it was all a bit of a rush.'

'You've let your home in England?'

'Yes.' So, even if she wanted to, she couldn't run for home… 'My sisters moved out when they married so it was just me, Grandma and Great-Uncle Basil. Grandma's arthritis was playing up and Basil wanted to take her somewhere warm for the winter so we decided to let the house to finance it—'

'And you were in a rush to escape from the horror of all that pink and white ice cream.'

'I shouldn't mock it.' She managed a somewhat watery smile. 'Ice cream has been very good to my family and, let's face it, art and fashion have never been safe career choices.'

'We do what we have to.'

'Yes…'

Leaving her to speak to the bank, he returned to the kitchen. She might think she had no appetite, but if it was put in front of her it was possible that she would be tempted.

When he returned, with a tray containing two bowls of *pasta al funghi*, a couple of forks and some napkins, she was staring into the fire.

'Sorted?' he asked, and she surprised him with a grin. 'What?'

'"*Sorted…*" You sound so Italian and yet you use English as if it was your first language. It sounds odd.'

'Not that odd. My mother is English.'

'That has to help,' she said.

'That and the fact that when she left my father she took

me with her to England and refused to speak another word of Italian for as long as she lives.'

'Tough on you.'

He shrugged but there was nothing like a reminder of that first endless cold, wet English summer hearing, speaking only an alien language, to dampen his libido.

Her eyes softened. 'How old were you?'

He handed her a fork, wishing he'd kept his mouth shut. 'Twelve, just coming up to my thirteenth birthday.'

'A bad age.'

'Is there a good one?'

She shook her head. 'I guess not, but it was tough enough to be faced with your parents splitting up without losing your home, your language.'

'My mother was angry, hurt…' He shrugged. 'She'd discovered that my father had been having an affair with the woman she thought was her best friend. She offered me the choice to go with her or to stay in Italy.'

'And you chose her.'

'She needed me more than he did.' He passed her a bowl of pasta. 'Eat…'

She looked at the dish she was holding as if unsure how it had got there but, as he'd hoped, she was too well-mannered not to eat food put in front of her. 'It smells very good,' she said politely and took a mouthful.

'Life is short,' he said as he settled at the far end of the sofa. 'Eat pasta every day.'

'I have to admit that on a cold, snowy Milan night it's the perfect comfort food.' Her brave attempt at a smile lit up her eyes, fringed with thick lashes and set in a soft smudge of charcoal. It went straight to his groin and he propped his foot on one knee in an attempt to keep that fact to himself. The kiss had been a mistake. Kissing anyone was a mistake… 'Of course, come spring I might be persuaded to make you a Bellini sorbet and then it would be a close run thing,' she added.

'A Bellini sorbet?' he repeated, mentally grabbing onto the thought of something ice-cold slipping down his throat.

'Fresh peach juice, Prosecco... The real thing, sparkling on the tongue, but frozen.' She raised her eyebrows. 'Oh, I see. You thought my sisters use mass-produced vegetable fat goo for their events business.'

He shrugged. 'The British are not famous for their ice cream.'

'Unlike Italians?'

'I believe you mentioned an ice cream van? If it's one of those stop-me-and-buy-one vans it won't be loaded up with Bellini sorbet.'

'True, but Rosie is a bit special. She goes to children's parties, hen nights, weddings...any fun bash that ice cream is going to enhance.'

'Is there a demand for that?'

'Huge. Of course, the fact that she makes the occasional appearance in a popular television soap opera means that we could book her three times over. We...they...my sisters...also make bespoke ices for weddings, corporate events and the like—that's the Bellini sorbet market—and now Sorrel, she's the sister with the business brain, is franchising a chain of retro American-style ice cream parlours.'

'And you design the interiors?'

With luck, talking would keep her mind off the non-existent flat until she'd finished the pasta. He prompted her to talk about how the business had evolved, looked at the photographs on her phone of the ice cream parlours she'd designed. She was very talented...

'So, you're a designer, an ice cream maker and you rescue kittens in your spare time?' he asked.

'Rescue is a two-way thing, Dante. People think that

cats are selfish, but I've seen them respond to need in their owners and in other animals.'

As she looked up at him from under those heavy lashes he found himself wondering who, in the kitten scenario, was rescuing whom. He sensed something deeper than a desire to paint, design, experience Italy behind her 'escape', but they were already way too deep into personal territory; he had no wish to hear more.

Maybe she sensed it too because she took another mouthful of the pasta. 'This is really good.'

'Wait until you try chef's *Risotto alla Milanese*. Arborio rice from the Po Valley, butter, dry white wine, saffron and Parmigiano-Reggiano.' Food was always a safe topic. 'I'm sorry you missed it but, with the weather closing in, Lisa sent everyone home.'

'Now that is really impressive.'

'Sending staff home early on a bad night?'

She shook her head, then said, 'Well, yes, but I was referring to your ability to name the ingredients in the risotto recipe.'

He shrugged. 'Nonnina used to make it for me,' he said.

'Nonnina? That's your grandmother, right?'

'Actually, she's Lisa's grandmother, my great-aunt, but everyone calls her Nonnina,' he said. 'Café Rosa was her bar until she finally surrendered to pressure from her son to retire and join him and his family in Australia. She used to let me help in the kitchen when I was a boy.'

She smiled. 'That's a sweet picture, but I think you were wise not to step into her shoes and take over the cooking.'

'Oh? And why is that?'

'You forgot the chicken stock.'

'Did I?' He sensed a subtext, something he was missing. 'Does it matter?'

'It does if you're the chicken.'

'Don't tell me,' he said, 'you find them wandering, lost

or abandoned, and put them in your pocket—no, in the basket of your bicycle. Do you put them in the bath, too?'

She grinned. 'I wouldn't advise you to try that with a chicken. They can't fly, but they do a very energetic flap and a panicky bird in a confined space is going to make a heck of a mess.'

'You are a fount of wisdom on the animal welfare front. So, what do you do with them?' he asked. 'Should the occasion ever arise.'

'I take injured birds to the local animal sanctuary, to be cared for until they can be released or found a good home.'

'Not to the vet?'

She tilted her head in an awkward little movement. 'I found a pheasant once. It had been winged by a shotgun and had taken cover in our hedge. I picked it up and carried it across the village to the vet, expecting him to take care of it. He didn't even bother to look at it, just wrung its neck, handed it back to me and told me to make sure my mother hung it for a few days before she cooked it.'

'*Perdio!* How old were you?'

'Nine.' She sketched a shrug. 'Grandma and I gave the poor thing a very elaborate funeral and buried it in the garden.'

'I hope your grandmother tore a strip off the vet.'

'No. She told me that he was an old school farm vet who thought he was giving a useful life lesson to a girl who lived in the country. No sentiment there.' She stirred the pasta with her fork. 'At least he was honest. He could have sent me on my way, promising to take care of the bird, and then eaten it himself.'

With his head now filled with the picture of a motherless little girl clutching a dead pheasant, he really wished he hadn't asked. And then her comment about the chicken stock registered. 'Are you a vegetarian, Angelica?'

'I don't eat meat,' she said.

'Is there a difference?'

'I don't wear fur, but I wear leather and wool and use it in my clothes. I don't eat meat, but I eat fish and cheese and eggs and I pour milk over my cereals.' She circled her fork over the dish she was holding to prove her point. 'I am fully aware of the hypocrisy.'

'I think you're being a little hard on yourself,' he said. 'Why didn't you say something earlier? When I ordered the risotto for you?'

'I was about to when events overtook us and actually this is perfect. One of my favourites,' she said, making an effort to eat a little more. 'Is it a problem for you?'

'Of course not; why would it be? It's just I'm surprised, that's all.'

She raised an eyebrow. 'Surprised? Why?'

'You are aware that you dress like a vampire?'

'Oh *that*,' she said, the corner of her mouth twitching into a smile. 'That's what Sean called me, the first time he set eyes on me. A skinny vampire.'

Sean? Who was Sean? Don't ask... 'That must have been some time ago,' he said.

'I was sixteen. I've put on a bit of weight since then,' she said, looking down at the soft curves of her breasts and then up at him and caught him doing the same.

For a moment nothing seemed to move and in his head, above the drumming of his heartbeat, he could hear Lisa asking how long it had been since he'd been laid.

Until tonight he hadn't noticed, hadn't cared, but then Angelica Amery had walked into his bar and it was as if she'd hit the start button on the part of him that, for self-protection, he'd switched off months ago. The part that could rage, react, *feel*. The moment he'd turned, seen her sparkling with snow, he'd known that all he had to do was put out his hand, touch her, and the life would come flooding back. And, like blood returning to a numb limb, the pain would follow.

He'd spent the last months concentrating on work, using it to create an impermeable membrane between his public life—devoting himself to this community, *his* community—and the vacuum within.

In a vacuum no one could hear you scream…

'Who's Sean?' he asked. She frowned at his abruptness. 'You said Sean called you a skinny vampire.'

'Oh, right. He's my brother-in-law,' she said. 'He and Elle have three little girls.' Her smile was something else, lighting up her face, making him want to smile right back. 'As for the vampire thing, it's just a look, Dante. I don't bite. Well, not often.' She scooped up another forkful of pasta. 'Just a little nip here, a little nip there but, unlike the kitten, I make it a rule to never draw blood.'

'A pity. I suspect that having you kiss it better would be an unforgettable experience.' Then, before she could speak, 'I'm sorry, that was—'

'No. I'm the one who has to apologise.' The pasta never made it to her mouth. 'I don't normally fling myself at total strangers.' She gave up pretending to eat and put down her fork. 'What am I saying? I *never* fling myself at total strangers. It must have been the shock—'

'Don't!' Without thinking, he'd reached out and put his hand over hers to stop her and the pulse in the tip of his thumb began to pick up speed, thrum in his ears. His brain did a desperate drive-by of all the meaningless phrases one used to cover awkward moments. None fitted. 'Don't apologise.' He didn't want her to apologise for kissing him so he said the only thing in his head—the truth. 'It's quite the best thing that's happened to me in a while.'

And that rushing in his ears had to be the sound of life pouring through the gaping hole she'd punched through his impermeable membrane.

Removing his hand, he abandoned his own supper and then, because he had to do something, he got up and opened the doors of the wood burner. 'What did the bank say?' he asked as he tossed in a couple of logs.

She didn't answer and he half turned.

'They took the details,' she said quickly. 'Asked me a load of questions. I got the feeling they thought, or maybe just hoped, that I'd shared my password with a boyfriend who'd done the dirty and cleaned me out.'

'It happens.'

'Not to me!' Perhaps realising that she'd used rather more vehemence than necessary, she said, 'My grandmother lost everything to a con artist not long after my mother died. He was elegant, charming, endlessly patient with us girls. He even bought me some black hair ribbons. It wasn't just Grandma. We all fell for him, even the dog. It took us a long time to recover. Financially and emotionally.'

'Is that why you're so angry with yourself?' he asked, standing up. 'You shouldn't be. You're as much a victim as if you'd been mugged in the street.'

'I know, but damn it, Dante, it was just so *perfect*. The living room had French windows that opened onto a tiny balcony with a distant view of the Duomo and there was a small second bedroom that I was going to use as a workroom…' She shook her head. 'I'm sorry. I know it doesn't exist but I'm still having trouble getting my head around this.'

'You know what's happened, but it's taking some parts of your brain a while to catch up.'

He knew how it was. He still had sleepless night reruns of the day he'd laid everything out for Valentina, giving her the choice to stay or walk away. She'd used everything she had—soft words and scorching sex—in a last-ditch effort to persuade him to change his mind. Trying to rewrite the scene, behaved better. She pulled a face. 'I guess.'

'A delayed flight, bad weather and then discovering that you're a victim of fraud would be enough to cloud anyone's thoughts.'

'Mine appear to be denser than mud.'

'Have you any idea what you will do?' he asked. 'Stay or go home?'

She lifted her shoulders. 'If I go home I'll be in the same situation as if I stay. Nowhere to live, no job, no money until the bank sorts out a refund. *If* the bank sorts out a refund.'

'What about your sisters?'

'Oh, they'd give me a room and a job like a shot but then I'll be stepping back into the role of baby sister. A big black cuckoo in the happy families' nest.' She glanced at her watch. 'It's late. Is there a B&B close by? A *pensione*? Somewhere that would take me in at this time of night?'

'Close enough.' He turned back to the fire and gave it a prod with the poker, sending up a cloud of sparks. 'Lisa has given you her room. It's the one opposite the bathroom.'

'Bathroom?' She frowned as she tried to make sense of that. 'Do you mean her room here? In this apartment? But I couldn't possibly—'

'There's a lock on the door,' he said before she could finish.

'What? No…' He couldn't be sure whether she had blushed or it was the glow from the fire warming her cheeks. 'I meant I couldn't possibly impose on you.'

'I think you should try,' he said. 'As you said, it's late and there's the additional problem—'

'I have some cash. And a credit card for use in emergencies. I'd say this counts as an emergency, wouldn't you?'

'Undoubtedly, but if you'd let me finish? I was going to

say that there's a problem with the kitten. He's not going to find much of a welcome in a hotel.'

'I could—'

'No,' he said. 'You couldn't.'

'You don't know what I was going to say.'

'You were going to say that you could put him back in your pocket and no one would ever know.' He raised an eyebrow, daring her to deny it. 'We all know how that turned out this evening.'

'Okay, so the kitten is a problem,' she admitted, 'but what about Lisa?'

'What about her?'

'If I have her room, where will she sleep?'

'Where she always sleeps,' he said. 'She keeps a few things here just in case there's an unannounced visit from her family, but she actually lives with Giovanni.'

'Really?'

'You think she's a bit old to be worrying what her parents think about her living with her boyfriend?'

'Well, yes.'

Dante had avoided looking at Angelica when he'd told her about the room. Forget the kitten, there was no way he was letting her leave after fainting so dramatically, but the flash of heat between them had complicated what should have been a simple offer of hospitality. She had to believe that there were no strings attached. No expectation that she follow through on a kiss that had fall-into-bed written all over it from the first touch.

He really had to stop thinking about that kiss.

'It's complicated.'

'I can do complicated,' she said. 'I have a very complicated family.'

'True.' He wanted to know all about them. All about her. Almost as much as he didn't… 'But nowhere near as complicated as a hundred-year-old family feud over a goat.'

'A goat?' Angelica looked startled, those hot crimson lips ready to laugh. If she laughed...

'Have you ever taken home a stray goat, Angelica?'

'Oh, please. Even I know that a goat in a well-tended garden is a recipe for disaster. They are particularly partial to roses and my grandmother loves her roses.'

'Goats will eat anything, but it's a story for late at night after good food and too much wine,' he said.

'Mine too,' Angelica said. 'Maybe we should save them for another night?'

'It's a date...'

No. Not a date...

Madonna, this was difficult.

One minute they'd been on the point of ripping one another's clothes off and maybe, just maybe, if he hadn't had time to think, it would have been all right. Now—thanks to an internet con and a stray kitten —Angelica might as well have a 'Do Not Touch' sign around her neck.

'You must be tired. I'll show you the room.'

'Yes... No...' The lace at her throat moved as she swallowed, the light catching the facets of the jet brooch. 'You and Lisa have both been incredibly kind but you don't know anything about me.' Then, and rather more to the point if she was going to be his roommate for the night, 'I don't know anything about you.'

CHAPTER FIVE

'Eat spinach tomorrow; today is for ice cream.'
    —from *Rosie's Little Book of Ice Cream*

'THAT'S NOT TRUE,' Dante said quickly. Too quickly. 'At least not the first part. I've learned a lot about you.' He shut the doors of the wood burner, carefully replaced the poker on its stand and propped his elbow on the mantelpiece, hoping that he looked a lot more relaxed about this than he felt. 'You're a talented designer. You have a wide knowledge of first aid. And ice cream. And you have a complicated family who you care deeply about.' It was there in her voice every time she mentioned them.

'That's not much to go on when you're opening your home to a total stranger.'

'Maybe not, but you're compassionate.' She had also turned every head when she'd walked into his bar—always a bonus—and was the first woman to make him feel like a man in over a year. He should focus on the compassion. 'Despite the fact that you were lost and it was beginning to snow, you still chose to rescue a helpless kitten. I am simply doing—'

'I am not helpless!' Geli said, shifting from calm to heat in a heartbeat, which brought a touch of colour to highlight those fine cheekbones.

'—doing my best to aid a damsel in distress,' he continued, rapidly editing out any reference to helpless or maiden. She was not helpless and no maiden kissed the way she had kissed him.

His reward was a snort of laughter, quickly suppressed. Whether it was at the thought of herself as a damsel or him as a knight errant, he had no way of knowing, but he was glad to have made her laugh, if only briefly.

'Sorry, Dante, but I don't believe in fairy tales.'

'No? All those orphans? All that abuse, abandonment, fear? What's not to believe?' he asked. 'You've just had a very close encounter with the hot breath of the wolf in disguise.'

'Nothing as beautiful as a wolf. Just the cold, unfeeling click of a mouse.' She straightened her back, sat a little taller. 'Okay, I've lost money that I worked hard for, but I'm not going to starve and I'm not going to be sleeping in a shop doorway.'

'Not tonight. And not while there's a room here.'

'I—'

'Tomorrow I'll take you to the *commissariato* so that you can report the fraud,' he said, hoping to distract her. 'You'll need some help with the language.'

'Is there any point? Catching Internet crooks is like trying to catch flies with chopsticks.'

'Made all the harder by the fact that those who've been caught often feel too foolish to report the crime. As if they are in some way to blame for their own misfortune. They're not. You're not,' he said, taking the half-eaten pasta from her.

The colour in her cheeks darkened. 'I know, but I was careless, forgot the basic rule and let my guard down. It will be tougher now to do what I planned, but I am not going to allow a low-life scumbag to steal my dreams and creep home with my tail between my legs.' She took a breath. 'I will not be a victim.'

Her words were heartfelt, passionate, and everything Italian in him wanted to cry out *Bravissima*, kiss her cheeks, wrap her in a warm embrace. His English genes knew better. She wasn't just angry with the criminals; she was angry with herself for falling for the con.

'Basic rule?' he asked.

'Always be suspicious of perfection. If it looks too good to be true, then it almost certainly is.'

'We fall for that one all the time, Angelica. The entire advertising industry is built on that premise. You were meant to fall in love with the apartment and it won't just have been you.'

She sighed. 'No. And it won't just be that apartment, will it? There'll be a host of perfect apartments and villas lined up for the unwary.'

'Undoubtedly. It's your public duty to warn the police that they are likely to be inundated with angry tourists who've paid good money for non-existent accommodation this summer. And maybe stop more people being caught.'

'I suppose…' She tilted her head a little. 'I read somewhere that in Milan the policewomen wear high heels. Is that true?'

'There's only one way to find out,' he said. 'Is it a date?'

'Another one? At this rate we'll be going steady…' Their eyes met and for a moment the air sizzled between them and he was the one swallowing hard. 'It's a date,' she said quickly.

'Can I offer you something else?' he asked. 'Tea, coffee, or do you want to go downstairs and raid the fridge for dessert?'

'Tea?' she repeated, grabbing onto something sane, something sensible. 'Proper tea?'

'Proper tea,' he confirmed.

'Well, now you're talking,' she said, uncurling herself from the corner of the sofa.

'What are you doing?' he asked as she gathered the dishes.

'Whoever cooks in our house is let off the washing-up,' she said, heading for the kitchen before he could tell her to sit down.

'It's a good system,' he said, 'but I do have a dishwasher.'

'You do?'

She looked around and her scepticism was understandable. Apart from the American retro-style fridge he'd installed when he moved in, the kitchen was pretty much as Nonnina had left it. A dresser, loaded with old plates, took up most of one wall, while a family-sized table dominated the centre and a couple of old armchairs stood by the wood stove in the corner—much used in the days when they could only afford to heat one room in winter and the main room was kept for best. It was comfortable, familiar and he liked it the way it was. Which didn't mean he was averse to modern domestic convenience.

'The twenty-first century is through here,' he said, opening the door into what had once been a large pantry but was now a fully fitted utility room. *'Il bagno di servizio.'*

'Magic! You have the best of both worlds.'

'I'm glad you approve.'

Valentina hadn't been impressed, but then his father had given her a personal tour of his apartment in the Quadrilatero d'Oro. He put the kettle on for tea while Angelica stacked the dishes in the machine. The light gleamed on glossy black hair that swung silkily about her shoulders as she moved. On the soft curve of her crimson lips as she turned and saw him watching her.

'It's snowing heavily now,' she said, looking out of the window. 'Will it last?'

'It could be gone by morning, or it could be set in for

days,' he said, but he wasn't looking at the snow piling up in the corners of the window. He was looking at her reflection. 'Whichever it is, there's nothing we can do about it.'

'Except enjoy it. If my mother were alive she'd go out and make a snowman.'

'Now?'

'Absolutely. It might turn to rain in the night and the moment would be lost.' The thought brought a smile to her lips. 'She got us all up in the middle of night once, when it had begun to snow. We made snowmen, had a snowball fight and afterwards she heated up tins of tomato soup to warm us up.'

'And was it all gone in the morning?'

'No, but we had a head start on all the other kids.' Her eyes were shining at the memory as she turned to him. 'She never let the chance for fun pass. Maybe she sensed that time was short and she had to make memories for us while she could.'

'Is that what you're doing? Following her example,' he added when she frowned.

'Always say goodbye as if it's for the last time. Live each day as if it's our last…'

'Are you saying that you want to go out and have a snowball fight?' he asked, not wanting to remember how he'd parted from his father.

'Would you come?' she asked but, before he could answer, she shook her head. 'Just kidding. It's been a long day.'

'And you've had a bad introduction to life in Isola,' he said, although, on reflection, it wasn't an evening which, given the option, he would have missed. 'On the other hand, a little excitement to raise the heartbeat is never a bad thing and you did say that you came to Italy for experience?'

As their eyes met in the reflection in the window he

wanted to rewind the clock, stop it at the moment her tongue had touched his lip... Then, as if it was too intimate, intense, she turned to look directly at him.

'Believe me,' she said, catching a yawn, 'it has delivered and then some.'

'You're tired.' She had neither accepted nor refused Lisa's room but, whatever doubts she might have had about staying, whatever doubts he might have about the wisdom of offering it to her, the weather had made the decision for them both. 'Lisa brought up your case,' he said, picking up the mug of tea he'd made her and leading the way to the room his cousin had dressed to make it look, to the casual glance, as if she was using it.

There was a basket of cosmetics on the dressing table, a book beside the bed. A pair of shoes beneath it, lying as if they'd just been kicked off.

'How long has she been living with Giovanni?'

'She followed him here from Melbourne just over a year ago,' he said, picking up Lisa's shoes and tossing them into the wardrobe. 'To be honest, I didn't think their relationship would survive the day-to-day irritations of living together.' Not that he'd cared one way or the other at the time.

'Is that the voice of experience?' she asked.

'I came close once.' He looked at her and she shook her head.

'Not even close,' she said.

'The village gossips?'

'They wouldn't have stopped me.'

'No...' He crossed to the shutters, stood for a moment looking down at the piazza. The snow was blanketing the city in silence, softening the edges, making everything look clean.

Angelica pressed her hands against the window and sighed. 'I love snow.' Her voice was as soft as one of the huge snowflakes sticking to the window and, unable to help himself, he turned and looked at her. 'It's like being in another world,' she said, 'in a place where time doesn't count.' And then she turned from the window and looked up at him.

Geli could feel Dante's warmth as they stood, not quite touching, in front of the cold window. Everything about the moment was heightened, her senses animal sharp; she could almost hear the thud of his pulse beating a counterpoint to her own, almost taste the pheromones clouding the air. She wanted to tug his shirt from his waistband and rub her cheek against his chest, scent marking him, catlike, as hers.

Lifting his hand in what felt like slow motion, Dante leaned in to her. Her skin tingled, anticipating his touch. Her lips throbbed, hot, feeling twice their normal size. The down on her cheek stirred, lifting to the heat of his hand, and she closed her eyes but his touch never came. Instead, there was the click as he reached over her head to pull shut one of the shutters and every cell in her body screamed *Noooo!*

'My room has an en suite, so the bathroom is all yours,' he said abruptly. 'There's plenty of hot water and no one will disturb you if want to soak off the day.'

No one would disturb her? Was he crazy? She was disturbed beyond reason.

She had nowhere to live, she'd lost her money but all she'd been thinking about was kissing Dante Vettori, ripping open the buttons of his shirt and exploring his warm skin. Imagining how his long fingers would feel curved around her breast—

Click went the second shutter and, released from the mesmerising drift of the snow, she was jolted back to reality and somehow managed a hoarse, 'Thank you.'

He nodded. 'If you need me for anything I'll be downstairs in the office, catching up with the paperwork.'

'I've been keeping you from your work?'

'I'd stopped to eat. That's why I was in the bar when you arrived. You know where everything is. Please…make yourself at home.'

'Dante…' He waited, hand on the door. 'Thank you.'

He responded with the briefest of nods. 'I'll see you in the morning.'

Geli didn't move until she heard the door to the flat close and then her shoulders slumped. How on earth had they come from the promise of a searing kiss to such awkwardness in the space of an hour, two at the most?

Halfway between the two, she discovered when she checked her watch, and that was the answer. Too much had happened too quickly.

If the kitten hadn't made such a dramatic appearance they would have been able to sit quietly over supper. Dante would have explained about the flat, helped her find a room for the night and then tomorrow she'd have come by to thank him and maybe, hopefully, pick up on the fizz of attraction that had sizzled between them.

Instead, they'd veered between meltdown lust and awkwardness and in an effort to cover that she'd revealed way too much about herself.

Her mother, black hats—where on earth had all that come from? And that pheasant… She hadn't talked about that since her sisters had arrived home on the school bus to find her and Grandma singing a heartfelt *All Things Bright and Beautiful* over its resting place beneath a climbing rose.

'Dio…' Dante, the image of Angelica with her hands pressed against the window burning a hole in his brain, pulled open the bottom drawer of his desk and took out a bottle of grappa.

He poured himself a shot, tossed it back and for a moment he let the heat of it seep through his veins.

Close. He'd been within a whisper of touching her, had almost felt the down on her cheek rising to meet him as, lips softened, eyes closed, she'd anticipated a rerun of that kiss. He clenched his hand in an attempt to eradicate the memory.

He might have stepped back, walked out of the apartment before he did something unforgivable, but it hadn't stopped his imagination reacting to what had been a non-stop blast to his senses ever since she'd walked into his bar and stopped the conversation dead. The steely fresh air smell of her hair, snowflakes melting on her cheek, on crimson lips, she'd looked like something from a fairy tale. A lost princess stumbling out of the darkness.

He'd turned, their eyes had met and in that first look he'd forgotten the pain. The heartache...

And then she'd said, 'Via Pepone.'

He should have let Lisa deal with her because by then the complications were piling up, but that first look had fired a lightning charge through his senses, jump-starting them from hibernation as she walked towards him. As he'd touched her hand. As she'd removed her glove, removed her coat in a slow, tantalising reveal of the briefest little black dress.

His hand at her waist as he'd swept her out of the bar had sent a shock wave of heat surging through him and he hadn't been able to let it go.

He'd wanted to know how her cheek would feel beneath his fingers, wanted to taste her. He wanted to undress her, hold her against his naked skin, bury himself in her until he felt warm again.

What she'd said, how she'd looked at him when she'd stood by the window had been an invitation to take it all. Not a lost princess stumbling out of the night but something darker—an enchantress, a sorceress and if this had been a fairy tale he would already be doomed.

He shook his head.

Angelica Amery was simply a woman in need and that was the problem.

The spontaneity of that fall-into-bed moment had been real enough but Lisa's terrible—or possibly perfect—timing had wrecked that. They'd both had time to think about it and they'd lost the moment when a simple, unplanned elemental explosion of lust might have led anywhere or nowhere.

Worse, because she didn't know him, Angelica might well have thought he expected to share the bed he'd offered her.

Anything now would be tainted by that uncertainty and while his body, jolted out of stasis, might be giving him hell for walking away, he had to face himself in the shaving mirror in the morning.

Work. That had been the answer when Valentina had demanded that he forget Isola, that he walk away from what he couldn't change because, sooner or later, the old houses would come down and his father, or someone like him, would replace them with high-rise flats and office blocks. Work had been the answer when he'd allowed himself to be seduced by her sensual inducement to change his mind when he'd known in his heart that it was already over.

He called up the paper he'd been working on, his plan for the future of Isola, but the words on the screen kept dissolving into images that had nothing to do with preservation orders or affordable housing.

Angelica's hands—tapping the map with a blood-red nail…slowly unfastening tiny buttons…a fingertip stroking the head of the kitten.

Angelica's mouth lifted to kiss him, the black lace choker emphasising the length of her white neck.

Angelica's face as she stood beside him at the window watching the snow blanketing the city—as she turned to him and he knew that all he had to do was reach out, touch her cheek and, for tonight at least, the dark emptiness of the void would be banished.

CHAPTER SIX

'In the winter dip your ice cream in sparkly rose-pink sprinkles.'
—from *Rosie's Little Book of Ice Cream*

CAFÉ ROSA WAS buzzing with morning activity. Men in working clothes were standing at the bar, a pastry in one hand, an espresso at their elbow. She was in Italy, where it cost more to sit down.

With so much whirling around in her mind Geli hadn't anticipated much sleep, but a soak in that huge bathtub with a splash of Lisa's luxurious lavender-scented bubbles and she'd gone out like a light the minute her head hit the pillow.

She'd taken the kitten's box into the bedroom with her in case it woke, hungry, in the night but it had been the sound of a distant door closing that woke her.

For a moment she hadn't known where she was but then the kitten had mewed and it had all come flooding back to her. The delayed flight, the non-existent apartment, Rattino. Dante…

She shook her head. Her life was complicated enough right now, without what might have become an awkward one-night stand. She might have inherited her mother's 'seize the day' genes—that she was feeling regret, the loss of something special missed, instead of relief proved that—but she'd had more sense.

She wrapped herself in her dressing gown, crossed to the window, rubbed the mist away with the edge of her hand. The early-morning sun was slanting across the city, lighting up colourful buildings—deep rose-pink, pale green, yellow; spotlighting a Madonna painted on a wall; glittering off the glass towers of high-rise blocks and snow-covered roofs.

Below her the pristine white of the snow had already been mashed to dirty slush by trucks bringing produce to the market stalls that had been erected along the street opposite. Everywhere there was colour, people wrapped up in thick coats and bright scarves, out and about getting on with their lives, and her heart gave a little skip of anticipation.

There was nothing like a good market to put a spring in the step!

She opened the bedroom door and stuck her head out. 'Dante?'

No response. Maybe he'd woken her when he'd left the flat. Not sure whether she was relieved or disappointed, she headed for the kitchen where she found a note pinned to the fridge door with a magnet.

Kitty comfort station in the utility room. Coffee and breakfast downstairs whenever you're ready. Lisa.

There was a litter tray ready and waiting for Rattino in the utility room, as well as two little plastic dishes filled with fresh minced chicken and milk and Geli found herself blinking rather rapidly at such thoughtfulness, such kindness. She'd read that in Isola she'd find the truest, most generous spirit of old Milan.

Clearly it was a fact.

She introduced Rattino to the first and watched as he dived into the second and then set his box on its side so that he could eat, sleep and do what came naturally at his leisure. Then she closed the door so that he couldn't wander and put the kettle on.

She found tea bags and dropped one in a mug and topped it up with boiling water. She found milk in the fridge and carried her must-have morning mug through to the bathroom. Hair dry, make-up in place, she layered herself in clothes that would see her through the day. A fine polo neck sweater, a narrow, high-waisted ankle-length skirt, stout Victorian-style lace-up boots, all black, which she topped with a rich burgundy velvet cut-away jacket that exactly matched her lipstick. She chose a steampunk-inspired pendant she'd made from the skeleton of a broken watch and, after a spin in front of the mirror to check that she was fluff-free, she went downstairs.

'*Ciao*, Geli!' Lisa called out as she spotted her. '*Come sta?*'

The men standing at the bar turned as one and stared.

'*Ciao, Lisa! Molto bene, grazie.* And Rattino thanks you for the litter tray. What do I owe you?'

She waved the offer away. 'Tell him to thank Dan. He called and asked me to pick it up on my way to work. Now, what can I get you? A latte? Cappuccino? Or will you go hardcore with an espresso?'

'*Vorrei un cappuccino, grazie,*' she replied, testing her phrasebook Italian.

'*Buona sceita!*'

She called out the order to someone behind her, piled pastries on a plate and came out from behind the bar and headed for a table in the centre of the room.

'How are you this morning, Geli?'

'Pretty good, all things considered. I thought I'd be tossing and turning all night, but I'd be lying if I said I remember a thing after I closed my eyes.' She couldn't say the same about Lisa who, up close, looked as if she'd had a sleepless one. 'Thanks so much for offering me your spare room. It was a lifesaver.'

'No point in paying for a hotel room when there's an empty one going begging,' she said, pushing the pastries towards her. *'La prima colazione,'* she said, taking one. 'Otherwise known as cornettos. The perfect breakfast food.'

'Thanks.' Geli took one and her mouth was filled with crisp pastry and cream. 'Oh, good grief,' she spluttered. 'That's sinful.'

Lisa grinned. 'Start the day the way you mean to go on,' she said then called out something in Italian to the men at the bar. They grinned, put down the empty cups they'd been nursing and made a move to go.

'What did you say to them?' Geli asked.

'To close their mouths before they catch flies.' She shook her head. 'You are going to be so good for business. Your make-up, your clothes—everything is perfect. Do you always make this much effort?'

'It goes with the territory. When you're a designer, you have to be your own walking advertisement.'

'It works for me. I'm no Milan fashionista, but I'd give my eye teeth for a jacket like yours.'

'I'll design a Dark Angel original for you when you come back from Australia. A very small thank you for being such a friend in need.'

'You don't have to do that.'

'It will be a totally selfish gift,' she assured her. 'You'll wear it and with those elegant shoulders you'll look fabulous.' She lifted her hands in a *job done* gesture.

'You're telling me that I'm going to be a walking shop dummy,' she said, grinning broadly.

'Walking and talking.'

'Oh, right. Everyone will want to know—' She stopped as Dante pulled out a chair and joined them.

Geli had wondered, as she'd taken her wake-up shower, if she'd imagined the attraction, or if it had simply been heightened by the drama of her arrival. A combination of being in Isola, being lost, the weather. Could anyone really hit all her hot buttons with no more than a look?

Apparently they could, even if it was a slightly crumpled, unsmiling version this morning.

'*Buongiorno*, Angelica,' he said. 'Did you sleep well?'

'*Buongiorno*, Dante,' she replied, her voice remarkably steady. It was the rest of her that felt as if it was shaking like a leaf. 'I slept amazingly well, under the circumstances.'

Dante, on the other hand, looked as if he'd been working all night and the urge to reach out and smooth the creases from his face was almost overwhelming. Fortunately, before she could do anything that idiotic he turned to Lisa.

'What will everyone want to know?' he asked.

'How on earth you managed to convince Geli that she should work for you,' she replied without a blush.

'Oh? And what is the answer?'

'You'll know that when you've persuaded her,' she said, getting to her feet. 'Off you go.'

'Lisa,' Angelica protested. 'My Italian is on the basic side of basic.'

'*No problema.* I might have an Italian father but I could barely utter a word when I arrived. Tell her, Dante,' she urged, turning a smile on her cousin that was so sweet it would give you toothache. 'There'll be a queue of regulars lining up to help her with the language and anything else she needs to make her stay in Isola a memorable experience before she can say *ciao*. Isn't that so?'

Geli, who had two older sisters, recognised one of those exchanges which, on the surface were exquisitely polite, while underneath there were seething undercurrents of hidden meaning.

'But you're family,' Geli protested, not sure what was going on, but not wanting to be in the middle of it.

'Unfortunately,' Dante said, his face expressionless. 'You can't fire family. It wasn't just the language; it was weeks before she could get an order straight or produce a decent espresso without me standing over her—'

Lisa snorted derisively and when he looked up she lifted an eyebrow a mocking fraction right back at him. 'I'm sure Geli is *much* smarter than me.'

He looked thoughtful. 'But nowhere near as devious, it would seem.'

'It runs in the family,' Lisa replied, moving aside as the waiter arrived with a tray containing her cappuccino, an espresso for Dante and two bowls of something pale and creamy. 'I'll walk you through the job when you come back from the *commissariato*, Geli. *Buon appetito.*'

'*Sì...grazie...*' she said, then, unsure what to say to Dante, she indicated the bowl in front of her. 'What is this?'

'*Zabaglione.* Whipped eggs, cream, sugar, a little Marsala. I usually leave out the wine before midday,' he added, 'but it's bitter outside.'

'So this is antifreeze?'

He laughed and the tension, awkwardness was defused. 'Let's hope so.'

She dipped in her spoon and let a mouthful, sweet and warming, dissolve on her tongue. 'Oh, yum. Pastries and pudding for breakfast. My mother would have so approved.' He looked up. 'When anything bad happened she'd make us cupcakes for breakfast. With pink frosting and gold stars.'

'Pink?' His brow kinked in amusement. 'Really?'

'Black frosting is just creepy.' She shrugged. 'Except at Halloween.'

Dante looked as if he was about to say something but the bleep of an incoming text distracted her and she searched in her bag for her phone. 'Oh, no… '

'Problema?'

'You could say that. I shipped my heavy stuff before I left. Who knew it would get here so quickly?' She showed him the phone. 'I think the driver is trying to the find the non-existent address I gave them.'

Dante read the text then replied to it before handing it back. 'I told him to bring it here.'

'Oh… This is so embarrassing.'

'Why?'

'This was supposed to be me standing on my own two feet. Being grown-up. Self-sufficient.'

'Would you like me to tell them to leave it on the pavement?' he asked.

'No!' She shook her head. 'No…I'm sorry, I didn't mean to sound ungrateful but this is my first excursion into the unknown, the first time I've ever done anything totally on my own and it's all going wrong.'

'It's hardly your fault,' he assured her. 'And it's just until Monday.'

Monday? 'Yes, absolutely. I'll have found a room by then.'

'That's Monday, when you can move into the apartment I've found for you. I'm afraid that, like the job, it is only temporary, but it will give you a little breathing space while you get yourself sorted out.'

'You see? Like that,' Geli said and then swallowed. 'I'm sorry. That sounded so ungrateful.'

'Yes, it did.'

She groaned. 'I bet you wish you'd listened to the

weather forecast and closed an hour earlier last night.' He didn't answer and she said, 'You're supposed to say no.'

The creases bracketing his mouth deepened slightly in what might just have been the promise of a smile. 'I'm thinking about it.'

She rolled her eyes. 'Okay, how much is this temporary apartment you've found to go with my temporary job?'

'Just the utilities. It's only for a month while Lisa and Giovanni are at the wedding, but it will give you time to look around.'

'Lisa and Giovanni?' She frowned. 'But I thought—'

'She wants me to give you a job so I offered her a deal. You get the job if she takes Giovanni as her plus one to her sister's wedding. They will need someone responsible to keep the pipes from freezing, make the place look lived in and feed the goldfish,' he added matter-of-factly. As if it was nothing. 'You are responsible, aren't you?'

'No goldfish has ever gone hungry on my watch,' she said, 'but why didn't Lisa tell me herself?'

'Because she wants you to stay here.'

'So that she doesn't have to take Giovanni?'

'No. His flight is booked.'

She went back over the conversation then shook her head. 'I seem to be missing something.'

'Lis believes that if we share the same apartment we'll inevitably fall into the same bed.'

The *zabaglione* took a diversion down her nose and Dante calmly handed her a paper napkin from the tray.

'That is outrageous.'

'I agree. I told her I never sleep with the staff, but apparently temps don't count.'

Never...? 'I wouldn't try that on an employment tribunal.'

'No,' he agreed with the wryest of smiles. 'And I did

point out that, since you had nowhere else to go, any move on my part would be open to the worst interpretation.'

And any move on hers might be seen as...

'So you suggested moving me out so that I'm available?' She should be outraged. She was pretty sure she was outraged... 'I don't believe we're having this conversation. No, scrub that. I don't believe you had this conversation with Lisa.'

But it went a long way to explaining that edgy undercurrent between them this morning.

'*Mi dispiace*, Angelica. It is, as you say, quite outrageous.'

'So you applied a little pressure of your own?' And when, exactly, had he come up with that idea? 'How does Giovanni feel about that?'

'The man is in love. He'll do whatever she asks.' The thought did not appear to give him great pleasure.

'I imagine you're banking on the fact that after a day of joy and celebration her family will realise that he doesn't have horns and a tail.'

'You're not convinced?'

'I don't know your family,' she said, 'and I don't know Giovanni, but I do know that weddings tend to be emotional affairs. There's the risk that, after a few glasses of the bubbly stuff, tongues will be loosened and fists will fly.'

'Maybe. Then they'll all get drunk, fling their arms around one another, vow eternal friendship and cry.'

'Or they'll all land in jail.'

'Or that.' He sat back. 'You don't have to take the job but if you'll just play along until they leave I'd be grateful.'

'I get that. What I don't understand is why throwing us together is so important to her.'

'We're doing each other a favour, Angelica. Does it matter if Lisa has her own agenda?'

Did it?

Lisa wanted to get them into bed together. Okay, so she'd been way ahead of her on her own account, but that was different. This was different… 'If you'll excuse me,' she said, sliding off her chair and standing up. It was time to leave. 'I'll pay for my breakfast and then I'll go and pack—'

He was on his feet, had caught her hand before she could move. 'Angelica…' She didn't pull her hand away, but she didn't look up at him. 'I haven't dated since my fiancée broke off our engagement a little over a year ago. Lisa thinks it's time I got back on the horse.'

He'd been dumped by the woman he loved? How unlikely was that? Then her brain got past the fact that any woman would dump him and she heard what he'd actually said.

'And I'm the horse?' she asked very quietly, aware that they were now the object of a dozen pairs of eyes. 'Gee, *grazie*, Dante. Or do I mean gee-gee *grazie*?' And, as everything suddenly fell into place, she took a step back. 'Is that what this has been about?' she demanded.

He tightened his grip on her hand. 'This?'

He'd known within minutes of her arrival that she was in trouble. All she'd seen was a man who could melt her underwear at twenty paces. All he'd seen was an opportunity. 'You've been using me from the beginning. Damn it, I should have known. If it looks too good…' she muttered, hurt, angry and feeling stupid. Again. 'Tell me, Dante, what would you have done without the kitten?'

'More to the point, what would you have done?' He closed the gap between them. 'You would still have needed somewhere to stay.' He reached up, touched her cheek with the tips of his fingers and the heat trickled through her, sweet and seductive as warm honey. 'There were two of us in that bedroom last night, Angelica. Which of us walked away?'

She flushed with embarrassment, well aware that it hadn't been her. That she'd wanted him with all the 'hang the consequences' recklessness of her Amery genes.

'I suppose I should be grateful that you weren't prepared to go that far,' she said, fighting the urge to lean into his hand. 'Oh, no, I forgot. You couldn't make a move in your own apartment. You need me off the premises so that it's not some totally sordid exchange that's open to misinter—'

'*Basta!*' His fingers slid through her hair, captured her head, shocking her into silence.

Around them, the café went quiet. He looked up and instantly everyone found they had somewhere else they needed to be. Then he turned back to her.

'I'm sorry, Angelica. You're absolutely right. We are both using you for our own ends but here's the deal. You get an apartment rent-free for a month and a temporary job if you want it. And, no matter what my cousin hopes might happen, there are no strings attached to either offer.'

'No strings? Well, golly, that's all right then.'

'Lis thinks she's helping,' he said, 'but I'm not ready for any kind of relationship. I don't know if I ever will be.'

'I don't imagine she's envisaging a "relationship",' she replied, making ironic quote marks with her fingers. 'Just a quick gallop to shake out the cobwebs. I'm a temp, re- member?'

'*Dio...*' he said a touch raggedly. At her nape, his hand softened but he didn't remove it and, despite her anger, she didn't step away. 'I was trying to be honest with you, Angelica. Nothing hidden. No con—'

Behind her, the café door opened, letting in a blast of cold air. 'Signora Amery?'

'Would you rather I'd prettied it up?' he insisted. 'Lied to you?'

Behind Dante, she saw Lisa watching them anxiously. Above her, Dante's face was unreadable.

She had left Longbourne determined to shake up her life, grab every experience that came her way. So far, Isola was delivering on all fronts. Make that all fronts but one. Not a problem. She was here to work, to learn, to grow as a designer, an artist. A little hot sex would have been a bonus but she wasn't looking for anything as complicated, as involving as a relationship. She had that in common with her mother, too. And, apparently, Dante.

The man at the door called out something in Italian and Lisa said, 'Geli...someone wants you.'

'Oh, for heaven's sake,' she muttered, then turned to the man standing in the doorway, '*Sono* Angelica Amery.'

'I'll see your boxes safely stored while you get your coat,' Dante said as the driver went to unload them. 'We'll go to the police station as soon as it's done.' He needed a little breathing space to recover from the sensory overload of being in close proximity to Angelica. A little cold air in his lungs.

'Would you like me to bring your jacket?' she asked.

'*Grazie*, Angelica. Thank you.' For a moment neither of them moved and the long look that passed between them acknowledged that it wasn't just the jacket he was thanking her for.

The last of the boxes was being stacked in the room opposite his office when she returned, dressed for the weather in the head-turning coat with pockets big enough to conceal a small animal. She'd added a scarf which she'd coiled in some fashionable loop around her neck and a black velvet beret with a glittering spider hat pin to fasten it in place.

Lisa was right. She certainly knew how to make an entrance. She was going to be a sensation at the *commissariato*.

'What is all this stuff?' he asked, indicating the boxes as she handed him his jacket and scarf.

'My Mac. A couple of collapsible worktables,' she said, walking around the boxes, touching each one in turn as she identified the contents. 'My drawing board, easel, paints, brushes, sketch pads.' The long full skirt of her coat brushed against the cartons as she moved among them.

'You intend to paint as well as design clothes?' he asked.

'Maybe...I haven't done anything serious since I switched to fashion for my post-grad. And I've been busy with the ice cream parlour franchise.' She stopped and bent to check a label. 'My sewing machines are in this one. And my steamer.' She looked up. 'I'll need to unpack the fragile stuff to make sure it's all survived the journey.'

'No problem. What about these?' he asked, indicating some of the larger boxes.

'Material, trimmings, buttons. It looks a lot when you see it in a small space,' she said.

'Buttons? You brought buttons with you? You can buy them in Italy,' he pointed out.

She smiled at that. 'I know, and I can't wait to go shopping, but these are buttons I've collected over the years. Some are very old. Some, like these—' she touched one of the tiny jet buttons at her waist and he tried not to think about the way she'd unfastened them last night...one by one '—are quite valuable.'

'Right.' He struggled with a dry mouth. 'Well, the bad news is that you're never going to get all this into Lisa's tiny one-bed flat.'

'Is there any good news?'

'This room isn't being used. You can work here until you find workshop space. Or a flat large enough to accommodate all this.'

'But—'

'I'll move these out of your way.' He indicated the few dusty boxes he'd pushed to one side. 'Will it do?'

'It's perfect, Dante, but we have to discuss rent.'

He'd anticipated that. 'No discussion necessary. In return for a month's lease, you can design an ice cream parlour for me. Whether you consider that good news is for you to decide. Shall we go?'

CHAPTER SEVEN

'There are no recipes for leftover ice cream.'
    —from *Rosie's Little Book of Ice Cream*

THE POLICE STATION was noisy, crowded, and Italian police-women, Geli discovered to her delight, really did wear high heels.

'How on earth do they run in them?' she asked. Anything to break the silence as she waited with Dante for a detective to come and talk to them.

'Run?'

'Never mind,' she said. 'Stupid question. They're all so glamorous I imagine the crooks put up their hands and surrender for the sheer pleasure of being handcuffed and patted down by them.'

She swallowed, unable to believe she'd actually said anything so sexist.

Dante said nothing. He'd said very little other than, 'Take care...' as they'd walked along the snow-packed street.

'Dante!' A detective approached them, shook him by the hand. *'Signora...?'*

'Giorgio, may I introduce Signora Angelica Amery?' Dante said, then, 'Angelica—Commissario Giorgio Rizzoli. Giorgio...' Dante explained the situation in Italian too rapid for her to catch more than a word or two. *'Inglese... Via Pepone...'*

'Signora Amery…' The Commissario placed his hand against his heart. *'Mi dispiace…'*

'He's desolate that you have had such a terrible experience,' Dante translated. 'We are to go through to his office, where he'll take the details, although he's sure you will understand that the chances of recovering your money are very small.'

'Tell him that I understand completely and that I'm very sorry to take up his valuable time.'

Reporting the crime took a very long time. Apart from the fact that everything had to be translated, it seemed that every officer on duty, from a cadet who was barely old enough to shave to one who was well past retiring age, had some pressing matter that only the Commissario could resolve. He was extraordinarily patient, introducing each of his men to her, explaining what had happened and smiling benevolently as each one welcomed her to Isola, offered whatever assistance was in their power to give and held her hand sympathetically while gazing into her eyes.

Dante, in the meantime, gazed out of the window as she repeated the well-rehearsed phrase, *'Mi dispiace, parli lentamente per favore…'*—begging them to speak slowly. If she didn't know better, she would have thought he was afraid to catch her eye in case he laughed. It gave her a warm feeling. As if they were partners in a private joke.

'Well, you promised me it would be an experience and I have to admit that it was almost worth being robbed,' she said as they paused on the steps, catching their breath as they hit the cold air. 'Tell me, are the women officers notably more efficient than the men?' He took her arm as they made their way down the steps, despite the fact that they had been cleared and gritted. 'Only I noticed none of them needed assistance.'

'I think you know the answer to that.'

He wasn't smiling and released her arm the moment

they hit the slushy, slippery pavement, keeping a clear distance between them as they walked back to the café, his face, his body so stiff that he looked as if he'd crack in two.

After about twenty paces she couldn't stand it another moment and stopped. 'Dante, last night…' He'd gone a couple of steps before he realised she wasn't with him and glanced back. 'This morning…' She swallowed. 'I just wanted you to know that I'm truly grateful for everything. I won't do or say anything to mess up Lisa's plans.'

He turned to face her. 'I appreciate that,' he said stiffly.

'And I'll design you the prettiest ice cream parlour imaginable. If you're serious about the workshop space?'

'It's yours, but this isn't the weather to be standing around in the street discussing interior decoration.'

She didn't move.

He shrugged. 'There's a small room at the back of Café Rosa that opens onto the garden. When I saw your designs it occurred to me that an American ice cream parlour might go down well with the younger element.'

'In that case, forget pretty—it had better be nineteen-fifties cool.'

'Maybe. Will your sister object to me borrowing her ideas?'

'There's no copyright in ideas,' she said. 'She borrowed the concept from the US after all and you won't be calling it Knickerbocker Gloria, using her branding or copying her ices. You'll be using gelato rather than ice cream, I imagine?'

'You're getting technical.'

'Just thinking ahead. Will you make your own *gelato* or buy it in, for instance? Is there anyone local who would make specials for you?'

'Good question. I'll think about it. Shall we go?'

'Yes…' She took a step, stopped again. 'No.' There was something she had to say. 'I want you to know that I understand why you were being completely—if rather brutally—honest with me this morning.'

'Do you?'

'You said it's no con—at least where I'm concerned. Lisa, well, that's between you and her.'

'Is that it?'

'Yes…' She rolled her eyes; he really wasn't helping… 'No.' He said nothing, although his eyebrows spoke volumes. But he waited. 'You might want to relax a little, walk a little closer, try and find a smile from somewhere because right now we look as if we're in the middle of a fight rather than about to fall into bed.'

'Do we?' And for a moment the question, loaded with unspoken reference to how close they'd come to the latter, hung there. Then he stuck his hands in his pockets, looked somewhere above her head. 'I owe you an apology, too.'

'If it's about the horse thing,' she said quickly as they continued walking, 'the least said the better.'

'Lisa put the words in my head last night and they leapt out when I wasn't paying attention,' he said and stuck out his elbow, inviting her to slide her arm beneath it. Her turn to do the thing with the eyebrows and he raised a wintry smile. 'You said it, Angelica—we're in this together.'

'Right.' She tucked her arm in his and he drew her closer, no doubt glad of warmth. 'And forget about the horse. I shouldn't be so touchy. I don't know what I'd have done last night if you hadn't been so kind.'

'You'd have managed,' he said as they walked back towards Café Rosa. 'You're a resourceful woman.'

'I'm glad you think so because I'd rather like to put my resourcefulness to the test,' she said as they reached the piazza. 'Will the bartending lesson keep for an hour?'

'Take all the time you need. Lisa managed to drag hers out for weeks.'

'How?' she asked. The fancy barista stuff might take time to master but the basics weren't exactly rocket science.

'I was too wrapped up in my own misery at the time to realise that she was playing the idiot in order to keep me busy. Doing her best to take my mind off Valentina.'

'Valentina? Your fiancée?'

'She's not my anything.' In the low slanting sun his face was all dark shadows. 'She's married to someone else.'

'So soon?' Not the most tactful response but the words had been shocked out of her.

'My father was ready to give her everything I would not.' Grey... His face was grey... 'And it seems that she was pregnant.'

His father?

They'd reached the first market stall and, while she was still trying to get her head around what he'd told her, he unhooked his arm and stepped away. 'Give me your phone and I'll put my number in your contacts.'

Geli handed over her phone but her brain was still processing his shocking revelation.

Valentina had been cheating on him with his father? No wonder he'd withdrawn into himself or that Lisa was so worried about him.

Dante slipped off a glove, programmed in his number and handed her back her phone. 'Give me a call if you need any help haggling over the price of designer clothes and shoes.'

'What...?'

He'd dropped an emotional bombshell and was now casually discussing the price of shoes. But there had been nothing casual or throwaway about his earlier remark. His mention of Valentina had been deliberate; he'd chosen to tell her what had happened before someone else—before Lisa—filled her in on the gossip. And then, just as deliberately because he didn't want to talk about it, he'd changed the subject.

'Oh, yes. *Grazie*,' she said, doing her best to sound equally casual as she dropped the phone back in her pocket. 'I love looking around a new market but I'm afraid that clothes and shoes are on hold until I find out if the bank is going to refund my money.' Concentrate on the most immediate problem. 'My first priority is to take a walk back to where I found Rattino and see if anyone is missing him. Do people put up "lost pet" notices around here?'

'I can't say I've noticed any. I suppose we could put up some "found" ones?'

'That's probably a lot wiser than knocking on strangers' doors when I barely speak a word of Italian,' she agreed.

'Not just wiser,' he said, 'it would be a whole lot safer. Do not, under any circumstances, do that on your own.'

'You could come with me.'

'Let's stick with the posters. Can I leave you to take a look around the market without getting into any trouble while I take a photograph of the rat and run off a few posters? I'll come and find you when they're done.'

'Trouble?' she repeated, looking around at the bustling market. 'What trouble?'

'If you see anything with four legs, looking lost, walk away.'

Geli explored the market, using her phone to take pictures of the colourful stalls and sending them to her sisters. Proof that she'd arrived, was safe and doing what came naturally.

She tried out her Italian, exchanging greetings, asking prices, struggling with the answers until her ear began to tune in to the language of the street as opposed to the carefully enunciated Italian on her teach yourself Italian course.

Despite her intention to simply browse, she was unable to resist some second-hand clothes made from the most gorgeous material and was browsing a luscious selection of ribbon and beads on a stall selling trimmings when Dante found her.

The stallholder, a small, plump middle-aged woman so bundled up that only her face was showing, screamed with delight and flung her arms around him, kissing his cheeks and rattling off something in rapid Italian. Dante laughed and then turned to introduce her.

'Livia, *questa è la mia amica*, Angelica. Angelica, this is Livia.'

Geli offered her hand. '*Piacere*, Livia.'

Her tentative Italian provoked a wide smile and another stream of unintelligible Italian as Livia closed both of her hands around the box of black beads she'd been looking at and indicated that she should put it in her bag.

'I sorted out her traders' licence a few months ago,' Dante explained. 'It's her way of saying thank you.'

'She should be thanking you.'

'I don't have a lot of use for beads and, since you are my friend, it would make her happy if you took them. You can buy something from her another day.'

'*Grazie mille*, Livia,' she said. 'Will you tell her I love her stall, Dante, and that I'll come back and buy from her very soon.'

He said something that earned her a huge smile then, after more hugs and kisses for both of them, Dante took the carrier she was holding and peered into it.

'You changed you mind about window-shopping, I see?'

She shrugged. 'I've got a job, rent-free accommodation for a month and a workshop that I'm paying for with my time. And now I've got some fabulous material to work with, just as soon as I unpack my sewing machine.'

'Do you need more time?' He looked around. 'I believe

there are still a few black things left—' She jabbed her elbow in his ribs and he grinned. 'I guess not.' He took a sheaf of papers from the roomy pocket of his waxed jacket. 'Shall we get this done?'

She took one and looked at the photograph Dante had taken of the kitten. 'He's quite presentable now that he's clean and dry. *Trovato*… Found?' He nodded. '*Contattare* Café Rosa. And the telephone number. Well, that's direct and to the point. Uh-oh…' She looked up as something wet landed on the paper and the colours of the ink began to run into one another as more snow began to fall. 'If we put them out now they'll be a soggy mess in no time,' Geli said. 'Have you got a laminator?'

'No.'

'Fortunately, I packed mine.'

While Dante, wrapped up against the weather, left on his mission to stick up the laminated posters of the lost kitten, Geli called her bank's fraud office and passed on the crime number the Commissario had given her.

'Okay?' Lisa asked, handing her a long black apron.

She shrugged. 'I've done everything I can.' She tied the apron over her clothes and watched Lisa's demonstration of the Gaggia and then produced, one after the other, a perfect espresso, latte and cappuccino.

Lisa, arms folded, watched her through narrowed eyes. 'You've done this before.'

'I was a student for four years. My sisters paid me for the work I did for them, but paints, material and professional sewing machines do not come cheap. Then, as now, I needed a job.'

'Right, Little Miss Clever Clogs, you've got your first customer.' She indicated a man standing at the counter. 'Go get him.'

Geli took a deep breath. *'Ciao, signor. Che cosa desidera?'* she asked.

He smiled. *'Ciao, signora...* Geli,' he added, leaning closer to read the name tag that Lisa had pinned to her apron. *'Il sono Marco.'*

'Ciao, Marco. *Piacere. Che cosa desidera?'* she repeated.

'Vorrei un espresso, per favore,' he said. Then, having thanked her for it, *'Che programme ha per stasera? Le va di andare a bere qualcosa?'*

The words might not have been familiar, but the look, the tone certainly were and she turned to Lisa. 'I think I'm being hit on. How do I say I'm washing my hair?'

'He wants to know if you have any plans for tonight and, if not, can he buy you a drink. So good for business...' she murmured.

'Definitely washing my hair.'

Lisa gave him the bad news and he smiled ruefully, shrugged and drank his coffee.

'What did you say?'

'That you're working tonight. Why?' she asked, thoughtfully. 'Have you changed your mind? He is rather cute.'

'Very cute.'

'Well, he knows where you'll be tonight. Maybe he'll come back.'

'Does that mean I've passed the interview?'

'When can you start?'

'It had better be this evening, don't you think? I wouldn't want Marco to think I was lying.'

'Heaven forbid. Come on, I'll run you through the routine and then you'd better go and put your feet up. It tends to get busy on a Saturday night.'

Half an hour later, Geli said, 'Can I make a hot chocolate to go? I'll pay for it.'

'There's no need. Staff get fed and watered.'

'It's not for me. One of the stallholders I met this morning is a friend of Dante's—'

'They're all his friends when they want something,' she said, pulling a face.

'Are they? Oh, well, anyway, she gave me some beads so I thought I'd take her a hot drink.'

'That's thoughtful, but it's on the house,' she said as Geli made the chocolate and poured it into a carry out cup with a lid. 'You don't know how grateful I am that you're staying, Geli. I really didn't want to leave Dante on his own.'

'Hardly on his own. He seems to know everyone.'

'Everyone knows him. They come to him for help because he'll stand up for them, fight their corner against bureaucracy and lead their campaigns to save this place from the developers. They don't care what it costs him. You're different.'

Geli shrugged, not wanting to get into exactly how different it was. The situation was already awkward enough.

'I mean it,' Lisa said. 'You're the first woman he's shown the slightest interest in for over a year and it hasn't been for lack of attention from women wanting to comfort him. He was engaged—'

'He told me what happened,' she said, cutting Lisa off mid gossip.

'You see? He never talks about that. I don't suppose he told you that they were both punishing him for not doing what they wanted?'

'Punishing him?' Geli shook her head. 'I…I imagined an affair.'

'Nothing so warm-blooded.' Lisa rubbed a cloth over the chrome. 'It hit him very hard.'

So hard that he couldn't envisage another relationship. That was why he'd told her. Not to forestall gossip, but so that she'd understand his reluctance to follow through on the obvious attraction. The classic 'It's not you, it's me…' defence.

'I'm just saying…' Lisa concentrated on polishing an invisible smudge. 'I wouldn't want you to be hurt.'

Really? A bit late to be worrying about that, Lisa…

Geli shook her head. 'I'm not interested in commitment. My sisters have all that happy-ever-after stuff, baby thing well covered. I'm my mother's child.'

She frowned. 'Your mother?'

'She didn't believe in long-term relationships. My sisters and I all have different fathers. At least we assume we do, since we all look quite different.'

'You don't know your father?'

'She used sperm donors.' It was her standard response to anyone interested enough to ask. Spilling out the truth to Dante had been a rare exposure. But then everything about Dante was rare. 'So much less bother, don't you think?'

'Um…' She'd rendered Lisa speechless? That had to be a first… 'Okay. Well, I suggest you come down at seven, while it's still quiet, and you can shadow Matteo. He'll look after you until you get the hang of things. Hold on…' She reached behind her. 'Take the menu to familiarise yourself with it.' She wrote something on the bottom. 'And that should deal with anyone pestering you for a date, although a shrug and *non capisco* will get you out of most situations.'

'Like this?' She shrugged and, putting on a breathy Italian accent, said, *'Non capisco.'*

Lisa grinned. 'Say it like that and I refuse to be responsible!'

Saturday night at Café Rosa was non-stop service of food and drink to the accompaniment of the jazz quartet from the night before. Everyone was very patient with her and Matteo caught any potential disasters before they happened. She had a couple more offers of a drink and dinner, which she managed to dodge without incident, although once Lisa was away there was no need to pretend that she and Dante might become an item—

'Geli…' She turned to find Lisa holding a tray loaded with coffee, water and a *panino*.

'You can take your break now. Will you give this to Dan on your way upstairs? And remind him that it's Saturday night. All work and no play…' She looked around. 'We seem to be between rushes at the moment. Take your time.'

Dante heard Angelica coming—it was disconcerting how quickly he'd come to recognise her quick, light step—but he didn't look up as she opened the door. If she saw he was busy she might not stop. His head might be telling him not to get involved, but his body wasn't listening and he needed to keep his distance.

'Lisa sent you some supper,' she said, placing it on the table behind his desk.

Of course she had. Any excuse that would throw them together…

He grunted an acknowledgement and continued to pound away at the keyboard.

'It's not good for you, you know.'

'What isn't?'

'Eating while you work.' Angelica backed up and propped herself on the edge of his desk. 'You'll get indigestion, heartburn and stomach ulcers.'

Nothing compared with what her bottom, inches from his hand, was doing to him. 'Haven't you got a café full of customers?'

'I'm on my break.' He continued typing, although it was unlikely he was making any sense. 'Lisa expects me to sit on your knee and ruffle your hair while I tell you about all the men who've hit on me this evening.'

'Did she say that?'

'Not in so many words, but she told me to remind you that all work and no play makes Dante very dull. And she told me to take my time. Of course, it could be that I'm so useless she's desperate to get me out of the way for half an hour.'

'Are you useless?'

'Not totally.'

No. He'd heard all about her virtuoso performance on the Gaggia from a very smug Lisa.

He stopped pretending to work and looked up. She'd swathed herself in one of the Café Rosa's long black aprons and her hair was tied back with a velvet ribbon. She looked cool and efficient but that full crimson mouth would turn heads at fifty paces.

'How many men?' he asked.

'Let's see. There was Roberto.' She held up her hand, fingers spread wide and ticked him off on a finger. 'Dark hair, blue eyes, leather biker jacket. *"Andiamo in un posto più tranquillo..."*' she said in a low, sexy voice.

'I'd advise against going anywhere with him, noisy or quiet.'

'He's bad?'

'His wife is away, looking after her sick mother.'

'What a jerk,' she said, using a very Italian gesture to dismiss him. 'What about Leo? He wanted to "friend" me on Facebook. Was that a euphemism for something else, do you think?'

'That you're thinking it suggests you already know.'

'Men! All they want is sex. Doesn't anyone ask a girl out on a proper date any more?'

'A proper date?' he asked.

'The kind where a man picks a girl up from her home, takes her to the movies, buys her popcorn and they hold hands in the dark—'

'Was that it?' He cut her off, trying not to think about Angelica in the dark with some man who might be holding her hand in the cinema but would have his mind on where else he was going to hold her when he got her home.

'What? Oh, no. Gennaro was very sweet, but I'm not looking for a father figure, and Nic, the guy who plays the saxophone, said *"Ti amo..."* in the most affecting way, but I think that was because I'd just taken him a beer.'

'That'll do it every time for Nic; even so, that's quite a fan club you've got there. Are any of them going to get lucky?'

'With Lisa keeping a close eye on me? She's doing a great job of protecting your interests.'

'She doesn't trust my personal charm to hold you in thrall?'

'I'm down there and you're up here working.' She lifted her shoulders, sketching a shrug. 'Out of sight, out of mind.' She blew away a wisp of hair that had escaped its tie. 'Did I mention Marco? He came in this afternoon when Lisa was showing me the ropes. I made him an espresso. He's downstairs now...' She stopped. 'You don't want to hear this when you're so obviously busy. I hadn't realised running a bar involved so much bureaucracy.'

'There's enough to keep me fully occupied, but I'm working on a development plan for Isola. One that doesn't involve pulling down historic streets,' he added.

'Oh, I see. Well, that's seriously important work and I'm disturbing you.'

Without a doubt...

'Don't forget your supper,' she said, rubbing the tip of her thumb across her lower lip. 'Is my lipstick convincingly smudged, do you think?' As she leaned forward so that he could give her his opinion, the top of her apron gaped to offer a glimpse of black lace beneath the scoop top of the black T-shirt she was wearing. It was clinging to soft white breasts and if that was the view that customers were getting as she served them it was hardly any wonder that she was getting hit on. 'Maybe I should muss up my hair a bit?'

'You want Lisa to think that we've been making out over my desk?'

'I'm doing my best to convince her that we're struggling to keep our hands off each other. Without a lot of help, I might add—'

As she reached up to tease out a strand, he caught her wrist.

'You want your hair mussed?' he asked, his voice sounding strange, as if he'd never heard it before.

She said nothing, but the tip of her tongue appeared briefly against softly parted lips, her pupils widened, black as her hair, swallowing up the silver-grey of her eyes and the catch in her breath was answered by his body's clamour to touch her, take her.

For a moment neither of them moved then he released her wrist, reached for the ribbon holding her hair and, as he tugged it loose, the silken mass fell forward, brushing against his face, enveloping him in the intimacy of its scent as she slid into his lap.

His fingers slipped through it as he cradled her head, angling his mouth to tease her lips open and, as he brushed against the sensitive nerve endings at her nape, a tiny moan—more vibration than sound—escaped her lips, her body softened against him and his tongue was swathed in hot sweet satin.

With one hand tangled in her hair, the other sought out the gap between her T-shirt and the black ankle-length skirt that hid her fabulous legs, sliding over satin skin to cradle her lace-covered breast, touch her candy-hard nipple.

She wanted this, he wanted it and he was a fool not to taste her, touch her, bury himself deep inside her—over his desk, on the floor, in his bed. It had nothing to do with emotion, feelings; this was raw, physical need.

It was just sex—

The four words slammed through his body like an ice storm. Colder than the snow-covered Dolomites.

'It was just sex...'

The last words Valentina had said to him.

'Okay, that should do it,' he said, lifting her from his lap and setting her on her feet before swinging his chair back to face his laptop. 'If that's all, I want this on the Minister's desk first thing on Monday.'

She didn't move but he didn't have to look to know that her hair was loose about her shoulders, her swollen lips open in a shocked O, her expression that of a kicked puppy. The image was imprinted indelibly on his brain.

He didn't expect or wait for an answer but began pounding on the keyboard as if nothing had happened while she backed out of the room, then turned and ran up the stairs. Kept pounding until he heard the door bang shut on the floor above and his fingers froze above the keyboard.

He stared at the screen, the cursor blinking an invitation to delete the rubbish he'd just written. Instead, he slumped back in the chair, dragging his hands over his face, rubbing hard to eradicate every trace of Angelica Amery. It didn't work. The scent of her skin, her hair was on his hands, in his lungs and, as he wiped the back of his hand over his mouth in an attempt to eradicate the honeyed taste of her lips, it came away bearing traces of crimson lipstick.

It would be two more days before Angelica moved out.

They were going to be two very long days and right now he needed air—fresh, clean, cold air—to blow her out of his head.

CHAPTER EIGHT

'You can't buy happiness but you can buy ice cream...
which is much the same thing.'
—from *Rosie's Little Book of Ice Cream*

GELI'S RACING PULSE, pounding heartbeat said, *Run—run for your life.* Falling in lust with a man who had made it clear not once, not twice but three times that while he might be aroused—and he had certainly been aroused—he was not interested in any kind of relationship was a recipe for disaster.

Sharing an apartment with that man, working with him was never going to work.

She threw open her bedroom window, stuck her head out and filled her lungs with icy air, hoping that it would cool not just her skin but freeze the heat from the inside out.

What was it about Dante Vettori that made her lose her wits? What had started out as a little teasing had ended with his arms around her, his mouth on hers, his hands spread wide over her skin. She shivered and pressed her hand hard against her breast, where his touch had created a shock of pleasure that racketed around her body like a pinball machine, lighting up every sensory receptor she had.

Maybe she should suggest some straightforward recreational sex so they could both get it out of their systems.

No strings. Except if he'd been a 'no strings' kind of guy he'd have been out there, taking anything on offer in an attempt to obliterate the heartbreak. A man who looked like Dante would not have been short of offers.

If he'd been a 'no strings' kind of guy they would have been naked right now.

He needed something more than that. Or maybe something less. Someone who didn't want anything from him but was just there…

She was good at that. She'd been rescuing broken creatures ever since she'd picked up that injured pheasant. She'd never tried rescuing a broken person before but there was no difference. They were edgy, scared and you had to earn their trust, too. No sudden moves. No demands…

She checked on Rattino, sat on the floor rubbing his tiny domed head, while she sipped iced water, rolled the glass against her mouth to cool her swollen lips and heated libido.

Having stretched the taking her time instruction to the limit, she found a clip and fastened back her hair, straightened her clothes, applied a fresh coat of lipstick. It was time to get back to work…

Dante was standing in the middle of the sitting room. He was wearing his jacket, had a bright red scarf around his neck and in his hands he was holding a battered cardboard box.

For a moment they stared at one another, then he said, 'I found this on the back doorstep.'

'On the doorstep?' What was he doing on the doorstep when he was so busy writing a report…?

'I needed some fresh air,' he said.

You and me both, mister, she thought, taking a step closer so that she could see what was in the box.

'Oh, kittens.' Two of them, all eyes, huddled together in the corner. 'Your notice appears to have worked.'

'I was under the impression that its purpose was to find the owner of Rattino so that we could return him to the bosom of his family,' he said, unimpressed. 'Not have the rest of his family dumped on our doorstep.'

She looked up. *Our doorstep...*

'In an ideal world,' she said, returning to the kittens, picking each one up in turn and checking it over for any sign of injury before replacing it in the box. 'They're thin but otherwise seem in good shape.'

'I imagine their mother is a stray who didn't come back from a hunting trip.'

'It seems likely. And would explain why Rattino went looking for food. He is the biggest. So what do you think?'

'What do I think?'

'Shall we call the black one Mole and the one with stripes Badger? We already have Ratty?' she prompted. '*Wind in the Willows*? It's a classic English children's book,' she explained when he made no response. 'Or would you prefer Italian names?'

'I think…' He took a breath. 'I think I'll go and take down those notices before anyone else decides to leave a box of unwanted kittens on the doorstep.'

'Right. Good plan. I'll, um, feed these two,' she said as he headed for the door. 'Introduce them to the amenities. Will you keep an eye out for their mother, while you're out? She wouldn't have abandoned them.'

'If she's been hit by a car—'

'You're right. She may be lying hurt somewhere,' she said. 'Hang on while I see to these two and I'll come with you. I know the kind of places she'll crawl into.'

Geli had no doubt that Dante would rather be on his own but, rather than waste his breath, he said, 'I'll go and tell Lisa that she's going to have to manage without you.'

'You'll make her evening.'

'No doubt.' His tone left her under no illusion that she wasn't making his. 'Wrap up well. It's freezing out there.'

Twenty minutes later, having fed the kittens, reunited them with their brother and changed her flat working shoes for a pair of sturdy boots, she was walking with Dante along the street where she'd found Rattino.

'Urban cats have a fairly limited range,' she explained, stopping every few yards to check doorways and explore the narrow street that had given her a fright the night she'd arrived. 'They avoid fights by staying out of each other's way whenever possible. Will you hold this?'

'Where is your glove?' he demanded when she handed him her flashlight and began to turn over boxes with her bare hand.

'In my pocket. I held the kittens so she'd smell them on me but she's not here—'

She broke off as he took her icy hand and tucked it into his own roomy fleece-lined glove so that their hands were palm to palm. 'Now we'll both smell of her kittens.'

She looked up at him. 'Good thinking.'

'I'm glad you approve,' he said and the shadows from the street lights emphasised the creases as, unexpectedly, he smiled.

Oh, boy... She turned away to grab one of the notices from a nearby lamp post and saw the wooden barriers surrounding the construction site where Via Pepone used to be.

'There,' she said. 'If she's survived, she'll be in there.'

'Are you certain?'

'As certain as I can be. Disturbed ground, displaced rodents, workmen dropping food scraps, lots of places to hide. Perfect for a mother with three hungry kittens. Maybe someone working on the site knew they were there and when he saw the notice brought them to us.'

'That makes sense.' He walked across to the site entrance and tried the gate. It did not budge.

'Is there a night watchman?' she asked.

'It's the twenty-first century.' He looked up at the cameras mounted on high posts. 'It's all high-tech security systems and CCTV monitored from a warm office these days.'

'Okaaay.' She reluctantly removed her hand from his glove and fished in her pocket for her own. 'In that case you'll have to give me a bunk-up so that I can climb over.'

'Alarms?' he reminded her. 'CCTV.'

'Which will deal with the problem of how I'd climb back out again with an injured cat. And the local *polizia* are so helpful. I'm sure they'll drive me to the vet before they arrest me.'

'Drive you to the vet, send out for hot chocolate to keep you warm and raise a collection to pay the vet's bill, I have no doubt. But you've had your quota of excitement for this week.'

'Well, that's a mean thing to say.' Their breath mingled in the freezing air and she pulled on her glove before she did something really exciting, like grabbing his collar and pulling him down to warm their freezing lips. 'Okay, your turn. What do you suggest?'

'I suppose I could climb over the fence and get arrested.'

'Your life is that short of excitement?'

'Not since you and that wretched kitten arrived.'

'You can thank me later. Any other ideas?' She waited. 'I sensed an *or* in there somewhere.'

He shrugged, looked somewhere above her head. 'Or I could make a phone call and get the security people to let us in.'

'Maybe sooner rather than later,' she suggested, stamping her feet.

He looked down at her for a long moment, then took out his cellphone, thumbed a number on his fast dial list and walked away down the street as he spoke to whoever answered. The conversation was brief and he wasn't smiling as he rejoined her.

'Someone will be here in a few minutes.'

'Well, that's impressive.'

'You think so?'

He looked up at the floodlit boarding high above the fence with an artist's impression of the office block that would replace Via Pepone. It bore the name of the construction company in huge letters. Beneath, smaller, was the name of the developer.

Vettori SpA.

Oh... 'That's not a coincidence, is it?' she said.

'My great-grandfather started the business after the war, repairing bomb-damaged buildings, working every hour God gave to save enough money to buy some land and build a small block of flats. My grandfather took over a thriving construction company and continued to expand the business until a heart attack forced him to retire and he handed it over to my father.'

This was his father's project? 'Was that who you called just now? Your father?'

Before he could answer, a security patrol van drew up in a spray of dirty snow. The driver leapt out, exchanged a few words with Dante in rapid Italian and then unlocked the small personal door set in the gates.

'Take care, Angel,' Dante said, taking her hand as they stepped through after him.

Angel? She turned and looked up at him.

'A construction site is a hazardous place,' he said.

'Yes...' With the ground frozen, no work had been done in the last couple of days and, as the patrolman shone his flashlight slowly across the site, there were few footprints to mar the pristine snow. Then she saw something...

'There!' She snatched her hand away to point to where the

light picked up a disturbance in the snow. Not paw prints but a wider trail marked by darker patches of blood where an animal had dragged herself across the ground, desperate to get back to her babies. 'She's hurt.'

'Wait…'

She ignored Dante, running across the yard, using her own small flashlight to follow the trail until she reached the place where the cat had wedged herself under pallets piled with building materials.

'Let me do this.' Dante knelt beside her, but she'd already stripped off her gloves and was holding out her hands so that the cat could smell her kittens. Crooning and chirruping, she dragged herself towards the scent until Geli could reach her and lift her gently from her hiding place. '*Dio*… She's a mess.'

'We need to keep her warm. Take my scarf,' she urged, but Dante pulled off his beautiful red cashmere scarf and wrapped it around the poor creature. 'We need to get her to a vet,' she said.

Dante looked at this angel, so passionate, so full of compassion.

He called the vet and then asked the security guard to drive them to his office. 'He'll meet us there. Come on; it'll be a squeeze, but it's not far,' he said, holding the door so that she could slide into the passenger seat, then squashing in after her, sitting sideways to give her as much room as possible. 'I'll breathe in when you breathe out and we should be okay,' he said, and she laughed. Such a good sound.

The vet was unlocking the door as they arrived, and Dante translated while Geli assisted him until his nurse arrived and they were no longer needed. Then they retired to the freezing waiting room.

'This is going to take a while,' she said, her breath a misty cloud. 'You should get back to your report.'

'It will keep.' He settled in the corner of the battered sofa and opened his jacket in invitation but she hesitated. Despite the last hour, she wasn't likely to forget the appalling way he'd behaved when she came up to his office. Okay, she'd been flirting a little but he should not have risen to it. Should not have kissed her, touched her and, when she'd responded with an eagerness that had wiped everything but need from his mind, he should not have rejected her.

He was a mess, he knew it, but the room was freezing and she wasn't going anywhere until she knew whether the cat was going to survive.

'Come on. You're shivering,' he said and, after what felt like for ever, she surrendered to the reality of the situation and sat down primly beside him. 'Snuggle up. You're letting out all the warmth,' he said, looping his arm around her and drawing her close, wrapping his coat around her.

She looked at him. 'Snuggle?'

'My mother used to say that. That's right, isn't it?'

'Yes.' She nodded and relaxed into him. 'My mother used to say that when we piled on the sofa to watch a movie on the television.'

'What movies did you watch together?'

'*Beauty and the Beast. Mary Poppins. The Jungle Book. White Fang…* We used an entire box of tissues between us when we watched that one.'

'Did White Fang die?' he asked, in an attempt to distract himself from the way her body was pressed against his, the tickle of her hair against his cheek.

'No, it was the scene where the boy had to send the wolf away for its own safety. He pretended he didn't love it any more. It was heartbreaking.'

'I can imagine.' He looked down at her. Or, rather, the top of her head. 'Is the cat going to make it, do you think?'

'It's hard to say. She seems to have taken a glancing

blow from a car. There's a lot of superficial damage, cuts and scrapes and a broken bone or two.' She turned her head and looked up at him and, despite his best intentions, it took all his strength not to kiss her again. 'It depends what internal damage has been done.'

'Yes, of course.' *Look away. Think about the cat.* 'How on earth did she manage to get under the fence and drag herself back across the site?'

'Cats are amazing and she's a mother. Her babies needed her.'

'They survived without her.'

Her face pressed against the collar of Dante's shirt, his neck, sharing his warmth, Geli heard a world of hurt in those few words.

'Only because I found Rattino and you put up that notice,' she said. 'Do you see your mother, Dante?'

He stared straight ahead and for a moment she didn't think he was going to answer her, but then he shrugged. 'Occasionally. She remarried, started a new family.'

'So you were able to return to Italy.'

'Just for the holidays. I was at school in England. Then I was away at university.'

'England or Italy?'

'Scotland. Then the US.'

Distancing himself from a father who was too busy with the new woman in his life to put him first, she thought. And from a mother who had found someone new to love and made a second family where he probably felt like a spare part...

She felt a bit like that, too, now that her sisters were married. It was no longer the three of them against the world.

'What did you read? At uni?' she asked. Anything to take away the bleakness in those dark eyes.

'Politics, philosophy and economics at St Andrews. Business management at Harvard.'

'St Andrews,' she repeated, with a teasing Scottish accent. 'And Harvard?'

He looked down at her, a smile creating a sunburst of creases around his eyes. 'Are you suggesting that I'm a little over-qualified to run a café?'

She made a performance of a shrug. 'What are you going to do with your degree except work as a researcher for a Member of Parliament? But business management at Harvard seems a little over the top. Unless you're planning world domination in the jazz café market?'

'Not ice cream and definitely not jazz cafés,' he said. 'The plan was that I gain some experience with companies in the United States before joining my father.'

'The fourth generation to run Vettori SpA?'

'Until Via Pepone got in the way.'

'Do you regret taking a stand?' she asked.

'Wrong question, Angel. The question is whether, given the same choices, I would do it again.'

'Would you?' she asked, shivering against him, not with the cold, where the snow had melted into her skirt and clung wetly to her legs, but at the thought of the boy who'd had his life torn apart, bouncing between adults who thought only of themselves.

'Maybe I was never meant to be the CEO of a big company,' he said, taking out his cellphone and thumbing in a text with the hand he didn't have around her shoulders. 'I hoped it would bring us closer together, but my father and I are very different. He thinks I'm soft, sentimental, trying to hang onto a past that is long gone. Incapable of holding onto a woman like Valentina Mazzolini.'

'When what you're actually trying to do is make a future for a place that you love.' A place where, sitting in Nonnina Rosa's kitchen as a boy, watching her cook, he'd been happy. Where he'd spent time as a youth on those long school holidays while his mother and father had been absorbed in new partnerships…

Isola was his home.

'Local politics seems to be calling me,' he admitted. 'There's no money in it, no A-list parties, just a lot of hard work, but maybe, in twenty or thirty years, if I've managed to hold back the march of the skyscraper and secure the spirit of old Isola in a modern world, they'll elect me mayor.'

'Tell me about Isola,' she urged. 'About your vision.'

'Vision?'

'Isn't that what the report you're writing is all about? Not just facts and figures, but your vision, your passion. The human scale?'

'That's the idea,' he said, 'but it's difficult to put all that into words that a politician can use. They need the facts and figures. It's dull stuff.'

'We're going to be here for a while and the only alternative is a pile of dog-eared Italian gossip magazines about people I've never heard of.' And she could have listened to Dante Vettori read the telephone directory. 'Go for it.'

'Go for it?'

'Tell me your plan, Dan.' He laughed—not some big ha-ha-ha laugh, it was no more than a sound on his breath, but it was the genuine article. 'Tell me why you love it so much,' she urged.

'It's real,' he said. 'This was a working class district with a strong sense of community. The park was closed and, with no green space, we made our own on a strip of abandoned land by the railway. The factories and the foundry are gone now, but people are still making things here because it's what they do, who they are. You know that, Angel. It's why you came.'

'Nothing stands still. There has to be change. Growth.'

'But you don't have to tear everything down. If they could just see—' He dismissed the thought with a gesture.

'What would you show them?' she pressed.

'The life, the music, the people.' And, at her urging, he poured out his love of Isola, his vision of the future.

'I don't think they'll wait twenty years,' she said when he fell silent. 'I think, given the chance, they'd elect you now.'

That raised one of his heart-stopping smiles. 'Maybe I should ask you to be my campaign manager.'

'Maybe you should.'

Their words hung in the air, full of possibilities, but she knew he hadn't meant it. It was just one of those things that slipped out when your mouth was working faster than your brain...

A tap on the outside door released them.

'I hope that's not another emergency.'

Dante didn't reply, but slipped out of his jacket and wrapped it around her while he went to investigate. He returned a few moments later with two carry-out drinks from Café Rosa and a box containing a pizza the size of a cartwheel.

'I didn't eat the supper you brought up,' he said, staring at the magazines for a moment before pushing them aside and opening the box to release the scent of tomatoes, cheese, basil. 'And you didn't get your break. It's a Margherita,' he added, glancing at her. 'No meat.' He checked the cups. 'This is yours. Hot chocolate.'

'*Posso abbracciarti,* Dante?' His only response was a frown. 'Did I mess that up?'

'That depends if you intended to ask if you could give me a hug.'

'You sent out for hot chocolate and my favourite pizza,' she pointed out. 'What do you think?' Then, grabbing a slice to cover her embarrassment, 'Don't fret. I was speaking metaphorically.'

'Metaphorically? Right.' Did he sound disappointed? She didn't dare look. 'Your Italian is coming along in leaps and bounds.'

'I'm memorising the phrasebook that Sorrel gave me.'

'Your sister?'

'The one who's married to an explorer.'

'And that was in it?'

'They've apparently moved on a bit since "my postilion was struck by lightning".' She took a bite of the pizza and groaned with pleasure.

'But they haven't got to grips with the metaphorical.'

She caught a trailing dribble of cheese with her finger and guided it into her mouth. 'It's a very small phrasebook.'

'Small but dangerous. Not everyone will get the subtleties of meaning.'

'Marco?' she suggested. 'He wasn't very subtle.'

'Nor was Roberto.'

'Oh, I've got him covered.' She adopted a pose. '*Non m'interessa*—I'm not interested. *Mi lasci in pace*—Leave me alone. *Smetta d'infastidirmi!*—Stop bothering me!'

'I take it all back. It is a most excellent phrasebook.'

'And this is the most excellent pizza. You texted Lisa?'

'I knew she'd worry when we didn't come back. And I thought you would welcome some warm food.'

'You thought right,' she said, helping herself to a second slice. Then she drank her chocolate, checked the time.

'Put your feet up,' Dante urged and, rather than unlace her boots, she picked up a magazine, placed it on the sofa and rested them on that. Then she eased the damp skirt away from her legs, tucked her feet up under her coat and invited him back into his jacket. He slipped his arms in and she leaned back against him as if it was the most natural thing in the world and, warm from the food, tired from what had been a very long day, she closed her eyes.

Dante watched with the envy of the insomniac as Angelica closed her eyes and was instantly asleep. Watched her as the silence grew deep around him and he closed his own eyes.

'Dante…'

He felt a touch to his shoulder and looked up to find the vet standing over him. He'd slept?

'It's over, Dante. She's in recovery.'

'The prognosis?'

'Fair. Cats are tough. We'll keep her here for a day or two and see how she does but, all things being equal, you can take her home in a couple of days.'

'Actually, she's a stray.'

'Good try,' he said, 'but she's going to need warmth, good food and care if she's going to make a full recovery. Tell the young lady that she saved her life. Another hour or two…' His gesture suggested that it would have been touch and go. 'You can see her if you want.'

'I'm sure she'll want to.'

'Come on through. Is there a spare slice of pizza?'

'It'll be cold.'

'My food usually is,' he said, helping himself to a slice and taking a bite.

'How much do I owe you?'

'My receptionist will send you a bill at the end of the month but I'll bring my family to the café at the weekend and you can give us all lunch. A small repayment for disturbing my evening.'

'My pleasure.'

Angelica stirred, opened her eyes, looked blank for a moment and then sat up in a rush as she saw the vet walking away with a slice of pizza in his hand. 'What's happened? How is she?'

'She's fine. We can take her home in a couple of days. Do you want to see her?'

'Please.' She stood up, picked up the magazine to return to the table and saw the front cover. An older man and a much younger woman arriving at some gala event. She didn't need to read Italian or check the names to know who they were.

He was Dante, twenty-five years on, just as she'd imagined him, with a touch of silver at the temple to lend gravitas. The woman, gold-blonde with ice-blue eyes, was wearing a designer gown that was a shade darker than her eyes and a Queen's ransom in diamonds.

He turned back to see what was keeping her and saw the magazine in her hand. He walked back to her and took it from her.

'The first time I saw her was at a party my father threw to welcome me to Vettori SpA. They were standing together but I was too self-absorbed to realise that he was in love with her. Even later, when he married her, I thought...'

'You thought he'd done it to hurt you.'

'Lisa told you that.' He shook his head. 'I was wrong. If I'd just taken a moment to look at him instead of her.' He looked bleak, utterly wretched and, unable to bear it, she touched his arm so that he looked up at her instead of the picture. 'He stood back and let me walk away with her.'

'Because he loved you both.'

'Maybe, but he chose her.'

Rejecting him for the second time. And yet Dante had called him tonight, asked him for help. For her.

Before she could think of the words to tell him that she knew how much it must have cost him, he tossed the magazine back on the pile at the end of the table. 'Shall we go and see how cat number four is doing?'

They went through to the recovery area where she was sleeping off the anaesthetic. Large patches of fur had been shaved off. There were stitches, her leg was in a cast and she'd lost most of her tail.

'She looks like Frankenstein's cat,' he said.

'It's temporary. She's been through the mill and she'll need a lot of TLC, but one day, when her fur has grown back and the pain has retreated, she'll smell a mouse or see a bird and, without thinking, she'll be up and away, purring with pleasure at being alive and on the hunt.'

He was very still beside her, not speaking, not moving. Then he said, 'My father took Valentina away and married her secretly in Las Vegas. No one knew about it for months.'

'Well, that makes sense. The gossip magazines would have gone to town. Paps following you around, hoping for some reaction. Speculation about whether you'd been invited to the wedding. Whether you'd show.'

He managed a wry smile. 'I suppose I should be grateful. In the end, their extended honeymoon was brought to an end when Valentina's grandmother died. The fact that she was very obviously pregnant made the front page of *Celebrità*.'

'That must have been a shock. Were you there? At the funeral?'

'No. My father sent me an email telling me that they were married, about the baby, asking me to stay away and I've done that.'

'Until tonight.'

He nodded.

'And he answered.'

'I imagine he's been waiting for my call.' He took out his gloves and pulled them on. 'When he realised that all I wanted was to get into the site to rescue a cat he was so relieved that he couldn't do enough.'

'Maybe he'll call you next.'

'If he doesn't, I'll call him.' He'd sounded matter-of-fact as he'd talked about what had happened but, when he turned to her, his normally expressive face was blank of all emotion. 'Shall we go?'

She paused on the step and, hunting for a way to change the subject, she looked up at the night sky. 'There are no stars.'

'It's the light pollution from the city.' Dante took her arm as her foot slipped on the freezing pavement. 'You have to go up into the mountains to see them.'

'In the snow? That would be magic.'

He looked down at her, his lips pulled into an unexpected smile. 'Would you like to go?'

Her heart squeezed in her chest. 'Now?'

'You're the advocate of seizing the day,' he reminded her. 'The forecast this evening suggested a warm front was coming in from the south. It could be raining tomorrow.'

For a dizzying moment she saw herself lying back in the snow, making angels with Dante, while all around them the world was sparkling-white, velvet-black and filled with diamonds...

This was why she'd come to Italy. For excitement, for moments like this. Her mother would grab the moment without a backward glance, without a thought for the consequences.

But she wasn't her mother.

'I have to check the kittens,' she said, sounding exactly like her responsible big sister, Elle. Elle who, just eighteen and with a college place waiting, had sacrificed her ambitions to stay at home and take a minimum-wage job so that she could feed her siblings, take care of her mentally fragile grandmother. Nurturing, caring, always there.

'Of course you do. And I have no confidence in the weather forecast. Experience suggests that we're going to be freezing for a while yet.'

They walked in silence for a while, their boots crunching against the frozen snow, their breath mingling in the bitter air, but Dante had offered her something special and she wanted to give him something in return. Something that would show him that she had not been rejecting him.

Something personal, something that she would only share with someone she— Someone she trusted.

'It's blonde,' she said.

'Blonde?' He glanced down at her.

'You wanted to know the natural colour of my hair. It's white-blonde.'

'Really?'

'I have to dye my brows and lashes or they'd be invisible. There must have been a Scandinavian roustabout with the Fair the year before I was born.'

'I can't imagine you as a blonde,' he said.

No, well, she'd seen the quality of blonde he was used to dating. 'I did once consider leaving a natural streak,' she said. 'For dramatic effect.'

'*Cara*…you are all the drama a man can take.'

'Is that a compliment? No, it's not… Anyway,' she said, rapidly moving on, 'Great-Uncle Basil said I'd look more like Lily Munster than Morticia Addams so that was that.'

'You are like no one, Angel. You are individual. Unique.'

Unique? 'Not exactly the kind of compliment a woman queues up to hear but I'll take it.'

'You don't need me to tell you that you're stunning, Angelica Amery. You have Roberto and Gennaro and Nic and Marco lining up to turn your head.' She laughed and he drew her closer to his side.

The café was closed when they arrived back and they went in the back way.

At the first landing Dante stopped. 'Go and tell the kittens that their *mamma* will be home soon. Have a warm bath. I've got a few things to do.'

'Do you ever sleep, Dante?'

'Not much,' he admitted.

'Not enough,' she said, lifting her cold hands to his face and smoothing her thumbs across the hollows under his eyes. 'You need to quieten your mind before you go to bed.'

The world stilled. 'How do I do that?' he asked.

'First you switch off your computer. Then you write a list of the things you have to do tomorrow so that you don't stay awake trying to remember them.'

'But I've turned off my computer,' he reminded her. 'How do I do that?'

'Use a notepad and a pen.'

'That's a bit old school.'

'Maybe, but that's the rule.'

'Okay, pen, paper, list. Then what?'

'You take a bath—don't have the water too hot; your body needs to be cool to sleep.'

He leaned against his office door, folded his arms. 'Go on.'

'Sprinkle a few drops of lavender oil on your pillow before you get into bed and, when you close your eyes, think about all the good things that happened to you today.'

'Good things? What do you suggest? Our trip to the police station? That I've been lumbered with two more kittens and their injured mother? Spent hours in a freezing—'

'Don't be such a grouch. You helped a stranger who was in a fix. Rescued a cat that would have died without you doing something big, something difficult. You spoke to your father.'

She rubbed her hand over his arm, a gesture of comfort to let him know that she was aware how hard it must have been to ask him for help.

He looked at her hand, small, white, with perfect crimson-tipped nails, lying against his shabby worn waxed jacket sleeve, and for a moment he couldn't think about anything but reaching out and wrapping his arms around her, just holding her.

'Think about how good that pizza tasted.'

He looked up, realised that she was looking at him with concern. He straightened, breaking the contact. 'Is that it?'

'No. Last thing of all, you should think about all the good things you're going to do tomorrow so that you wake up happy.'

'Is that more of your mother's wisdom?'

'Yes...' Her eyes sparkled a little too brightly. 'Can I give you that hug now, Dante?'

'A metaphorical one?'

'Actually, I think you deserve the real thing,' she said, stepping close and, before he could move, she'd wrapped her arms around him, her cheek was against his chest. 'You have been a one hundred per cent good guy today, Dante Vettori. Think about that.'

Dante closed his eyes and inhaled the scent of this woman who had blown into his life like a force of nature.

She smelled of pizza and chocolate, there was a hint of antiseptic where she'd washed after handling the cat. And something more that he was coming to recognise as indefinably his Angel...

'You can hug back,' she murmured after a moment. 'It doesn't hurt.'

How could she be so sure? How could you want something so much and dread it at the same time? But ever since she'd asked him to hug her while they were waiting for the vet, leaning against him as she'd put her feet up, he'd been thinking about how it would feel to really hold her, to kiss her, live for the moment. What would happen if he followed through on those kisses without any thought of the past or the future?

Selfish thoughts. Dangerous thoughts. But if anyone

deserved a hug it was Angelica and he tightened his arms about her, holding her close for a long perfect minute, but she was wrong about it not hurting. It hurt like hell when, after a while, she pulled away.

CHAPTER NINE

'If you licked the sunset, it would taste like Neapolitan ice cream.'

—from *Rosie's Little Book of Ice Cream*

GELI STOOD AT the top of the stairs hugging her arms around her, holding in how it felt to have Dante's arms around her. Not in some crazy mad moment when one or both of them had temporarily lost control, but the kind of hug you'd give a friend in a shared moment. Special, real...

He was special. She could not imagine how hard it must have been for him to call his father and ask for his help but he'd done it for her. Okay, he'd done it for the cat, but if it hadn't been for her he wouldn't have been out there in the freezing night looking for a stray cat in the first place.

He *was* special and she would be his friend and if that was all he could give then she'd ask for nothing more.

Dante watched as Angelica ran up to the top floor to check on her precious kittens then went into his office and sat down at his desk. He'd left his laptop on and the screen-saver was drifting across the screen waiting for him to touch a key and continue with his dry, full of facts report that, despite all the promises and encouragement from the minister, would be filed and forgotten.

He turned the machine off, pulled a legal pad close, uncapped a pen and wrote the number one in the margin.

Quieten his mind. Make a list…

It began easily enough as he jotted down half a dozen of the most urgent things he had to do in the coming week. He added a note of something to include in his report. Crossed that through. Wrote: *vision, passion*… He underlined the last two words. What was it Angelica had asked him? *'What would you show them?'*

The life, the music but, above all, the people. Not some slick documentary film but real people talking straight into the camera, telling those who would tear this place down what was so great about it. Why they should think again.

He sent a text to Lisa, wishing them both *buon viaggia, buona fortuna,* so she'd see it when she woke. He hoped he'd done the right thing. That Lisa and Giovanni's love would heal the rift between their families. If it did they would have Angelica's crazy arrival to thank for that.

Angelica—

She had never had a father, had lost her mother at a pitifully early age. She might wear the protective black she'd hidden behind as a child but on the inside her world was richly coloured and filled with wonderful memories. Tragedy, need, had not shattered her family; it had bound it together.

She'd asked him if he saw his mother and he'd implied that she hadn't had time for him. The truth was that he'd been so angry that she'd found someone else—had *looked* for someone else when he'd sacrificed his world to stay with her—that he'd walked away. He could hear Angelica telling him that he should be grateful that his mother had been strong enough to look forward, move on. Be grateful for the small half-sisters she and her husband had given him and reach out to make them part of his world.

This evening, when he'd called his father to ask for a

favour, they'd spoken as if they were strangers and yet
assistance had arrived within minutes. Angelica had assumed guilt, but all he'd heard was the fear of a man with
his head buried in the sand.

He looked at the phone lying beside the pad, then
picked it up, flicked through the photographs, staring at
one he'd downloaded from *Celebrità* for a long time before he sighed, thumbed in a text to let his father know
that they'd found the cat, adding his thanks for his prompt
response. There was more, but some things had to be said
face to face. He added his initial and pressed send then,
with the phone still in his hand, he texted his mother to let
her know that he'd call her in the morning.

He tapped the end of the pen on the pad for a moment,
added one final item to his list and then went upstairs.

The apartment was quiet. The kittens were curled up
together in the shelter of their box. And, hanging from the
knob of his bedroom door, was a small linen drawstring
bag with a hand-embroidered spray of purple lavender. It
contained a little glass phial with a handwritten label—
lavender oil and a date—and a note.

> *Gloria—as in Knickerbocker Gloria of ice cream
> fame—produces this from her own garden. It's a bit
> magic, but then she's a bit of a witch.*
>
> *I've done with the bathroom so use the tub—a
> shower will only wake you up.*
>
> *Dormi bene. Sogui dolci. G.*

Sleep well. Sweet dreams.

The café did not open on Sunday and Geli got up early to
the sound of bells ringing across the city, fed the kittens,
gathered cleaning stuff from the utility room and, with a
sustaining mug of tea, went down to her workroom.

Dante had cleared out everything but her boxes and she set to work cleaning everything thoroughly before setting up her work tables and drawing board, putting together her stool. Her corkboard was hung and was waiting for the scraps of cloth, pictures—anything and everything that would inspire her.

Three hours later, everything was unpacked, her sewing machines tested, her Mac up and running and all the boxes flattened and neatly stacked away in the corner, ready to be reused when she found somewhere of her own. Not that she could hope to find somewhere as perfect as this.

It was a fabulous space, and she took a series of pictures on her phone which she sent to her sisters, attached to an email explaining that there had been a problem with the apartment she'd rented but that she had found temporary accommodation and everything was great. She might even make a snowman later.

Elle replied, asking for a picture of the snowman.

Sorrel wanted to know: *what problem?* And actually her sister was probably just the person to fight her battle with the bank if things got sticky. She'd chase them up on Monday.

Right now she just itched to sit at her drawing board and begin working on an idea for a design that had been forming in her head ever since she'd seen those black beads in the market. Dusty, hungry; it would have to wait until she'd had a shower and something more substantial than a pastry for breakfast.

She was heading for the bathroom when Dante, dishevelled and wearing only a robe, emerged from his room and her heart jumped as if hit by an electric current.

'Angel—' He was sleep-confused, barely awake, giving her a moment to catch her breath. Gather herself. 'What time is it?'

'*Buongiorno*, Dante,' she said with what, considering

the way her heart was banging away, was a pretty good stab at cool amusement. 'Did you sleep through your alarm?'

He dragged a hand through his hair and his robe gaped to expose a deep V of golden skin from his throat to his waist, the faint spatter of dark hair across his chest. Releasing the knee-weakening scent of warm skin.

'I don't have an alarm clock,' he said, leaning against the door frame as if standing up was still a work in progress, regarding her from beneath heavy lids. 'I don't need one.'

'No?' She knew what the time was, but raised her wrist and pointedly checked her watch. 'You intended to sleep until ten o'clock?'

'Ten? *Dio*, that lavender stuff is lethal.'

It wasn't just the lavender that was lethal. Wearing nothing but a carelessly tied robe, Dante Vettori was a danger not just to her heart, her head, but to just about every other part of her anatomy that was clamouring for attention... 'You had a late night,' she reminded him.

'So did you but it doesn't appear to have slowed you down.' He reached out and she twitched nervously as he picked a cobweb from her hair. 'What on earth have you been doing?'

'Giving the storeroom a good clear-out.' Forcing herself to break eye contact, she brushed a smear of dust from her shoulder. 'I wanted to set up my stuff so that I can start work.' She should move but the message didn't seem to be getting past the putty in her knees. 'Give me ten minutes to clean up and I'll make breakfast.'

'Ten minutes.' He retreated, closing the door, and she slumped against the wall. A woman should have some kind of warning before being confronted with so much unfettered male gorgeousness.

Really.

She had just about got some stiffeners in her knees

when he opened the door again. 'I took your advice and made a list,' he said.

He had? 'Good for you. Clearly, it helped.'

'That's to be seen. One item concerns you.'

'Oh?'

'You won't be moving.'

'I won't?' Her heart racketed around her chest. He wanted her to stay... And then reality kicked in. 'Did Lisa change her mind about taking Giovanni to the wedding?' she asked, concerned.

'No. They should be safely on their way by now.'

'Well, that's good. For them,' she added in case he thought her only worry was about having somewhere to live.

'Let's hope so but, in the meantime, you're going to be here all day, working a shift or on your designs and you can't keep rushing across town to look after an injured cat and a bunch of kittens.'

'It's a kindle,' she said. 'The collective noun. It's a kindle of kittens, a clowder of cats. Would it be necessary to move them? As you said, I'll be around in the day and you'll be here in the evening, at night.'

'Not all the time. I've had my head stuck in this damned report when I need to be out there, drumming up support. Making a noise. I'll be going to Rome some time this week. And I've decided to supplement the report with a DVD.'

'A picture says a thousand words?'

'That's the idea. I thought I'd put together a short film. There'll be library footage of people at last summer's jazz festival, the collective lunches at the *giardino condiviso*, the "green" construction projects and the creation of the street art.'

'That's a start but you'll need people. Interesting faces, characters.'

'Two minds with but a single thought... I'll intersperse

the clips with people talking about why they love this place. Not just the old guys who've been here for ever, but the young people who are drawn here. You, for instance.'

'Me?'

'You're so excited about it. And, as Lisa said, you're good for business.'

'Oh, I see. I'm going to be the hot totty that keeps the old guys watching.'

'Not just the old guys.' He straightened. 'Anyway, that's for next week. I was talking about the cats and it's going to be easier if you stay here and I move into Lisa's flat.'

'You...?' According to Lisa, the heating was on a thermostat, a cheap timer switch would turn the lights on and off and, in any case, she was going to have to go and feed the goldfish and check that everything was okay while he was away. 'Is that really necessary?'

'Cara...' He lifted a hand and, although his fingertips barely brushed her cheek, her body's leaping response was all the answer she needed. Of course it was necessary. She would be here, in his space, all day, all evening, either in the café or working on her designs.

He'd made no attempt to deny the frisson of heat, the desire that simmered whenever they were in the same room, but he'd made it clear in every way that, despite the attraction between them, he was still mourning the woman who'd abandoned him.

He might be mourning for Valentina, but right now he was there, leaning against the doorframe, arms folded and very much awake beneath those slumberous lids as he called her *'cara'* in that sexy, chocolate-smooth accent.

She'd probably be doing him a favour if she reached out, tugged on the tie that was struggling to hold his robe together, pushing him over the edge so that he could blame her for his 'fall'.

She wouldn't have to push very hard. He wanted it as

much as she did and she had him at a disadvantage. Once her hands were on his warm satiny skin, his resistance would hit the floor faster than his robe and neither of them would be thinking about anything except getting naked. But afterwards he'd feel guilty, there would be awkwardness and she didn't just want his body, luscious as it was. She was greedy. She wanted all of Dante Vettori.

'Are you sure you'll be able to handle the goldfish?' she asked, stepping back from the danger zone.

'Are you mocking me, Signora Amery?'

'Heaven forbid, Signor Vettori.'

She was mocking herself. She'd come to Isola looking for artistic and emotional freedom. Marco, gorgeously flirtatious, would have been perfect for the kind of sex without strings relationship she had envisaged. Or even the elegant Gennaro. Throwing Dante Vettori in her path on day one was Fate's cruel little joke.

'Now, if you'll excuse me, I have a litter tray to clean.'

Dante shut the door and leaned back against it. He'd made his list then soaked in a tub, filled with water that was not too hot, in a bathroom still steamy and scented with something herby that Angelica had used. Sprinkled a few drops of lavender oil on his pillow before lying back and recalling all the good things that had happened that day. He'd implied it would be hard but a dozen moments had crowded in...

The moment he'd walked into the café that morning, seen Angelica and experienced the same heart-stopping response as the night before. Watching her laugh. Avoiding her eyes as every male in the *commissariato* had paid court to her, knowing that they would be laughing just for him. The weight of her body against his as she'd slept while the vet operated on their stray...

And then he'd thought about all the good things he'd do today so that he'd wake up happy.

He'd have breakfast with Angelica. Bounce ideas off her, about his film. He'd call the vet for an update on the cat because she'd be anxious. Afterwards, they could go into the city for lunch and he'd show her the Duomo, wander through the Quadrilatero so that she could window-shop at the great fashion houses. Finally, supper in front of the fire. And bed. With her? Without her?

He'd have woken very happy if, when he'd opened his eyes, she had been lying beside him, her silky black hair spread across the pillow, her vivid mouth an invitation to kiss her awake…

He tightened his hand in an attempt to obliterate the peachy feel of her skin against his fingertips, the soft flush that warmed her cheeks, darkened her eyes, betraying her, even while she attempted to distance herself with words. They both knew that all he had to do was reach out to her and she would be in his arms.

It had been there from the moment he'd looked around and their eyes had met; in that first irresistible kiss. Romantics called it love at first sight, but it was no more than chemistry bypassing ten thousand years of civilisation, sparking the atavistic drive in all animals to procreate. A recognition that said, *This one. This female will bear strong children, protect your genes…*

That was how it had been with Valentina. She'd been at the party thrown to welcome him home, welcome him into the Vettori fold. She was there when he'd arrived, standing with his father, a golden, glittering prize, and he'd been felled by the metaphorical Stone Age club.

He was still suffering from the after-effects of the concussion and, whatever Lisa advised, whatever the temptation—and he'd been sorely tempted—he would not use Angelica as therapy.

Before he could weaken, he took a bag from his wardrobe, packed everything he was likely to need in the next week and then took a wake-up shower. An espresso, a quick run-through of the heating system and he'd be gone.

And then he opened his bedroom door and the smell of cooking stopped him in his tracks.

'An English breakfast,' he said, dropping his bag in the hall and walking into the kitchen. 'That takes me back to those first days when my mother rented a house in Wimbledon. Sunday mornings and everyone walking their dogs on the Common.'

'Pastries for breakfast are all very well,' Angelica said without turning around, 'but a long day should start with something more substantial.'

'I noticed that you'd bought oatmeal.'

'Oatmeal is for weekdays. Sunday demands *il uovo strapazzato, la pancetta e il pane tostado.*'

'You've been at that phrasebook again.'

'I've moved on to food and drink. Sadly, I can't offer you *la marmellata.* I forgot to buy a jar when I was in the shop.'

'Eggs, bacon and toast with marmalade? Really? I thought you were looking for new experiences, not clinging to the old.'

'So you don't want any of this?' she asked, looking back over her shoulder as she waved a wooden spoon over the scrambled eggs, crisp thin bacon.

'Did I say that?'

Her mouth widened in a teasing grin. 'That's what I thought. You can make the coffee while I dish up. Then you can tell me all about this ice cream parlour you want me to design.'

She was brisk, businesslike, keeping her distance, which should have made their enforced intimacy easier to handle. It didn't. 'You're eager to start?' he asked, concentrating on the espresso but intensely aware of her standing a few feet away.

'I imagine you want it to be open in time for the spring?' She turned to him, a frown buckling the clear space between her lovely brows. 'Or was it just something you said to shut me up about paying rent?'

'No…' He shrugged. 'Maybe. I didn't want an argument, or rent complicating the accounts, but I do have a room that isn't earning its keep and the more I think about it the more the idea grows on me. We'll take a look after breakfast if you've got time.'

Breakfast…

On the intimacy level, that word rang every bell.

'This is it.' Dante stood back and Geli stepped into a large square room with French windows that opened out onto a snow-covered courtyard. He'd warned her that the heating wouldn't be on and she was glad of a long cardigan that fell below her hips and the scarf she'd looped around her neck. 'What do you think?'

With an injured cat to nurse and three lively kittens to look after, an ice cream parlour to design, an inconvenient lust for a man who was locked in the past and snow, Geli thought that this was so not why she'd come to Italy.

She walked across to the window and looked out. There was the skeleton of a tree and a frosted scramble of bare vines on the walls that promised green shade in the summer. An assortment of tables, chairs and a small staged area in the corner were hidden beneath a thick coating of snow, undisturbed by anything other than a confused bird, floundering in an unexpectedly soft landing.

Dante joined her at the window. 'It looks bleak on a day like this but in the summer—'

'I can see,' she said.

The snow would melt, the vines would flower, the kittens would be found good homes and designing an ice cream parlour would be a small price to pay for a temporary workspace. She'd find somewhere to live and Dante... Maybe her heart would stop jumping every time she saw him, every time he came near.

Meanwhile, there was this very tired room to bring to life.

She drew a rough square on the pad she was carrying and then fed out a tape measure. 'Will you give me a hand measuring up?'

He took the end and held it while she read off the basic dimensions—length, width, height of the room. She made a note and then added detailed measurements of the positions of doors, windows, lighting and electrical sockets.

'Have you any thoughts on a colour scheme?' she asked.

'Anything but pink?' he volunteered.

'Good start,' she said. 'I thought we might carry through the dark green from the café. It will tie the two parts together and look cool in the summer. I'll add splashes of colour that we'll carry through to the courtyard with pots filled with flowering plants.'

'That's very different to the designs you showed me. Rather more sophisticated.'

'You're right. I see a space and I get carried away with my own ideas of how it should look.'

'But?'

She shrugged. 'This is a sophisticated venue. If I was doing this in a UK high street I'd be using bright colours to catch the eye. I'd want nineteen-fifties American cars, a vintage soda fountain and a jukebox with fifties-era records, but you have live music and Italy has a fabulous car industry,' she said as she gathered her stuff and headed for the door.

'Keep the jukebox. We can turn it off when there's live music.'

'Okay, but you need to think about who is actually going to use this space. Who do you want to attract? Young people looking for somewhere to hang out? I doubt ice cream and fifties pop is going to do it. Most of our sit-down customers in the UK are young teenage girls, families—birthday parties for kids do really well—and women meeting up for a chat over a treat.'

'And the stand-up ones?'

'That's the takeaway trade.'

'Of course.'

'Having second thoughts?'

'No…I can see a daytime and early evening market for this, but you're right. It needs to fit in with what's going on outside.'

'You'd better give me some idea of your budget. Are you thinking Ferrari or Fiat 500?'

'I hadn't given it much thought.'

She grinned. 'My ideal client.'

'Show me what you've got and I'll have a better idea of what it's likely to cost,' he said, heading back to the rear lobby where he'd left his bags.

'The major capital expenses will be the freezer counter for the ices, jukebox and, depending on the look you want, furniture.' She looked around, already seeing it on a summer evening with the doors thrown open, musicians on the stage. 'There'll undoubtedly be some rewiring needed, the floor will need sanding and refinishing and whatever wall treatment you decide on.'

'I'm going to have to sell an awful lot of ice cream to pay for that.'

'I'll draw this up on my CAD program today and put together some ideas for you to look at.'

'Great. Give me your pen.'

She gave it to him and he leaned in to jot something down on the corner of the pad she was holding. Too close—so close that she could see a single thread of silver in amongst the glossy dark hair.

'This is my email address…' He looked up, catching her staring. 'Send me your ideas. It'll be light relief from the politics. Is there anything else?'

Yes… 'No.'

He nodded. 'I'll leave you in peace, then.'

About as much chance of that as a hen laying a square egg, she thought. He might have slept like a log but she'd tossed and turned all night. Getting up had been a relief.

'You've got my number. Give me a call if you have any problems,' he said as he shrugged into his heavy jacket, found his gloves in the pockets, continued searching… Swore softly under his breath. 'I left my scarf at the vet's office.'

The soft, very expensive scarlet cashmere scarf that he'd wrapped around the injured cat. The kind that usually came gift-wrapped, with love, at Christmas… Not this last Christmas, she suspected, but the one before.

As he turned up his collar she took off her own scarf and draped it around his neck. 'Here. This will hold you.'

He opened his mouth as if to say something, clearly thought better of it and left it at, 'Thanks.' Then concentrated on tucking in the scarf and fastening the flap across his collar. 'I'll ring the vet later. To ask about the cat,' he added.

'I usually switch my phone off when I'm working, but you can leave a voicemail.'

'Angel…'

'Yes?'

'You know how to set the alarm? The kitchen staff will turn it off when they arrive.'

'Lisa took me through it. Matteo is in charge while she's away. I start at seven for the morning shift,' she added, 'and work until everyone goes home when I'm on the evening shift.'

'He'll probably close up early. Once people get home they won't come out in this.'

'Very wise of them, if not great for business.' He didn't move. 'Will you come in for breakfast?'

'If I have time.'

'How about if I suggest chef puts porridge on the menu as a cold weather special? With fruit, cream, a drizzle of honey and, to give it a little Italian panache, a dash of Marsala to keep you warm while you're out doing your Zeffirelli thing.'

'Hold that thought.' He reached for the door handle and, still holding it, said, 'Will you be in it? The film. It was your idea.'

'It was?'

'You said, "What would you show them?"'

'So I did.' She lifted her shoulders in an awkward little shrug. 'If it will help. Do you want me in English or Italian?'

'Either. Both. Whatever comes out. Nothing polished or rehearsed. Just you.'

She managed a wry smile. 'I think I can guarantee that. You'll need an editor to pull it together.'

'I don't want a slick tourist promo. I'm looking for something raw, something from the street.'

'Why don't you use a student? Does the university have a media school?'

'Another great idea.'

'I'm full of them,' she said and, since he didn't seem in any hurry, 'for instance, do you have any contacts in local television?' He seemed thrown by the question. 'An historic part of the city struggling to retain its identity?' she prompted. 'It's the sort of thing that would get airtime in the early evening magazine programmes at home.'

'I suppose so.' He did not sound enthusiastic and she didn't press it.

'Okay, what about the local press? And social media? Politicians use it to target supporters and make themselves look good, but it's a two-way street. You can target them. Put your film on YouTube, post a link on their Facebook page and Twitter account and get everyone involved to share, leave comments, retweet.' He was still looking at her as if she had two heads and she shrugged. 'I did all the early promo for Rosie, our ice cream van, and I learned a lot. Mostly about how desperate the media are for stories that will fill airtime and the big empty spaces in their pages.'

'I'm sorry. You're right, of course. I'll give it some thought.'

For a moment neither of them said anything.

'Angel...'

'Dante...'

'What?' he asked.

'You should go. The goldfish will be getting lonely.' Hungry... She meant hungry...

CHAPTER TEN

'Forget science. Put your trust in ice cream.'
—from *Rosie's Little Book of Ice Cream*

DANTE SLUNG HIS bag and laptop case on the passenger seat of his car. Then he undid the neck flap of his jacket and touched the scarf that Angelica had placed around his neck.

He had other scarves, and had been about to say so, but this one was warm from her body and as she'd draped it around his neck he'd caught that subtle scent that seemed to stay with him whenever he touched her. He stood in the cold garage, lifted it to his nose, breathed in, but it was nothing he could name—it was just Angelica.

And it made him smile.

Geli settled at her computer, called up the CAD program, put in the dimensions of the room then began to play with ideas, searching through her boxes for fabrics and colours to create mood boards.

Dante called and left a voicemail to let her know that Mamma Cat was recovering and that he'd pick her up first thing on Monday.

When she found herself picking up her phone and, like some needy teenager, listening to the message for the tenth time, she deleted it and drove herself crazy trying to find the right combination of words—in Italian—that would bring up freezer counters and jukeboxes. Something her phrasebook was singularly useless at providing. It would be the perfect excuse to call Dante, but she told herself not to be feeble and eventually she got it and printed out photographs of the ones that inspired her schemes.

That night she tried her own remedy, listing all the good things that had happened that day and could only come up with one. Dante had touched her... And that wasn't good. At all.

'I'll take over here,' Matteo said as she began to make yet another espresso. 'Dante's taken the cat upstairs and he wants to know what to do with her.'

'Oh, right. I won't be long.'

She took off her apron and took the stairs two at a time. A cat carrier had been left in the kitchen but there was no sign of Dante. No doubt he was picking up something he needed from his room.

She took a breath, knelt down to look through the grille at the cat. 'Oh, poor lovely. Shall I take you to see your babies?'

'The vet sent antibiotics,' Dante said. She looked up. He was wearing a dark suit, silk tie, a long elegant overcoat and looked, no doubt, like the man who'd been destined to run the family business. All it needed was a red cashmere scarf to complete the image. Instead, he had the black one, hand-knitted by her grandmother, draped around his neck. 'One tablet in the morning until they're gone. She's had today's dose.'

'I'll take care of her. You're going to Rome now?'

'I've got a taxi waiting. Will you take the carry basket back to the vet?'

'Of course.'

'You'll need your scarf,' he said.

'No,' she said, her hand on his to stop him as he began to unwind it. 'It's freezing out there and I have others.'

'If you're sure. Thank you.' He reached in his pocket, took out a key and placed it on the kitchen table. 'Here's the spare key to Lisa's place. The lights are on a timer switch and I've set the heating to run continuously on low, but the goldfish will get lonely.'

'I'll take care of him. Go… *Arrivederci! Buon viaggia!*'

He smiled again, touched her cheek lightly with the back of his fingers. '*Arrivederci, cara.* Take care.'

Cara…

It meant nothing. Italians used it all the time. The market traders, the waiters, the customers all called her that.

It was only when she was watching Mamma Cat, purring as her babies rubbed against her, that she realised what he'd said.

The goldfish will get lonely…

There was no more snow but the temperature remained below freezing. While daytime business was brisk, with everyone looking for hot food and drinks to keep them going, Dante was right; once they were home nothing was going to tempt them out again.

Geli worked the early morning shift when there was a rush for espresso and pastry, but finished at nine, leaving the rest of the day to the regular staff, who were short of evening tips. The money would have been useful but she nagged the bank and, with no distractions, she got an awful lot done. She hardly had any time to think about Dante.

Okay, she thought about him when he surprised her with a text to let her know he'd arrived safely and a photograph of a frosty Coliseum to show her that Rome was freezing, too.

Obviously, she replied—it would be rude not to—and

in return sent him a photograph of Mamma Cat, recovered enough to give her kittens a thorough wash.

She couldn't help thinking of how brilliant he'd been about the cat when she dropped off the carry basket and paid the vet's bill using her credit card, despite the receptionist's insistence that she'd send a bill at the end of the month. It was wince-making but there was no way she was letting Dante pay it.

She thought of him later, too, when the vet's nurse called at the café on her way home with a bag containing his scarf, stiff with blood and mud, and was disappointed to discover that she was not going to be able to hand it over in person.

Shame she didn't bother to wash it, Geli thought sourly, but it had simply been an excuse to see Dante. The scarf was ruined.

She gave him the bad news the next day, when she emailed him photographs of the mood boards she'd prepared for three different schemes for his ice cream parlour and colour-wash impressions of what each of them would look like.

The first was a full-on US fifties-style diner, with booths and a jukebox and hot rods. In the second she replaced the booths and paid tribute to Milan with ultra-modern furniture and an artwork motif of sleek Italian cars. For the third she used her own vision of the room. Dark green walls, the mix-and-match furniture painted white and a sparkly red jukebox. She suggested shelf units for the walls, with bright jars of toppings and blown-up details of ice cream sundaes on the walls and, through the open French windows, a glimpse of planters overflowing with flowers. It was the simplest, least expensive and, in her opinion, would be the most adaptable.

He responded instantly.

You're right. Let's go with number three. D.

She smiled, and replied.

You have excellent taste. How are the meetings going? G.

It was only polite to ask.

Slowly. Important men make a point of keeping you waiting so that you'll understand how generous they are in
sparing you five minutes of their valuable time. D.

He didn't mention the scarf.

They're all too busy sending tweets and posting pictures
of themselves doing good works on Facebook to waste
time on real people. Social media is the way to go. G.

And she attached a picture of Lisa's goldfish, peering
at her out of the bowl, to which she added a speech bubble
so that he appeared to be saying, 'Tweet me!'

She went to the Tuesday market and bought more beads
from Livia for a project and looked at some wonderfully
soft cashmere yarn in the same clear bright scarlet as
the scarf that had been ruined. She passed over it and
picked up half a dozen balls in a dark crimson that exactly
matched the colour of her nails.

Dante, clearly bored out of his skin hanging around
waiting to talk to people, sent her a text asking how the cat
was doing. She took a photograph of Mamma Cat looking
particularly Frankensteinish and then she opened a new
page on her Facebook account that she called *A Kindle
of Kittens*.

She posted snippets of the story, pictures of the kittens
and then the one of Mamma Cat. Then she added a speech

bubble to the photograph of Mamma Cat, saying, 'Like me on Facebook' and sent it to Dante with the link.

He immediately 'liked' the page and left a comment.

I'll keep the black one. D.

The black one? Was he making some kind of veiled reference to her? She shook her head and replied.

She's all yours.

The icon on his post was for Café Rosa's Facebook page and when she checked it out she discovered that it was simply a listing of the musicians who would be appearing and the artists who were exhibiting there with some of their work. Nothing personal.

Elle and Sorrel sent her identical texts.

Who is D?

She replied:

He's my landlord and my boss. Why didn't you warn me that it would be freezing here?

She sent Dante a text, asking him how he was sleeping.

I've been making a list, remembering the things I've done, thinking about what I'm going to do the next day. It's not working. D.

That's politics for you. Concentrate on the small pleasures. Every life needs ice cream. G.

And thinking about him was unavoidable when she

curled up on the sofa in the evening with her headphones on as she worked on her Italian and knitted his scarf, her head against a cushion that smelled faintly of the shampoo he used.

Fortunately, there were distractions.

She had called in at a fashion co-operative where local designers displayed high quality one-off pieces, and designs that could be produced in small quantities for boutiques. She wasn't sure if they would accept work from a non-Italian, but she was living and working in Isola and that, apparently, was enough. She'd worn her coat and had photographs of other pieces on her phone and she'd been invited to bring along a finished piece for consideration.

Of course, she'd had to tell Dante and he'd been thrilled for her.

Marco came in every day, still hoping that she'd change her mind about spending the evening with him. He was charming, good-looking and she knew she was mad not to get out for a few hours, try and get Dante out of her head, but he wasn't the man to do it. She wasn't sure if such a man existed.

Dante laughed at a video Angelica had posted on the kittens' Facebook page of one of the kittens chasing a strand of wool and falling asleep mid-pounce. It earned him a stern look from the Minister's secretary. She was right. It wasn't funny.

He could hear Angelica saying, 'Pull it, pull it...' and the rumble of a man's laughter in the background.

Who was pulling the wool? Marco, Nic, Gennaro...?

He told himself that he had no right to care. But he did. He cared a lot.

He'd been cooling his heels in a dozen offices since he'd arrived, been given a dozen empty promises and he'd scarcely noticed. The only thing he'd cared about were the texts from Angelica. The photographs she sent him.

A selfie of her with Livia, and a stack of beads she'd bought. A bowl of porridge lavishly embellished with fruit, honey and cream. Some balls of wool she was using to knit him a scarf to replace the one that had been ruined. He'd seen Nonnina knitting and he knew that every inch of the yarn would have been touched by her as it slid through her fingers...

She hadn't said one word about the kitten-botherer.

He put the phone away and stood up. 'Please give the Minister my apologies,' he said, picking up his laptop bag and heading for the door.

'You're leaving?' she asked, startled. 'But you have an appointment with the Minister.'

'I had an appointment with the Minister over an hour ago and now I have to be somewhere else.'

'But—'

'I'll tweet him.'

He stood on the steps of the Ministry, breathing in the icy air as he pulled on his gloves, wrapped Angelica's scarf around his neck.

He'd spent four days chasing his tail in Rome, waiting for people to see him and getting nowhere. No surprise there. He'd known how it would be and yet he'd come anyway.

Wasting his time.

Running away from what had to be done. Running away from his feelings for Angelica Amery.

On Thursday evening, Geli settled down with her head-phones on, working on her Italian while she added a few more inches to the scarf.

Listen then repeat...

Buongiorno. Desidera?

'Buongiorno. Desidera?'

Buongiorna. Mi dà uno shampoo per capelli normali per piacere.

'Buongiorna. Mi dà uno shampoo per capelli normali per piacere.'

Si, ecco. Abbiamo questo...

Geli heard another sound over the lesson and lifted one ear of the headphones. Someone was at the door. She checked her watch. They'd be clearing up downstairs and this would be Matteo bringing her some little 'leftover' treat.

She switched off her iPod, stuck her needles in the wool and went to open the door and the smile of welcome froze on her face.

It was the same every time—no, not the same; this time it was worse. Or did she mean better? The heart kick, putty knees and a whole load of X-rated symptoms were getting a lot of practice.

'Dante... You're back,' she said stupidly.

'Despite the best efforts of the airline and the weather to keep me in Rome for another night,' he said. 'I waylaid Matteo on his way up here with this,' he went on, indicating the small tray he was holding. Not coming in, despite the fact that she'd stood back to give him room. 'Is there something I should know?'

'Know?' For a moment she didn't understand what he meant. Then the penny dropped. Did he think that she and Matteo...? Shocked that he could believe her so fickle—and just a bit thrilled—make that a whole lot thrilled—that he actually cared—she managed a puzzled frown. 'Didn't you ask him to come up and check that I was okay every night before he went home? Bring me up a little treat? What is it?' she asked, reaching for the cover. 'Chef was making cheesecake—'

'No,' he said, moving it out of her reach.

She looked up. 'It's not cheesecake?'

'It's chocolate truffle tart. And no, I did not ask him to come up here bothering you.'

He did! He thought that she was encouraging Matteo and he was not amused. Considering that he'd made it plain more than once that he wasn't interested—okay, they both knew that he was interested, but he wouldn't, couldn't do anything about it—his attitude was a bit rich, but it still gave her a warm, fuzzy feeling that wasn't helping the knee problem one bit.

'He wasn't bothering me,' she said, leaving him standing on the doorstep. 'On the contrary,' she called back as she headed for the kitchen, leaving him to follow in his own good time. 'I'm assuming there's enough of that tart for two?'

She took a couple of cake forks from the cutlery drawer then, as she heard the tray hit the kitchen table, she stretched up to take two plates from the rack. Before she could reach them, Dante caught her wrist and turned her to face him.

'Was it Matteo pulling the wool?'

She didn't pretend not to know what he was talking about, but met his gaze head-on. 'You didn't have to fly back from Rome to ask me that,' she pointed out, quite rationally, she thought, considering that she was backed against the work surface, that the front of his overcoat was pressed very firmly against her sweater. That his breath was warm against her cheek. That his hand had slid from her wrist and his fingers and hers were somehow entangled… 'You could have just sent a text.'

His fingers tightened over hers. 'What would you have replied?' he demanded, his eyes darkened with an intensity that might have scared her if it hadn't been making her heart sing. He cared…

'I'd have replied that Matteo brings me cake every evening as an excuse to play with the kittens.'

'The kittens?' he repeated, confused. 'Why would anyone even notice the kittens when you're here?'

She leaned into him to hide a smile too wide to fit through a barn door.

'He's besotted with them.'

'The man's a fool.'

'No… He's going to take one, maybe even two of them, when they're old enough to leave their mother.'

'Not the black one.' His face softened as he looked down at her. And this time there was no doubt about his meaning. 'Not Mole.'

'Molly. She's a girl.' Her legs were trembling. 'I told you, Dante. She's all yours.' And then, because she had to say something to break the tension, 'Do you like chocolate tart?'

'I like this.' He took the forks from her, placed them on the work surface behind her, took her face between his hands, brushed his lips over hers. 'I've been thinking about this.'

'This' was a kiss, angled perfectly to capture her mouth. Tender, thoughtful, tasting lips, tongue, nothing hurried or snatched, he bombarded her senses with a flood of heat until, like the city bells on Sunday morning, they were clamouring for attention. Screaming, *Nooooo*…as he drew back a little to look at her.

'I've been thinking about you, Angelica Amery, and all the good things I'm going to do with you.'

Okay, enough with the talking—

She reached for the buttons of his overcoat but he put his hand over hers, stopping her, and she looked up. 'You have too many clothes on.'

'Not for where we're going.'

What? 'I don't—'

'This is date night,' he said. 'I've called for you at your door and I'm going to take you stargazing. We'll also eat, talk and, at some point during the evening, I'll undoubtedly hold your hand.'

'Just my hand?'

'It's our first date. Your rules.'

'No. I was just—'

He touched his finger to her lips to stop her saying that she was just… Actually, she didn't know what she was 'just' doing. Mouthing off that all men saw when they looked at her was an opportunity for sex? A bit hypocritical when the whole idea of old-fashioned commitment terrified the wits out of her.

His hand moved to her cheek. 'It's not just about sex, Angel.'

She swallowed. 'It's not?'

He could read her mind now? She'd thought she had a problem when she'd discovered that her apartment didn't exist, that her money was gone, but this was trouble on a whole new level.

This wasn't about mere stuff. This was about taking the biggest risk imaginable.

'No.' His hand cradled her cheek, his touch warming her to her toes as he looked straight into her eyes. 'I've learned that the hard way. There has to be more if a partnership is going to clear the hurdles that life throws in your way. Survive the knocks.'

'That's a heck of a lot to put on a first date, Dante.'

'I know, but if you don't start out with the highest expectations it's always going to be a compromise. Are you okay with that?'

Was she? He'd been totally honest with her from the beginning and she'd tried to be the same. She hadn't been coy, hadn't tried to hide the way she felt whenever she was within touching distance of him. But this was exposing the soft nerve tissue, the stuff that hurt when you poked it.

'You want the truth?'

'*Parla come magni, cara.* Speak as you eat. I have always told you the truth,' he reminded her.

'I remember,' she said. 'Even when it hurt.'

'Even when it hurt,' he agreed, easing back a fraction, as if preparing for bad news, and the bad news was that she wanted to grab him, hold him close.

'The truth is that it scares the pants off me. The metaphorical pants,' she added quickly, trying to keep this light.

He didn't smile. 'Do you want to tell me why?'

'I've spent my entire life losing people. My father, half of everything I am, was gone before the stick turned blue—unknown, unknowable. No name, no picture, just an empty space.'

'Your mother didn't tell you anything about him?'

She shook her head. 'And when she was there it didn't matter. She filled our lives, Dante, and I never thought about it, about him, but when she died—'

He put his arms around her, drew her close. 'You realised you would never know. That you'd lost not just one but both your parents.'

'Then along came Martin Crayshaw—obviously not his real name—and for a while he was everything a storybook father should be until, having stripped us clean, stolen our lives, he disappeared without so much as goodbye.'

'Did the police ever catch up with him?'

'My grandmother was in a state of nervous collapse and Elle, my oldest sister, was only just eighteen. She was afraid that if the authorities discovered what had happened Sorrel and I would be taken into care.'

'She didn't report it?' She shook her head. 'How is your grandmother now? You are very close, I think.'

'Better. Much better. Great-Uncle Basil's arrival has given her something I never could. He takes wonderful care of her now. They are the dearest of friends.'

'And your sisters fell in love, got married, have families of their own.'

'I'm happy for them. They married wonderful men and I love my nieces and nephews to bits, but it's as if I've been left behind.'

'No, Angel. They haven't left you behind; they've simply moved on to the next stage in their lives.' His lips brushed her hair. 'Relationships change. When my mother made a new life for herself, started a new family, I was so angry…'

'Angry?' she repeated, surprised. 'I can't imagine that.'

'One of the things I put on that list you said I should make was to call her.'

She leaned back a little so that she could see his face. 'Did you?'

'We had a long talk. Cleared away a lot of the dead wood. I've been doing a lot of that.'

'So that there's room for fresh new growth.'

'I knew you'd understand.' He caught her hair between his fingers and pushed it back so that she couldn't hide behind it. 'I told her all about you and your lists. About that moment when I first saw you, the front of your coat plastered with snow and looking exactly like the princess in a fairy tale book she used to read to me when I was little. About Rattino's unscheduled appearance. That made her laugh. She wished she'd been there to see it.'

'Hmm, I suspect it's one of those experiences that improves with the rose-tinted spectacles of time.'

'The sort of thing you tell your grandchildren when they ask how you met.'

Grandchildren? This was their first date…

'And I told her that you were knitting me a scarf to replace the one she sent me at Christmas because it was ruined when we rescued Ratty's mother.'

'Your mother gave you that scarf?'

'Yes…' She saw the moment when he realised what she'd actually thought. 'Did you imagine that I would wear something that Valentina had given me?'

'I… It was a beautiful scarf,' she said.

'Yes, it was.'

'Now I feel really bad. Maybe I could have rescued it if I'd tried harder, but I have to confess that I really enjoyed putting it in the rubbish.'

He roared with laughter. 'My mother said that you sounded like a keeper.'

'She doesn't know me, Dante. You barely know me.'

'It's been a steep learning curve,' he admitted, 'but so far I like everything I've seen.'

'Ditto,' she said, pleased, awkward. 'I'm glad you talked to her.'

'I have you to thank for that,' he said, 'and I'll tell you something—the hardest part was picking up the phone.'

'Are you saying that I need to pick up the metaphorical phone?'

'It's just a date, Angel.'

She shook her head. 'No, it's not,' she said. They both knew it was a lot more than that. 'We're both trailing baggage. We should both probably start with something less intense.'

'I'm doing my best here.'

'It's not working but, given the choice between staying here and knitting a scarf or having you hold my hand while we look at the stars—'

'The stars have it?'

She shook her head. 'You had me at holding hands. The stars are a bonus.'

'In that case, I think we'd better get out of here before my good intentions hit the skids. You need to go and wrap up in something warm. I'll go and put Matteo out of his misery and tell him that he's got overtime babysitting the kittens.'

CHAPTER ELEVEN

*'Love is an ice cream sundae with all the marvellous
toppings. Sex is the cherry on top.'*
—from *Rosie's Little Book of Ice Cream*

THEY WERE BOTH unusually quiet as Dante drove out of the
city. He was, presumably, concentrating on the traffic—
driving in Italy was not to be taken lightly—while she was
absorbed in the change in their relationship. Wondering
what had happened in Rome…

Then Geli, sneaking a glance at his profile, lit only by
the glow from the dashboard, discovered that Dante was
doing the same and practically melted in her seat.

'Where are we going?'

He returned his full attention to the road. 'Does it matter?'

'No. The only thing that matters is that I'm going there
with you.'

And in the darkness he reached across and took her
hand, holding it lightly until he slowed to turn off the high-
way and they began to climb into the mountains.

After a while, the lights of a village appeared above
them but, before they reached it, he turned off and pulled
onto an area that had been levelled as a viewing point.

'Wait…' Dante came round, opened the door and helped

her from the car, keeping her arm in his as they walked to the barrier and looked out over the valley.

There was no moon, but the Milky Way, so thick that it was hard to make out individual stars, silvered the flat dark surface of a lake far below them.

'What lake is that?' she asked. 'I know Como is the nearest but there don't seem to be enough lights.'

'No, that's Largo D'Idro.' He glanced at her. 'It's the highest of the lakes but very small. There are no tourist boats doing the rounds of celebrity villas because there are no celebrities. It's popular for water sports.'

'But not in this weather. There's snow right down to the shore. I thought the lakes had a famously mild climate?'

'Nowhere is mild in February,' he assured her, 'and the lakes have been known to freeze over in severe winters.'

'They don't tell you that in the tourist brochures.'

'Maybe that's because we like to keep it to ourselves. There's something rather magical about sitting in a steaming hot tub when the air temperature is below freezing.'

She gave him a thoughtful look. 'Is that what you have in mind?'

'On our first proper date?' He took her hand and held it. 'You will be escorted to your front door and maybe, if I'm lucky, you'll have enjoyed yourself enough to risk a second one.'

Geli thought that she was more than ready for an improper date; that hot tub sounded like a lot of fun. But she had complained that men never asked women out on dates any more and, while she wasn't totally convinced that he was going to kiss her on the cheek and say goodnight at the door, she would go along with it.

'In that case, if we're going to act like kids, it's time to make snow angels.' She looked around, caught his hand and, tugging him after her, headed towards a gently sloping area of untouched snow. 'The stars will look even better if we're lying down.'

She flung herself down into the snow, laughing as she swept her arms and legs wide to make an angel while Dante looked on.

'If you don't get down here and join in I'm going to feel stupid,' she warned. 'You are also blocking out the stars.'

'I just love watching you.'

Geli stilled.

'What happened to you in Rome, Dante?'

'Nothing happened. Everything happened. For months my head has been filled with the past, the mess we all made of it. While I was in Rome all I thought about was you. How much I enjoyed getting your emails and texts. How much I wished you were there with me.'

'And yet you're standing up there and I'm down here.' She held out her hand. 'I promise you, this is a lot more fun if you join in.'

He took it and then lay beside her in the snow. About to tell him that the magic only happened when you made your angel, she pressed her lips together. He had missed her. Now they were lying together in the snow, looking up at the stars and Dante Vettori was holding her hand. That was all the magic she could handle right now.

'Do you know the constellations?' she asked.

'Some of them…'

They lay there in the snow pointing out the stars they recognised until the cold drove them in search of warmth, food and they drove up to the ski resort where, in a restaurant lively with an après ski crowd, they shared an *antipasti* of grilled vegetables and a *risotto alla pescatora*, rich with prawns, squid and clams.

As they finished their meal with ice cream and espresso, Geli said, 'No meat and nothing to drink. I'm a tough date.'

'I don't drink and drive, I didn't have to have the grilled

vegetables and I would have chosen the risotto even if I'd been on my own. Are you free tomorrow?'

'The dating rules say that I shouldn't be that easy,' she said. 'I'm going to sound desperately sad and needy if I say yes.'

'I'm doing the asking so that makes two of us, but this isn't something we can do next week. I have an invitation from one of the big fashion houses to their pre Fashion Week party. It's tomorrow,' he said, 'or you're going to have to wait until the autumn and hope I'm still on their party list.'

'You're kidding me?' Milan Fashion Week was as big as it got. Invitations to parties thrown by the designers were like gold dust.

'They probably think I'm my father. Dante, Daniele... What are you doing?' he asked.

'Just checking that my chin isn't down there on the floor,' she said. 'Do you think he'll be feeling slighted? Your father?'

'He won't notice. Valentina presents a local evening television show so she gets invited to everything.'

'Oh... I had no idea.'

'Lisa didn't tell you?'

'No. She started to talk about her but I said that you had already told me what happened and she got the message.' But it explained his reluctance to contact local TV about his film. 'Will Valentina be there? With your father?'

'More than likely, but this is not about them. I'm asking you. Would you like to go as my plus one?' And then Dante told her who the invitation was from and she nearly passed out with shock.

Her mouth was moving but nothing was coming out and she fanned herself with one hand while indicating that she'd be with him in a moment with the other. He caught the fanning hand, said, 'I'll take that as a yes.'

'No—'

'No?' He sounded genuinely shocked, as well he might.

'You don't have to put yourself through this for me.'

'She's married to my father, Angel. If he and I are going to have any kind of relationship we have to move on. But you're right. Maybe what I'm asking...' He linked his fingers through hers. 'Will you do this for me?'

'You want me to be your wing man?'

'Above and behind me? No, my angel, I want you beside me all the way.' And he leaned across the table and kissed her.

His lips tasted of coffee and pistachio ice cream and, like every kiss they'd shared, it was all too brief. She'd waited long enough...

'Dante—' He waited. 'You do realise that this isn't actually our first date?'

'It isn't?'

'Don't you remember? When you insisted on taking me to the *commissariato*—'

'I certainly remember that. I hope there wasn't an emergency while you were there because no one would have heard the phone.'

She rolled her eyes. 'No, think... You said, "Is it a date?"'

'And you said yes.'

'Actually, I asked if it was "another" date. Made some stupid comment about going steady. We'd already made a date to sit up late one night and tell one another stories. I think we can quite legitimately count this as a two-in-one. A double date for two.'

'So you're saying—be patient with me, I don't want to get this wrong—that this is our third date?'

She just smiled and he raised a hand in the direction of a passing waiter. *'Il conto...'*

* * *

Dante opened his eyes, saw Angelica's dark hair spread across the pillow, her lovely mouth an invitation to kiss her awake and thought for a moment that he was dreaming.

He kissed her anyway and, like Sleeping Beauty, she opened her eyes, smiled, hooked her hand around his neck and drew him down to her so that she could kiss him back. A morning kiss, new as the dawn, as welcome as the spring.

'*Ciao, carissima,*' he said, his hand tracing the profile of her body as she turned towards him; the lovely curves he'd explored with such thoroughness during a night in which he'd been reborn. '*Come posse servirvi?*'

She frowned, mouthed the words then, her smile widening into soft laughter, she said, 'Did you really ask how you can serve me?'

'Would you like tea?' he asked, his hand lingering on her thigh. 'Or I could carry you to the shower and get creative with the soap. Or—' a blast of Abba's *Dancing Queen* shattered the silence '—*Dio!* What is that?'

'The alarm on my phone.' She rolled out of bed and he watched her walk, naked, to her bag, find her phone and turn it off. She looked back at him. 'Your service will have to wait, I'm afraid. I have to go to work.'

'Matteo is not expecting you. I told him that you had other plans today.'

'What? You can't do that.' He loved how shocked she was. How committed…

'I'm the boss. I can do what I like.'

'But it's market day. They'll—'

'They'll manage,' he said, peeling himself off the bed, wrapping his arms around her. 'Now, where were we, *mio amore*? Tea, shower—' he nuzzled the lovely curve of her neck '—or is there some other way I can serve you?'

She kissed his neck, ran her hand down his back. 'Why don't we start with the shower and see how it goes from there?'

Geli's hand was shaking as she called Elle. She hadn't the faintest clue what she was going to say to her; she only knew she had to hear that calm voice.

'Sorry, I can't talk right now. Leave a message and I'll call you back when whatever crisis I'm having is sorted.'

A message? Which one would that be? *I'm going to a swanky party thrown by one of the world's most famous fashion designers. I can't stand up because Dante Vettori spent the night melting my bones. I'm in love...*

No, no, no! It had been the most thrilling, tender, perfect sex, outshining anything she could have imagined in her wildest fantasy, but Dante was right, love was more than that.

It was lying together in the snow in a universe so quiet that you could hear a star fall. It was making the toughest phone call in the world in order to find a cat which might already be dead. It was small things, like texts that said nothing except I'm thinking of you.

'Just me,' she said. 'Nothing important, just looking for some big sister advice about what to wear to a bit of a do. Love to everyone. Catch up soon.'

Clothes... Concentrate on clothes.

She was standing in front of her wardrobe when Dante returned from Lisa's flat. 'You were an age. Was there a problem?'

'You could say that. The goldfish was floating on the top of the tank. I've been at the pet shop trying to find a match.'

'Any luck?'

'We found one with similar markings. It's a bit bigger, but with any luck Lisa will put that down to a growth spurt.'

'And if she doesn't?'

'You'll just have to own up.'

'Thanks for that.' She turned back to the wardrobe and the two dresses hanging over the doors. 'Have you heard from her since she arrived?'

'Just a text to let me know that she arrived safely. What are you doing?'

'I'm trying to decide which dress to wear tonight. The black or the burgundy-red.'

'So nothing taxing, then.' She gave him what Elle called 'the look'. 'Obviously, you'll wear the black but you'll look fabulous whatever you wear, *cara*. Meanwhile, I have something important to say. I need you to concentrate.'

Heart in her mouth, she turned to him. 'What is it?'

'It's this. *Posso baciarti, carissima*?'

'Testing my Italian, *carissimo*?' she asked, raising her arms and looping them around his neck. *'Voglio baciare si...'*

His answer was a long slow kiss, followed by an intimate lesson in advanced Italian.

It was the accessories that finally settled the matter of what she would wear. Her black dress had been refashioned from a fine jersey vintage dress that she'd found in a trunk in the attic.

The sleeves had been cut in one with the dress and she had narrowed them below the elbow. The neck was a simple V, cut low, but merely hinting at her breasts and she'd used a series of darts to bring it in at the waist. Worn as it was, it was timelessly elegant. Tonight, she'd cinched it in with an eight-inch-wide basque-style black suede and silver kid belt that was fastened at an angle by a series of small diamanté buckles.

When she was finally satisfied that every detail was perfect, she picked up a tiny silver and black suede clutch and her long black velvet evening coat and went through to the living room.

Dante, looking jaw-droppingly handsome in a tux, was standing in front of the fire, one hand on the mantel, the other holding a glass, his face burnished by the flames as he gazed into some dark abyss. Then, as he lifted the glass, he saw her and it never made it to his mouth.

'Angel...' He put down the glass, crossed to her, took the coat from her, holding onto one of her hands. 'Pretty gloves,' he said, admiring the fingerless black lace mitts she was wearing. 'I want to kiss you but you look so perfect.'

She lifted her hand so that he could kiss her fingers and he took his time about it, kissing each one in turn before turning her hand over and kissing her palm.

'What a gentleman,' she said, laughing, to disguise the fact that she was practically melting on the spot, and tapped her cheek. 'You can't do much damage there.'

He touched his lips to the spot.

'Or there.'

She lifted her chin so that he could kiss her neck, by which time he'd got the idea and continued a trail of soft kisses along the edge of the neckline of her dress. When he reached the lowest part of the V he slid his hand beneath the cloth and pushed it aside, then audibly caught his breath as he realised that she wasn't wearing anything underneath it. *'Mia amore...'*

He settled her silver and jet necklace back into place, carefully removed his hands, stepped back and held out her coat. As she turned and slipped her arms into the sleeves, he said, 'Have you grown?'

She hitched up her skirt a few inches to reveal the slender steel vertiginous heels of her intricately laced black suede boots.

He studied them for a moment, then her belt, then he looked up and smiled. 'I am so going to enjoy undressing you when we get home.'

By the time the limo approached the red carpet, Geli was shaking with nerves. 'All the women will be wearing designer dresses, diamonds,' she said.

'You *are* wearing a designer dress. And every one of those women will wish they were wearing that belt.'

'You think so?'

'Believe me. They'll know that every man in the room will be wishing he was the one unfastening those pretty buckles tonight.'

'Now I'm blushing.'

'Then it's just as well I'll be the only man in the room who knows for sure what you're not wearing tonight.' It was probably as well that the car stopped at that moment. Dante climbed out, offered her his hand, said, 'Big smile, Angel…' and she stepped out of the car to a blaze of flashlights from the army of paparazzi waiting for the celebrities.

The room was like a palace in a very grown-up fairy tale: everything beautiful, everything perfectly arranged, a stage set for exquisitely dressed players who moved in a circle around the legendary central character who was their host, and she watched, fascinated, as the famous—Hollywood stars, supermodels—paid court.

Dante introduced her to some people he knew, she drank a little champagne, ate a little caviar and wished she hadn't. He went to fetch her a glass of water and, as she turned, searching the crowd for a sight of Valentina or his father, she came face to face with the Maestro himself.

'*Signora…*'

'Maestro. *Piacere... Mi chiamo* Angelica Amery. *Sono Inglese.* My Italian is not good.'

'Welcome, Angelica Amery,' he said, switching to English. 'It's always a pleasure to meet a beautiful woman, especially one with so much courage.'

'Courage?'

'I believe that, including the waitresses, you are the only woman in the room not wearing a dress designed by me. This vogue for vintage clothes will put us all out of business.'

'*Mi dispiace,* Maestro, but I could not afford one of your gowns or even the one I'm wearing for that matter. This belonged to my great-grandmother.'

'She was a woman of great style, as are you, *cara.* And I adore your belt. The asymmetrical slant of the buckles complements the era of the dress so well. Where did you find it?'

'*Grazie*, Maestro. I designed it myself. I was inspired by an Indian bracelet I saw on the Internet.'

'Quite perfect.' He nodded, held out his hand before moving on and when she took it he raised it to his lips. 'Come and see me next month. We will talk about your future.'

'*Grazie...*' But he was already talking to someone else and, when she looked down, she realised that he'd tucked his card under her lace mitten.

He'd given her his card. Asked her to come and see him. He'd said her belt was 'quite perfect'...

She stood for a moment trying to breathe, trying to take in what had just happened and then spun round, searching for Dante so that she could tell him.

Taller than most in the room, he should be easy to spot, even in this crush, and after a moment she spotted his broad shoulders jutting from a small alcove. He had his back to her but, as she took a step in his direction, she saw who he was talking to.

Valentina Vettori was older than she'd realised, older than Dante, but even more beautiful in the flesh than in her photograph despite, or perhaps because, her eyes were brimming with tears.

It was like watching a car crash you were unable to prevent. The way she reached for him, the way he took her into his arms and held her while her tears seeped into the shoulder of his jacket. And all the joy of the last twenty-four hours, the triumph of the evening, turned to ashes in her mouth.

Valentina had been his lover—he'd grieved for her loss for over a year.

He'd only known her for a week.

Look away, she told herself. *Look away now...*

It was a moment of the most intense privacy and no one in the celebrity-hunting crowd had noticed. No one cared but her.

As she dragged her eyes from the scene in the alcove she saw someone else she recognised. Make that no one but her and Daniele Vettori who, glass in hand, was looking around, clearly wondering where his wife had got to.

'Signor Vettori,' she said, walking towards him, hand outstretched. 'I am so glad to meet you. I wanted to thank you for your help the other night.' His smile was puzzled but he turned to look at her. '*Sono* Angelica Amery,' she said. 'The crazy cat lady.'

'Signora Amery... *Piacere*.' He took her hand. 'I did not realise that you were English. You are here with Dante?' He sounded surprised. Looked hopeful.

'I'm a dress designer—in a very small way,' she added. 'Dante thought I might enjoy this.'

'And are you?'

'Very much.' Until two minutes ago she had been on

top of the world. 'Is your wife with you?' she asked as his eyes wandered in search of her. Anything to keep him focused on her.

'She's here somewhere, making up for lost time networking. We were very late. Alberto—our son—wouldn't settle. We have a nanny but Valentina... I'm sorry; you do not want to talk about babies.' He smiled, gave her his full attention. 'Where is my son?'

'He's gone to find me a glass of water. It's rather a crush.'

'Please, take this.' He offered her the glass he was holding. 'My wife is breastfeeding so she's avoiding the champagne.'

'Oh, but—'

His smile deepened and it was so much like his son's that a lump formed in her throat. 'There's a price to pay. You will have to stay and talk to me until Dante returns.'

'That's not an imposition, it's a pleasure.' She took the glass from him, hoping that her hand would not shake as she took a sip.

'Did you meet Dante in England, Signora Amery?'

'Please, everyone calls me Geli.'

Everyone except Dante...

'*Grazie*, Geli. *Mi chiamo*, Daniele.'

'Daniele... And, in answer to your question, no. I came to Isola to work. Dante helped me when I had a problem with my apartment.' She had to chase up the bank. She'd let things slide; there had been no urgency, but now—

'Angelica...' She physically jumped as Dante placed his hand on her shoulder, standing possessively close. He was paler and there was the faintest smear of make-up on the shoulder of his jacket that only someone who knew what to look for would see, but he had remembered her water. 'It appears that I'm redundant here.'

'Not at all.' She took the glass from him and handed it

to his father. 'Daniele merely loaned me this glass until you returned. It was for Valentina but she seems to have disappeared.'

'I saw her a minute ago. I believe she was heading in the direction of the cloakroom.'

'Then I will wait here with you if I may,' Daniele said.

The two men looked at one another for a long intense moment before Dante put out his hand and said something in Italian that Geli did not understand. And then she was holding two glasses as the two men hugged one another.

And she was the one blinking back tears when Valentina found them, linked her arm in Daniele's and said something to her in Italian, speaking far too quickly for her to understand.

'Geli is English, *cara*,' Daniele said, taking the fresh glass from Dante and handing it to her. 'She is the heroine who searched my construction site in the snow and saved the injured cat.'

'*Alora*… Such drama. You are so brave…' Her expression was unreadable and she could have intended anything from genuine admiration—possibly for risking her nails—to veiled sarcasm. '*Come*… How is she? The cat?'

'She is healing fast and contented now that she is with her kittens,' Geli assured her.

'Then all is right with her world.' She looked at Dante and for a long moment it was as if she and Daniele were not there. Then she snapped on a smile and said, '*Dolci*…' before turning to her. 'Sweet… I do not know if you are aware but I present an early evening magazine programme on regional television. We are always looking for light stories. Good news. Maybe we could feature your cat and her kittens? Are they photogenic?'

Geli, astonished and not entirely sure what to make of her invitation, turned to Dante but, getting no help there, said, 'Well, Mamma Cat is a looking a bit like Frankenstein's monster at the moment, shaved patches and stitches, but the kittens more than make up for that.'

'Perfect. Will you do it? Obviously, the programme is in Italian, but I can translate for you or—' Geli waited for her to suggest that Dante came along to translate '—we could film them at home and I can do a voice-over.'

'*Grazie*, Valentina. I'm working on my Italian but it might be kinder to your viewers if you did the talking.' Valentina's smile was strained and, on an impulse, she began telling her about the drama of Rattino's appearance, giving it the full action treatment as she described Lisa's horror, the women leaping on chairs, her diving under the table. By the end of the story they had gained a small audience and everyone was laughing.

'*Bravissima!*' Valentina clapped. 'That! I want that! We'll use subtitles. *I gattini*…where are they now?'

'They're in our apartment,' Dante told her. 'Why don't you come and see them? Come to lunch tomorrow, both of you. I have a gift for Alberto—' his father looked wary rather than pleased '—and I have a project that I'd like to discuss with Valentina.'

'Oh?'

'Angelica is an artist and we're making a film about the need to preserve the heart of Isola.'

'From people like me?'

'It isn't personal, Papà. It was never personal.'

There was another of those long looks, but after a moment his father nodded. They chatted for a few more minutes before Valentina spotted someone she had to talk to and the party broke up in a round of very Italian hugs. Only Geli saw that, while her husband was occupied with her, Valentina took the opportunity to whisper something in Dante's ear, saw his nod of acknowledgement, imperceptible to anyone who wasn't watching closely.

'Would you like to go on somewhere?' Dante asked as they climbed into their car.

'No. Thank you.'

'You can't know how glad I am you said that. Did you have a good time? I saw you talking to our host.'

'Did you? Actually, he was congratulating me on being the only woman present with the courage not to be wearing one of his gowns.'

'Amore...' he exclaimed. 'I never thought. I'm so sorry.'

'Why? It is what it is and when I explained that this dress had belonged to my great-grandmother he forgave me.'

'Are you serious?'

'That my dress is eighty years old or that he forgave me?'

'Madonna, mia! Either...both. Is it really that old?'

'My great-grandmother kept a ledger of her clothes. When she bought them, how much they cost, where she wore them. This one is by Mainbocher, the man who designed the dress Wallis Simpson wore when she married the Duke of Windsor. Great-grandma didn't wear it after that. She disapproved of divorce, disapproved of the abdication...disapproved of pretty much everything, apparently, except beautiful clothes.'

She knew she was talking too much but Dante, it seemed, was disinclined to stop her. Maybe he was interested in vintage fashion...

'We have trunks full of clothes in the attic, not just hers, but my grandmother's too. She was a sixties dolly bird, a contemporary of Twiggy, but that's more Sorrel's era. Lucky for us that Elle had no idea of the value of vintage clothes when she was selling off the family silver to pay the creditors.'

Talking too much and all of them the wrong words.

'The dress is perfect, Angel. You were so busy looking at everyone else that you didn't notice that they were all looking at you.'

He reached across the back seat of the limo to take her hand but she pretended she hadn't noticed, lifting it out of his reach to check the safety of a long jet earring.

'The Maestro admired my belt, too,' she said. 'It's a Dark Angel original.'

'I hope you told him so.'

'I did… He kissed my hand, gave me his card and asked me to go and see him next month. When the shows are over.'

'I think that is what you call a result.'

'Beyond my wildest dreams,' she assured him. And maybe that was it. The jealous gods only let you have one dream at a time… 'And you, Dante? Did you accomplish everything you wanted tonight?'

He sighed, leaned back. 'Everything is not for mortal men,' he said, eerily reflecting her own thoughts, 'but as much as I could have hoped. The fact that you were already talking to my father made it a great deal easier.'

'Did it? You sounded rather cross.'

'No…' He shook his head. 'How did you come to be talking?'

'Oh, the usual way. You know how it is at parties. We were in the same space at the same time. I was looking for you so that I could tell you about meeting the Maestro. He was looking for his wife and about to see her crying into your shoulder so I distracted him by introducing myself as the crazy cat lady.'

'Then I'm not imagining the touch of chill in the air. Congratulations, Angelica. You have not only made a hit with the one man in Milan famously impossible to impress, but appear to have excelled yourself in diplomacy.'

'My sisters would be astonished on both counts,' she

assured him. 'I usually say exactly what I think and hang the consequences.'

'I applaud your restraint but, since we're alone, feel free to share your thoughts with me.'

She closed her eyes. That was it? No explanation, no attempt at justification? No reason for her to forget what she'd seen and…no, she would never forget the tenderness with which he'd held Valentina. She knew how that felt and she wasn't in the mood to share.

'I'm thinking that you took me to the party as an excuse to see Valentina. That, sooner or later, she will leave your father and come back to you and he knows it.' When he still said nothing, made no attempt to deny it, she added, 'And I think that new goldfish will be nervous, all alone in a strange tank. You should keep him company tonight.'

CHAPTER TWELVE

*'Eat ice cream for a broken heart. It freezes the heart
and numbs the pain.'*
—from *Rosie's Little Book of Ice Cream*

DANTE TOLD THE driver to wait, walked Angelica upstairs
to the door of his apartment, unlocked it and waited while
she walked in, turned to him, blocking the way.

'Angel—'

'Don't… Don't call me that.'

'I just wanted to thank you for everything you did this
evening. You were kinder than any of us had a right to expect and we are all in your debt for ever.'

'I didn't do it for you. I did it to spare your father's
feelings.'

'I understand, but whatever you think you saw…' He
wanted to tell her that what she'd seen was not what she
imagined. She was right about Valentina—he had thought
that meeting her on neutral ground with hundreds of other
people present would be easier for both of them. He had
been as wrong about that as Geli was about everything
else. Valentina had almost fainted with shock when she'd
seen him, had been desperate for reassurance that he
wasn't about to blow her life apart.

Now he was the one clinging on, hoping that Angelica would remember that he'd respected her enough to be

honest with her about Lisa's motives when he could have gone for the easy lie.

She'd been angry then, too, but not for long. She'd thought things through and accepted that he had been doing what was right.

All he could do was hope that, given time, she would understand that tonight—

'Hello, you're back early.' Matteo, slightly tousled, as if he'd been asleep, appeared from the living room. 'I thought you'd be going on somewhere.'

'It's been a long day,' he said. 'Any problems?'

'No.' He grinned stupidly. 'Actually, I've been talking to my mother. She's at home all day and she'd be really happy to take care of the cats. If it would help?'

Not in a million years. Right now, the only thing anchoring Angelica in his life was the cats and they were going nowhere.

'We'll talk about it tomorrow. Go down and wait in the car. I'll give you a lift home.'

'Thanks. *Ciao*, Geli.' He grabbed his coat from the hook and thundered down the stairs.

When he had gone, Angelica opened her mouth as if to say something, but closed it again. Closed her eyes as if it was too painful to look at him. He felt the shock ripple through her as he cradled her face, wiping away the tears squeezed from beneath her lids with the pads of his thumbs, but she didn't pull away.

'Carissima...' Tears clung to her lashes as she opened her eyes. 'May I offer some words of wisdom from a woman it is my honour, my privilege to know?'

'Please, Dante,' she protested, but she was still there, the door open.

'Cherish the good things that happened to you this evening, hold them close. They do not come often.'

'I know...'

'Make a list of all the things that hurt you so that you won't lie awake turning them over in your head.' Her mouth softened a little as she recognised her own advice returned with interest and, encouraged, he continued, 'Take a bath, not too hot. Sprinkle a little lavender oil on your pillow and then, while you wait for sleep, think of all the good things that you will do tomorrow so that you'll wake happy.'

She swallowed. 'Good things?'

'The early shift in the café, flirting with Marco and all your other admirers.' She shrugged. 'The appointment with your client to finalise the scheme for his ice cream parlour.' She might move out, but she wouldn't walk away from a promise and it would keep her close. Give him hope.

'That's not in my diary.'

'It's in mine. Ten o'clock.'

Another shrug.

'And then lunch with—'

'You expect me to have lunch with you and... With all of you?'

'I believe, in fact I'm certain, that if you will talk to my father about our film he'll be more receptive.'

She frowned. 'Why would he listen to me?'

'Because you are a beautiful woman. My worst moment tonight was seeing you with him, watching him flirting with you. He has Valentina and yet he still cannot help himself.'

'Maybe he's protecting himself,' she said. 'Making an exit plan. Preparing to be left.'

'Something you'd know all about, *cara*?'

'What?' She shook her head. 'What are you talking about?'

'You told me yourself that you're scared to death to risk your heart, always holding something back, protecting yourself from hurt in case you're left behind by those you love. Wearing mourning black in case they die.'

She opened her mouth to protest, but nothing emerged.

'It isn't going to happen. Valentina will stay with him because he gives her everything she ever wanted.'

'Not you.'

'She was the one who left, *cara*. I would never have made her happy and she had the sense to know that. The courage to go after what she wanted.'

'Taking part of you with her. You still love her, Dante. Admit it.'

'You're right. She took something of mine, but love?' He shook his head. 'I was dazzled, infatuated, but in the end it was just sex.'

Enough. He'd said enough. He had to go before he heard himself begging to stay and he took her hand, placed his key in her palm and closed her fingers around it. 'Take this.'

'But it's your key.'

'Now it is yours.' He bent to kiss her cheek and she leaned into him, drawn to him despite everything, and it took every ounce of self-control not to put his arms around her, hold her.

To his infinite regret, she'd seen him hold Valentina and it would be there, between them, until she could trust him, believe that he was hers, body and soul. He could show her in everything he did, but only she could choose to see.

'Dormi bene, mio amore. Sogui dolci.'

Something inside Geli screamed a long desperate *Noooooo!* as Dante turned and headed down the stairs. The hand he'd kissed reached out to him but he did not look back and when she heard him hit the lower flight, she closed the door and leaned back against it, clutching the key he'd given her.

'Now it is yours.' What did that mean?

That he had locked himself out until she invited him in? But this was his apartment... No, wait. This evening, when Valentina had asked him where the cats were, he'd said that they were in 'our apartment'. Not his, but *our* apartment. And Valentina hadn't batted an eyelid.

But she'd cried in his arms. And whispered something in Dante's ear before walking away.

What? What had she said to him? She tried making her lips form the words but it was hopeless.

She gave up, fetched a tub of ice cream from the freezer and ate it while the bath filled. Then she slid beneath the water and, letting its warmth seep into her, she blanked out Dante and his whole wretched family and did as he'd advised, focusing her entire mind on that moment when one of the world's most famous dress designers told her that her belt was 'quite perfect'.

She sprinkled a few drops of lavender oil on her pillow and then lay in bed and wrote down everything she could remember about the evening. What she'd worn down to the last stitch and stone—she should start keeping a clothes journal like her great-grandmother. She wrote how Dante had looked as he'd stood by the fire waiting for her because he was beautiful and she loved him and it was a memory to hold, cherish.

So much for nothing serious, not for keeps but for fun. If it had been that, then what had happened this evening would not have mattered.

So not like her mother...

She wrote everything she could remember about the limousine, about being snapped by the paparazzi as she'd walked the red carpet, the people she'd seen, every word that the Maestro had said to her.

Every word that Dante had said.

'Our' apartment. 'Our' film...

His certainty that Valentina would not leave his father because she had everything she was looking for. If that was true, why had she been crying into his shoulder? Guilt, remorse…?

What had she whispered in Dante's ear?

It was the last thing she thought before *Dancing Queen* dragged her out of sleep.

Dante arrived on the dot of ten and they had a straight-forward client/designer meeting downstairs in the room that was to be converted into an ice cream parlour, making final decisions about colours, furniture, artwork. They chose the ice cream cabinet and Dante used his laptop to go online and order it. Then he turned it around so that she could see a vintage jukebox he'd found.

'It plays old seventy-eights.'

'Boys' toys,' she muttered disapprovingly. 'It'll cost you a fortune to find records for it. And you won't get anyone later than…'

'Later than…?'

'I don't know. They pre-date my grandmother. Frank Sinatra?'

'That's a good start. See if you can find *Fly Me to the Moon.*'

She rolled her eyes but made a note then reached for her file as he picked it up to give it to her. Their hands met and, as he looked up, she might have forgotten herself, grabbed hold of him—

'I'll organise the decorators,' he said, standing up. 'Will you supervise them?'

'It's part of the job.' She checked her watch. 'If that's all, I have to go and change for lunch.'

The cleaning staff had been in. There were fresh flowers and a soft cat bed had been placed near the freshly lit fire, glowing behind the glass doors, for Mamma Cat and her kittens.

She checked on the cats, changed into her black mini-dress, topped it with the red velvet jacket that Lisa had so admired and wore the laced boots from the night before. Her reflection suggested that it was too much.

It looked as if she was competing. She was at home and she should be more relaxed, informal, allow their guests to shine.

Our apartment…

She changed into narrow dark red velvet trousers and a black silk shirt which she topped with a long, dark red brocade waistcoat and ditched the boots for ballet flats.

Better. But, for the first time in her life, she wished her wardrobe contained at least one pink fluffy sweater. Because although she didn't want Dante to be right, deep down she knew he was.

She picked up his key and slipped it into the pocket of her waistcoat. It was a pledge of some sort. Of his sincerity, his commitment, maybe.

If only she knew what Valentina had whispered to him.

Her phoned beeped and, grateful for anything that would delay the moment when she'd have to go downstairs to the café, she picked it up and discovered a reply to the somewhat sharp message she'd sent to the bank.

Her balance had been restored, along with five hundred pounds for her inconvenience. What? Banks didn't pay up like that unless they were being harassed by consumer programmes. Clearly they'd discovered some monumental error…

She had no excuse to stay now. Only the cats, but Matteo was desperate to give them a home.

She checked the clock. She couldn't put it off any longer. It was time to go, in every sense of the word.

She could hear Dante talking to someone on the phone as she passed his office. The door was slightly ajar; she didn't stop but she couldn't help wondering who he was talking to. That was how it was when you weren't sure. It was how Daniele must feel every day of his life but she couldn't live like that.

She was checking the table that had been set up in the corner when Dante joined her.

'Lunch first and then we'll go upstairs for coffee so that Valentina can meet the cats. Did the basket arrive?'

'Yes. Good thought. They'll look adorable.'

'If they're going to be on television they need more than a cardboard box…' He turned as the door opened and Valentina appeared in a gush of air kisses.

'*Ciao*, Geli. *Ciao*, Dante… Daniele had to park around the back somewhere. He's just coming. Can you get the door for him?'

Dante was calling out to Bruno behind the bar to bring water and menus as he opened the door so he didn't immediately see what was hampering his father.

Then he turned, looked down and saw Valentina's sleeping baby nestled in a softly padded buggy and in that moment Geli understood everything.

Valentina's tears, Daniele's uncertainty, Dante's grief.

He had not been mourning the loss of his love, but the child she had carried, given birth to and then placed in his father's arms.

In the excitement created by the arrival of the baby, the staff crowding around to coo over him, Geli reached out a hand to him and he grasped it so tightly that it hurt while he arranged his face into a smile.

Hours later—actually, it was no more than two but it had felt like a thousand—Geli shut the door behind their visitors and turned to Dante.

'Your father knows, doesn't he?' she said. 'That the baby is yours.'

'He had a fever when I was a child. That's when I first came to stay here with Nonnina. Valentina is his fourth wife but there have been no more children when, as you can see, he loves them…so I imagine there was some damage. I should have told you. I would have told you, but last night—'

'Don't…' She did not want to think about last night. That familiar, horrible sense of loss— 'We have known one another just over a week. Okay, we've probably spent more time together than some couples spend in months, but it's still new. We're still learning about one another. And that is a huge secret to share with anyone.'

'Secrets are poison. Valentina nearly fainted when she saw me last night. She was sure I was there to make trouble, to tell my father that Alberto isn't his child. Blow their lives apart.'

'Are you saying that she doesn't know that he knows?'

'Apparently not. That's when she cried, when I told her. With relief and joy, I think, to realise just how much he loved her.'

'I see.' And remembering the way Valentina had gone straight to her husband, put her arm in his—not a guilty wife returning to her husband's side, but one who knew how much she was loved—she did see.

'You asked me once if I regretted my choice, do you remember?'

'You said it was the wrong question. That I should be asking if you'd make the same decision again.' Could she ask it? Could she live with his answer… 'Would you?'

'The truth?'

'Parla come magni, caro.'

He smiled as she quoted his words back at him and her heart broke for him. After that first shocked moment he'd been so generous, admiring the baby, holding him, handing him back to his father to put in his buggy for a nap when it must have been tearing his heart out.

'There will always be regret, Angel, but a baby's place

is with his mother and his mother's place is with the man who will make her happy. I can only hope that, should I be given the chance, I'd have the strength, the wisdom, the humanity to make the same decision.'

'You'd do that for them?'

'What should I do? Demand DNA tests? Give the readers of *Celebrità* a scandal to thrill them over the breakfast table? Make his mother the centre of vicious whispers?'

'No.' She shook her head. 'No…'

'I created a trust fund for Alberto when he was born, *cara*. And today, when you took Valentina to your workshop to show her your designs, Papà agreed to sign documents giving me legal access to Alberto, and to name me his guardian in the event of a divorce.'

'Will Valentina agree to that?'

'She knows that he will always be a part of my life,' he said. 'I want you to know that.'

'I treasure your trust. You are a very special man, Dante Vettori.' And to show her confidence, her trust, she took his key from her pocket and offered it to him.

'You are returning my key?'

'No, *caro*, I'm not returning it; I'm giving it to you for safe keeping.'

He took the key, put it in his pocket and then took her hand. 'I've missed you.'

'It was ten hours, Dante,' she said, stepping into his arm. 'But I've missed you, too.'

'Did I tell you that you look lovely today?'

'Make the most of it. I'm going to buy a pink fluffy jumper at the market on Tuesday. And if you don't kiss me right now, I'll wear it on television.'

His kiss was thorough and then, as a demonstration of how seriously he took her threat, he picked her up and carried her through to the bedroom and kissed every single part of her.

Later, when she was lying in his arms, he said, 'Tell me about this pink jumper thing. Is it going to be an ongoing threat? Not that I'm complaining.'

'I'll tell you when you can relax.' She looked up at him. 'Can I ask you a question?'

'Ask away.'

'What did Valentina whisper in your ear last night?'

'You saw?'

'I saw.'

'She said, *"Si prega di essere felice..."* I'd told her that I'd met someone and, having met you, she was urging me to be happy.' He leaned down and kissed her. 'A command that I'm delighted to obey.'

'Uh-oh.'

'Cara?'

'I've had a text from Elle. I knew opening the ice cream parlour at Easter was a mistake. They're all coming to see it.'

'They're flying to Milan to see an ice cream parlour?'

'Professional interest?' she offered.

'Cara...'

'Okay, they're coming to check you out. Sorry, I've tried to be as casual about us as I can be, but the less you say, the more big sisters read between the lines.'

'Is there anything I should know? Topics not to be mentioned?'

'Just be yourself and they'll love you. But I have to find somewhere for them to stay.'

'I'll call Papà and ask if the villa at Lake Como is going to be free.'

'It's not. Valentina told me that they're going to the Lake for Easter. She rang to invite us while you were out. I thought that maybe we could go down on Sunday for the day so that you can spend time with Alberto but...'

'But nothing. There's plenty of room.' He took out his phone. 'Four adults, three children, one baby, right?' She nodded and he made the call. 'They're delighted to have them and we'll stay over until Tuesday. It'll give you plenty of time to catch up with your sisters.'

'Did I ever tell you that I love you?' she said.

'Not since breakfast. Are we done here?'

She looked around at the rich green walls, the huge brilliant print—just the corner of an ice cream sundae with all the focus on a huge, glistening red cherry—the white-painted furniture, vintage jukebox and gleaming ice cream counter waiting to be filled.

Outside in the courtyard, tubs of red and white flowers were overflowing from old stone troughs and she'd threaded tiny white solar-powered fairy lights through the vines that would light up as dusk fell.

'It looks done to me.'

'Then come with me. I have something to show you.'

He took her outside and unlocked the front door of the tall narrow building next door that had, until the owner retired a few weeks ago, been a hardware store.

'More expansion plans?' she asked. 'Only I'm a bit busy.'

She'd been working flat out since the photograph of her talking to the Maestro had appeared in an Italian lifestyle magazine reporting his interest in her belt. Now it seemed everyone wanted one.

He had offered her a job in return for the rights to reproduce it but, flattered as she was, she didn't want to be a nameless designer producing ideas for a designer 'brand'.

She had her own label and was collaborating with a student who could do amazing things with leather to produce variations on her design in gorgeous colours.

She'd also had an order for a dozen of her spider web beaded silk chiffon tops for a Milan boutique.

'I know how busy you are and that you need more space,' he said. 'Welcome to your *atelier*.'

'What? No...'

'No?' Dante repeated. 'You do not think this would make appropriate showroom space for your designs?'

'A showroom...' She spun around, imagining everything painted white, shelves, a display table, one brilliantly coloured piece in the small window. 'You know it's perfect.'

'I'm glad that's settled. There's a room out the back for office and storage and two rooms on the next floor for workshop space. And on the top floor...'

She turned to him, knowing what was coming. She'd told him, that first night in Isola, about her dream. A house with three floors. One for sales, one for work and one to live in.

'There's a little apartment. Just big enough for one?'

'Well, it's a bit bigger than that. I thought we could knock it through.'

She frowned. 'Knock it through? I don't understand. Have you bought this?'

'No. At least not recently. I inherited some money from my maternal grandfather when I turned twenty-one and Nonnina wanted to raise the money to help her son set up in business in Australia. She owned the whole block and it seemed like a good investment, even if part of the deal was that she stayed on, rent-free, until she decided to retire. Papà would buy it in a heartbeat if it was for sale.'

'*Madonna*, Dante, you know how to take the wind out of a girl's sails.'

He shrugged. 'So you're good with that? Extending the apartment? Only we'll need more space when we're married.'

And, while she was struggling to get her chin under

control, he produced a small leather box from his pocket and opened it to reveal a large solitaire diamond.

'Dante, *caro*, my love, are you sure? There's no hurry...'

He did not pretend that he did not understand but said, 'This is different in so many ways from Valentina. We are not just lovers, Angel, we're friends. *Siete la mia aria...* You are the air I breathe. *Voglio stare con te per sempre...* I want to stay with you for ever. *Ti amo.*' And then again in English, so there could be no mistake. 'I love you, *mia amore.* I would leave here and go to the ends of the earth to be with you.'

She dashed away a tear, took the ring from the box and gave it to him, holding out her hand, and as he placed it on her finger she said, '*Siete la mia aria,* Dante. *Voglio stare con te per sempre...* I would live in a cave with you.'

There were two weddings. The first was in Isola early in May. They said their vows in the *municipio*, with Giovanni standing as his best man and his own bride, Lisa, as her very best woman. Afterwards everyone was invited to a party in the communal garden. The feast was lavish but still everyone brought something they had made to add to the table. Geli's family returned to Isola for the occasion, bringing with them her grandmother and Great-Uncle Basil. Nonnina flew with her son from Australia to be with Dante and meet his bride. A fiddler played so that they could dance and later, as dusk fell, a jazz quartet filled the air with smooth, mellow music while the square was lit up with thousands of tiny white fairy lights.

Six weeks later, in midsummer, Geli and Dante repeated their vows in the Orangery at Haughton Manor, just as Geli's sister had done a few years earlier, followed by a picnic in the park with Rosie in attendance to provide all the ice cream anyone could eat. This time her sisters were her best women, her small nieces her bridesmaids and Great-Uncle Basil gave her away.

Over the vintage cream slipper satin vintage gown she'd adapted for both occasions, Geli wore a luscious new belt made from shocking-pink suede, which made the front page of *Celebrità* and its English version, *Celebrity*.

An order book for a limited edition of the design was filled the same day.

* * * * *

A faint smile curved his lips.

"I'm a curious man and you're a beautiful woman. A plus B equals C."

"That's not the way algebra works."

Finn chuckled lowly. "You're right. That's not algebra. That's my own special equation."

He was making light of the whole thing and it would be best if she did, too. But his kiss had shaken her to the very depths of her being. And she was sick of men never taking her seriously, tired of being considered a pleasant pastime and nothing more.

"Very cute," she muttered, then quickly turned away from him and walked over to Harry's playpen. "But I've had enough laughs for one night. I'm putting Harry and myself to bed."

Mariah was bending over to pick up Harry when Finn's hands caught her around the waist and tugged her straight back into his arms.

"If you thought that was for laughs, then maybe I'd better do it over."

Before she could react he'd already fastened his lips over hers. And this time there was no mistaking the raw hunger in his kiss.

***

Men of the West:
Whether ranchers or lawmen, these heartbreakers can ride, shoot—and drive a woman crazy…

DADDY WORE SPURS

BY
STELLA BAGWELL

MILLS
BOON

Published in Great Britain 2015
by Mills & Boon, an imprint of Harlequin (UK) Limited,
Eton House, 18-24 Paradise Road, Richmond, Surrey, TW9 1SR

© 2015 Stella Bagwell

ISBN: 978-0-263-25151-7

23-0715

Harlequin (UK) Limited's policy is to use papers that are natural, renewable and recyclable products and made from wood grown in sustainable forests. The logging and manufacturing processes conform to the legal environmental regulations of the country of origin.

Printed and bound in Spain
by CPI, Barcelona

After writing more than eighty books for Mills & Boon, **Stella Bagwell** still finds it exciting to create new stories and bring her characters to life. She loves all things Western and has been married to her own real cowboy for forty-four years. Living on the south Texas coast, she also enjoys being outdoors and helping her husband care for the horses, cats and dog that call their small ranch home. The couple has one son, who teaches high school mathematics and is also an athletic director. Stella loves hearing from readers. They can contact her at stellabagwell@gmail.com.

To my husband, Harrell.
You still look sexy in spurs, my darlin'!

Chapter One

Was this baby his son?

Finn Calhoun stared in wonder at the four-month-old boy cradled in the woman's arms. The child's hair was curly, but it wasn't bright copper like his own. Still, it was a light shade of auburn. Finn's eyes were the color of the sky, while the baby's eyes were a much darker blue. There were also the dimples creasing his fat little cheeks. Finn possessed those same dimples, too. But that was hardly proof the little guy belonged to him.

A man was supposed to have nine months to adjust to the idea of becoming a dad, Finn thought. He'd had all of two days to ponder the notion of having a child. And though he liked to consider himself a man with his boots firmly planted on the ground, the idea that he might be a father had left him feeling as if he'd been shot out of a cannon and hadn't yet landed.

"Would you like to hold him?"

The gently spoken question broke through Finn's dazed thoughts, and he lifted his gaze to Mariah Montgomery, the baby's aunt.

Gauging her to be in her midtwenties, he noted that her slender frame was concealed beneath a pair of worn blue jeans and a sleeveless red checked blouse. Crowblack hair waved back from a wide forehead and was fastened at the nape of her neck with a white silk scarf. Cool gray eyes regarded him with cautious regard, while a set of pale pink lips pressed into a straight line.

Since meeting him at the door five minutes ago and inviting him into the house, Finn hadn't seen any sort of pleasurable expression or welcoming smile cross her face. But Finn could overlook her somber attitude. She'd surely gone through hell these past few weeks.

A month ago, her sister Aimee had died in a skiing accident. Since then she'd had to deal with grief and instant motherhood. Now she was meeting Finn for the first time. And she had no idea if he was a worthless bum who'd taken advantage of her late sister, or a nice guy who'd been caught up in a long-distance love affair. She only knew that Finn's name was listed on the baby's birth certificate as the father.

His head whirling with questions and reservations, Finn stepped forward. "Do you think holding him would be all right?"

She shot him an odd, almost suspicious look. "Why wouldn't it be all right? Fathers do hold their sons. And Aimee named you as the father."

Her voice held a thread of skepticism. As though she was far from convinced he was the boy's father. Well, Finn could've told her that for the past two days, he'd also been swamped with doubts. No matter that the timing of the child's birth calculated perfectly back to the weekend he'd spent with Aimee, a two-day affair hadn't necessarily created a baby. Even so, he wasn't about to dismiss the possibility that he was the father.

Keeping these thoughts to himself, he said, "Some babies don't appreciate being handed over to a stranger. And I don't want to make him cry."

Mild surprise pushed the suspicion from her face. "Oh. So you're familiar with babies?"

"I've never had one of my own," he admitted. "But I spent quite a bit of time with my nieces and nephews when they were small."

That hardly seemed to impress her, but she did move a step closer.

"I see. Well, Harry is a friendly little guy. He likes most everyone."

The breath suddenly rushed from Finn's lungs. "Harry? Is that short for Harrison?" he asked, his voice little more than a hoarse whisper.

"That's right. I always call him Harry, though."

The yellow and blue furnishings of the nursery faded to a dazed blur, prompting Finn to wipe a hand over his face. He'd never felt so humbled, so shaken in his life.

"Harrison is my first name," he told her. "But I—I guess you already knew that. You saw it on the birth certificate."

Her cool gray gaze connected with his and for one brief moment, Finn thought he spotted a flash of compassion in her eyes. Could she possibly understand that his emotions were riding a violent wave? Maybe she understood he wasn't the sort of man who could casually make a baby, then walk away without a backward glance.

She said, "I'm sorry. When I spoke to you on the telephone, I was so focused on how to give you the news about Aimee that I didn't think to tell you Harry's name."

Hearing that Aimee had died from a tragic accident had been enough to knock Finn sideways. Then before he could recover, she'd hit him with the news of the baby and that supposedly he was the father. After that he'd been too stunned to ask for details. He'd managed to scribble down the child's location and a phone number, and the rest of the conversation had passed in a blur.

"To be honest I don't recall much of our conversation. I was pretty shaken up. All I could think about was getting up here," Finn admitted, then shook his head. "I can't believe Aimee even remembered my first name. Everyone calls me Finn—that's my middle name."

He held his arms out and Mariah carefully handed the boy to him. Once he had the baby's weight cradled safely in the crook of his arm, the realization that he could be touching his son for the very first time swelled his chest with overwhelming emotions.

Bending his head, Finn placed a kiss on the baby's forehead, while unabashed tears burned the back of his eyes. Father or not, he couldn't ignore the deep and sudden connection he felt to the child in his arms.

"This isn't the way a man is supposed to be introduced to his son," he murmured thickly. "The child should be newly born from his mother's womb with his eyes squinched and his skin all red and wrinkled. He should be there to hear him crying and sucking in the first few breaths of his life."

Lifting his head, he looked to Mariah for answers. "If Harry is truly mine, then I've lost so much—memories and moments that I'll never have. Why didn't Aimee tell me she was pregnant?"

With a frustrated shake of her head, she turned and walked to the far side of the nursery. As Finn watched her go, his gaze was instinctively drawn to the sway of her curvy hips encased in faded denim and the long black tail of hair swishing against her back. He hadn't expected Aimee's sister to look so young or pretty. In fact, during the brief time he'd known Aimee, she hadn't said much about her sister. Only that she had one and that the both of them lived on the ranch.

As Finn had made the drive up here to Stallion Canyon in Northern California, he'd held the notion he'd be meeting an older woman with a family of her own, who'd kindly taken in her little nephew until the father could be located. He couldn't have been more wrong. Mariah was an attractive single woman. Not only that, there was a fierce maternal gleam in her eye. One that said she wasn't about to hand Harry over to him without definitive proof.

"Several weeks passed after Harry was born before Aimee finally told me you were the father. After that, I tried to persuade her to contact you, but she always stalled without giving me a reason. I don't know why. Unless it was because some other man actually fathered Harry. Maybe she got tangled up with a married man. Or she didn't want you involved. I'm just as confused as you are about the whole thing."

It was becoming clear to Finn that Aimee hadn't revealed much, if anything, to her sister about their weekend romance in Reno. But he didn't consider that odd. He hadn't said anything about that weekend to his brothers, either. Not until two days ago when he'd learned about the baby. Before then, his time with Aimee had been a private, personal thing.

"I've never been married. I made that clear to Aimee." He shook his head with confusion. "We met and after having a whirlwind weekend together, I thought she'd taken our time together seriously. Before we parted I gave her my number and she promised to keep in touch. But I never heard from her again."

Her expression rueful, she said, "We were sisters, but we had our differences. She didn't talk much to me about her personal life. But after Harry was born—well, we eventually got into a heated argument."

Her wavering voice had broken in spots and as Finn watched her struggle to hold back tears, it suddenly struck him that this whole ordeal was far more difficult for her than it was for him. Mariah had lost a member of her family. Finn's connection to Aimee had been little more than a brief, star-crossed encounter.

Finn was wondering if he should offer some comforting words when she suddenly went on, "I warned her that if something happened to her, Harry would need his father. I didn't— I never thought something actually would happen. I was only trying to push her into contacting you. But then she really died. Now I have to live with those words I said to her. Even though I said them with good intentions."

Finn was suddenly struck with the urge to go to her and place a reassuring arm around her shoulders. But he held back. They'd met only a few minutes ago. She might not appreciate him getting that close. Especially when the two of them appeared to be the only two adults in the house.

"We all say things we wish we could change or take

back," Finn told her. "But in this case I hardly see where you crossed the line. Harry's father should've been contacted long before his birth. I don't understand why she was keeping it a secret."

She made a helpless palms-up gesture. "Frankly, Aimee had been giving me the impression that the father was someone else. A guy she'd been involved with off and on for a long time. When she told me about you and showed me the birth certificate, I was shocked."

Finn's mind was so jammed with questions, he didn't know where to begin or what to think. "What else did she tell you about me?"

Shrugging, she said, "Not much. Just that you lived in Nevada and liked horses. Later, after the accident, I found your number in her address book."

With the baby cuddled safely to his chest, Finn moved across the room to where Mariah was sitting stiffly on the edge of the rocking chair. The two sisters couldn't have been more different, he thought. Where Mariah was dark and petite, Aimee had been tall, with caramel-brown hair and hazel eyes. Their personalities appeared to be equally opposite, too. Aimee had been full of smiles and laughter, whereas this young woman seemed to be all serious business.

"I don't know what to think about all that, Ms. Montgomery. But if she said I'm the father, then I surely must be." He looked down at the precious baby snuggled in the crook of his arm. Three days ago Finn had been a thirty-two-year-old man with nothing on his mind but his job of managing the Silver Horn's horse division. The possibility of having a child never entered his thoughts. Now here he was holding a baby who could very well be his son. The whole thing seemed surreal. "I met Aimee at the mustang training competition in Reno. After the first round was over I made a point of searching her out. To offer a price for her horse. She refused to sell him."

"But she didn't refuse to go to bed with you," Mariah said pointedly.

Her blunt way of putting it spread a wave of heat over his face. More than a year ago, when he'd said goodbye to Aimee, he'd never imagined that anything so life-altering as a baby had occurred between them. And he certainly hadn't expected Aimee to lose her life on a ski slope less than seventy miles from the Silver Horn.

"We spent the weekend together in Reno. It wasn't like either one of us set out to make a baby."

"I'm not so sure about that, Mr. Calhoun."

The suggestive remark caused his jaw to drop. "You think I—"

"Not you," she interrupted. "I'm talking about Aimee. I've always believed she deliberately set out to get pregnant. If not by you—then someone else."

The idea of Aimee using him to get pregnant was incredible. She'd hardly seemed the conniving type. And why would she have done such a thing?

He said, "I'll admit that two days wasn't long enough for me to know everything about Aimee. But I find it hard to believe she was luring me into a pregnancy trap, or shotgun wedding, or anything close to it. She didn't try to attach any strings to me. My mistake was trusting her when she said she was on the pill. But as you can see I'm here and more than ready to take responsibility for Harry."

Bending her head, she said in a low voice, "I'm sorry. I shouldn't have said any of that. When my sister met you in Reno—well, her plans might not have included a baby at all. It's just that she had—"

"Look, if you were going to tell me about Bryce, I already know. She told me how he'd been a longtime boyfriend. But she'd broken things off with him."

Her head popped up. "Aimee mentioned Bryce to you? That's surprising. She wasn't one to share personal things."

"Sometimes it's easier to talk about yourself to someone you just met. Especially if your plans are to never see them again," he added wryly.

Her expression turned curious. "You think she'd never intended to see you again?"

"I didn't then, obviously. But I do now."

The baby began to squirm and Finn looked down to see that the infant was chewing on his tiny fist. Drool was dripping off his chin and Finn carefully wiped it away with his forefinger. Just touching the baby's face and looking into his dark blue eyes filled Finn's heart with a fierce protectiveness. If Harry was his son, he wouldn't let anyone or anything keep him from taking the baby home to the Silver Horn. And that included the black-haired beauty who was eyeing him as though he were the devil himself.

Across the small nursery, Mariah was having all sorts of trouble dragging her gaze away from the rugged Nevada cowboy. A few minutes ago, when she'd opened the door and found herself standing face-to-face with Finn Calhoun, she'd felt as though the ground had shifted beneath her feet.

She'd expected Finn's appearance to be a bit more than average, otherwise Aimee would've never taken a second glance at him. But this guy was leaps and bounds beyond average.

At least two or three inches over six feet, he towered over her. Broad shoulders sat over a long torso that narrowed down to a lean waist and tall, muscular legs. Yet his hard, wiry body was only a part of his striking appearance, she realized. His face was a composite of tough angles and slopes. A jutting chin, hollow cheekbones and rough-hewn lips were softened by a pair of dazzling blue eyes partially hidden by a thick fringe of copper-colored lashes. Slightly darker hair of the same color curled wildly around his ears and against the back of his neck, while a set of white teeth made a startling contrast against his tanned skin.

Oh, he was a looker all right, Mariah decided. But that didn't necessarily make him daddy material. Especially if he used those looks to go around seducing women. Still, in all honesty, she didn't know if this man had done the seducing or if Aimee had been the initiator of their romance. And it hardly mattered now. The only question that should be on her mind was whether he'd actually fathered little Harry.

Reining in her wandering thoughts, Mariah said, "Aimee dated Bryce for over three years and wanted to marry him, but he kept putting her off. He was divorced and wasn't ready to try marriage again. That's why—well, Aimee once told me she was tempted to get pregnant so that Bryce would feel obligated to marry her. But she said he was always too careful about such things and she wasn't sure how she could manage it. I told her she was crazy to even consider such a scheme. Being pregnant wouldn't necessarily force Bryce into marrying her, anyway."

His eyes narrowed with suspicion and Mariah could see that he was stung by the notion that Aimee might have used him, especially to coerce another man into marrying her.

"That's one of the most conniving, deceitful things I've ever heard. If that's the way Aimee's mind worked, then she might've had other affairs. Harry's father might be someone you never heard of!"

The anguished look on his face implied he wanted Harry to be his son. The notion surprised Mariah. Most single guys his age would be running backward at the idea of taking on the responsibility of a baby.

Her gaze continued to roam his rugged face and the big hands gently cradling the baby. "Look, I'm just saying she harbored those ideas. I have no proof she was trying to carry them out with you or any man. For my sister's sake, I'd like to think Harry was innocently conceived."

"With me?"

An awkward silence followed his question, and with each second that passed, the more Mariah had to fight to keep from jumping from the rocker and rushing out of the nursery. Something about this man and her sister sharing a passionate weekend together was an image she wanted to push from her mind.

"Well, I'd hate to think she falsely put your name on the birth certificate. And I'd sure hate to think that Harry's father might always be a question mark."

He looked down at the baby. "I'd never let that happen to this little guy."

Feeling like a jumble of raw nerves, she restlessly crossed her legs and began to tap the air with her bare foot. The movement must have caught his attention because she suddenly noticed his gaze slowly slipping from her face and traveling downward, over her leg and onto her foot.

Heat instantly flooded her cheeks and she mentally scolded herself for not slipping on her shoes before she'd answered the door. But it was a warm May afternoon and certainly pleasant enough in the house to go without footwear.

You're reacting like a foolish teenager, Mariah. Finn doesn't find anything fascinating about your pink toenails. And he hasn't come to Stallion Canyon to ogle you in any form or fashion. He's here because of Harry and no other reason.

Clearing her throat, she blocked out the scolding voice in her head and tried to form a sensible question. "So you're saying you want Harry to be your son?"

To her relief, his gaze returned to Harry and as he studied the child, she could see something that looked an awfully lot like love move over his features. The sight smacked Mariah right in the middle of her heart. A man was supposed to care that much for his child, she thought. Yet a part of her had been hoping Finn would be the irresponsible type. That he'd gladly hand the responsibility of raising Harry over to her. But it was becoming clear that he had no intention of stepping aside. So where was that going to leave her?

He said, "This wasn't the way I'd planned on becoming a father. But now that I have Harry in my arms, it feels right and good."

She folded her hands together atop her lap and tried to keep the confused emotions swirling inside her from showing on her face.

"So you believe he's actually your son?" she asked guardedly.

"I do. I think you'd have to agree that he takes after me. The red in his hair and dimples in his cheeks."

"Maybe. But that's hardly proof."

Frowning, he moved closer to where she sat, and Mariah instinctively placed a hand on each arm of the rocker and both feet flat on the floor.

"Something in your voice says you're hoping I won't be the father," he said tersely.

A blush scalded her cheeks. "I only want what's best for Harry."

He eyed her with cool conviction. "I don't know what sort of man you think I am, Ms. Montgomery, but—"

"Please, call me Mariah," she interrupted. "Calling me Ms. Montgomery makes me feel like I'm in the classroom."

Distracted now, he latched onto her last word. "Classroom? You're a teacher?"

"High school. History. That surprises you?"

Confusion flitted across his rugged face. "Aimee insinuated that Stallion Canyon was a profitable horse ranch. I just assumed the ranch was your livelihood, too."

A dead weight sank to the pit of her stomach as she slowly pushed herself out of the rocker. "I'll explain in the kitchen. It's time for Harry's bottle and I'm sure you could do with some coffee or something."

"Coffee sounds good," he agreed. "Lead the way."

With the baby cuddled safely against his chest, Finn followed Mariah out of the nursery and down a hallway that eventually intersected a small breezeway. Once there, she turned left down another short hallway until they reached a wide arched opening.

"We used to have a cook, but we had to let her go," she tossed over her shoulder. "Hopefully, you can tolerate my coffee-making."

They stepped into a rectangle-shaped kitchen with a ceiling opened to the rafters and a floor covered with ceramic tile patterned in dark blues and greens. To the right side of the room a round oak table and chairs were positioned near a group of wide windows covered with sheer blue curtains. To the left, white wooden cabinets with glass doors lined two whole walls, while a large work island also served as a breakfast bar.

Glancing over her shoulder, she said, "Have a seat at the bar or the table. Wherever you'd like. I'll get the coffee going, then heat Harry's bottle."

Since he was closer to the bar, Finn sank onto one of the padded stools and propped the baby in a comfortable upright position against his left arm. So far the tot seemed to be a good-natured boy. He hadn't yet let out a cry or even a fussy whine, but living in the same house with Rafe's two children, Colleen and Austin, had taught Finn that a baby's demeanor could change in an instant.

"What was wrong with the cook?" he asked curiously. "Burned the food?"

Greta, their family cook back on the Silver Horn Ranch, had been with them for more than thirty years. He couldn't imagine anyone but her making their meals and ruling the kitchen.

Over at the cabinet counter, Mariah was busy pouring water into a coffeemaker. He was still trying to grasp the fact that she was a teacher. Apparently, being in a classroom full of kids was a more comfortable job to her than sitting atop a horse.

You're wondering too much about the woman, Finn. It doesn't matter what she does for a living or for fun. Once you take Harry away from here, you probably won't see her again. Unless she comes to the Horn to visit Harry from time to time.

Was that the way it was going to be? Finn asked himself. Was it already settled in Finn's mind that Harry belonged to him? That the baby belonged on the Silver Horn with him?

Mariah's voice suddenly interrupted the heavy questions pushing through his thoughts.

"Cora was a great cook. She'd worked here for years. But after Dad died, money got tight. We had to start cutting corners."

There was an embittered tone to her voice. One that shouldn't belong to someone so young and pretty, he decided. Sure, she'd obviously had to deal with her fair share of raw deals. But that didn't mean she needed to keep dragging those disappointments behind her.

"Aimee talked about your father passing away," he told her. "I could see she was still pretty cut up about his death."

"Aimee and Dad were very close. She was just like him—obsessed with horses. Especially the wild ones," she added bluntly.

Was Mariah trying to say that Aimee had possessed a wild streak? Had Aimee shared her bed with Finn because she'd liked living recklessly? Or had she, as Mariah had implied, used him to get pregnant? Whatever the reason, it was clear that Aimee hadn't been completely honest with him, and that left Finn feeling like a fool for ever getting involved with her in the first place.

The baby let out a short cry and Finn looked down to see that the child was gnawing on his fist. "Harry, you must be hungry or teething," he said to the boy.

Finn's voice caught the baby's attention and Harry went quiet as he stared curiously up at him. Finn used the moment to touch his forefinger to the baby's hand, and instantly the tiny fingers latched tightly around his. Harry's response filled Finn with a fierce love and protection he'd never experienced before. Father or not, the baby needed him.

As another thought suddenly struck him, he glanced over to where Mariah was gathering mugs from the cabinet. "Do you have a copy of Harry's birth certificate?"

"I have the original. It's safely stored with my important documents. Harry's name is registered as Harrison Ray Calhoun—the Ray being our father's name." She turned a pointed look on him. "So where do we go from here? A DNA test?"

He'd been waiting for her to say those three little letters. The birth certificate stated Finn as the father, but Mariah wasn't yet ready to accept that as complete validation. And perhaps she was right. After all, a child's parentage was a serious matter. Yet seeing Harry and holding the little guy in his arms had caused some kind of upheaval inside Finn.

He didn't understand what had come over him. All he knew was that this child had suddenly become everything to him. The idea that a clinical test could say otherwise chilled Finn to the very bottom of his being.

"I suppose that would be the logical thing to do. That way his parentage would never be in doubt," Finn said with slow thoughtfulness. "I just wish it wasn't necessary. I don't want Harry to grow up and learn that the identity of his father was ever in question."

Forgetting her task, she walked over and placed a hand on Harry's back. "I don't necessarily want that for him, either. But I want him to have the 'right' father."

He slanted her a wry look. "Don't you mean you want him to have the right 'parent'?"

Her long black lashes lowered and partially hid the thoughts flickering in her gray eyes.

"What do you mean?"

The threads of his patience were quickly snapping. "Don't act clueless. You want to keep Harry for yourself. You're hoping like hell that I won't be the father."

Her mouth fell open. "I never said that."

"You didn't have to. I can see it all over your face. Hear it in your voice."

Shaking her head, she turned her back to him. "If that were true, then why did I call you? I didn't have to, you know," she said, her voice heavy with resentment. "I could've kept Harry all to myself."

He instinctively cradled the baby closer to his chest. "Yeah, you could've left me in the dark. But then you couldn't have lived with your conscience. Or with Harry, once he grew old enough to start asking about his father. You'd have to make up a lie to tell him why you didn't make an effort to contact me. Then one lie starts leading to another. You're not that kind of woman. The kind that can live on a bed of lies."

She whirled around to face him and Finn was struck by the moisture collecting in her eyes. He didn't want to hurt this black-haired beauty. She'd already been hurt enough. But she needed to understand that he wasn't a fool. Or at the mercy of her wants and wishes.

"You don't know what kind of person I am! We've only just met." A sneer twisted her lips as she raked a disapproving gaze over him. "But then I need to remember you jumped into bed with Aimee right after you met her. I suppose you thought you knew her, too!"

His jaw tight, he said, "Your crude observations don't embarrass me, Mariah. But they do have me wondering. Maybe *you'd* like an invitation into my bed."

Her eyes widened with disbelief, then turned to cold steel. "That's the most insulting, despicable thing I've ever heard!"

"Is it?" he asked softly.

A scarlet blush crept over her face. "Look, Mr. Calhoun, the only thing you need to concern yourself with is the result of Harry's DNA test. And the faster we can get those done, the happier I'll be!"

Chapter Two

Finn watched Mariah stalk to the opposite end of the kitchen and thump a pair of empty mugs onto a plastic tray. He'd never spoken that way to any woman before and he wasn't quite sure what had prompted such a thing to come out of his mouth. Except that ever since he'd arrived on this ranch, she'd been subtly goading him. As though she considered it okay for her to judge him as a cad for having a romantic interlude with Aimee. As if she were infallible and would never stoop to such human impulses.

With a heavy sigh, he rose to his feet and walked over to where she was pulling a baby bottle filled with formula from the refrigerator. After giving him a cursory glance, she shut the door on the appliance and moved over to a microwave. Finn felt compelled to follow.

"I'm sorry, Mariah," he told her. "I shouldn't have said that to you. I was way out of line."

While the microwave whirred, she kept her back to him. It wasn't until the bell dinged that she retrieved the bottle, then turned to face him.

"Then why did you say it?" she asked stiffly.

The icy stare she'd stabbed him with earlier was gone. Now her gray eyes were dark with shadows, and Finn realized his question had touched far more than just her female pride. The notion made him feel even worse.

"Because you seemed set on judging me for spending a weekend with Aimee. That's not— Well, for your information, I don't go around having affairs, short or long, on a regular basis! Yet you want to make me out as a cad. What's the matter with you? Are you a prude or something?"

Outrage popped her mouth open and Finn expected her to flounce off in huff. But after a moment, her shoulders sagged and she glanced away. "Making a baby is a serious thing," she murmured.

She was avoiding his question, but he was hardly going to point that out to her now, Finn decided. Besides, he had the feeling that before this ordeal with Harry was finished, he was going to find out plenty about Mariah Montgomery.

"That's why I'm here," he said curtly. "Because there is a baby. A baby who's lost his mother."

She reached for Harry then, but Finn continued to hold him firmly against his chest. "Give me the bottle. I'd like to feed my son."

Her chin came up to a challenging angle. "It's yet to be determined whether Harry is your child, Mr. Calhoun."

"You decided that. I didn't. I agreed to a DNA test because you wanted one and my family back home wants one. But as far as I'm concerned, Harry has Calhoun blood running through his veins. And by the way," he added, "call me Finn. When you say Mr. Calhoun you make me think you're addressing my grandfather."

"All right, Finn. I guess I should appreciate your frankness. At least I'm not in the dark about where you stand with Harry."

She handed him the bottle. Finn carried it and the baby back over to the breakfast bar. After he'd taken a seat on one of the stools, he cradled Harry in a comfortable position in the crook of his left arm and offered him the warm bottle.

"Here's your dinner, little one," he told the baby. "Go for it."

The infant latched onto the nipple with a hunger that brought a faint smile to Finn's lips. Oh, what a stir this little guy was going to make on the Silver Horn, he thought. Especially with his grandfather Bart, who was all for the expansion of the Calhoun family.

He looked up as Mariah approached the bar carrying a tray with the coffee and containers of cream and sugar. As she placed it a safe distance from his elbow, she asked, "Would you like cream or sugar? Since you have your hands full, I can fix it for you."

"Just black. Thanks," he said, grateful that she was being somewhat hospitable. Especially after that sexual taunt about inviting her into his bed. No telling what she was thinking about him now. Her impression of him had most likely slipped from cad to pervert. But why her opinion of him should matter, he didn't know. Except that something about Mariah Montgomery got under his skin. He wanted to see approval in her eyes and a smile on those lovely lips.

Cradling one of the mugs with both hands, she stood a couple of steps away, watching Harry feed. After a long stretch of silence, she asked, "Where did a bachelor like you learn how to feed a baby?"

"My sister, Sassy, has two kids. A son, J.J., and a daughter, Skyler, born three months ago. And two of my brothers have small children."

"Playing with your little nieces and nephews is not the same as actually caring for them," she said bluntly.

Defending himself to this woman was definitely getting old, Finn thought, but he was going to do his best not to let his impatience show. Sparring with her wouldn't help matters. "I've done more than just play with them," he informed her. "I've babysat Sassy's kids while she and her husband went out for the evening. So I know about bottles and diapers and those sorts of things."

"You, a babysitter? That's hard to imagine."

Ignoring that jab, he said, "Sassy trusts me to care for her kids like they're my own. And I'm glad to do it for her."

"So the two of you are close," she said thoughtfully. "Aimee and I were that way once. But time and…other things caused us to grow apart."

The contents of the bottle had lowered to the point where Finn was forced to tilt it higher so Harry would ingest formula rather than air. She watched him make the adjustment, then seemingly satisfied that he knew how to feed a baby, she took a seat on the stool next to his.

Using his free hand, Finn reached for the mug of coffee, then carefully leaned his head away from Harry to take a sip. The brew was stronger than what he was normally used to, but it tasted good. The long drive up here, coupled with the stress of meeting Mariah and the baby, had worn him down.

After downing several sips of the coffee, he asked, "Do you have any other relatives living close by?"

"No. Our parents divorced when Aimee and I were small, and ever since, our mother has lived in Florida near her parents."

"Do any of them ever come to visit?"

A bitterness twisted her features. "Not hardly. Aimee and I were lucky to get a birthday or Christmas card from any of them. Now that I'm the only one left, it'll be easy for them to forget they have family back here on a dusty ranch."

So Mariah clearly wouldn't be getting any emotional support from that branch of the family. The idea bothered him greatly. Mariah was so young. She needed someone to embrace and encourage her through the loss of her sister and the transition it was making on her life. She needed a loving family surrounding her. But she had none.

He said, "I guess you can tell that Aimee didn't share much about her family life with me. But to be fair I didn't ask her a lot of personal questions. We mostly talked about horses and the things we had in common. I thought we'd have plenty of time for family talk later. I never believed...well, that things would end up like this."

Over the rim of her mug, she regarded him solemnly. "After you left Reno did you ever try to contact her?"

"Sure. I called several times. But the phone signal would break or she'd never answer. I even left messages on her voice mail, but she never returned them. I finally decided she wanted to put our weekend behind her. So I did the same."

She turned her head away and Finn could hear a heavy sigh swoosh out of her.

"I should apologize to you, too, Finn. You were right. I wanted to think of you as a cad. I'd made up my mind even before you arrived that you were the one who'd left Aimee in the lurch. That was easier than thinking my sister was…callous or indifferent or—" Her head swung back and forth. "Guess it doesn't matter now."

Aimee's true intentions toward Finn or her baby had died with her. And none of it could change the future now, Finn thought—unless the DNA test proved some other man had fathered Harry. But already his mind was balking at that idea. Something deep within him recognized that Harry was his child.

He glanced down to see that the baby was sound asleep, his lips slack around the nipple. Carefully, he eased the bottle from the boy's mouth and placed it on the bar.

"You don't need to apologize," he told Mariah. "We're both in the dark about each other and Aimee and how Harry came to be.

"So you don't have any other relatives around who could help you with the ranch? What about your dad's parents?" he asked.

She shook her head. "They died a few years ago within a few months of each other. Both had struggled with serious health problems."

"Sorry to hear that," he said gently.

Her sigh was wistful. "Aimee and I adored them both. After our parents divorced we lived with them for a while, then Dad purchased this ranch and the three of us moved up here. Having Stallion Canyon was his dream come true."

Finn glanced thoughtfully around the warm kitchen and tried to imagine what it had been like when her father and sister had been living. Had the three of them gathered at the dinner table and talked about their dreams and plans? Had there been jokes and laughter or arguments and worries?

"So this house—this ranch has been your home for many years," he stated the obvious.

Rising from the bar stool, she walked over to the cabinet and poured more coffee into her mug. "Since I was eight. And I'm twenty-eight now. So yes, this has been home for all my adult life. But not much longer," she added dully.

"So you're planning on moving?" he asked.

She said, "As soon as the real estate agent can sell the ranch."

There was a hollow sound to her voice, as though moving from this home had no effect on her. Finn didn't understand why the notion should bother him, but it did. A family ranch with a long history represented pride and hard work. It meant passing a home and legacy from one generation to the next. Had Mariah stopped to think of that, or was getting away from here more important? After twenty years she was bound to have deep roots and sentimental ties to the place. Could she be putting up a front? Pretending to him and even herself that it didn't matter where she lived?

"You're going to sell it? Damn, that's pretty final, isn't it?"

Glancing over her shoulder, she frowned at him. "I'm a teacher. Dad and Aimee are gone and I have no use for the land, the barns or the equipment. I've already gotten rid of all but ten of the horses. And I only have those because I can't find buyers. One of them is a prize stallion and I was holding out for a better price, but I'm almost to the point of giving him and the rest away. Cutting out the feed bill would help stop the ranch from sinking into deeper debt."

One thing he'd learned about Aimee during their brief time together was that Stallion Canyon and its horses had meant everything to her. But apparently Mariah didn't feel any such pull. Had it always been that way? he wondered. Or had hard times embittered her?

"My mistake," he said. "When I drove up earlier, I thought I saw a man at one of the barns. I assumed the ranch was doing business."

"That was Ringo," she explained. "He comes by twice a week to haul in feed and generally check on things. To save money I take care of the daily feeding."

Harry was the only reason Finn had traveled up here to Stallion Canyon. The ranch's financial condition, or its lone proprietor, was none of his business. But little by little Mariah was somehow drawing him into this place and her plight.

"Am I understanding you right, Mariah? You're selling the ranch because it's going under?"

She returned to her seat at the bar. "You're asking some very personal questions," she said.

Their gazes connected, and as he studied her gray eyes, he felt something stir in him. The sensation had nothing to do with the baby in his arms and everything to do with the moist gleam on her dusky lips and the subtle scent of flowers drifting to his nostrils.

Hellfire, what's wrong with you, Finn? One Montgomery sister has already had your baby. Now you're looking at this one as though you'd like to try for a second!

Trying to shake away the accusing voice in his head, he countered, "You've been telling me some very personal things."

She drew in a deep breath and his gaze instinctively fell to the rise and fall of her breasts. The gentle curves beneath the red checked blouse were just enough to fill a man's hands, he mentally gauged, or comfort a crying baby.

She said, "Normally I keep such things to myself. But if you are really Harry's father, then you need to hear about his mother's side of the family. As for me selling the ranch, I shouldn't have brought that up."

Finn's gaze roamed over her delicate features and crow-black hair. She was hardly the glamorous sort, but there was a sweet sort of sexiness about her that he found very hard to resist.

"Aimee told me your father died suddenly of a heart attack. There are five of us Calhoun brothers and we lost our mother about nine years ago to an accident. It's hell to lose someone you love."

She stared at the liquid inside her cup, and Finn got the impression she was purposely trying to keep from connecting with him in a personal way. Maybe the sight of him reminded her of Aimee. Or maybe she saw him as the villain, here to take Harry away from her. The idea made him feel like a jerk.

"At least you had a big family to support you. But I'm surviving. And I'm determined to move on with my life."

Over the years Finn and his family had dealt with troubles and sorrows, but they'd always had one another to lean on. Mariah had been facing everything on her own. He couldn't imagine how that felt, or what it would do to his spirit.

"I guess losing your father threw the ranch into up-heaval," he spoke his thoughts out loud.

Her expression rueful, she said, "That was the beginning of the downfall. After we buried Dad, Aimee promised she could keep Stallion Canyon profitable. And in the beginning I trusted her. She was a very good trainer. As good as Dad."

"At Reno I could see how competent Aimee was with her mustang. Your horses should've been bringing in top dollars. What happened?"

Mariah released a heavy sigh. "At first she worked very hard. And back then she had capable assistants to help her. But something caused her to change. She started spending money on frivolous things and ignoring her work. I tried to be patient, because I knew how much she was hurting over Dad's death. Each morning she walked out to the barns, she had to deal with working without him. On top of that, her relationship with Bryce was going nowhere. Then she got pregnant. After that the ranch quickly went downhill."

Listening to Mariah now, it sounded as though Aimee had been a troubled soul long before he'd met her. Yet he hadn't glimpsed that side of her. All he'd seen was her laughter and smiles. The realization proved that he'd misjudged her badly. Did that mean any woman could fool him? Even this one?

"I suppose you're thinking I'm partly to blame for your problems," he said ruefully.

"I can't blame you for the choices Aimee made. And anyway, you might not be the man who got Aimee pregnant."

So she was going to hold on to that notion, he thought

grimly. Well, he supposed she had that right. Just as much as he had the right to believe Harry was his son.

The thought had him looking down at the boy in his arms. The child was so tiny and vulnerable, so precious. He wanted to hold the sleeping baby's face next to his own, to breathe in his sweet scent and let the wonder of being a father settle deep inside him. He might have been gullible with Aimee, but he wasn't about to let Mariah dupe him. Especially when it came to Harry's parentage.

But what if Harry's DNA doesn't match yours, Finn? You'll have no argument to keep the boy. Maybe you ought to ask yourself if you're playing a fool's game.

Silently cursing the voice of warning in his head, he looked up to see Mariah's attention fixed on a nearby window. As he studied her pensive profile, he wondered if there was a special man in her life. Even though she wasn't married, there was still the possibility she had a boyfriend or fiancé. For all he knew, she might even have ideas of marrying and keeping Harry as her child.

Crazy or not, the mere idea of losing the baby in his arms left him cold inside. It changed the whole landscape of the future he'd been mentally painting for himself and his son. Harry gave him a purpose that he'd never had before, and he liked it.

"I believe I am that man," Finn said. "Aimee put my name on Harry's birth certificate. She did that for some reason. I only wish she'd contacted me. I could've helped—before things here on the ranch started falling apart."

She glanced at him, her expression wry. "We needed help all right. About a month before her accident, we were forced to sell off part of the horses just to keep the

bills paid. Seeing them go opened Aimee's eyes somewhat. But it was already too late."

Finn frowned with confusion. "If money was that
tight, how did she get the money to go on a skiing holiday?"

"Two of Aimee's girlfriends paid for the trip. They
were hoping a break from the baby and the ranch would
help her get her head on straight. Now they blame themselves for her death."

"Do you blame them?"

Frowning, she looked at him. "No. Accidents can
happen anywhere."

"You've never told me exactly how Aimee died. Do
you believe it truly was an accident?"

The widening of her eyes told Finn his question had
surprised her.

"Why, yes, I do. Her friends said that one minute they
were all headed down the slope together and everything
was fine. Then a steep embankment appeared several
yards on down the path. One of the friends managed to
swerve around it, but Aimee and the other girl chose to
ski over it. Both of them ramped the ledge and fell on
the other side. There was soft powder on the ground that
day, but something about the twisted way she landed
severed Aimee's spinal cord."

"I'm sorry," he said quietly. "But after all you've said
about Aimee it got me to wondering if maybe she was
depressed or wasn't herself and—well, that she was deliberately being reckless."

Her brows pulled together in a scowl. "I'd be the first
to admit that Aimee liked to live on the edge. Most normal folks would be terrified to climb on a horse that had
bucking on its mind. But my sister relished the challenge

and excitement. Still, as for that day on the ski slope, no, I believe it was an accident. Nothing more."

Finn was thankful for that much, at least. He hated thinking the responsibility of mothering Harry and the weight of the floundering ranch had pushed Aimee to the point where she hadn't cared whether she lived or died.

Still, the facts of Aimee's accident didn't change what was happening to Mariah now. She was on the verge of losing everything, he thought bleakly. How was she going to pick herself up and start a new life without her home? Without Harry?

Shoving the troubling questions aside, he said, "Aimee's death. Harry being born. There's some reason it all happened. And no matter the circumstances of how he was brought into the world, just holding this little guy in my arms makes me feel like a blessed man."

She said nothing to that. Instead, she stared at him, her gaze frozen on his face. While Finn waited for her to say anything, silence stretched between them like a taut highline.

After several more moments passed without a response, he finally asked, "Is something wrong?"

She jumped to her feet and cleared her throat. "I'm sorry," she said, her voice choked. "Please excuse me."

Before Finn could react, she was rushing toward the arched doorway and as he watched her retreating back, he knew there were already tears on her face.

Damn it! Now what?

With a heavy sigh, he rose to his feet and carried the sleeping baby out of the kitchen and back to the nursery.

As soon as he walked into the room, he spotted Mariah standing by a window near the crib, gazing out at the rugged landscape in the distance. Was she think-

ing about leaving this ranch? No doubt everything about
the place reminded her of her father and sister. Or was
it the fear of losing Harry that had caused her to break
down in tears?

Finn placed the baby in the crib and covered him with
a light blanket. It wasn't until he straightened from the
task that he noticed Mariah was looking over her shoulder at him. Thankfully, there were no tears on her face,
but Finn didn't miss the redness of her eyes. The sight
hit him far harder than it should have.

"I'm sorry for rushing away like that, Finn," she said
huskily. "Everything suddenly piled up on me."

He moved from the side of the crib and went to stand
next to her. "I hardly need an apology," he told her. "But
it would be nice to see a smile on your face."

Turning slightly, she cast him a sidelong glance.
"I'm not in a smiling mood," she admitted. "Harry is
on my mind. I'm thinking this ranch should eventually
be handed down to him. It should remain his home. But
sooner rather than later it's going to belong to someone
else. And if it turns out you're his father, then none of
that will matter anyway. You'll be wanting him to live
with you."

"That's my plan. If Harry is my son, then he's going
home with me. The child belongs with his father."

Her mouth fell open, snapped shut, and opened again.
"I can't let that happen, Finn."

A cool chill rushed through him. "Excuse me, but if
DNA proves Harry is mine, then I have every right to
take him."

Her expression bleak, she turned her back to him.
"Okay, I'll admit that as his father you'd have the right.
But that's not all there is to it," she said in a low tone. "I

mean, Harry is used to me. I've been his mother since… well, practically since he was born. To pull him away from me would be traumatic for both of us. Besides, I don't know anything about you. I wouldn't be much of an aunt if I simply turned him over to you without learning who you are."

Finn's first instinct was to remind Mariah that he'd already been robbed of the first few months of his son's life because her sister had deliberately left him in the dark. But now was not the time to get into a bitter battle with her, he decided. It wouldn't help his cause to have her thinking he was a hothead who had no business dealing with a baby. She'd learn soon enough that he was Harry's father and that he wasn't about to allow her, or anyone, to come between him and his son.

Drawing in a deep breath, he tried to remain cool and collected. "I have all kinds of identification with me. And if you'd like to call and speak with someone about me or my family, I can give you plenty of character references."

Biting down on her lip, Mariah closed her eyes and tried to calm the churning fear inside her. What could she say? How could she make this man understand that Harry was all she had left in the world? He was her little boy. If Finn Calhoun took him away from her, she didn't think she could bear the pain.

If the test revealed he was Harry's daddy, there'd be no way she could prevent him from taking custody of her baby—unless he was unfit to be a parent, and he hardly looked that. This hunky cowboy looked like a man who was in complete control of himself and everything around him.

Bracing herself with a deep breath, she turned back to him and was immediately struck again by his huge presence. She couldn't put her finger on it, but there was something about Finn that set him apart from the other cowboys who'd worked on Stallion Canyon. He had enough confidence for two men and the looks to go with it. But that wasn't exactly the reason her gaze kept returning to him. There was something about his blue eyes and the hard curve of his lips that invited her to draw near him. And that could prove to be dangerous.

With her mouth feeling as though she'd eaten a bowl of desert sand, she said, "I don't need a bunch of your friends mouthing your superlative qualities to me. I need to see for myself what sort of man you are."

His rusty brown brows pulled together in a frown while his keen gaze rambled lazily over her face, and Mariah suddenly wished she'd dressed that morning in a shirt that buttoned tightly at her throat and wrists. At least then she might not be feeling so downright naked.

After a long, pregnant pause, he said, "Most folks consider me a respectable, hardworking man. How do folks around here feel about you?"

For a moment she was taken aback. She hadn't been expecting him to turn the tables on her. "I have a few friends," she said. "And the school where I teach wants me back next year. Does that tell you anything about my reputation?"

A corner of his lips curved slightly upward and Mariah found she couldn't tear her eyes from the provocative image. How many women, besides Aimee, had felt the pleasure of those hard lips on hers? she wondered. Was he the kind of man that frequently pursued women in general, or did one in particular have to catch his attention before he went after her?

His low chuckle caressed her senses, and longing suddenly pierced the empty spots inside her. How nice it would be to hear his laugh each and every day, to be able to laugh with him. To feel his hands touching her, protecting her, loving her.

"You said you wanted to get to know me. Could be that I'd like to know more about you, too. Do you have a boyfriend? Or fiancé?"

Rattled even more by his questions, she moved around him and returned to the side of Harry's crib. He'd laid the baby on his back and tucked a lightweight blue blanket around him. The idea of the tall, tough cowboy caring so gently for the baby caused her eyes to mist over once again.

"No boyfriend. And definitely not a fiancé."

"And why is that? You don't want to be married?"

She made an indifferent shrug, even though a tangle of emotions was suddenly choking her. "I'm waiting for the right man to come along," she mumbled.

She wasn't about to add any more to her explanation. She hardly wanted him, or anyone else for that matter, to know that she'd never gotten over losing the only man she'd ever cared about to another woman. And considering the woman had been her sister, Mariah wasn't sure she'd ever get over the betrayal.

Slowly, she sensed his presence moving alongside her, and then the faint scent of him drifted to her nostrils. He smelled like a man who'd been bathed in desert wind and kissed by hot sunshine, and for one brief moment she wondered what it would be like to press her nose against his throat, to breathe in that evocative scent. To let herself forget that he'd once been Aimee's lover.

He said, "You must be waiting for Mr. Perfect."

The huskiness of his voice was such a sensual sound it caused goose bumps to form on the backs of her arms.

"That's none of your business," she said.

"Probably not. But I'm a curious kind of guy. I've been trying to figure out how a woman who looks like you is living out here alone—without a man to care for her. Protect her."

And make love to her. Mariah could hear the unspoken words in his voice as clearly as she could hear Harry's soft breathing behind them.

The fragile grip she had on her senses was coming close to snapping. "Aimee was always the one who wanted a man in her life. Not me."

"That could change—if you met a man you couldn't live without."

Everything inside Mariah had quickly gone hot and shaky. And she wondered wildly how he would react if she suddenly turned and placed her palms against his chest. If she were to tilt her face up to his, would he want to kiss her? Oh my. Oh my. Why were these crazy, wicked thoughts going through her head? Why was he making her forget that she was a practical woman?

"I'm just trying to survive, Finn. I'm not foolish enough to believe a knight will come riding through here on a big white horse and make all my troubles go away."

A wry grin tugged at his lips. "He might come riding through here on a big brown mustang. Ever think that might happen?"

Her laugh was short and caustic. "If that ever happened I'd run him off with a loaded shotgun. Once these last ten are gone, I never want to see another mustang. If it hadn't been for the wild horses I might have persuaded Aimee to get out of the business before we went broke. But she was obsessed with the damned things. And now—"

As her words trailed away, his hand wrapped gently around her upper arm, and the touch splintered her resolve to remain indifferent to him. Heat from his fingers was rushing to her cheeks, then plunging downward, showering her whole body with sparks.

"You're blaming the wrong thing for your troubles, Mariah. At one point, those horses were running free, caring for themselves. They didn't ask to be captured and confined."

Mariah's chin dropped against her chest. She sounded like a pouting child, blaming her problems on everything and everyone but herself. But grief, worry, anger and resentment had been playing with her emotions for so long now. And for just as long, she'd been trying to hide her emotions, to pretend that she was strong and unaffected. And now something about Finn was pulling her feelings right out in the open.

"Sorry. I'll admit my thinking is twisted. But Aimee refused to consider any other job. With her it was the horses or nothing. And that's where the ranch was headed—with nothing."

The subtle tightening of his fingers on her arm had her lifting her face up to his, and as her gaze probed the depths of his blue eyes, her heart thumped so hard she could feel it banging against her ribs.

"Look, Mariah, horses can get into a person's blood. Caring for them, working with them, loving them. It becomes sort of an addiction. One that's impossible to shake. Even when you know they're costing too much money or taking you down a wrong path."

"So you're saying your job has to involve horses or you wouldn't be happy?"

"I'd be miserable without horses around me."

Disappointment washed through her. Which was ridiculous. Finn's dreams and desires had nothing to do with her. Except where Harry was concerned. She didn't want the child to have a father like hers, who'd spent every weekend at horse shows and every waking minute of the day at the training barn.

"You and Aimee would have made a perfect pair," she said stiffly.

His gaze rambled over her face. "It takes more than a shared love of something to make a perfect partnership. The fact that Aimee wasn't interested in building a relationship with me proves that much."

She grimaced. "As far as men go, Aimee didn't know what she wanted."

"Thanks," he said with sarcasm.

Her gaze connected with his and Mariah's heart gave a hard thump. "Tell me, Finn, if you'd known about Aimee's pregnancy would you have married her?"

His expression didn't flinch, or his gaze break away from hers. "That's hard to say. Aimee might not have wanted marriage. And as it is, I'm not sure I would've wanted it, either. When I do marry I want it to be for love, not out of obligation."

"So you weren't in love with my sister?"

"There wasn't enough time for that. But who knows, if Aimee had given us a chance, we might've fallen in love and gotten married."

Hearing this sexy cowboy talk about loving and marrying Aimee bothered her in more ways than she cared to admit. Maybe because she'd never had a rugged man like him give her a second glance. Not as long as Aimee had been around to monopolize all the male attention.

"Then you'd be my brother-in-law right now. And a widower."

"Yeah."

Mariah was so busy trying to read the emotions in his eyes that long moments passed before she realized the room had gone quiet and Finn's hand was still wrapped around her arm.

Move, Mariah. Step away from him before his touch begins to feel too good to resist. Before your dreams start down a very foolish path.

"I—please—excuse me, Finn. I have to go."

Before she could let herself weaken, before he could guess the longing on her face, Mariah pulled away from him and raced out of the nursery. She didn't stop until she was inside her bedroom with the door shut firmly behind her. And by then she was trembling from head to toe.

With her shoulders slumped against the door, she covered her hot face with both hands and sucked in several deep breaths. She'd been through too much to let herself break down now. She needed to show Finn that she was a strong, capable woman. More than that, she needed to convince herself that he was a man she couldn't fall in love with.

Chapter Three

Finn sat at the kitchen table, his hands wrapped around a mug of half-burned coffee, as he tried to decide what to do next. He'd been sitting there for more than half an hour, waiting for Mariah to show her face again. Since she'd run from the nursery, he hadn't heard her stirring, and he was starting to wonder whether he should search her out and apologize, or tell her he was leaving for town.

Neither option appealed to him. He wasn't ready to leave the ranch just yet. Not until the two of them had made definite plans concerning Harry. And he hadn't done anything he needed to apologize for—except maybe make her face the reality of Harry's being a Calhoun.

Rising from the table, he walked over to a set of double windows and studied the view behind the house. From this spot, he could just make out a corner of one large barn, a smaller shed and a maze of connecting corrals. Except for a few birds and the wind twisting the leaves, nothing was moving. It was a sad and lonely sight, he thought grimly.

"I see you've helped yourself to the coffee. I'm glad. I haven't been a very good hostess."

He hadn't heard her enter the room, and the sound of her voice had him quickly turning to see her walking toward him. While she'd been in her room, she'd put on a pair of faded red cowboy boots and released her hair from its ponytail. Now the long black waves framed her face and rested on her shoulders. Her nose looked as though she'd patted it with a powder puff, while a sheen of pink glossed her lips. She looked sweet and sexy and totally unassuming. And as Finn stared at her, he felt a strange sensation slowing coursing through him. Was this how it felt to be mesmerized by a woman?

"I dug into your brownies, too," he told her. "They're good. Did you make them?"

A faint smile touched her lips. It was the first one that Finn had seen on her face and the sight encouraged him. Maybe the short break from him and the baby had put her in a better mood.

"Thanks. I like to bake and cook. Now that Cora is gone I get to do plenty of it."

"I've been listening for Harry. Does he usually cry when he wakes up?"

"Depends if he's wet or hungry. Most of the time he's a happy baby. I'll find him wide-awake just cooing and looking around." She walked over to the cabinet and dumped the last of the syrupy black coffee into the sink. "We had an intercom system put in after Harry was born. It was rather expensive. But I can go anywhere in the house or out on the porches and still be able to hear every little sound he makes."

"Dad had one installed in the ranch house years ago. It was rarely used until Rafe and Lilly had their babies. That's my brother and sister-in-law. They have two kids. A girl, Colleen. And a boy, Austin. He's just a few months older than Harry."

She looked at him with interest. "So Harry would have cousins to play with. That is, if he truly is a Calhoun."

Obviously she was going to point out the question of Harry's parentage at every turn of their conversation, he thought drearily. Well, if it made her feel better, then so be it. She'd have her bubble busted soon enough.

"Six little cousins. The Calhoun family is big. And I don't figure it's quit growing yet."

"Hmm. Must be nice. To be in a big family. I wouldn't know." She rinsed out the coffee carafe, then placed it back on the warmer. "So tell me about yourself and your family. What do you do back in Nevada?"

Rising to his feet, he carried his cup over to where she stood, then rested his hip against the cabinet counter. "I manage the horse division of the Silver Horn Ranch. Along with the cattle, we raise quarter horses for show, cutting and ranch use."

Mariah stared at him while trying not to appear shocked. Aimee had simply told her that Finn was a horseman and Mariah had presumed he'd worked as a wrangler for some ranch, or was simply a guy who liked horses. Aimee had never mentioned anything as impressive as the manager of a horse division.

Her head swung back and forth. "We? Uh—you have other men helping you?"

"Why, yes. I thought—" Tilting his head to one side, he studied her. "Apparently Aimee didn't tell you that my home is the Silver Horn."

Confused now, she said, "No. She didn't. And I'm not familiar with that name. Should I be?"

Her question put a look of amused disbelief on his face.

"Most folks on both sides of the state line have heard of the Silver Horn. But with Aimee gone and Stallion Canyon up for sale I guess you don't keep up with ranching news."

As long as her father had been alive, Mariah had been proud of Stallion Canyon. Ray Montgomery had poured his heart and soul into the land and the horses, and along the way had provided his daughters with a good home and security. But once he'd died, everything had taken a downhill slide. As the burden of debt had grown heavier on Mariah's shoulders, she'd started to resent the place that had been her home for twenty years. Yet now, hearing Finn speak as though the ranch was done and finished left a hollowness inside her.

Resting her hand on the cabinet counter, she turned so that she was facing him. "So this Silver Horn where you work—it's a big outfit?"

He nodded. "I don't just work there. I live there, too. It belongs to the Calhoun family. My great-grandfather started it many years ago. These days my grandfather Bart—I call him Gramps—is the director of the whole shebang. We run a few thousand head of cattle and usually have two to three hundred horses on hand."

Mariah was stunned. Why had Aimee kept something like that from her? Had her sister gone after Finn because she'd known he was wealthy, then later changed her mind about pursuing a relationship with him? Dear Lord, it was all so strange, so mind-boggling.

She tried not to sound as dazed as she felt. "Your ranch must cover a lot of acreage."

"We own several thousand acres and lease that much more from the BLM—the Bureau of Land Management," he told her.

Mariah felt like a fool. Not only because Aimee had kept her in the dark, but because she hadn't looked into Finn's background before she'd called to tell him about Harry. At least she would've known what sort of man she'd be facing. But then, a man's material worth didn't necessarily speak for his character, she reasoned. And she was quickly learning that Finn wasn't a man who could be summed up in one short visit.

"I apologize if my questions sound stupid. But Aimee didn't tell me anything about you. Except that you lived in Nevada and liked horses."

He shrugged. "Guess that was all that mattered to her. When I told her I lived on the Silver Horn, she seemed to be familiar with the ranch. But we didn't talk about it that much. She asked about our remuda and the brood-mares and a little about the ranch house. It didn't seem important to her."

Her thoughts whirled as she gathered the few dirty dishes scattered over the countertop and piled them into the sink. "So Aimee understood you were wealthy?"

"I figure she made that assumption. But I never told her any such thing. Only a braggart starts spouting off information like that to a woman he's just met," he said.

"I don't expect you share the balance of your bank account with the men you meet."

Pulling back her shoulders, she said, "I don't meet that many men. But if I did, they wouldn't hear about my finances. I just wondered…"

"If Aimee pursued me because of my wealth?" he asked wryly. "I think the fact that she didn't attempt to continue our relationship tells you how much she appreciated my money."

Mariah thoughtfully swiped a soapy sponge slowly over a saucer. "I don't mean to pry, Finn. I'm just trying to understand why my sister put off contacting you about Harry. Could be she was worried about you getting custody—since you could provide more financial security for him. Far more than she ever could. But that doesn't make much sense, either. Because she wasn't afraid to put your name on the birth certificate."

He moved a step closer and Mariah's nerves twisted even tighter.

"I don't think you ought to be worrying over Aimee's motives anymore," he said. "Harry's future is the main issue now. And that brings us to the DNA test. Do you think we can get that taken care of tomorrow?"

Her throat went tight as she glanced over at him. "You're not wanting to waste any time, are you?"

"Dallying around won't tell us anything. And my job on the Horn is—well, pretty demanding. I need to get back there as soon as possible."

"I suppose I can call the school and let them know I need to take a couple hours off in the morning. Long enough for us to go to the health department and get the samples taken," she said guardedly. "That way you can go on back to Nevada. And receive the results in the mail."

"That isn't going to happen."

His instant retort had her dropping the sponge and squaring around to face him. "What does that mean?"

"It means I'm not about to leave here without Harry."

The determination in his voice sent a chill slithering down her spine. "And what if you're not his father? All that waiting will be wasted."

His clear blue gaze traveled over her face in a way that made Mariah forget about breathing.

"Let me be the judge of that," he said quietly.

Shoving a hand in her hair, she pushed it off her forehead, while silently yelling at her heart to slow down. Otherwise, she was going to faint right at his feet.

Drawing in a steadying breath, she said, "You must be feeling confident that Harry is your child."

"I am. And deep down you believe I'm his father, too. Don't you?"

Clamping her jaw tight, she was determined not to let him see her cry, to let him know that the thought of losing Harry was shattering her whole being.

Turning back to the sink full of dishes, she picked up the sponge and twisted it until soapy foam covered both hands. "I'll believe what the DNA test says," she said hoarsely. "Nothing less."

She was fighting back tears when she felt him move behind her and place his hand on her shoulder. Mariah squeezed her eyes shut as heat raced up the side of her neck and down her arm.

"Mariah," he said gently, "I'm not an ogre. I can see how much you love Harry. But a man who could leave his son—well, he wouldn't be much of a man. Would he?"

Swallowing hard, she turned to face him, but the moment her gaze met his, her self-control crumbled and she began pounding her fist against his chest. "No, damn you! I wished I'd never called you! I'd have my baby and you'd never know the difference!"

By the time he grabbed her flying fists and anchored them tightly against his chest, she was sobbing, her cheeks drenched with tears. But what this man thought about her no longer mattered. All she cared about was Harry.

"Hush, Mariah. Please, don't cry."

He gently drew her forward, until her wet cheek was pressed against the middle of his chest and his hand was stroking the back of her head.

Even if Mariah had wanted to resist, the solid comfort of his arms, the tender touch of his fingers upon her hair, was a balm to her raw nerves. A man hadn't touched her this way in ages. She hadn't wanted one to touch her. Until now.

Eventually, the warmth of his arms eased the chill inside her and dried the tears in her eyes. By then, his masculine scent and the hard muscle beneath her cheek were turning her thoughts in a totally different direction.

He murmured against the top of her head. "Better now?"

The husky note in his voice shivered through her like a cold drink on a hot day. So good. So perfect. But she couldn't keep standing here in his arms, letting her erotic thoughts get out of control.

Quickly, she stepped back from his tempting body and wiped fingers against the traces of tears on her cheeks.

"Forgive me," she whispered. "I'm behaving like a

shrew. But I——" Her gaze met his and her heart very nearly stopped as she spotted a sensual gleam in his blue eyes. Had the embrace they'd just shared affected him, too? Or were her scattered senses making her see things that weren't really there?

His lips took on a wry slant. "Forget it, Mariah. I can take a few punches. Besides, you made your point. You chose to call me. Otherwise I wouldn't have known anything about Harry. Unless by some chance I ran across some of her old friends at a horse show, and even then, I probably wouldn't have made the connection of me being her child's father."

His expression softened. "I'm grateful that you made that call, Mariah. Even though I understand how much it's breaking your heart."

Blinking at a fresh wave of tears, she turned back to the sink and thrust her hands into the water. Better there than pounding them against Finn's chest and making a complete neurotic fool of herself, she thought dismally.

A shaky breath shuddered past her lips. "Harry deserves a father," she said bluntly.

He moved a few steps away and Mariah went limp with relief. For the first time in her life, she couldn't trust herself near a man.

"The afternoon is getting late," he said, "and I haven't gotten a room in town yet. Can you recommend a good place to stay?"

She glanced over her shoulder at him and suddenly without warning, she heard herself saying, "You don't need to drive back to town. You're welcome to stay here. There are plenty of empty bedrooms and you'd be close to Harry."

And to me.

The voice in her head came out of the blue. Just as her unplanned invitation had come from a place inside her she hadn't known existed. Dear Lord, she must be cracking up. Earlier, she'd wanted rid of this man. Now she wanted to get closer to him. This cowboy was putting some sort of hypnotic spell on her.

"It's nice of you to offer, Mariah, but I don't expect you to put me up for the night."

The arch of his brows said her invitation had surprised him. But it couldn't have surprised him any more than it had her.

"Dad would've already insisted you be our guest," she reasoned. "I wouldn't feel right doing any less."

"But you live here alone."

She frowned. "What's that got to do with it?"

"I wouldn't want to make you feel uncomfortable."

Heat rushed to her cheeks. "I trust you to be a gentleman. And you look like a strong guy—you can help me with the barn chores."

The broad smile he gave her was like a dazzling ray of sunshine. It warmed Mariah as nothing had in a long time.

"You just got yourself a ranch hand and a houseguest. Thank you, Mariah."

She inclined her head in agreement. "If you'd like to fetch your things, I'll show you where to put them."

"I'll be right back," he promised.

Once he was gone from the room, Mariah leaned weakly against the cabinet and wondered if she just made the biggest mistake of her life. Opening her home to Finn wasn't going to make him change his mind about taking Harry.

Oh, come on, Mariah. Inviting him to stay here on

*the ranch had nothing to do with Harry. You want him
around because looking at him is a constant thrill. Hearing his voice shivers over your senses like sweet, slow
music. And touching him made your whole body ache
for more.*

Disgusted with the mocking voice in her head,
Mariah left the kitchen and hurried toward the block
of bedrooms located at the back of the house. As she
collected clean linen for Finn's bed, she assured herself that she wasn't about to be charmed by the Nevada
horseman. She had more important and pressing issues
in her life to deal with. Like finding out whether Finn
actually was Harry's father.

Later that evening, Finn stood in the middle of the
ranch yard, surveying the barns and surrounding landscape. From what he could see from his limited view,
the ranch was a beautiful property. Run-down in places,
but still very usable.

Not far to the east of the barns and corrals, forest-
covered mountains formed a towering green wall. To the
west, the land swept away to an open valley floor dotted with a mixture of hardwoods and evergreens. Some
twenty to thirty miles beyond the valley, tall blue mountains etched a ragged horizon against the sky. Stallion
Canyon was a much greener land than that of the Horn,
and the beauty of it made Finn long to straddle a horse
and explore the foothills and meandering streams.

He wondered if Mariah ever had the urge to ride over
the ranch, or had the financial difficulties she'd been
under robbed all pleasures she'd taken from the place?

Damn it, he wished he could quit thinking about the
woman. Quit wondering why she'd invited him to stay

here on Stallion Canyon. Especially when his presence only seemed to upset her.

You didn't have to accept her invitation, Finn. You could have told her a quick "no thank you." Instead, you couldn't accept fast enough. So you could be near Harry, you told yourself. Bull. Admit it, you want to be near Mariah, too.

Fighting away the condemning voice in his head, he walked over to a long shed row running the length of a large red barn. A black stallion was hanging his head over a stall gate, and Finn was instantly drawn to the horse.

"Hey there, handsome guy," he greeted the animal. "I'll bet you'd like it if I got you out of there, wouldn't you?"

The horse nudged his nose against Finn's hand and he obliged the animal by gently stroking his face. After a moment, Finn moved his hand on down the strong, arched neck. There, beneath the long curtain of black mane, he found the alpha angles of a BLM freeze brand, which was made by freezing a copper iron with liquid nitrogen before pressing it to the animal's hide. The process turned the hair on the horse white, rather than burning it off. The white symbols the BLM used could be translated to reveal what state the horse had originally come from, its age, and its own individual code number.

The sight of the markings against the horse's black coat tugged at something deep within Finn. The stallion had once run wild and free over the mountains and plains. Most likely he'd had his own harem of mares and had fought valiantly to keep his family safely at his side.

Now this majestic animal was confined behind fences, and though he was getting more nutrition and care than he could've ever possibly obtained out on the

range, Finn would love to see him running free on miles
of grazing land, with a band of mares racing close behind him.

The image brought back all the arguments he'd had
in the past with his father and grandfather over the mustangs. For three or more years now, Finn had fought to
incorporate wild horses into the breeding program on
the Silver Horn, but Orin and Bart had strongly resisted.

Now that Finn was standing face-to-face with this
regal animal, his determination to work with a herd of
mustangs grew even stronger. Sooner than later, he was
going to take a stand for what he wanted. And he wasn't
going to back down.

The ring of his cell interrupted his thoughts and he
reluctantly pulled the instrument from a leather holder
fastened to his belt.

"Hi, Dad," he greeted. "What's up?"

"I've been ringing your phone for the past two hours!
We've been sitting on pins and needles back here waiting to hear from you!"

"Sorry. These past few hours have been like a roller
coaster. I've just now gotten a chance to grab a quiet
moment."

Orin said, "You sound exhausted."

Finn's gaze drifted away from a pen of mares and over
to the house. Seeing Harry for the first time and dealing
with Mariah's emotional reactions had done something
to him. He wasn't the same man who'd driven away from
the Silver Horn Ranch early this morning. But trying to
explain that to his father would sound ridiculous.

"It's not every day that a man sees his son for the first
time. A son he didn't know he had."

A long pause followed, then Orin said, "Sounds like

you've made up your mind pretty damn quick about this baby."

"The boy resembles me, Dad. His hair is auburn and curly. And he has my dimples. Aimee named him Harrison Ray after me and Mr. Montgomery. Mariah calls him Harry, and I've already found myself calling him Harry, too."

"Hmm. Right after you were born Dad called you Harry. Until your mother ordered him to stop. Still, a name doesn't make him yours. Or red hair and dimples."

"No. But I have a feeling inside me and it's telling me that Harry is mine," Finn reasoned. "I was right about Sassy being my sister. I'm right about Harry, too."

Orin sighed. "Could be you're letting your wants interfere with your reasoning. These past few years your brothers and sister have been having children. It's only natural for you to want the same."

Finn wiped a weary hand across his forehead and tried not to let his father's suggestion annoy him. It was true his siblings were having babies left and right. But that hardly meant Finn wanted the same for himself. Hell, he didn't even have a steady girlfriend. And rarely found the time to go out on a casual date, much less make room in his life for a wife and child.

Finn said, "Well, don't worry, Dad. Monday morning Mariah and I are taking Harry into town and having a DNA test done."

"Good. Was this the aunt's idea, or yours?"

Finn grimaced. "We both thought it was the best way to resolve the issue."

"Well, apparently she isn't grabbing the first chance to push the baby off on you. Has she or any of her family demanded money yet?"

It wasn't like his father to bring up the issue of money. Especially where a child's welfare was concerned. But this was an unusual circumstance, one that had left Finn feeling a little embarrassed. Having one-night stands wasn't his style. But the revelation of Harry had certainly made him look like an irresponsible lothario. Now his father was probably thinking Finn's philandering was going to cost the family a fortune.

Biting back a groan, he said, "There is no Montgomery family to speak of, Dad. It's just Mariah. And she's hardly out for money." Resting a shoulder against the board fence of the stall, Finn gazed at the back of the ranch house some fifty yards away. When he'd left to come out here to the barns, Mariah had been in the kitchen preparing some sort of dessert she planned to bake. She'd been quiet and reflective, and Finn didn't have to wonder what was on her mind. "I am concerned about her, though. She considers herself Harry's mother. Giving him up is going to crush her."

"She needs to remember she's only the aunt. Whether it's you or some other man, Harry has a father and he has every right to his son."

Finn absently reached over and stroked the stallion's jaw. "It's not just the issue of Harry. Without her dad and sister to train the horses, the ranch is going broke. She's been forced to put it up for sale. If I take Harry she'll be losing him and her home. So I'm not exactly dealing with a pleasant situation up here, Dad."

His father was silent for so long Finn thought the connection between them had broken.

"Dad, are you still there?"

"Yes, son. Just thinking. How old is this woman, anyway?"

Finn mouthed a curse word under his breath. "She's twenty-eight. But what the heck does her age have to do with anything?"

"Finn, you're not up there to fix Ms. Montgomery's problems. This is about a baby and whether you're the father. I hope you remember that."

What did his father think he was? A teenager, whose brain was dictated by raging hormones instead of common sense? The idea clamped his jaw tight.

Finn's silence must have made a point. After a moment, Orin asked, "Are you okay, son? Do you need for me or one of your brothers to come up there?"

His slouched stance suddenly went rigid as he straightened away from the fence. "No! I'll handle this in my own way!"

"There's no need for you to get defensive, Finn."

He was more than defensive. He was disappointed and hurt that his father didn't trust him to use a lick of sense about Harry or Mariah, or any of it.

"Look, Dad, don't expect me to just brush Mariah's feelings aside. Maybe that's the way Gramps would do it. But not me!"

"Okay, Finn. You want to keep your family out of it, so handle it your own way."

It was all Finn could do to keep from yelling out a curse word. "I'm not trying to keep my family out of this. But this is my baby. Not yours or Clancy's or Rafe's or Evan's or Bowie's. I think I have enough sense to decide what my son does or doesn't need!"

"Fine," Orin said bluntly. "So what are your plans? When do you think you'll be coming home?"

"I'll be staying here on Stallion Canyon until we get the results of the DNA test," Finn told him.

"But that could be weeks! I know you haven't forgotten when you and Sassy had the test. It felt like we waited forever on those results."

"I'm hoping the process has speeded up since then," Finn said. "Will you be able to handle my job until I get back? If not, Colley can. He knows as much about horses as I do."

"I can handle it."

His father sounded snippy, but Finn wasn't going to fret about that. The Silver Horn ranch had an endless number of hands and the money to keep everything running in tip-top condition. Moreover, his father had all sorts of family surrounding him and supporting him with whatever endeavor or problem arose.

Mariah had none of those things. Maybe his father could be indifferent to her plight, but Finn couldn't. His feelings had already gotten mixed up with hers. And he didn't have a clue as to how to untangle them. Or whether he even wanted to.

"Thanks, Dad."

"Don't thank me. Just get yourself home—where you belong."

"I'll keep you abreast of things."

Finn ended the connection and jammed the phone back into its leather holder. That was the first time in his adult life that he'd ended a conversation with his father on a tense note, and the realization bothered him. But as much as he loved and respected his father, it was time that Finn stood alone as his own man.

And whether the decisions he made about Harry and Mariah turned out to be right or wrong, or made with his head or his heart, they had to be Finn's own decisions.

Chapter Four

The conversation with his father was still buzzing in his head as Finn walked over to a tall board corral. Inside the enclosure, a group of mares stood dozing beneath a pair of aspen trees. The only mustangs that had ever run over Horn range were the wild ones that just happened to stray onto the ranch's property. When that occurred, the ranch hands were promptly sent out to round up the wild horses and haul them back to their allotted range-land. But if Finn had his own land, he could put as many mustangs on it as he wanted. He could breed and train them without any interference from his family.

Up until now, he'd only dreamed of finding a piece of land in the Carson City area that possessed sustainable grazing and water supply. But now that Harry had come into his life, the idea of becoming more independent had not only germinated; it was rapidly growing.

"I was beginning to think you'd gotten kicked in

the head or something. You've been out here for a long time."

Mariah's voice had Finn turning to see her walking toward him with Harry riding happily in the crook of her arm. A billed cap was on the baby's head to shield his eyes from the late evening sun, while Mariah's red boots had been replaced by a pair of brown ones that were scuffed and scarred with wear.

"Sorry I worried you," he said. "I've been taking my time looking things over." He didn't add that he'd been talking to his father. Sharing the gist of their conversation would only upset her.

When she joined him at the fence, Finn immediately reached for Harry and positioned the boy against his shoulder. Soft baby scents instantly drifted to his nostrils, and the bright, eager gaze in the boy's blue eyes touched something deep inside him. Harry would grow to be a man of the land. Somehow Finn was certain of that. Just as certain as he knew that having a son was going to change the direction of his own life.

Mariah said, "Before Dad died, horses were everywhere. The barns were always freshly painted, the fences erect. Hay and grain would be stacked to the ceiling and there were plenty of ranch hands to deal with the chores. Now it's a ghostly place."

The pensive note he heard in her voice told Finn she wasn't quite as indifferent to her longtime home as she'd first led him to believe.

"It would thrive again," he told her. "In the right hands."

Her sigh was so faint it was barely discernible to his ears. "Maybe the next person can make it successful again. But if I had all the money in the world I wouldn't sink it back into this place."

If one of his brothers spoke in such a negative way about the Silver Horn, Finn would be livid. Passing down the land and legacy was important to every Calhoun family member. If necessary, each one of them would fight with his dying breath to save what their forefathers had worked so hard to build. It was hard to understand Mariah's lack of fight to save her home.

He studied her profile. "I can't decide if you love this place or hate it."

"I don't hate the ranch or the horses. I guess my feelings are mixed," she admitted.

"Considering all that's happened, I'd probably be feeling mixed up, too."

Her head turned toward him and Finn watched the warm wind play with the baby-fine tendrils at her hairline. The black curls were a vivid contrast against her creamy skin, and for a moment Finn wondered how her skin would taste. How would she react if he placed his lips against her temple?

As the erotic questions swirled through his head, Harry's squirms reminded Finn where that sort of thinking had gotten him. The last thing he needed right now was to let his libido lead him down a reckless path with this woman.

"Forgive me if I sound like a bitter, ungrateful person," she said. "I'm not really. It's just that—well, I lost Dad, then Aimee. Then all of a sudden it was just me and little Harry. And everything around me seems to be slipping away."

Finn wanted to reach over and lay a steadying hand on her shoulder. He longed to see her smile and hear her promise she was going to be happy again no matter where her plans took her. But the past seemed to be overwhelming her.

"I'm going to be frank, Mariah. I'm not sure that getting rid of your home is the right answer for you."

Turning her back to him, she rested her forearms on one of the lower rails of the board fence and stared out at the broodmares. There was no grass in the paddock; only a few spindly weeds dotted the dusty ground. Obviously, the mares were getting fed daily, but it wasn't the sort of nutrition they needed to produce sturdy foals. Now was hardly the time for him to point that out to Mariah, though.

No time would be right for that, Finn. This isn't your place, your horses or your woman. Someone else will have to deal with Mariah's problems. Not you.

The sound of her voice suddenly drowned out the one going on in his head.

"Aimee used to talk about Harry growing up and taking over the reins of Stallion Canyon. But if it turns out that he—well, goes with you to Nevada, then this place won't matter. You'll have plenty to pass on to him."

So that was it, Finn thought. Losing Harry was taking away her purpose, her drive to fight for her home.

He gazed down at the baby, who was happily taking in the sights and sounds of the outdoors. Even though he'd only met his son a few hours ago, plans for his future were already building in Finn and taking hold of his heart. How would he feel if the DNA said Harry belonged to some other man? All his dreams would suddenly be snatched away. The way he was going to snatch them away from Mariah if he left with Harry.

Stop being so damned softhearted, Finn. You're the one who's been wronged. If Harry truly is your son, then you've missed seeing him born and lost the first four months of his life. All because this woman and her sister didn't see fit to tell you a baby was coming.

Mentally shaking away the pestering thoughts, he said to Mariah, "Harry will ultimately inherit my share of the Silver Horn. But right now my main objective is to give him a home."

As soon as the remark passed his lips, her head jerked around and she stabbed him with a resentful stare. "Excuse me, but Harry hasn't exactly been homeless."

Seeing he was going to have to be more careful with his words, Finn said, "Sorry. That didn't come out exactly right. I meant a home with me."

"That depends on the DNA test." She turned and motioned toward a connecting barn. "It's time to do the evening feeding. If you'd be kind enough to see after Harry, I'll get to work."

She started walking toward the end of the big white barn and Finn automatically fell into step beside her. "I'd be glad to watch Harry. But I'm curious. What do you normally do with the baby while you tend to your outside chores? Doesn't anyone come around to help you with him?"

"A nanny keeps him during the weekdays while I'm at school. But she leaves in the evenings before feeding time. When he was smaller I put him in his stroller and parked it in a safe spot where I could keep an eye on him. But now that he's grown enough to sit in a propped position, I put him in a little wagon with side boards. He enjoys that even more than the stroller. Especially when I pull him along behind me. Follow me and I'll show you."

Inside a large, dusty feed room filled with sacks and barrels of mixed grain, rubber buckets, galvanized tubs, and scoops, Mariah pulled out a red wagon with wooden side boards. The inside was lined and padded with a thick blanket.

"I made a seat belt for him with the straps from a child's old car seat. And I use this baby pillow to prop in front of him for extra support. It works great," she told Finn. "I don't have to worry about him toppling over or trying to pull himself out. Just sit him here and I'll show you how to buckle him up."

He placed Harry at the back end of the wagon and Mariah clipped the safety straps across the boy's chest. All the while, she was incredibly aware of Finn standing next to her.

These past few hours, her emotions had been on a violent roller coaster. The lonely woman in her was relishing every moment of his rugged presence. But part of her was weeping at the thought of his taking her baby away. Her only hope of hanging on to Harry was to have Finn's DNA be a mismatch. But would that really solve anything? Harry deserved a father. She'd have to keep searching, and the next man might not be daddy material at all.

"Very ingenious," he said with a grin. "You ought to put these things on the market."

Straightening to her full height, she tried her best to smile. "I'd rather just keep the little invention to myself."

She hurriedly moved away and began scooping grain into one of the heavy rubber buckets. One, two, three. She continued counting until she reached six, then started on another bucket.

From the corner of her eye, she could see Finn watching her. What was he thinking? Earlier this afternoon, there'd been odd moments when she'd thought she'd seen masculine appreciation in his eyes, maybe even a hint of attraction. But that could've been her imagination working overtime. After all, it had been so long since she'd had a man look at her in a sexual way that she wasn't sure she would recognize the signs.

"Can I help you measure the feed?" he asked.

"No thanks. I can handle this. Just take Harry on outside so he won't breath in the grain dust."

For a moment she thought he was going to protest, but after a shrug of one shoulder, he grabbed the wagon tongue and pulled Harry out of the feed room. Once he was out of sight, Mariah bent her head and drew in a long, bracing breath. She had to collect herself. The man was going to be around for several more days. She couldn't fall apart every time he came near her.

By the time she carried the feed buckets out of the barn, she noticed Finn had parked the wagon beneath a canyon mahogany so that Harry would be shaded. As soon as he spotted her at the gate to the mares' paddock, he left the baby to join her.

"Harry is perfectly content, so let me help you with one of those," he said, while reaching for one of the buckets.

"Thanks," she told him. "Just pour it into one of those long troughs. I'll fill the other one."

Once the mares were lined up at the trough, the two of them made their way out of the small paddock.

"I hope you're giving the mares adequate hay. Carrying babies, they especially need the nutrition."

Mariah would be the first to admit she didn't know a whole lot about horse care. Not when she compared her equine knowledge to Aimee and her father. Still, it irked her to have this man telling her what she needed to be doing with her own animals.

"I do," she answered. "But I'm not sure how much longer I can keep it up. Hay is expensive. If I don't sell the horses soon I may have to turn them out on the range and let them scavenge for whatever grazing they can find."

He stopped in his tracks and stared at her in disbelief.

"Mariah, no! All five of those mares are near foaling. They need to be monitored closely. If they have trouble—"

"Look, Finn, I realize you mean well. But I can't afford the best hay or grain. I can't even afford a vet. If the mares have trouble foaling the most I can do is call on Ringo to help. Together we'll try our best to get the foals delivered safely."

"Is he a vet?"

Her short laugh was like a mocking snort. "He's a mechanic by trade. He kept Dad's tractors and trucks running. All he knows is to pour out feed, toss hay and make sure the water troughs are full. But he'll do whatever he can to help."

He sighed and stroked his fingers against his jawline as though she'd just thrown him a heavy problem, one that he had no idea how to deal with. Mariah could've told him that she'd been feeling that same heavy burden for months now.

Frowning, she asked, "What's wrong? None of this is your problem. So you needn't concern yourself."

"I'm sorry if it seems like I'm intruding—"

"You are intruding," she interrupted.

"But I'm concerned about the mares."

For as long as Mariah could remember, it had always

been horses first in the Montgomery family. Many times she'd longed to have her father's undivided attention, even for only one day. Now she was seeing the very same thing with this man.

"So am I. But I'm doing the best I can." She glanced over her shoulder to make sure Harry was safe before she continued walking.

Three long strides and he was back at her side. "I'm only trying to help, Mariah."

She heaved out a heavy breath. "Then find me a buyer. Quick."

"For the horses? Or the ranch?" he questioned.

"Both."

"Tell me, Mariah, what if someone came along right this minute and bought you out?" he asked. "Do you have a plan?"

Did he really care or was he just being nosy? she wondered.

"My plan is to be happy," she said. "No matter where I go. Or what I do."

His lips took on a sardonic twist. "Really? I'm not sure you know how."

Later that evening, Mariah cooked a quick meal of salad and spaghetti. Afterward, Finn helped her clean the kitchen and then excused himself to his bedroom to make a phone call.

While Finn was occupied, Mariah gave Harry a bath, then carried him to the nursery where she dressed him in blue pajamas printed with cats and dogs.

"Okay, little guy. Let Mommy brush your red curls and then you'll be all ready for a visit from the sandman." While she hummed a lullaby beneath her breath, she pushed the baby brush through Harry's fine hair until a red curly strip stood up in the middle of his head. "Wow! What a handsome guy you are now!"

Harry cooed and gave her a toothless grin. Laughing at his precious face, Mariah bent her head and pressed kisses to his fat cheeks, which in turn made the baby giggle loudly.

Behind them, Finn knocked lightly on the door facing. "Am I interrupting?" he asked.

He'd interrupted everything, Mariah thought. Especially her peace of mind. For weeks now, she'd been convinced that selling the ranch and starting a new life elsewhere was exactly what she needed and wanted. Now, he had her questioning her own feelings and wondering if she was about to make a giant mistake.

"No. I'm only getting Harry ready for bed. He usually falls asleep around this time in the evenings. Was there something you needed? If your room isn't comfortable, there's another guest room just down the hall."

"As long as I have a place to lay my head, I'm happy," he told her. "This time of the year I spend most nights sleeping on a cot in the foaling barn, anyway. Thankfully, most of the Horn mares have already delivered, and breeding next year's foals has started."

"Sounds like you have lots of babies coming at once. You must be a busy man in the spring."

"It's hectic. One of these mornings I expect to look in the bathroom mirror and see that my hair has turned white. But I love this time of year. New babies—new beginnings. It's exciting."

He walked over to where she had Harry lying atop the small dressing table, and as he stood beside her, she was suddenly remembering the few moments she'd stood with her cheek pressed to his chest. His arms had felt so warm and strong, and the scent of him had filled her senses with erotic thoughts. Just thinking of it now warmed her cheeks and left her feeling horribly foolish. If she'd been the one he'd made love to, if she'd been the one who'd borne his child, things would be so different now, she thought. Because she couldn't imagine loving this man only once. Unlike Aimee, she would've done everything in her power to keep him in her life.

He said, "Actually, I wanted to discuss something with you. Whenever you have a free moment."

She glanced over to see he'd removed his long-sleeved shirt and replaced it with a gray T-shirt. The cotton jersey fabric clung to his broad chest and revealed a pair of heavily muscled arms. The sight rattled her senses so much that she swiftly jerked her gaze back to the safety of Harry's sweet face.

"Uh—let's go to the back porch," she suggested. "It's cooled off nicely and there's a playpen back there for Harry."

"Sounds good."

With Finn carrying the baby, they walked through the house and onto the back porch. The long planked floor stretched the full length of the back of the house and was protected from the weather by a tin roof. At one end several pieces of wicker lawn furniture were grouped together. Behind the chairs, next to the wall of the house, was a small playpen equipped with blankets and a small pillow.

"I'll just hold Harry for a while," he said.

He eased his long frame into one of the chairs and Mariah took the seat opposite from him. As she watched him settle Harry in a comfortable position against his chest, she couldn't help but notice how gentle he was with the baby. It was a reassuring sight. If Finn truly was Harry's father, he'd be a loving one, at least.

"You have a beautiful view out here with the pine trees and the mountains in the distance. How many acres does Stallion Canyon cover?"

"Close to six thousand," she answered.

"You get much rain up here?"

"No. Hardly any in the summer. A little more in the autumn season. Normally we do get a fair amount of snow, though, and that helps. Dad always kept a few of the hay meadows irrigated. But the irrigation system needs repairing. Like everything else around here."

He didn't reply, and she wondered what he was thinking as he stared off toward the western horizon where a purple haze was darkening the skyline. Yes, Stallion Canyon was a beautiful place. Strange that it had taken this man to make her remember just how beautiful.

He said, "I've been doing some thinking this afternoon. About you and Harry."

Something about the quiet tone in his voice made her go on sudden alert. "What about us?"

His gaze returned to her face and Mariah's heart thumped with anticipation. In spite of the serious expression on his face, there was an appealing look in his blue eyes and it melted her like spring snow beneath a warm sun.

"I wanted to ask if you'd be willing to travel to the Silver Horn and stay for a while." He held up a hand before she could reply. "That is, if the DNA proves Harry to be my son," he added.

Without even knowing how she got there, Mariah

was instantly standing on her feet. "To Nevada? With you and Harry?"

He shot her a crooked grin and Mariah's gaze was drawn to his white teeth and the faint dimples bracketing his lips. He was the most masculine man she'd ever encountered, and each time she looked at him the act of breathing grew more difficult. Being around this man for only a few hours had already shaken her. A steady dose of his company would no doubt turn her into a complete fool.

"Yes. With me and Harry and the rest of the family," he said easily. "Harry is accustomed to you. It would be much easier for him to make the transition to a strange place if you were with him. We have plenty of room. And you wouldn't have to lift a finger. Just be there for Harry's needs."

Finn was inviting her to his home in Nevada. The idea staggered her. What normal woman with a beating heart could resist such an opportunity? But he was getting way ahead of himself. And she couldn't let her romantic notions run wild.

Her mouth was suddenly so dry she had to swallow before she could manage to say a word. "Aren't you assuming quite a bit? You can't be certain of what the DNA test is going to say. Before either of us makes plans regarding Harry, we need to see the results."

"We'll waste the time and the money on the DNA test to put your mind at ease. But I can tell you right now— I'm Harry's father."

She couldn't let his confident attitude shake her. "We'll see," she replied. "But in the meantime, I have two more weeks of school. I can't go anywhere."

He looked disappointed and Mariah wondered if his reaction was because of her or Harry.

Don't be ridiculous, Mariah. The man didn't invite you to his home for romantic reasons. He's already convinced that Harry is his son. He's only thinking about the baby's welfare. Not you.

He slanted a thoughtful glance at her. "Well, could be that the results will return about the time you finish your school term. Would you be willing to make the trip then?"

She stared at him in disbelief. Was having her with Harry really that important to him? She couldn't imagine it. Not when he could easily hire a full-time nanny. "I'd have to think about that. I have so many responsibilities here. The ranch, the horses and—"

The remainder of her words trailed away as he suddenly rose from the chair and carried Harry over to the playpen. As he carefully deposited the baby on his back, he said, "Before you say anything else, Mariah, let me get Harry settled."

After pulling a light blanket up to the boy's waist, he offered him a rubber teething ring. Once Harry was happily chewing on the ring and kicking his feet, he left the baby and came to stand next to her. The nearness of his tall, lanky body towering over hers whipped her senses into a wild frenzy.

He said, "Before my invitation, you'd pretty much written this ranch off. Now all of a sudden you can't leave it."

Darkness had settled over the backyard, but there was enough light slanting through the windows of the kitchen to illuminate the porch. She watched in fascination as patches of golden glow and gray shadows played across his rugged features.

"My feelings concerning the ranch have nothing to do with it," she countered. "Other than the little work Ringo does around here, I'm the sole caretaker. I have to be here to keep things going."

"That's no problem. I'll hire someone to take care of the horses and whatever else is needed done around here."

Her heart was suddenly racing at such a frantic pace, she unconsciously pressed her fingers to the middle of her chest. "You'd do that?"

A faint smile brought the dimple back to his cheek. "Of course I would. If Harry goes to the Horn I want him to be happy. Having you with him would surely help him make the transition."

Naturally his concern was all about Harry. But for one moment there, Mariah wanted to believe he was thinking of her. She wanted to think he was extending the invitation so she wouldn't feel so cut off from Harry. Dear God, she was turning into a mushy idiot.

Unable to look him in the eye, she turned her back to him and gulped in a breath of fresh air. She had to get a grip before she fell to pieces right here in front of him. "I see. Well, if you do take Harry—I'm not sure that my going along would be wise. He'd get to thinking I belonged there with him. And eventually I'd have to leave. He wouldn't understand why I was gone."

Her last words were choked and she quickly bent her head in an attempt to conceal the tears that were rushing to her eyes. She didn't want Finn to see a shattered woman. She wanted him to believe that she was strong enough to survive anything. And with or without Harry, she would survive, she forcefully reminded herself. She had no other choice.

Suddenly his hands wrapped around her upper arms and their warmth rushed through her like a fierce wild-fire, scorching her senses and melting her resistance.

"You could be right about that, Mariah. I'm only try-ing to think of a way to make this easier for all three of us."

Agony twisted her insides as she turned back to him. "That's impossible, Finn. Besides, what if you're not the father? Other than Bryce, I wouldn't have a clue who it might be. What would happen to Harry if some stranger laid claim to him? The whole idea makes me shudder with fear."

His eyes narrowed thoughtfully. "Hmm. All this time I believed you didn't want my DNA to match. Now it sounds like you do."

A blush stung her cheeks. "Okay. Maybe I was hop-ing that…just a little," she admitted. "But this afternoon I've been doing some thinking, too. And I've decided that you—"

When she couldn't find the words to go on, he fin-ished for her. "I'm the lesser of two evils?"

Somehow her face grew even hotter. "Something like that," she mumbled. "I don't know all that much about you yet. But I can see you'd be good to Harry."

"What about Aimee's old boyfriend? Is he the father-ing sort?"

"Bryce?" She shook her head. "Not at all. From what Aimee said, he didn't want kids with his first wife. And he didn't want them with Aimee. If he turned out to be the father, God help us."

His hands tightened on her upper arms. "Don't worry.

I'm the father," he murmured. His hands eased their grip on her arms and slid slowly upward until they were resting upon her shoulders. "And if we put our minds together and concentrate on doing everything for Harry's sake, then everything else will take care of itself."

As his last words trailed away with the night breeze, Mariah saw his gaze settle on her lips. After that she wasn't sure if he bent his head first or if she rose up on her toes, but something caused their faces to come together. And then his lips were fastening over hers, his arms pulling her tight against his hard body.

Too dazed to think, Mariah's lips automatically parted beneath his. Her arms slipped up and around his neck, while the front of her body nestled itself against a slab of masculine muscle. It didn't matter if this was all for Harry's sake. All that mattered was that he was making her feel like a woman. A woman who was needed and wanted.

Her senses were spinning faster and faster, until everything was a blur. She couldn't move or think. But she could certainly feel. The search of his hard lips upon hers was tugging her to a dark, sweet place that beckoned her to move closer, to stay in the enchanting web of his arms.

But suddenly his head lifted and a cool wind brushed across her face and touched her heated lips. Gulping in a deep breath, she opened her eyes to see that he was gazing down at her. It was then she noticed that his hands were resting at the base of her throat, where a vein throbbed against his fingers.

"Mariah," he whispered.

He made her name sound like a sexy plea and it was all she could do to keep from groaning aloud.

"Why did you do that?" she asked hoarsely.

A faint smile curved his lips. "I'm a curious man and you're a beautiful woman. A plus B equals C."

"That's not the way algebra works."

He chuckled lowly. "You're right. That's not algebra. That's my own special equation."

He was making light of the whole thing and it would be best if she did, too. But his kiss had shaken her to the very depths of her being. And she was sick of men never taking her seriously, tired of being considered a pleasant pastime and nothing more.

"Very cute," she muttered, then quickly turned away from him and walked over to Harry's playpen. "But I've had enough laughs for one night. I'm putting Harry and myself to bed."

She was bending over to pick up Harry when Finn's hands caught her around the waist and tugged her straight back into his arms.

"If you thought that was for laughs, then maybe I'd better do it over."

Before she could react, he'd already fastened his lips over hers. And this time there was no mistaking the raw hunger in his kiss.

Mariah didn't know how long she stood there in his arms, his lips feasting on hers. She eventually heard herself groaning and then he was stepping away, staring down at her flushed face.

"Sweet dreams, Mariah."

He walked off the porch and into the shadows that stretched toward the barns. Mariah stood there until she'd regained her breath, then collected Harry from the playpen and hurried into the house.

Chapter Five

"Is anything wrong with your eggs? If they don't suit you I can cook more."

Finn looked up from his plate and across the breakfast table to Mariah. With Harry sitting in a high chair next to her, she was offering the baby a spoonful of mushy-looking oatmeal. Harry appeared to be enjoying every bite, even those that were dripping onto his chin.

"The eggs taste fine." To prove it, Finn shoveled up a forkful of the fried eggs he'd covered with green chili sauce. "I was just thinking, that's all."

Thinking, hell. That was hardly what he'd been doing since he kissed Mariah last night. His mind had been whirling like a dust devil. What had possessed him to kiss her, not once, but twice? It wasn't like him to lose his head over a woman he'd just met! At least, not since that brief fling with Aimee. And looking at Harry ought to remind him of the results of that particular instant attraction. Yet this thing he was feeling about Mariah was different. It was more than attraction. She made him forget all common sense.

"If you're thinking about that kiss, then don't," she said stiffly. "I've already forgotten it and you should, too."

"Then why did you bring it up?" he countered.

She frowned as pink color spread across her cheeks and Finn could only think how pretty she looked, even when she was vexed. This morning she was wearing a black button-up blouse with little sleeves that barely covered the ball of her shoulder. Her black hair was tied back from her face with a white silk scarf, but it hardly contained the long waves falling around her shoulders. Her bare skin glowed like a pearl that had been polished between two fingers, while her lips glistened moist and soft. She looked fresh and erotic and oh, so young. And Finn was finding it impossible to keep his eyes off her.

She said, "Because you have a miserable look on your face and I suspect you're regretting you kissed me once. Much less twice."

"I'm not regretting anything," he muttered. And given the chance, he'd do it again. But he wasn't about to let her in on that secret.

"Oh," she said stiffly. "So when you first get up in the mornings, it's normal for you to look like you could commit murder."

Groaning, Finn wiped a hand over his face, then reached for the china cup filled with steaming coffee. "Sorry. I have a lot of things on my mind. And about last night—I don't usually go around kissing women like that. But I—"

"Thought it might be a good tool of persuasion? Or you needed to end the day with a few kicks?"

A sleepless night, added to all that had happened to him yesterday, had left Finn feeling addled this morning, and Mariah's brittle comments were only compounding the sluggishness of his brain.

He sipped the coffee in hopes it would clear the heavy fog behind his eyes, while across the table she used her fork to push the bacon and eggs from one side of her plate to the other.

"Those kisses had nothing to do with Nevada or Harry or fun," he said crossly. "Can't a man be near a woman just for the simple pleasure? Why does there have to be ulterior motives behind a couple of kisses?"

Sighing, she said, "I just don't like being used. That's all."

"Neither do I. So let's forget it," he suggested. "It's a new day. Let's start over. What do you say?"

She looked across the table at him and Finn noticed her gray eyes were full of lost, lonely shadows. The sight made him feel like a heel. It made him want to cradle her in his arms and tell her she was special. That he would never intentionally hurt or use her.

A tentative smile tugged at the corners of her mouth. "That's a good idea. So, tell me, now that you've slept on it, are you still planning on staying until we get the test results?"

She was giving him a crack to wriggle through. If Finn was ever going to change his mind about being in this woman's company for the next several days, he needed to do it now. But Harry was too important and he wasn't going to leave this ranch without him.

He reached for the thermal pot sitting in the middle

of the table. As he warmed his coffee, he said, "I'm staying."

Her fork paused in midair. "Oh. Did you bring enough things with you for a lengthy stay? I mean, like extra clothes and that sort of stuff."

Cradling his coffee cup with both hands, he leaned back in his chair. "Enough. But I think I'll drive into town this morning and pick up a few more things I could use while I'm here. If you and Harry need anything, make a list and I'll pick it up for you. Or better yet, you're welcome to come with me."

She shook her head. "Thanks, but I have too much to do here in the house before I go back to work in the morning."

"I'm sure Harry can always use formula and diapers," he pointed out. "Let me know what kind and I'll pick some up."

She looked like she wanted to argue, and Finn decided she was reluctant to relinquish any part of Harry's care to him. Which was only natural, he supposed. But how long was it going to take before she finally let go of the baby? When the DNA made it clear Finn was the father? Or did she ever plan to let go?

"Okay. I'll make a list," she said.

"Good."

Finn ate the remaining bacon and eggs on his plate, then drained his coffee cup. By the time he was finished, Mariah had already risen from her chair and started gathering dirty dishes from the tabletop.

"I need to get to the barn and start feeding," she said. "I'd be grateful if you could watch Harry. It would save me bundling him up and taking him out with me. It's rather cool this morning."

Finn left the table and carried his dirty dishes over to the sink. "You stay in and watch Harry. I'll tend to the feeding."

She walked over to him. "I know I mentioned you helping out around here. But I don't expect you to do my chores."

"Look, Mariah, I'm not used to being idle. Besides, caring for horses is a pleasure for me." He walked over to the bar, where he'd left his hat. As he levered the brim over his forehead, he said, "By the way, if you're still in a hurry to get rid of the mustangs, I think I can come up with a new home for them."

Her eyes narrowed with speculation. "A new home? Where?"

"I need to make a few phone calls before I say more. We'll talk about it later." On his way out of the kitchen, he paused at Harry's high chair and squatted down to the baby's level. Emotions swelled in his chest as he touched a forefinger to the dimple in Harry's cheek. "That grin of yours is going to melt all the girls' hearts."

As though he understood, Harry kicked both legs and squealed. Across the way, Mariah laughed softly and the warm sound had him looking over to see a tender smile on her face. The expression made her features even lovelier.

"I think Harry has already melted a few hearts," she said. "Including yours."

Straddling a river, the little town of Alturas sat in a valley with a ridge of tall mountains to the east, forest to the north and flat wetlands to the south. A wide main street was lined on either side by quaint shops and businesses, some housed in buildings that had been

around for a century or more. As Finn negotiated his
truck through the sparse Sunday traffic, it dawned on
him that this community had been Mariah's life for the
past twenty years.

Would she still continue to live here once he took
Harry home to the Silver Horn?

*Why wouldn't she? Her teaching job is here. Her
friends and acquaintances. Once the ranch sells, she'll
probably move to a little rental here in town. And eventually, she'll find a man to marry. She'll raise children,
not horses. And after a while, you and Stallion Canyon
will be nothing more than a dim memory to her.*

The voice going off in Finn's head continued to nag
at him, even after he finished his shopping and stopped
at a little diner on the edge of town. After having a slice
of pie and a cup of coffee, he climbed back in his truck,
but made no move to start the engine. Instead, he pulled
out his cell phone and punched the number to his oldest
brother. According to his watch, it would be another hour
and a half before his brother and family left for church.

After the third ring, Clancy's voice boomed in Finn's
ear.

"Hey, Finn! How's it going? Dad told us you've seen
the baby. What's he like?"

The mention of Harry sent a spurt of joy through
Finn. "He has red in his hair and dimples in his cheeks.
And he's a happy little guy. You'll fall in love with him."

"Sounds like you already have."

"Yeah. I guess I have," he admitted.

Clancy said, "I might as well tell you that Dad's concerned about you. He says when you two talked yesterday you didn't sound like yourself."

"That's because I was disagreeing with him," Finn

said. "He's not a bit happy about me staying up here until the DNA results get back."

"Oh. He didn't mention that. But I could tell he was steamed about something. So this means you'll probably be up there two or three weeks?"

Pushing the brim of his hat to the back of his head, Finn wiped a hand across his forehead. "Something like that. I don't want to leave without the baby, Clancy. I'm already convinced he's mine. But Mariah, that's Harry's aunt, wants proof."

Clancy's reaction was a heavy sigh.

"What's the matter?" Finn asked. "You think I'm being selfish for taking that much time off from my job?"

"No," Clancy was quick to reply. "If anyone on the ranch deserves time off, it's you, Finn. Dear Lord, you and Rafe both put in far more hours than any one man should. I just don't want you to have any trouble with this woman. I mean, where the baby is concerned."

Finn could've told Clancy that he was already having trouble with Mariah. But the problem had nothing to do with Harry. It was all about Finn keeping his hands off the woman.

Finn said, "Once the DNA comes back, I don't think she'll give me any problem."

"I'm glad to hear it. And Finn, don't worry. Now that Dad is in full swing again, he can handle the horse division until you get back home."

For several years after their mother had lost her life to a tragic fall, their father, Orin, had retreated into a private shell. Instead of riding the ranch and overseeing the care of the livestock, he'd rarely emerged from the house. But thankfully that had changed when a daughter he hadn't known about had suddenly walked into his life.

Sassy had renewed their father's zest for living. These days he was back to being a rough-and-ready cowboy and had acquired a girlfriend to boot.

Finn rubbed fingers against the furrows in his brow. "There's something else, Clancy. Mariah has ten mustangs. A stallion, four geldings and five broodmares, all of which are soon to foal. I haven't told her yet, but I'm going to buy them."

He expected to hear a gasp out of Clancy. Instead, silence stretched on and on.

"Clancy? Did you hear me?"

"Yeah. Sorry. I don't know what to say. Except that you're asking for trouble. Dad and Gramps aren't going to bend."

Finn muttered a curse under his breath. "Don't worry, I'll find a home for them—as far away from the Horn as I can find."

"Finn, are these horses something you want? Or are you doing this to help Harry's aunt?"

His jaw clamped down even harder. "I'm thirty-two years old, Clancy. Not fifteen. Since when do I have to explain my motives about horses or women or anything else to you?"

"You don't," Clancy quipped. "And what the hell is the matter with you, anyway? Becoming a father normally doesn't turn a man into a smart-ass."

Finn bit back the tart retort on his tongue and sucked in a deep, calming breath. "Okay, so I'm being a jerk. I'm sorry. I—thought you'd understand about the horses. Instead you sound like Dad."

"I just don't want you making any impulsive decisions. The baby should be enough on your plate right now without bringing a bunch of mustangs into the picture."

"Harry and the mustangs go together."

"What does that mean?"

Finn turned the key in the ignition and the truck's engine sprang to life. "I can't explain it now, Clancy. I gotta go."

"Okay. And Finn, I honestly want everything to work out for you. Call me if you need me."

"All I need is for you to trust me, Clancy."

More than a half hour later, back on Stallion Canyon, Mariah stood on the front porch with Harry propped on her hip. After ten minutes, the baby's weight was getting heavy and she desperately wanted to take a seat in one of the wicker armchairs positioned behind her. But she was afraid the man standing on the steps would take it as a sign to join her and she'd already had more of his company than she could stand.

Presently, the stocky, dark-haired man somewhere in his midthirties was gazing out at the western range. Without much spring rain, the grass was sparse, but a bevy of tiny wildflowers had bloomed across the meadow. For some reason she didn't like this man eyeing the ranch as though it was already his. Yet if he was a potential buyer, she needed to remain cordial.

"This is a mighty pretty place, Miss Montgomery," he said. "A man could do a lot with this property."

"A woman could do a lot with it, too," she replied. "If she had enough financial backing to do it with."

He looked back at her. "Does that mean you'd like to keep the place?" A knowing grin narrowed the corners of his eyes. "You know, with the right man and woman working together—"

The sound of an approaching vehicle halted his words and Mariah looked around to see Finn's truck rolling to a stop in the driveway. Thank God he was finally home, she thought with a rush of relief. But what was he doing with hay stacked higher than the cab?

"Is that someone you know?"

"Pardon me," she told him, then shifting Harry to a comfortable position against her shoulder, she walked past the man and out to the front yard gate.

As Finn joined her, he darted a suspicious glance at the man standing on the steps. "Is anything wrong?" he asked.

"Not exactly."

"Then he's company?"

Leaning her head closer to Finn's, she lowered her voice. "I've never met him before. He says he drove out here to talk to me about buying the ranch."

His blue gaze connected with hers, and in that moment Mariah was shocked at how familiar it felt to be near him like this and how dear his features had already become to her.

"You told me you've listed the property with a real estate agent," he said with a frown. "If that's the case, he should be dealing with that person. Not you."

With a hand at her back, he urged her toward the house. "Come on. I'll deal with this."

When they reached the steps, Mariah remained close by Finn's side as she quickly introduced the two men. "Mr. Oakley says he lives down in Likely," she informed Finn. "That's a little town south of here."

The stranger directed an appreciative grin at Mariah

and she instinctively cuddled closer to Finn's side. From the moment the strange man had arrived, he'd been leering at her to the point where she'd begun to doubt whether he was actually here about seeing the ranch. Yet if he was truly a potential buyer, she was hardly in a financial position to send him packing just because he was giving off creepy vibes.

"That's right," the man said. "I work on a little spread down there. But I heard this place was on the market. And from what I can see it's a dandy. A man could do well for himself here."

Finn's lips tightened to a thin line. "Mr. Oakley, I assume you know how to use a telephone?"

The man looked at Finn with comical confusion. "Yeah." He patted a leather pouch attached to his belt. "I've got a cell phone right here."

"Then why didn't you use it before you drove up here?"

Oakley looked as if he'd just been boxed on both jaws. "I—beg your pardon?"

Finn said, "If your interest is in buying this ranch, then you need to be talking with the real estate agent. Not bothering Miss Montgomery by showing up here out of the blue on a Sunday morning."

Stunned that Finn was giving the man such a stinging lecture, Mariah's gaze swapped back and forth between the two men. Oakley's face was beet red, while Finn's features appeared to be chiseled from concrete. What had come over Finn? She'd wanted him to deal with the pushy stranger, but she'd expected him to do it in a polite manner.

"For your information, I did call the agency," Oakley said. "I didn't get an answer."

"Then you should've kept calling until you did get an answer," Finn retorted.

The stranger's eyes narrowed as he stared at Finn. "Who are you, anyway?" he asked curtly. "I thought Miss Montgomery owned this ranch."

Next to her, Mariah could feel Finn go tense and then suddenly his arm was wrapping possessively around her shoulders.

"I am this baby's father. That's who I am," Finn said tersely. "And if I were you, I'd get out of here right now. I don't want to see you around here again. Ever."

Without a word, Oakley stomped off the steps and skirted his way past Finn and Mariah.

Leaving her side, Finn followed a few steps behind the man, then waited at the yard gate until he'd climbed into his truck and driven away. Before the dust from the tires drifted off to the southeast, Mariah carried Harry into the house and placed him in a small playpen she'd erected in the kitchen. Once the baby was settled, she walked back out to the porch to find Finn climbing the steps.

"What was that about?" she asked.

He stepped onto the porch. "Just giving the man the send-off he deserved. He was up to no good and I didn't see any point in playing nice."

"Up to no good?" She shook her head. "Maybe he was a little flirtatious, but that had nothing to do with him being a potential buyer for this ranch. Now you've scared him off!"

He shot her a disgusted look. "Are you kidding me? Would you honestly want a creep like him to own this place? A home you've lived in for twenty years?"

"That's not the point!"

With little more than an inch standing between them, he stared down at her, and Mariah felt her insides begin to tremble. Not with anger, but with raw desire. And the uncontrollable attraction she had toward the cowboy aggravated her as much as his authoritative attitude.

"You're telling me it doesn't matter who winds up here?" he demanded. "Just as long as you have the money?"

"You make it all sound nasty!" she shot back at him. "And you're doing that to make me forget about your— rude behavior!"

"Maybe you'd better explain that," he said tightly.

"Yes, Oakley was a creep. But you could've gotten rid of him in a nicer way."

"Nice, hell! If you think a man like him understands nice, then you're too damned naive to be living out here alone!"

Furious now, she said, "You don't own this ranch. And you certainly don't own me. From now on I'll handle my personal business."

His nostrils flared and though the sparks in his eyes were fueled by anger, the sight of them made her wonder if he made love with the same sort of unleashed passion. The notion sent a shiver of excitement slithering down her spine.

"You think— Oh, to hell with it," he muttered.

He turned to leave the porch and Mariah instantly snatched hold of his forearm.

"Finn, I'm trying to understand your behavior," she said, her voice growing softer with each word. "But you're not making it easy."

He turned back to her and Mariah's heart lurched into a wild gallop as his hands closed over her shoulders.

"Then I need to make things plainer, Mariah. Maybe

I ran that creep off because I don't want him, or any man, thinking they have a snowball's chance in hell of doing this."

This? The question had barely had time to zing through her thoughts when she saw his head lowering to hers. Yet the realization that he was about to kiss her wasn't enough to make her step back. If anything, she wanted to step into him. She wanted to feel his arms around her once again, to experience the taste of his hard, searching lips.

In a feeble attempt at resistance, she planted her palms against his chest, but before she could push a measurable distance between them, the warmth of his muscles seeped into her hands and raced up her arms. The sensation was so pleasurable, she couldn't move, much less make her lungs work in a normal fashion.

"This shouldn't be happening again."

The breathless words rushed past her parted lips but did little to slow the downward descent of his head.

"Probably not," he whispered, his mouth touching hers ever so softly. "But I don't think either of us is going to stop it."

Chapter Six

Mariah had never been kissed outside in broad daylight, not like this. It made her feel exposed and naked and even a bit wicked. Finn's lips were making a hungry foray over hers, turning her into a melted mess, making it impossible for her to think.

Closer. That was the only thing she wanted, needed. With that one thing on her mind, her hands instinctively moved to the back of his neck, the front of her body arched into his, while their lips rocked back and forth to a rhythm only they could hear.

Her head began to whirl until she was certain she was floating off into the blue sky. Her breathing stopped and her heart pounded. If the kiss ended, she'd surely die, she thought. But eventually it did end when Finn finally lifted his head.

Sanity rushed into Mariah's brain and with it came the reality of how lost she'd become in Finn's embrace.

Her fingers were tangled in the hair at the back of his neck, while his hands were splayed against her back, holding her upper body tightly against his.

Through a foggy haze, she stared up at him. "Finn," she whispered hoarsely, "I don't know what's happening to me. To us!"

Not waiting to hear what, if anything, he had to say, she pulled away from him and hurried to the other side of the porch. With her back to him, she stared out at the distant mountains and tried to gain control of her labored breathing. She was trembling all over and her body felt as though a wildfire had ignited inside her and was now spreading from her head to her feet.

The sound of his boots moving across the porch floor alerted her to his approach. Even so, she wasn't ready for the contact of his hand as it rested gently against the back of her shoulder. Until she'd met Finn, she'd had no idea that the simple touch of a man's hand could have the power to shake her like an earthquake.

"Mariah, if it makes you feel any better I'm just as confused as you are. I didn't come here looking to start up a relationship with you."

She swallowed to ease the aching tightness in her throat. "I'm sure you didn't. So what—"

"Am I doing?" he finished for her. "The only thing that's clear to me is when I'm near you I lose control. And I think it happens to you, too."

She turned to face him and her heart was suddenly crying for her to step into his arms, to confess how much the warmth of his embrace chased away her loneliness. But that would be inviting trouble. The sort she didn't need at this point in her life. She had very little experience with men. Especially one as rugged and sexy as

Finn. Hot, brief flings were his style. Not waking up in the same bed with the same woman for the rest of his life.

"Yes. It—" Glad he couldn't see her face, she closed her eyes and licked her swollen lips. "I'm not going to deny that I'm attracted to you. That would be pretty pathetic, wouldn't it? When I just kissed you like—well, like I wanted you."

His fingers tightened on her shoulder and for some inexplicable reason Mariah felt the urge to cry. To brace herself, she bit down hard on her lip and drew in a deep, cleansing breath.

"I want you, too, Mariah."

Such sweet, simple words. But his wanting wasn't the same as hers. She wanted him for more than just a day or night. And she wanted more than just his physical touch. She wanted even the simplest form of his company. To see his smile, hear his voice, watch the ever-changing moods in his sky-blue eyes.

A few years ago, during her college days, she'd thought she felt these things for Kris. But now she realized how lukewarm her feelings for him had been compared to the intensity of her reactions to Finn. And what did it all mean? That she was falling in love with a man she'd met less than twenty-four hours ago? No. Dear heaven, no. His life was back in Nevada on that rich ranch. He'd never think of her in a long-term way.

Bracing herself, she turned and faced him. "It's nothing more than chemistry, and we need to deal with it in an adult way."

"Speak for yourself. I pretty much feel like an adult right now."

She groaned with frustration. "Yesterday we were total strangers, Finn!"

A slow grin spread across his face and Mariah's gaze went straight to his lips. Even now, she wanted to forget the right or wrong of it and tilt her mouth back up to his. Oh my, she had to get a grip and fast.

"If you ask me, a kiss is a pretty good way for us to get to know each other."

She stepped around him before she was tempted to give in to the urge of touching him again. "You need to understand that I'm nothing like Aimee!"

"What the hell does that mean?" he barked.

She started toward the door. "It means I won't go to bed with you just because it would feel good!"

"Thanks for the warning," he flung at her, then stomped off the porch.

Mariah didn't wait to see where he was going. With her eyes full of tears, she hurried into the house.

A few minutes later at the barn, Finn backed his truck up to the door of the feed room and began to unload sacks of grain and alfalfa bales from the bed. As he stacked the feed and hay neatly to one side of the room, Mariah's parting words continued to eat at him.

Damn it, did she think all he wanted from a woman was to get her into bed? Having a brief fling with Aimee didn't make him a playboy. But apparently in Mariah's eyes it did. And after the way he'd been grabbing her up and kissing her, he could hardly blame her for thinking that way.

Using his knee to shove the last bale into place, Finn stepped back from the stacked hay and pulled a bandanna from the back pocket of his jeans. As he wiped the sweat from his face, words of warning from his father and brother swirled through his mind, adding to his frustration.

Deep down, he realized his family was right. Now more than ever, he needed to use common sense. He couldn't let a pair of soulful gray eyes and warm lips turn him into a randy fool.

"What is all of this?"

At the sound of Mariah's voice he quickly glanced over his shoulder to see her standing in the doorway of the feed room. After stomping off the porch in a huff not more than twenty minutes ago, he certainly hadn't expected her to show up here at the barn.

"Where's Harry?" he blurted the question.

"He just went to sleep. He's safe in his crib and I only intend to be here for a few minutes."

"What's the matter? You didn't jab enough barbs in me a while ago? You decided to come out here to the barn and try to cut me a few more times?"

Her lips tightened. "I didn't walk out here to the barn to discuss that—that kissing episode on the porch. We've said enough about it. I came out here because I saw your truck was loaded with hay. And I didn't ask for it."

Relieved that she wasn't going to keep harping about that kiss, or whatever the hell it had been, he turned and walked over to the open doorway. "That's right. You didn't ask for it. I took it upon myself to buy some things for the horses."

The look of disapproval on her face changed to one of concern. Her mouth opened, then after a moment's pause, snapped shut. When it opened a second time he expected to hear a loud protest. Instead, she simply said, "All right. Give me the bill and I'll write you a check."

"That won't be necessary," he told her.

Her shoulders straightened to a stiff line. "It's necessary to me."

He shook his head, while wondering how one moment he could be so on fire to make love to her and the next he wanted to yell with frustration. "We need to talk," he said.

"There's nothing you can say about this—"

"It's not about the hay or the feed." He stepped out of the barn and shut the door behind him. "Let's go to the house. I'll meet you there as soon as I move my truck."

"I'll be in the kitchen," she told him.

A few minutes later, Finn entered the kitchen carrying several packages. As he placed them on the breakfast bar, Mariah left the cabinet counter where she'd been peeling apples and joined him.

He gestured toward the sacks. "I got all the things you had on the list and a few more. There's a little something for you, too," he added sheepishly.

She cast him a guarded glance. "Me? I didn't write anything on the list for myself."

Reaching for the sack closest to her, she pulled out diapers, formula, tiny T-shirts, matching shorts and two pairs of jeans that snapped on the inside of each leg. She couldn't imagine this man strolling through the baby department, picking out clothes for Harry. It only gave her further proof that he wasn't about to shy away from fatherhood.

As she thoughtfully smoothed a finger over the blue fabric, he said, "He might already have plenty of clothes. But I thought they were cute."

"Very cute," she agreed. "I'm surprised you didn't find a Western shirt to go with the jeans."

"I would have, but the store where I bought that stuff didn't have any. And with it being Sunday the Western store was closed," he said. "But give me time and I'll have a stack of shirts for him. And when his feet get big enough, he'll get a pair of boots. Just like mine."

Clearly, Finn was already becoming very attached to Harry. He truly believed he was the father. If his DNA wasn't a match to Harry's, it would crush him. And strangely, Mariah didn't want Finn to go through that heartbreak. Even though it meant he'd be taking the baby to Nevada.

She glanced down at Finn's snub-toed brown boots. To her they looked like they were made from expensive alligator hide. And they probably were. She couldn't imagine him wearing anything fake.

"Considering the size of your foot, that might take a while."

He grinned and Mariah was relieved that the angry tension between them was easing.

"They do make baby-sized boots, you know."

"Yes. And I have no doubt you'll find a pair." She reached for the second sack and removed a little stuffed horse, a bright green teething ring, and lastly, a shiny gold box tied with a pale pink ribbon. The fact that he'd bought her a little gift made her feel awful for losing her temper with him.

"Is this mine?"

"Yes. And don't worry," he told her. "It won't explode or jump out at you."

She pulled the ribbon loose and lifted the lid to see a necklace lying on a bed of velvet. The tiny silver cross attached to a delicate chain was so touching and unexpected she couldn't utter a word.

After a weighty stretch of silence, he said, "It's nothing fancy. But it's real silver. And I thought it suited you."

She swallowed hard. "It's lovely," she murmured. "But you shouldn't have gotten me anything. What you paid for this would've bought a week's work of groceries."

Tangled emotions stirred inside Finn as reached for the necklace. "A woman shouldn't always be practical," he said huskily. "Let me put it on for you."

Expecting her to argue, he was somewhat surprised when she lifted her long hair off her neck and presented her back to him.

Moving closer, Finn positioned the little cross in the hollow of her throat. With the scent of her hair filling his nostrils and her soft skin beckoning every male cell in his body, the temptation to drop his head and press kisses to the back of her bared neck was so strong it caused his hands to tremble.

"Sorry," he murmured as he fumbled with the delicate clasp. "I'm not very practiced at this sort of thing."

"Neither am I," she said softly.

The poignant note in her voice caused his fingers to pause against the nape of her neck. One minute she was all fire and the next as soft as a kitten. And either way, he wanted her. It was that simple, Finn thought.

"You're a beautiful woman, Mariah," he said huskily. "I'm sure other men have given you jewelry before."

She was quiet for long moments and then she turned and smiled wanly up at him. "My dad gave me a bracelet for Christmas one year. And once in grade school, a boy gave me a ring that he'd gotten out of a crank machine.

That little piece of plastic turned out to be much more heartfelt than a diamond I received…well, later on."

A diamond? So she had been deeply involved with a man at one time, he thought. Like a match striking against stone, jealousy flared inside him. He didn't want to think of Mariah loving another man so much that she'd wanted to marry him.

"You were engaged?"

Her head bent downward to hide her face. "For a brief time—a few years ago. It means nothing now."

"If you were wearing his ring it must have meant something back then," he ventured to say.

"I thought it did. But later I realized I was confused about him…and myself."

"Well, that happens," he told her. "I was confused once, too."

She looked up at him and Finn noticed how her fingers were clasping the silver cross as though it were a lifeline.

"You've been engaged before?" she asked.

He grimaced at the memory of Janelle. She'd been a big part of his young life and for a long time he'd expected her to be a part of his future. But she'd had other ideas. Losing her had forced him to grow up. It had also made Finn decide he wanted no part of marriage until he was certain he could deal with the intricacies of a woman's emotional needs.

"Not exactly engaged," he admitted. "We were a steady couple for a long time in high school. It ended before I asked her to marry me."

Curiosity flickered in her gray eyes. "Were you planning to ask her?"

He shrugged while remembering the humiliation he'd

felt when Janelle had turned away from him to marry an older man. "Yes. But at a later time. You see, I was only nineteen. I wasn't ready."

"Oh. Yes, things do get confusing at that age." Turning her head to one side, she licked her lips. "Well, thank you, Finn. It was very thoughtful of you to remember me with a gift."

His gaze took in the strands of black hair resting against the pale creamy skin of her cheek, the silver-gray depths of her eyes and the moist pink curve of her lips. Something about her made his body ache to make love to her, yet at the same time his heart yearned to keep her safe and protected. The conflicting feelings inside him were seesawing back and forth, refusing to settle on common ground.

"The necklace is just a small token—for being such a good mother to Harry. I truly appreciate what you've done for him, Mariah."

Her gaze drifted over to the stuffed horse he'd purchased and he watched a melancholy expression creep over her features.

"It's been a labor of love, Finn."

An uncomfortable lump collected in his throat. He tried to clear it away as he turned and took a seat on one of the bar stools. "Uh—what I wanted to talk to you about, Mariah—there's a reason I don't want any money for the feed and hay. And it has nothing to do with charity. I want to purchase the horses from you."

The look on her face turned to one of disbelief. "The horses? All of them?"

He nodded. "The stallion, the geldings and the mares. Just shoot me a fair price and I'll write you a check. With one stipulation, that is. That I don't have to ship them out immediately. I'd like for them to stay here until the test comes back and we—uh, get everything settled about Harry. By then I'll have found a place to put them. Besides, from the looks of the mares, they're all getting close to foaling. It would be much safer for them to deliver before they have to travel."

Her thoughtful gaze roamed his face. "You're not going to haggle over the price?"

Finn shook his head. "I trust you to be fair."

Easing onto the stool next to his, she stared at the floor. "This past month I've prayed for a buyer to show up. Now you've come along and answered my prayers. But I don't feel good about it." Her head swung back and forth. "Doesn't make much sense, does it? I should be happy. But I—"

"Feel like you're turning loose a part of yourself. I understand."

Thrusting a hand through her hair, she looked at him. "How did you know I felt that way? I didn't even know it myself until this moment."

The torn look in her eyes bothered him far more than it should have. "I know how I'd feel to be giving up a part of my home—what this place had been built on. I figured it would be the same for you. If it will make you feel any better, I can assure you I'll give the horses the best of care."

"I have no concerns about that." Biting down on her bottom lip, her gaze turned away from his. "All right. I'll sell the horses to you. Just give me a bit of time to think over the price. In the meantime, I'm curious about one thing, though."

"What's that?"

She looked at him. "You said you'd have to find a

place to put them. I don't get it. You live on a huge ranch. Surely you have space for ten more horses."

Avoiding her gaze, Finn rubbed the heels of his palms against his thighs. "Not these horses—they're mustangs. My father and grandfather refuse to have any wild horses on the ranch."

Totally surprised, she said, "Oh. I thought you'd have a say in things on the Silver Horn? I mean where the horses are concerned?"

He frowned. "I manage the horse division of the ranch. I oversee the breeding, foaling, training and care of all the equines on the ranch. That includes show horses and working horses."

"Well, clearly they believe you know your job. I don't understand."

He didn't understand it, either, Finn thought grimly. After all these years, he wanted to think his father and grandfather respected his ideas and plans. Instead, they refused to consider them. "The Silver Horn has its own foundation breeding. The same bloodlines have continued on for a hundred years or more. Dad and Gramps don't want it tampered with. You see, they're all about tried-and-true tradition."

"But you could keep the mustangs in a separate area," Mariah argued. "If the ranch covers thousands of acres, what could they possibly hurt?"

"The Silver Horn image."

She mulled that over, then finally replied, "Your folks must be snobs."

"Only where horses and cattle are concerned." The notion had him grunting with wry amusement and then he cast her a meaningful glance. "If I didn't know better, Mariah, you sound like you're proud of those mustangs."

"Well, they were my father and sister's dream. And though there've been plenty of times in my life that I wish I'd never seen a horse, I guess a part of me is proud that Stallion Canyon was founded on mustangs. But I can't keep hanging on to them," she said huskily. "It's not possible. Much less practical."

"And you must be practical."

She left the bar stool and returned to the cabinet. As she sliced an apple into a plastic bowl, she said, "Dad and Aimee were always dreamers. I was always the one who worried over the ranch's finances. And I'm still worrying over them. A person with money has the luxury of being sentimental rather than sensible. I'm not in the position you are, Finn. I have to think about surviving."

So she'd never been the happy-go-lucky sort. Was that the reason her engagement had ended? Finn wondered. Because she'd been all business and no fun?

Hell, Finn. It doesn't matter why or how her engagement ended. That part of her past has nothing to do with you. She loved a man once and he wasn't you. So what? You're not looking for love or marriage.

The need to comfort her suddenly pushed away the irritating voice in his head and he walked over to where she stood and rested his hip against the cabinet. "Mariah, money doesn't fix everything. It doesn't stop you from losing loved ones. Wealthy people get hurt and betrayed. They also get sick and lonely and lost. Just like poor folks do."

She closed her eyes and it was all Finn could do to keep from bending his head and placing his lips on hers. Kissing her stirred more than libido, he realized. It made him dream and want and wish for things that, up until now, he'd never considered important. And he wasn't quite sure if that was a good thing or bad.

"I don't expect selling the horses and the ranch to feel good. But I have to climb out of this hole some way." She opened her eyes and attempted to smile. "Now if you'll excuse me, I'd better go check on Harry."

He didn't want her to go. He wanted to pull her into his arms, stroke her hair and whisper words of reassurance in her ear. He wanted to feel her body go soft and yielding against his, to know that she trusted him completely. But she didn't trust him. He wasn't sure she trusted anybody.

And as he watched her scurry out of the room, Finn decided she was like a little wounded bird, determined to fly away from the very person who wanted to help her.

Chapter Seven

Bright and early the next morning, Mariah and Finn left the ranch to take Harry to the health department in town. After a qualified nurse took swabs from both Finn's and the baby's mouths, she managed to get to school just in time to start the second-hour class, while Finn took Harry back to the ranch, where Linda was waiting to take over her usual role as nanny.

Now a few hours later, Mariah was sitting in a small staff lounge with her friend and fellow teacher, Sage Newcastle, as the two women enjoyed the last few minutes of their lunch break.

"You're actually going to Nevada with this man?" Sage asked in a shocked voice. "I don't believe it!"

Mariah looked over at the blonde thirty-one-year-old divorcée, who'd given up on marriage but not romance.

"Shh! I said I'm considering it. But I don't want the whole staff to know about it!" When Aimee had become a single mother, Mariah had been forced to deal with all sorts of gossip. The rumor mill would surely run rampant if any of the school staff learned she was going to make a trip with Harry's father.

"Besides," she went on, "we only took Harry to the health department this morning to get the DNA swabs sent off. And until I learn that Finn is the father I don't plan on going anywhere with him."

Sage glanced at her with concern. "Having that Nevada cowboy in the house must be causing you a lot of extra work. You look exhausted."

Mariah had to bite her lip to keep from groaning. No way did she want Sage to know she'd lost sleep the past two nights because her mind was fixated on Finn. The way he smelled. The way he looked. The sound of his voice, his laughter. And then there were his kisses. She'd relived them over and over in her mind, as though she'd never been kissed before.

That's because you hadn't been really kissed, Mariah. Not until Finn took you into his arms and like a starving man, made a meal of your lips. Now you're besotted with the way he touched you. The way he made you drunk with desire.

"Yoo-hoo, Mariah! Are you with me?"

Shaking away the mimicking voice in her head, Mariah focused on her friend's earlier remark. "Finn isn't causing extra work. It's—well, everything is going to be in limbo until the DNA comes back."

Sage reached over and placed a comforting hand on Mariah's forearm. "I'm not sure I would've had the courage to call Mr. Calhoun and tell him about Harry. I'm afraid I would've kept the baby all to myself."

"My conscience wouldn't let me do that," she said ruefully. "Harry deserves to have a father."

"Will this Finn make a good one, you think?"

Sage's question caused images of Finn and Harry to flash in the forefront of her mind. She couldn't deny that Harry had already bonded with Finn. And Finn handled the baby as though he were the most special thing on earth. "Finn will make an excellent father. I have no doubts about that."

She didn't add that Finn was a wealthy man and would be able to give Harry every wonderful opportunity in life. That part of the puzzle hardly seemed important now. As he'd told her last evening: money didn't equal happiness. And she figured if Finn didn't have a dime, he'd still have a grin on his face.

Sage said, "Well, that's a relief. Uh—you haven't really told me much about the man. Does he look anything like Harry?"

Mariah shrugged. "Actually, the more I look at the two of them together, the more similarities I see."

"Hmm. Then he must be handsome. Because Harry is adorable," Sage said. "You know, the more I think about it, the more I think you should have me over for dinner one evening. Before Finn goes back to Nevada."

Mariah rose from the long couch where the two women had been sitting and gathered up a stack of books and papers from the corner of a nearby table.

Deliberately changing the subject, she said, "It's almost time for the bell to ring."

"I'm right behind you," Sage told her.

They left the lounge and started down a wide corridor of the high school building. Teenagers were already

scurrying past them, while others were opening and closing lockers lined along the walls.

In spite of the stress that went along with teaching
young people, Mariah loved her job. To her, the idea of
helping a child develop into a productive adult made up
for the long hours and minimal salary. The school was
her second home and without it these past few months,
she would've been truly lost.

"You know," Sage said wryly, "I don't think you want
me to meet Harry's dad. That tells me he's either really
an ogre, or a dreamboat you want to keep to yourself."

Mariah's chuckle held little humor. "He's a cowboy,
Sage. Not your type at all."

Sage's grin was a bit naughty. "I'll bet he's your type,
though. You—" She broke off as her gaze zeroed in on
the silver cross dangling in the hollow of Mariah's throat.
"Oh, how pretty! It looks like a piece from that famous
silver designer. Is it?"

Surely not, Mariah thought. Finn wouldn't have spent
that sort of money on her. On the other hand, his concept
of a lot of money would be quite different from hers.

Unconsciously touching a finger to the cross, she said,
"I have no idea. The necklace was a gift."

Sage's brows shot up. "Your birthday won't be for
several months. Who—?"

Thankfully, the bell sounded, giving Mariah the perfect excuse to leave Sage's question dangling. "Gotta
run. See you later."

Back on Stallion Canyon, Finn was finishing the last
of his lunch on the patio. Across from him, Harry's nanny
had taken a seat in one of the wicker chairs and settled
the baby comfortably in her lap.

This morning when he and Harry had returned from town, Finn had found Linda Baskin already here and waiting to take over her duties of caring for Harry. A tall, slender woman with a long blond ponytail threaded with streaks of gray, she appeared to be somewhere in her midfifties. Her complexion was ruddy and weather-beaten, her brown eyes crinkled at the corners. For the most part she was quiet and reserved, but friendly enough.

Last night, Finn had tried to convince Mariah that the nanny was no longer needed. He could certainly take care of Harry while she was at work. But Mariah wouldn't hear of it. She'd argued that he'd be wanting to spend time outdoors with the horses and he couldn't do that with a baby on his hip.

Yet now that Finn had met Linda, he realized that Mariah's reasoning to keep the nanny around was much more complex than giving him free time with the horses. The woman was totally enamored with Harry. Another fact that nagged at Finn. Linda would also be lost whenever he took his son home to the Horn.

Picking up a glass of iced tea, he leaned back in his chair and crossed his boots at the ankles. "Have you known the Montgomerys long?" Finn ventured to ask her.

"Twenty years or more," she said. "I met Ray and the girls when they first moved here. We all went to the same church, you see."

The baby was chewing his fist, while a stream of drool dripped from his chin. Last night Mariah had rubbed a soothing gel over his gums and predicted the tooth would be appearing soon. He wanted to be around to see Harry's first tooth appear and the many other firsts the child would have. But then, so did Mariah.

And this woman, too. Until this moment, Finn had never stopped to think about the connections a child created to all the people around him or her.

"That's a long time," Finn commented.

She handed Harry the green teething ring that Finn had purchased for him yesterday. The baby immediately jammed the piece of plastic in his mouth.

"I watched the girls grow up and Ray work to make this ranch into a fine home." She turned a wistful look toward the barns. "I never thought he'd die like he did. But then life is unpredictable, isn't it?"

Something in Linda's quiet voice told Finn that she was more than just a family acquaintance to the Montgomerys.

"That's why we should enjoy every day," he said, then asked, "Did you know Mariah is selling the ranch? She's already sold the horses to me."

With her gaze still on the barns, she said in a flat voice, "Yes, I know about the ranch. And the horses, too."

Finn had been wondering if Mariah had anyone close that she could talk to about private matters. Obviously Linda was that person.

"What do you think about her decision? About the ranch, that is."

"If it wasn't for her, this place would've already been sold through a sheriff's auction. She's gone as far as she can go. I don't like it. But that's the way it is. For now, at least."

Finn gazed thoughtfully toward the paddock where the mares were pastured. Beyond it, a ridge of forest-covered mountains curved toward the east. He figured with a bit of rain the foothills would hold some hearty grasses.

"Such a shame," he said thoughtfully. "I haven't seen much more than this area around the ranch yard, but what I see is beautiful."

Her features were stern as she looked at him. "Why don't you buy it?"

For a moment Finn was too stunned to know how to answer. "Me? I live on my family's ranch. I don't need this one."

She frowned. "Some men are independent and some aren't. I took you for the independent sort. But then, I'm not always right about people."

Finn had never expected to be having this sort of conversation with Harry's nanny, but now that she'd opened up, he couldn't resist the chance to find out more about Mariah's family.

"Now that we're on the subject, what sort of man was Ray Montgomery?" he asked.

A soft light entered the woman's brown eyes. It was the sort of look that was born from deep affection.

"A good, simple man. This ranch, the horses and his girls. That's all that mattered—all he wanted."

"Did you ever meet his ex-wife?"

Her brown eyes suddenly squinted. "That's a strange thing for you to be asking."

Finn shrugged. "I'm trying to get an idea of Harry's maternal family. Especially since they seem to be out of the picture. Mariah tells me her mother lives in Florida, but she never sees her."

She sighed. "Selma decided she didn't care for country life. She left the family long before Ray and the girls moved here. And that's the way it's stayed."

Finn tried to imagine his own mother leaving her

children behind, but it was impossible. Up until the day she'd died, Fiona had loved her five sons utterly.

"It takes a strong woman to be a rancher's wife," Finn mused aloud. "But why turn her back on her daughters?"

Harry began to fuss and squirm, prompting Linda to lift the baby to her shoulder and gently pat his back. "Because the girls wanted to live with their father and Selma never forgave her daughters for making that choice."

"Mariah hasn't mentioned ever having a stepmother around. Guess Ray never remarried."

The stark expression that spread over Linda's face spoke volumes to Finn.

"No," she said. "He remained single until he died."

Feeling as though he'd opened a diary that he had no right reading, Finn rose to his feet and gathered up the leftovers from his lunch. After putting the things away in the kitchen, he returned to the patio and picked up his hat.

"Going back to the barns?" Linda asked.

He tugged the brim of the felt low onto his forehead. "I have horses saddled and ready to be exercised."

"Be safe with those mustangs, Finn. I don't think Mariah could survive if you had an accident."

Finn stared at her. Was Linda trying to imply that Mariah cared for him? The idea was ridiculous. Sure, she'd kissed him as though she liked it. But that hardly meant she had feelings for him.

He chuckled sardonically. "Mariah isn't all that interested in my safety. In fact, she doesn't much care for men who wears spurs. And there's no chance of me ever taking mine off."

Before Linda could make any response, Finn left the patio and headed quickly toward the barns.

* * *

Later that evening when Mariah returned home from work, she dropped her tote and handbag on the coffee table, then walked straight to the middle of the living room where Linda had spread a blanket on the floor in front of the television. She was sitting cross-legged with Harry lying on his belly next to her. The baby was doing his best to get traction with his toes and push himself forward.

Bending down, she picked him up and cuddled him tightly against her shoulder. "How is my little man?" she crooned to the baby.

"Give him two or three more months and he'll probably be sitting on his own and crawling everywhere." She studied Mariah's drawn face. "You look drained. School must have been tough today."

"No more than usual." Closing her eyes, Mariah pressed her cheek against the top of Harry's head and tried to swallow away the tightness in her throat. The DNA test was off to the lab. Whether Finn was the father or not, once the results were determined, her life and Harry's would never be the same. The idea left a perpetual knot in the pit of her stomach.

Rising to her feet, Linda patted her shoulder. "It's Monday. Tomorrow will be better. Want a glass of tea or something?"

"Maybe later. I need to change clothes. Uh—how did you get on with Finn?"

"We understand each other, I think," Linda said, then gestured in the direction of the open doorway. "He's been down at the barns since lunch. I hope you're right about him being a horseman. That stallion isn't safe to be around and it's been four hours since I've seen him."

Concern fluttered in the pit of Mariah's stomach. Finn might be an expert horseman, but that didn't rule out accidents happening. "Finn should be able to handle himself around Rimrock. But I'd better go check on him just the same."

Mariah handed the baby over to Linda and quickly left the room. Once she reached the hallway, she didn't bother going to her bedroom to change out of her dress clothes. Instead, she exited the house through the kitchen and made a beeline to the main horse barn.

Along the way, her gaze desperately searched the ranch yard for a sign of Finn. As crazy as it seemed, he'd already become a part of her life. The image of him lying in the dirt, hurt or worse, sent a rush of icy fear through her. If something had happened to him, she'd be devastated.

Quickening her steps, Mariah reached the shed row where the stallion, Rimrock, was stalled along with four geldings. The gates to all five stalls were swung wide with no horses to be seen. A hurried glance told her the stalls had been shoveled all the way to the dirt floor, but no clean shavings had yet been added. At the far end of the shed row, near the tack room, a shoeing stand, a rasp and hoof nippers were lying on the ground.

Finn had certainly been busy. That much was clear. But where was he now? A glance at the paddock to her right told her the mares were all there, munching contentedly at a manger full of alfalfa.

Suddenly the wind swirled from the north and with it came a cloud of dust from the other side of the barn. Mariah hurried around the huge building, then stopped in her tracks and stared in amazement at the training arena some fifty yards away.

Finn was riding Rimrock in a slow lope, directing the horse in large looping figure eights. Dust boiled from the stallion's hoofs, sending brown clouds swirling around animal and rider.

Slower now, she walked over to the arena and stood just outside the wire mesh fence to watch. Finn was handling Rimrock as though he was a docile kid pony, instead of a high-strung stallion that hadn't had a person on his back since her father had passed away.

Only a few moments clicked by before Finn spotted her. With a short wave, he drew Rimrock to a walk and directed the horse in her direction. As horse and rider grew closer, she noticed Finn was wearing a pair of hard-worn chinks with hand-sewn buck stitching. The butterscotch-colored leather was scratched and scarred from the top of his thighs all the way down to his knees, while in some spots the fringe edging the legs was either missing or broken off to a shorter length. A pair of long shanked spurs with clover rowels worn smooth on the edges were strapped to his boots. Apparently he carried the tools of his trade with him at all times, she decided.

One thing for certain, no matter what angle Mariah looked at him from, he was all cowboy. And the sight of him sitting astride Rimrock was more than enough to set her heart to pounding.

"Hey, Mariah," he greeted her with a grin. "How was school today?"

Beneath the shade of his broad-brimmed hat, she could see his gaze traveling up and down the length of her. No doubt he was wondering why she was out here in the dusty ranch yard in a skirt and high heels. But she wasn't about to confess she was so worried about him she'd hurried straight out here instead of changing clothes.

Her heart suddenly hammering, she struggled to tuck strands of loosened hair back into the twist at the back of her head. "School was fine. From the looks of the stalls you've been busy today."

The saddle leather creaked as Rimrock took a restless side step. Finn gently touched his spur into the horse's side to make him return to the spot where he'd initially reined him to a stop.

"I've been occupied."

He rested a forearm across the horn of the saddle and Mariah could see he was as much at home on a horse as he was in a chair at the breakfast table.

She said, "In case you hadn't found them, the clean shavings are in the tractor shed."

"I found the shavings. But I'm in no hurry to spread them. I'm going to turn the horses out for a while. They need to graze and run. And they especially need to socialize with one another."

Mariah spluttered. "You're letting them loose? I hope you're not planning to put the geldings in with Rimrock. He's wild. He might kill them!"

Finn chuckled and Mariah's backbone immediately stiffened. Aimee had often laughed at her, too. Her sister had considered Mariah's knowledge concerning horses, and men, and fashion, amusing and even more lacking. It hurt to think that Finn considered her naive, too.

"He doesn't appear wild to me." He patted the stallion's neck. "Besides, the geldings have legs. If need be, they'll scoot out of his way. But Rimrock understands the geldings are not—uh, let's just say, all men. So he hardly feels threatened by their presence."

Shading her eyes with her hand, she continued to gaze up at him. "Dad was the last person to ride Rimrock four years ago. He was very unruly then. How did you get him to behave like this?"

A slow grin exposed his teeth and it struck Mariah that she'd spent half the day dreaming about those lips, while the other half had been on Harry. She could only hope she'd made sense while she'd been lecturing her students on California history.

"I just told him we were going to be buddies. That's all."

He climbed down from the horse and came to stand directly in front of Mariah. The fence between them did nothing to protect her senses from his overwhelming presence, and with each passing moment she felt her breaths grow slower and her heart beat faster.

"That simple, huh?"

He grinned and the warm light in his eyes sent pleasure spreading through her like a ray of sun after a long, cold rain. Being away from him only for a few hours had seemed like an eternity, and now that he was standing so near, it was all she could do to keep from reaching through the fence and latching onto his shirt. Just to touch him in any small way gave her pleasure. The kind of pleasure that was hard to resist.

"I've been riding since I was just a wee tot. And everyone tells me that I have a kinship with horses. I'm sure your dad had it, too."

Ray Montgomery had been a good horseman, but he'd had to work hard to learn the trade. Mariah figured it all came natural to Finn. As natural as the dimples in his cheeks and the easy way his lips had moved over hers.

In an effort to clear her straying thoughts, she drew

in a deep breath and blew it out. "A tot? Exactly how old were you when you took your first ride?"

"I'm told my grandfather carried me in the saddle when I was only a few weeks old."

"A few weeks! Your mother must've been going out of her mind with fear!"

Chuckling, he said, "Not really. She'd already seen my three older brothers on a horse when they were only babies. By the time I came along, she was used to it."

"So this means if Harry turns out to be your son, you'll be putting him on the back of a horse in the near future?"

His grin deepened. "No 'ifs,' Mariah. Only when. And once the test reveals I'm the father, then I plan on doing lots of things with Harry. And that includes riding him on a gentle horse."

Even though the idea of Harry being on the back of a thousand-pound animal was terrifying, she didn't say anything. Because in the end, if it turned out that Harry was his son, she'd have no rights to the child's upbringing.

After a stretch of silence, he asked, "What? No loud protest?"

"No." She smoothed a hand down the front of her skirt, then turned away from him. "And now that I see you haven't been kicked in the head or bucked off with a broken leg, I'd better be getting back to the house. I'm keeping Linda from going home."

He arched a brow at her. "Oh. So you were worried about me?"

Heat flared in her cheeks. "Linda said she hadn't seen you since lunch. We were both concerned."

A sly glint appeared in his blue eyes. "It's nice to have a woman worrying over me."

"I'm not worried now." She turned to go only to have him reach through the fence and snag a hold of her shoulder.

"Wait, Mariah. Before you leave, I want to talk to you. Let me tie Rimrock and I'll come around there," he told her.

Finn tethered Rimrock to a post, then exited the arena through a nearby gate. As he walked down the fence to where Mariah stood, he was struck by how different she looked. Compared to the blue jeans and work shirts he'd seen her in the past two days, she looked far different in a slim gray skirt and thin white blouse. Although the feminine clothes were cut modestly, her curves filled them out in all the right ways. And the black high heels covering her pretty little feet were as sexy as all get-out.

Halting a short space away from her, he tried not to gawk, but ever since they'd parted ways at the health department this morning, he hadn't been able to get her image out of his mind. Now his eyes seemed to have a mind of their own. Instead of looking out at the mountains or the mares behind her shoulder, they continued to travel over her mussed black hair, the thrust of her breasts and the enticing way her hips curved out from her tiny waist.

"You have something you want to say?" she asked.

Clearing his throat, he said, "Uh—yes, the fences—I wanted to ask you about them."

"What about the fences?"

The fabric of her blouse was just sheer enough to

show a hint of lacy undergarment, and the sight stirred up thoughts that he'd been trying all day to forget.

With a mental shake of his head, he gestured toward the open land to the west. "Do you know if the fences are upright? And is the land sectioned off with cross fences? I'll need to know before I let the horses out to pasture. I don't want them wandering too far away from the ranch yard or getting on your neighbor's land."

A thoughtful frown furrowed her brow. "Sorry. I don't know how long it's been since the fences have been inspected. Dad used to make routine checks to ensure they were all intact. But after he died Aimee wasn't too concerned about fences. All she ever worried about was the arena and the stalls."

"That's a hell of a way to run a ranch," he said frankly.

One of her slender shoulders made a negligible shrug and the movement drew Finn's gaze to the white fabric opened at her throat. The silver cross he'd given her was lying against her creamy skin and he found himself wondering if she was wearing the piece of jewelry because she liked it, or the man who'd given it to her?

She said, "Looking back on it now, after Dad died we should have hired a man to manage the ranch. He might've done a better job than me of dealing with Aimee's neglectful ways."

"No use fretting about the past now. I'll check the fences myself. I'm sure there are a few old roads traveling over parts of the ranch. I'll drive out this evening and inspect what I can before dark. Would you like to go with me?"

Her lips parted and Finn's gaze homed in on the moist curve of her lower lip. He'd kissed plenty of girls over the years, but none of them had tasted quite as sweet or seductive as Mariah. And that was worrisome. How did a man forget something that good?

"I suppose I could join you," she said guardedly. "But what about Harry? I'd have to ask Linda to stay and watch him."

She was being agreeable and that was enough to put a grin on his face. "No need for that. The weather is nice. We'll take him with us. Isn't that what parents do when they go on a family outing—take their baby with them?"

Confusion flickered in her eyes. "But we're not parents."

Unable to stop himself, Finn moved closer and gently cupped his hand along the side of her face. "For now we're Harry's parents," he said softly.

"Yes. I suppose. For now."

Her eyes suddenly misted over and before he could say anything else, she pulled away from him.

As Finn watched her walk away, he realized the taste of Mariah's lips wasn't only one thing he'd eventually have to forget about the woman. The depth of emotion in her gray eyes, the touch of her hand, the heady scent of her skin and the sweet husky lilt in her voice. Those things would haunt Finn long after he was back on the Horn and Mariah had moved on with her life.

Did that mean he was falling in love with her?

Hell, Finn, that's a stupid question. You've only known Mariah for three days. A man can't lose his heart to a woman that quickly.

Maybe not, Finn thought uneasily. But a moment ago when she'd walked away with tears in her eyes, he'd felt like a part of him had gone with her.

Chapter Eight

For now we're Harry's parents.

Later that evening as Finn drove the three of them over the western section of the ranch, his words continued to roll through Mariah's thoughts. To imagine the two of them as Harry's parents, even temporary ones, was bittersweet.

As a young girl growing up without a mother, and with a father who'd been absorbed in his work, Mariah had dreamed of having a real family of her own. One that was loving and whole and could never be torn apart. When she'd met Kris during her college studies, she'd thought all those dreams were going to come true. Dark-haired and conservative in nature, he'd been the first guy who'd given her a serious glance and she'd naively fallen for his attention. Now she realized what a Pollyanna she'd been to trust him. Even more to believe in her dreams. Real families were fairy tales. At least, in her world they were.

But with Finn sitting only inches away and Harry safely ensconced in his car carrier in the backseat, she couldn't stop herself from dreaming, or smiling.

For nearly an hour Finn drove the truck alongside a network of boundary and cross fences that were located closest to the ranch yard. Once he'd determined the repairs needed, he decided to follow a dim, overgrown road that would lead them to a portion of the ranch that ran alongside a river.

Eventually, the truck crested a small rise and a stretch of open land lay before them. In spite of the dry spring, the ground was covered with clumps of grass and long-stemmed yellow flowers that bowed with the evening breeze.

Finn braked the truck to a stop to take in the sight. "Oh, Mariah, this is awesome," Finn declared. "I'm going to guess this is the area where your father grew alfalfa."

She nodded. "That's right. And about a mile on west from here is a second meadow that was used for grass hay. There's some of the irrigation system over there." She pointed to their left, where long pipes connected to large spoke wheels sat at the edge of the tree line. The weeds growing around the equipment revealed how long it had been sitting idle.

"Did your dad pump water from the river or is there a well around here somewhere?"

"Both. Depending on how much irrigating he wanted to do. The well is somewhere over there by the wheel line."

"Let's get out of the truck for a better look," he suggested. "We'll leave the doors open and stay right by the truck so we can keep an eye on Harry."

"All right."

The jostling of the truck had lulled Harry into a deep sleep. Mariah covered him with a light blanket to protect him from the cool evening air before Finn helped her to the ground.

Once they were standing together at the side of the truck, Mariah gazed around her and drank in the beauty of the nearby mountains juxtaposed with flat river land. Other than the faint sounds of insects and the rustle of leaves, a peaceful silence encompassed them.

"I'd almost forgotten how beautiful it is here," she murmured. "When Aimee and I were small we used to ride horses to this meadow. In the summer we'd take off our boots and wade in the river. 'Course, we never told Dad about the wading," she added with a wistful smile.

Finn moved close enough to slip an arm around the back of her waist. The warm weight of it filled her with an odd mixture of contentment and excitement.

"So you did have some good times here on the ranch."

Pleasant memories suddenly flooded through her, causing her heart to wince. "Lots of them," she said lowly. "But that was before Aimee and I grew apart. And before Dad left us."

He looked down at her, his eyes full of misgivings. "I wish you'd change your mind about selling the ranch, Mariah."

"Why?"

His hand tightened on the side of her waist. "Because I have a feeling and it's telling me you belong here."

Her rueful laugh came out sounding more like a

choked sob. "You don't know me well enough to make that call."

With hands on both sides of her waist, he turned her toward him. Mariah's heart thumped with anticipation.

"I've already learned a lot about you, Mariah. There are so many things I can see in your eyes that tell me what you're thinking and the kind of woman you are."

Unable to stop herself, she rested her palms against his chest. "And what sort of woman am I?" she asked huskily.

His head bent toward hers until a scant space was the only thing separating their lips.

"A woman I want to see smile. A woman I want to make love to."

By the time his voice died away, his lips were hovering over hers, robbing her breath and her senses.

"Finn," she whispered.

His arms tightened around her. "Tell me you want me, Mariah. As much as I want you."

His words were enough to make her tremble. "I do want you, Finn. Very much."

She heard him groan and then everything else faded away as he began to kiss her. Not in a gentle way. But in a hungry, all-consuming way that weakened her knees and forced her fists to snatch hold of the front of his shirt.

Just when she was certain she was going to faint from lack of oxygen, Finn lifted his head. But the reprieve only lasted long enough for her to haul in one deep breath before his mouth attacked hers once again from a different angle.

A tiny particle of Mariah's brain recognized that something was happening between her and Finn. Something that went far beyond the heat fusing their mouths together. She wanted to tear his clothes away, to beg him to make love to her right here on the ground.

The reckless abandon racing through her was like lightning racing across a summer sky. And when his hand cupped her breasts and his mouth made a downward descent along her neck, she groaned with raw, unleashed desire.

It wasn't until he'd unbuttoned the top of her blouse and pressed his lips against the valley between her breasts that a brief flash of sanity warned her to end the embrace. But the pleasure of Finn touching her, wanting her, was something she'd never had before. She couldn't give it up.

Nearby, a night bird suddenly called. Then called again. The sound must have shaken Finn out of the erotic fog that had wrapped around them. He lifted his head, then eased back far enough to allow the cool night air to drift between them.

Totally shaken, Mariah turned and attempted to catch her breath and wrangle her scattered senses back together.

Behind her, she could hear the ragged intake of Finn's breath and she wondered if his world was tilting as much as hers. Or was making love to a woman second nature to him? It had certainly felt like it, she thought.

"Dusk is falling," Finn said after a moment. "Are you ready to head back to the ranch?"

The fact that he was giving her a choice to leave this magical place made her feel somewhat more in control of herself, but only a little.

She cleared her throat. "Yes. I—think we'd better."

He moved up behind her and closed a hand over her

shoulder. "I can't apologize for any o~~~~ said gently. "When I touch you it feels ve~~~ like something I should be ashamed of."

Her eyes squeezed tight, she fought against the turn and fling herself back into his arms. Oh, how g~~ it would feel to let herself go, to simply enjoy this man's touch without worrying about tomorrow. She deserved that, didn't she? To simply allow herself to be a woman?

Trembling through and through, she turned and gave him a wobbly smile. "It feels very special to me, too, Finn. But I'm not sure if it's the right thing for me. I don't do this sort of thing for fun and games."

"That didn't feel like a game to me."

She could find no appropriate reply to that, and with a hand at her back, he urged her around to the truck.

On the way back to the ranch, Mariah remained quiet and so did Finn. The episode at the meadow had swiftly altered everything between them. Now as she gazed out at the darkening landscape it was as though she were seeing it for the first time. The same way her father must have seen it twenty years ago. And the images put a very real pang of loss in her heart.

Much later that night Mariah woke up without reason and glanced at the digital clock on the nightstand: 1:20 a.m. She groaned. For hours she'd lain awake, reliving Finn's every touch, every word, until finally sleep had overtaken her mind. Why had she suddenly woken? Had she been dreaming?

The quietness of the house settled around her at the same time an uneasy sensation pricked her senses. Something was wrong.

Tossing back the covers, she rapidly tied a light robe

...er gown and hurried across the hallway to Harry's nursery. Beneath the dim glow of the night-light, she could see the baby was sleeping soundly and she sent up a prayer of relief.

Still, something didn't feel right, and that perception deepened when she walked down the hall and saw the door to Finn's room standing wide open. As a respect to her privacy and his, he always kept the door shut whenever he was in his bedroom. Seeing it open and the room dark meant one thing. He wasn't there.

Panic suddenly struck her and she raced on bare feet out to the kitchen. A night-light next to the sink illuminated the room enough for her to see that Finn wasn't there. And with the rest of the house in darkness that could only mean he was outside.

Grabbing up her cowboy boots from the mudroom, she jerked them on and dashed out the back door. The temperature had fallen drastically since she'd gone to bed, but she hardly noticed the chill as she instinctively ran toward the barns.

Lights were burning beneath the shed row, but Finn wasn't anywhere in sight.

Slowing to a trot, she glanced into each stall. By the time she reached the end, Finn was still nowhere in sight.

Pausing to give the frantic beating of her heart a chance to catch up, she called loudly, "Finn? Where are you?"

"Over here, Mariah."

Relieved, she followed the sound of his voice to the back of the barn where a small pen was equipped with a lean-to shelter. Beneath the overhang of the tin roof, she could see the shadowy image of Finn kneeling over a downed horse. Her short-lived relief was suddenly pierced with alarm and she quickly let herself into the enclosure.

"Finn, what's wrong?"

"I came out here to check on the mares before I went to bed. Thank God I did. This one is trying to foal. But both of the baby's front feet are together. The head won't follow that way. One foot needs to be forward more."

"Oh, no! This is her first foal, Finn. Should I call the vet?"

"I've already called one. But it'll probably be another hour before he can get here." Finn gently rubbed the mare's sweaty flank. "I've got to do something before then or it will be too late for both of them."

Mariah could hardly bear to hear the animal's groans as she strained to expel the baby from her. She'd never helped with any of the foaling before. Her father had taken care of those things. Along with Aimee's help. Mariah had always been told her help wasn't needed. "Is there anything I can do?"

He glanced up, his gaze making a rapid sweep over her. "You're going to freeze in those nightclothes. And what about Harry?"

"Harry is sound asleep in his crib."

His expression stern, he said, "I don't want him left in the house alone. You'd better get back."

"I'm not leaving you out here unaided," she practically shouted. "You might need help before the vet arrives."

Rising to his full height to emphasize his point, he repeated, "I said I don't want Harry in the house alone!"

Seeing that there was no point in arguing the matter, she started out of the pen. "Fine," she muttered. "We'll do this your way."

Not waiting to hear his response, she left the barn area and hurried to the house. Inside, she pulled a jean jacket over her robe, then went straight to the nursery and gently swaddled Harry in a heavy quilt. The child never stirred. Even when she made a beeline back to the barns.

After she'd settled the sleeping baby in his wagon, she positioned it in a safe position outside the mare's pen.

By now, Finn was too involved with the troubled delivery to notice her whereabouts, until she reentered the pen and joined him beneath the overhang.

"I brought Harry back with me. He's sound asleep and warmly bundled," she told him, then gestured toward the straining mare. "Is she any better?"

Finn dismally shook his head. "No. And too much time has already passed. I'm going to try one more thing to see if the baby will turn itself. If it doesn't, then I'll have to try to do it myself."

She drew in a sharp breath. "Have you done that sort of thing before?"

"Only a handful of times. Mostly, there's no need. The Horn has a resident vet that handles the ranch's emergencies."

The evident worry on his face urged Mariah to lay a reassuring hand on his shoulder. "If you've done it before you can do it again. I have every faith in you. But let's pray you won't have to."

He shot her a grateful look. "I don't want to lose this mare and baby. Right now I've got to get her up and walking. Hopefully that might relieve enough pressure of the uterine walls to give the foal enough room to turn itself."

Mariah moved out of the way and Finn wasted no

time in getting the suffering mare to her feet and walking her around and around the small pen. Five minutes passed, then ten. All the while Mariah continued to pray for the mare's and baby's safety.

Eventually the mare balked and started lowering herself back to the ground. Finn dropped his hold on the lead rope and allowed her to stretch out.

"Finn! What's happening? Is she dying?" Mariah asked frantically.

Finn knelt closer to the mare and began to examine her. "No. I think she's telling us the baby will come out now. Yes! Here it comes! Just the way it should."

Mariah watched in wonder as first one little hoof emerged. A few inches behind, the second hoof appeared, and then the head. After that, the mare had no trouble delivering the rest of the foal.

For the next half hour, Mariah watched Finn deftly deal with the pair, who appeared to be in good condition, especially considering the prolonged birth. When the lights of a vehicle announced the arrival of the vet, she scooped up Harry.

"The vet's here," she told Finn. "I don't want him to see me in my nightclothes. I'm going back to the house."

As she started off, he called to her. She paused long enough for him to walk over to her.

"Yes?"

A crooked grin twisted his weary features. "Thank you."

His tender words of appreciation added to the incredibly tense moments they'd shared over the mare all came together at once to cause Mariah's eyes to mist over. "I didn't do anything," she said.

"Just being here was exactly what I needed."

Her heart melting, she touched his hand and then scurried back to the house.

* * *

Another hour and a half passed before the vet finished administering care to the new mother and baby. Once the doctor packed up and drove away, Finn walked slowly back to the house.

He should've been dog tired. He'd been at the barn for hours and the fear of losing the mare and baby had been worse than stressful. But the joyous outcome had wiped all his weariness away. Now, in spite of his watch reading close to three in the morning, he was wide-awake.

When he reached the back door, a light was on in the kitchen. But when he stepped inside and spotted Mariah sitting at the breakfast bar, he was more than surprised.

"It's late," he said. "You should be in bed."

He hung his hat and jacket on a hall tree located a few steps away from the door. When he turned back around, Mariah was standing in front of him, her pale face strained, yet hopeful.

"The mare and baby?" she asked anxiously.

She honestly and truly cared. The realization filled him with incredible joy. "Both fine. The filly is already on her feet and nursing."

She let out a tiny groan of relief and then suddenly she was wrapping her arms around his neck and burying her face in his chest.

"Oh, Finn. I was so worried about you—and them."

Finn didn't bother to wait or wonder what had brought on this show of affection. She was holding him, touching him as though she never wanted to let him go. And that was all that mattered. With a hand beneath her chin, he tilted her mouth up to his and kissed her hard and quick. "Mariah, my sweet. Before I went out to check on the mares, I was fighting myself to keep from going to your bedroom."

Pink color stained her cheeks and he kissed the soft, heated skin while his nostrils pulled in the sweet, musky scent of her hair. Having her in his arms was like an incredible dream, one that he wanted to remember long after it ended.

"And I was lying awake," she whispered. "Hoping you would."

"And now?" he asked.

"Now all I can think about is being next to you. Like this."

Groaning deep in his throat, he lifted her into his arms and carried her straight to her bedroom.

The room was dark, but a yard lamp outside the window slanted strips of faint light across the bed and floor. The rumpled bedcovers exposed a wide expanse of white sheet.

Finn placed her in the middle of the bed, then stood staring down at her, allowing himself a moment to let his mind catch up with desire that was already gripping his body.

"I washed my hands at the barn," was all he could manage to utter. "But my clothes are dirty."

She pushed herself to a sitting position and reached for him. "I don't care about that," she whispered. "I'm going to take them off you anyway."

Her boldness sent a thrill of anticipation through him, and when her hands grabbed his belt and tugged him forward, he went willingly down beside her.

Wrapping his arms around her, he pulled her tight against him and pressed his lips to the middle of her forehead. "I can't believe this is happening," he mouthed against her. "After we came home from the meadow you were—so withdrawn. I was sure you were wishing you could wipe out everything that had happened with us."

Her hands came up to cradle his face. "I wasn't regretting, Finn. I was thinking. About myself. And you. I don't want to be afraid anymore. Afraid to let myself make love to you—to let myself be a woman."

Emotions he didn't quite understand poured into him and suddenly he felt as though he was ten feet tall and walking on air.

"Mariah, my sweet."

Finding her lips, he began to kiss her deeply, his mouth searching for the same wild excitement he'd felt when they'd kissed in the meadow. And he wasn't disappointed as it crashed into his head as quick as thunder after a violent flash of lightning.

Desire hummed along his veins as she opened the front of his shirt, then flattened her palms against his heated skin. While his lips continued to devour hers, he felt her fingers begin a search of their own. They lingered at his flat nipples, then slid to the small of his back before coming to rest on the waistband of his jeans.

Tearing his mouth away from hers, he climbed off the bed and started stripping away his clothing.

Mariah levered herself up on one elbow and watched him peel off a pair of navy blue boxer shorts. "I was going to do that," she complained.

"Next time, baby. We'll go slower. Right now I can't wait to touch you—get inside you."

With his clothing lying in a heap on the floor, he leaned over her to remove her gown and robe. Once they were tossed over his shoulder, he rejoined her on the bed, where she immediately rolled into him and swung her leg over his hips.

The sensation of her warm flesh touching his robbed his breath, and suddenly the pleasures attacking his senses were almost overwhelming. He wanted to taste her lips, her breasts, every curve and nuance of her body. He wanted to touch and hold and feel her soft skin sliding against his.

He'd torn his mouth from hers and was circling his mouth around one pert nipple when her fingers slid into his hair and gently tugged to garner his attention.

Tilting his head back, he saw that her gray eyes were half closed, her long black hair fanned against the white sheet. The swollen curves of her lips beckoned him. But then, so did the rest of her body, and he wanted to explore every inch of it. But if she was having reservations, he'd have to find the strength to get up and walk out of the room.

His throat thick, he shoved out the question. "Is something wrong?"

"No. But I think I should tell you that I haven't done this—well, in a long, long time."

Shifting slightly away from her, he propped his head on one hand and used the other to gently push a curtain of tangled waves from the side of her face. Uncertainty darkened her eyes, and the corner of her lips trembled.

Her vulnerability pierced him and all he wanted at that moment was to protect and reassure her. "Sweetheart, don't be scared. I'll be as gentle as you want me to be."

Her head moved back and forth against the mattress. "That's not worrying me," she mumbled. "I'm inexperienced. And I...just don't want to disappoint you."

Groaning with disbelief, Finn cradled her head against the curve of his neck. "Oh, darling, you couldn't do that. Having you in my arms—loving me. That's all I need from you." Tilting her head back, he traced a fingertip across her cheekbone. "Do I need to wear protection?"

Relief eased the tension on her face. "I'm on oral birth control. But maybe you'd feel safer with more protection—I won't mind."

Oddly enough, the idea of creating a baby with Mariah felt natural and right to him. What did that mean? That he was too full of lust to care? Or that Mariah had already become very, very special to him?

Squeezing those questions to the far fringes of his mind, Finn kissed her softly. "I don't need to feel safe. Not with you."

He heard the soft intake of her breath and then everything faded away as he brought his lips down on hers and her arms wrapped tightly around him.

He kissed her until his breath was gone and he was forced to tear his mouth away. While his lungs gorged themselves on oxygen, his hands made a sweeping exploration of her curves. Over her breasts, down her rib cage and across her flat belly. And then finally, the heated juncture between her thighs.

When he touched her there, she moaned and arched against him, inviting his fingers to slip inside. The slick warmth made his loins ache with need, and though he wanted to linger and enjoy each sensation to the fullest, his body refused to wait.

Rolling her onto her back, he poised himself over her and in the semidarkness of the room, her gaze locked with his. The connection sent a shock of awareness through him and suddenly he was almost afraid to make the final, ultimate link with her. Because he understood it would be irrevocable and life changing.

"Finn." As she breathed his name, the upper part of her body lifted from the mattress and molded itself against his. "Don't think. Or worry. Or make me wait another second," she pleaded.

Even if he'd wanted to, he couldn't turn back now. His heart, mind and soul were screaming for the chance to absorb her sweetness, to draw in the very essence of her being and hold it fast inside him.

"Mariah."

Her name was but a whisper as he blindly thrust himself into her welcoming body. Delicious heat instantly wrapped around him, rocking him with vibrations of pleasure so intense that his teeth snapped together.

Beneath him, Mariah's hips shifted upward, drawing him deeper within her. The movement was very nearly his undoing, but after a steadying breath, he regained enough control to begin a steady thrust.

Hot. Sweet. Perfect. On and on it went until his mind no longer belonged to him. At some point Mariah had taken control of his every movement, every thought that entered his brain. He'd become a willing prisoner and he never wanted her lips to release his, her arms to let go. If there was such a place as paradise, she was quickly leading him straight to it.

Somewhere in the back of his mind, he registered her soft moans and the frantic foray her hands were making upon his chest, across his belly and buttocks. Each touch of her fingers, each kiss of her lips upon his skin, scorched him, tightened every cell in his body until blood was roaring in his ears and his gasps for air were harsh and rapid.

"Finn. Oh, Finn."

The sound of his name coming from her lips was all it took to break the last fragile thread of his control. With his hands clenching her buttocks, he held her hips tight against his until a burst of light exploded behind his eyes and suddenly he was breaking into tiny pieces. The ragged bits flew to the ceiling, then floated aimlessly around the dark room before they finally settled slowly back to his sated, sweaty body.

Yet even after the axis of his world righted itself, Finn recognized that a part of him was now missing. And he had the very real and scary feeling that the lost piece of him was his heart.

Chapter Nine

Three days later, Mariah was in her classroom, gathering the books and papers scattered across the desk top. Less than five minutes ago, the final bell for the day had sounded and the students had scattered out the door. Except for tall, brown-haired Lucia. With a heavy backpack fastened to her shoulders and a sweater tied around her waist, the teenager paused at the corner of Mariah's desk.

"Did you need to talk to me about something, Lucia?"

Winding a finger through the end of her ponytail, the girl nervously chewed on her bottom lip. Mariah wished she had the right to give her a reassuring hug. Although Lucia made excellent grades, Mariah understood the girl's home life was not the best in the world.

"It's not about our assignment for tomorrow, Ms. Montgomery. I've just been wondering. Since school is almost out for summer…I mean…will you be coming back next fall?"

Next fall? For the past few days Mariah hadn't allowed herself to think too much about the future, even the near future. Enjoying the fleeting time she had with Finn was all that mattered. But Lucia's question was forcing her to picture the future and at this moment, it looked very uncertain.

Frowning thoughtfully, she asked, "What makes you ask that?"

The teenager blushed. "Well, uh, some of the kids have been saying that you're going to Nevada. I sure hope that isn't true, Ms. Montgomery. I'd really miss you."

Mariah had no idea how the rumor had gotten started about her going to Nevada. She didn't think Sage had spoken to anyone about it, but that day in the lounge when they'd been discussing the subject, someone could have overheard their conversation. Now apparently the rumor was all over the school.

Smiling at the girl, she reached for a tote bag. "Don't worry, Lucia. If I go to Nevada it will only be for a short visit. I'll be back for the next school year."

Grinning with relief, Lucia bounced on her toes. "That's great, Ms. Montgomery! Really great!"

Mariah smiled, then glanced pointedly at her wristwatch. "The bus will be leaving in a few minutes. You don't want to miss it."

"Oh! I gotta run!"

The teenager raced out of the room and Mariah thoughtfully began to load the tote bag with the things she needed to carry home.

Home to Stallion Canyon. Strange, how much that

image had changed in her mind. For the past few months, she'd thought of little else but selling the place and moving to a new home and a new life. She'd wholeheartedly believed everything would be better for her and Harry if the ranch was out of their lives once and for all.

But now that Finn was here, everything had changed. She was seeing the ranch as it had been years ago, a beautiful home where she'd lived and loved and laughed with her father and sister. And hope had begun to stir within her. Hope that the impossible might happen and she could somehow manage to keep Stallion Canyon.

Face it, Mariah. You've fallen in love with Finn. He's the reason Stallion Canyon looks so good to you now. With him living in your house and sleeping in your bed, the place feels perfect to you. But sooner or later, with or without Harry, he'll be leaving. And then what will you have? Besides a broken heart?

Mariah shoved a stack of tests papers into the tote and refused to let the mocking voice prick the happy thought of going home to Finn. The time would come soon enough to face the sad fact of losing her home, her baby and her man.

Back on Stallion Canyon, Finn sat in the kitchen, gently nudging the toe of his boot against the floor to keep the old rocking chair in motion. Harry had already finished a bottle and now his blue eyes were closed in sleep. Finn needed to rise and carry the boy to his crib, but each time he held Harry in his arms he was fascinated with his tiny features and the little hands that were already learning to grip. He loved feeling the baby's warm weight resting against his chest, while he dreamed of the day his son would become a man.

"Harry is going to be as tall as me, don't you think?"

Across the room, Linda continued to fold laundry atop the breakfast bar. "Probably. But do you ever wonder if you might be setting yourself up for a disappointment? It's not right to talk about the dead, but I have to say that Aimee was no angel."

Maybe she hadn't been perfect, Finn thought. But that hardly mattered anymore. Mariah was the only woman he could think about. Making love to her these past few nights had changed him. Now as he looked toward the future, he could see only her and Harry in his life. If that meant he'd fallen in love with her, he didn't know. He only knew that she'd become just as important to him as little Harry.

"The DNA isn't back yet. But Harry is mine," Finn said with confidence.

"Hmm, and then what? You'll be taking him home to Nevada?" she asked.

He hadn't expected Linda to prod him about his personal plans. At least not until they had complete confirmation of the baby's DNA. But considering the time and emotions the woman had invested in Harry, she had a right to ask.

"That's right. That's where my home is." He looked at her. "Why? You didn't think I'd be leaving him here, did you?"

She cast him a sly look. "Actually, I was thinking you might be considering making your home here. What with all the fencing and other work you've been doing around here, you'd think this was your ranch."

For the past four days, Finn had been working diligently to patch sagging wire and leaning fence posts so he'd have a secure pasture to turn out the geldings.

Or he'd told himself that was the reason. In truth, he should be making arrangements to get the horses and mares shipped back to Nevada. Instead, he wanted to find every excuse he could to keep them here, and more important, to keep himself here.

"I like keeping busy. And this place needs lots of work to get it back into shape."

Frowning, she picked up a towel and shook out the wrinkles. "So someone else can buy it?"

Finn looked down at the sleeping baby. In years to come, Stallion Canyon should be handed over to Harry, or at the very least shared with any children that Mariah might have in the future.

Mariah having children with some other man. The ranch being sold to a stranger. The thoughts were agonizing to Finn, and yet sooner rather than later, they were realities he would have to face.

He looked over to Linda. "The real estate agent called Mariah last night to let her know that two different men are interested in the property. One wants to harvest the timber on it. The other one wants to plow the meadows and grow potatoes."

Both ideas sickened Finn. Stallion Canyon was a wild, beautiful mixture of mountain ridges and valley floors that stretched along a narrow, winding river. It wasn't meant to be stripped of timber or plowed into fields. It was a land to raise horses, not lumber or vegetables.

Linda scowled. "I suppose they'll be coming out to look the place over. I hope I'm not here when either of them come. I—well, Ray is surely turning over in his grave. That's all I can say."

She picked up the basket and left the room. Finn rose to his feet and carried Harry to the nursery. As he carefully put the baby to bed, the whole situation gnawed at him like an empty stomach begging for a bite of food. Mariah, Harry and Stallion Canyon. This past week all three had begun to feel as though they belonged to him. Was he thinking liked a damned fool? Or was he thinking like a man who'd finally figured out what he wanted in life?

Back in Alturas, Mariah was about to leave the school parking lot when she spotted Sage hurrying toward the driver's side of her car.

Mariah pressed the button to lower the window. "What's wrong? Car won't start?"

Sage smiled. "No problems. I wanted to catch you—I thought we might stop by the Silver Slipper and have an ice cream together before you go home."

"You're a sweetheart to ask, but I really don't have the time. Linda will be expecting me."

Sage frowned. "All you have to do is pick up your cell and call her. I'm sure she wouldn't mind staying with Harry another thirty minutes. Besides, Harry's father is there. He can look after his son."

Yes, Finn was there. The fact made her heart smile. It made her want to rush home and spend every precious minute she could with him. "He's been staying pretty busy around the ranch. Besides working with the horses, he's been repairing fences and working on the irrigation pump."

Sage's expression turned to sly speculation. "Hmm. Why would Finn be doing all that? He'll be leaving soon and you're selling the ranch."

Actually, Mariah had been asking herself the very same things. She could understand the time and work he put in on the horses. They belonged to him. But the ranch was a different matter. Was he doing it for her? Because he knew she had no money or means to make upgrades to the property?

"Finn isn't the sort of man who can just sit around. He wants to keep busy."

Sage didn't look at all convinced, but mercifully dropped the subject.

"Well, call Linda," she said. "I'll meet you at the Slipper."

Assuming that Mariah would agree to follow, Sage turned away from the window to leave.

Mariah called out to her. "Sage, I don't have time. It's not just keeping Linda overtime. I have—things to do. Supper to cook for Finn."

Sage's brows shot up. "Oh? Sounds like this whole thing has turned into a family situation to me."

Mariah sheepishly glanced away from Sage's inquisitive face. If her friend only knew how she'd been making love to Finn these past few nights, she'd be properly shocked. But nothing about sharing her bed with Finn felt shocking. It felt right and special. And though she was probably crazy for thinking of her and Finn and Harry as a family, she couldn't help it.

"So what if it is?"

Sage groaned. "Oh, Mariah, don't tell me you're really falling for the guy? I mean, I know I've always wanted you to find somebody and I've been teasing you a bit about him. But seriously he's—well, he's one of Aimee's castoffs! You can't be getting serious thoughts about the man!"

Mariah's fingers unconsciously touched her fingers to the cross dangling against her throat. Aimee had already ruined one relationship for Mariah. She couldn't let her sister's memory interfere with her feelings for Finn. If she did, she'd be letting Aimee win a second time.

With her foot on the brake, Mariah pulled the gearshift into Drive. "I have to go," she said curtly. "I'll see you tomorrow."

Reaching a hand through the window, Sage squeezed Mariah's shoulder. "I'm sorry, Mariah. I shouldn't have said that. It was an awful thing to say. Finn is your business, not mine."

"Forget it," Mariah muttered. "I'll see you tomorrow."

She gave the other woman a halfhearted wave and quickly drove away.

At the same time on Stallion Canyon, Finn was working in the meadow, attaching a huge pipe to the irrigation pump, when his cell phone rang. Tossing the heavy wrench aside, he reached for the phone and was somewhat surprised to hear his father's voice on the other end of the connection.

"Did I catch you at a bad time?" Orin asked.

Still working to catch his breath, Finn said, "No. Just doing a bit of plumbing on an irrigation system. I think I'm close to having it going again."

"Irrigation system? Finn, what in hell is going on up there? I thought this trip was all about a baby."

Finn wiped a hand across his sweaty brow. "It is about Harry. But I can't just sit idle while we're waiting on the DNA results to come back. There's plenty of work to be done around here."

Orin spluttered. "There's a hell of a lot of work to do here on the Horn, too. Your home, remember?"

The testiness in Orin's voice put a grimace on Finn's face. "Yes, Dad. I remember. Is anything wrong there?"

Orin sighed. "No. I was calling just to check on you. I didn't mean to go off like that. It's just been—well, different with you away this long, Finn. I miss you. I want you to hurry up and get back here."

Finn leaned his back against the wheel on the irrigation line as warring emotions tore through him. From the time he was born, the Silver Horn had been his home, and he loved his family with every fiber of his being. But now there were new feelings growing inside him. For Harry and Mariah. And for Stallion Canyon. In spite of his ties back in Nevada, and in spite of the uncertainty of the future, he felt his roots sinking into this fertile land.

"Well, I've missed seeing everyone there. How are the horses? Any problems?"

"Not really. We've bred the last two mares. So the spring breeding is all wrapped up. Dandi, the yearling with the curly mane, cut her foot. We're not sure how. But Doc Pheeters has sewn it and seems to think it won't be a problem. Other than a scar."

"That's good." Finn's gaze wandered over the meadow. With the pump going, he could irrigate until the grass was growing thick and lush. The mustangs would thrive here. If only he had more time. But he expected that one day next week the DNA test would arrive in the mail. And then Mariah would be out of school and he'd have no reason to linger here on Stallion Canyon. Unless she asked him to stay. "Uh—did Clancy speak with you about the mustangs?"

There was a long pause. "No. What are you talking about?"

Damn it, he should have known Clancy wouldn't say

anything to their father about the mustangs. His brother didn't want to hear Orin yell any more than Finn did.

"I purchased ten mustangs from Mariah. They were the last ones she had here on the ranch. Five mares, four geldings and one stallion. A few nights ago, one of the mares foaled a filly, so I actually have eleven now. The baby is precious, Dad. She's bright chestnut with four white feet and a snip on her nose. She's going to be a real looker. And the other four mares will be delivering soon."

The pride that Finn was feeling was quickly smashed as Orin muttered several curse words. And for a split second Finn considered ending the call. But this was his father, and sooner or later he was going to have to deal with the situation. Might as well be now rather than later, he decided.

"What are you thinking, Finn? You know you can't put them on the Horn! Hell, your grandfather is probably going to have a stroke when he hears about this."

Angry and hurt, Finn pushed away from the irrigation wheel to stare across the sea of grass where spots of river glittered through the limbs like diamonds hanging from a Christmas tree.

"Then don't tell him!" Finn said tightly. "Because neither of you have anything to worry about. I damn well don't plan on bringing them to the Horn!"

"Then what are you planning to do?" Orin demanded.

"I haven't decided yet. But you can be sure of one thing. Wherever the mustangs go, I'll go with them! Now I have to go. Good-bye, Dad."

"Finn! Listen to me! I—"

Finn ended the connection and drew in several deep breaths in hopes it would cool his boiling blood. He'd probably just burned a bunch of bridges with that last shot he'd flung at his father, but Finn wasn't going to regret it. It was high time that his family realized he was a thirty-two-year-old man with dreams and desires of his own. He couldn't live his life according to a Calhoun edict.

That night as Mariah and Finn sat at the dinner table, she worriedly watched as he pushed the food around on his plate. From the moment he walked into the house this evening, he'd seemed preoccupied. Now as her gaze slid over his rugged features, she could see lines of fatigue around his eyes and mouth. But she had a feeling it wasn't fatigue that was making him withdrawn. Something else was wrong.

"If you don't care for the pork chops, Finn, I'll be happy to fix you something else."

His expression rueful, he glanced across the table at her. "I'm sorry, Mariah. The food is delicious. You've cooked everything just right."

To prove his point, he shoveled up a forkful of mashed potatoes and gravy and lifted it to his mouth.

She reached for her iced tea and took a long sip before she casually asked, "How's baby Poppy?"

A halfhearted grin crossed his face and the weak reaction told Mariah that something was definitely wrong. Normally, the mere mention of the newborn filly would light up Finn's whole demeanor. Tonight there was a sadness dimming his eyes and the sight troubled her greatly.

"She's getting spunkier every day. I might turn them into the meadow with the geldings tomorrow and give the baby a chance to stretch her legs."

"What about the mares?" Mariah asked, as she offered Harry a spoonful of pureed fruit.

"I'm happy with how they're looking. The brown mare's milk bag is getting full so I expect her to deliver in the next day or two."

Harry smacked his hands on the high chair tray and opened his mouth for another bite. As Mariah continued to feed the baby, she said, "I hope all the babies are born before it's time for you to ship them back to Nevada."

The silence that followed her comment had her looking over to see him staring moodily toward the windows behind her shoulder. Mariah decided it wasn't the time to prod him with questions. At best, her time with Finn was limited; she didn't want to waste it by picking and prodding at him.

After a moment, his gaze snapped back to hers and though he attempted to smile, she could see his heart was hardly in it. "Yes, I hope it will work out that way, too."

The remainder of the meal passed with Finn saying very little and Mariah focusing on feeding Harry the last of his food. Afterward, Finn helped her with the dishes, then excused himself to attend to chores at the barn.

While he was out of the house, Mariah readied Harry for bed, then graded a stack of test papers. She'd just finished the schoolwork and was carrying Harry toward the nursery when she heard Finn enter the house through the back door.

Changing directions, she met him in the breezeway. "I was on my way to the nursery to change Harry's diaper," she told him. "Was everything all right at the barn?"

An annoyed frown put a crease between his brows. "Everything was fine. Why do you keep asking me?"

Losing her patience, she snapped, "Maybe because

you're acting like you've lost your best friend. And you won't tell me what's wrong."

Not waiting on his reply, she turned and walked straight to the nursery. She'd laid Harry on the dressing table and was in the process of unsnapping the legs of his pants when she heard Finn's boots tapping against the tiled floor of the nursery.

"Let me do that," he said softly as he brushed her hands out of the way.

Saying nothing, she stood to one side and watched him deftly deal with Harry's soiled diaper, all the while talking to the boy in a hushed, gentle voice. When he had Harry dressed again, he positioned him over his shoulder, then turned toward Mariah.

"I'm sorry for snapping at you, Mariah." He blew out a heavy breath. "I have a lot on my mind—but that's no excuse."

Mariah had a lot on her mind, too. And all of it had to do with him and Harry. And where she might fit into their lives.

Placing her hand on his arm, she gave him a wobbly smile. "I'm sorry, too. Would you like to go sit on the back porch? I can make us some coffee if you'd like."

"Sounds nice. I'll take Harry with me," he told her.

A few minutes later, Mariah stepped onto the back porch, carrying a tray with the coffee and a few slices of pound cake. As she placed it on a small table, she looked over to see that Finn was sitting in the rocker with Harry already asleep in his arms.

He said, "Harry looked around for a minute or two and then his eyelids got droopy. I must be a dull daddy. Each time I hold him, he falls asleep."

Mariah smiled. "He feels contented and safe when you hold him. That's why he falls asleep."

"Well, now that you're here with the coffee, I'll put him in his playpen."

He carried Harry over to the playpen and covered him with a quilt to protect him from the cool evening air. Once he'd resumed his seat in the rocker, Mariah served him the coffee and cake, then sank into the chair angled to his left arm.

As she helped herself to a cup, he said, "I finished working on the irrigation pump this afternoon. So far it's working as it should."

"That's great. You must be a regular handyman. Dad always called a repairman out whenever it went on the blink."

He shrugged. "Dad made us boys learn to do other chores besides ride horses and chase cows. He always reminded us that ranching was much more than taking care of livestock."

"Sounds like your father is a wise man."

He turned a thoughtful gaze toward the mountain ridge to the east as he sipped at the coffee. "I used to think he could do no wrong. And I still love and respect him. But—"

Mariah gripped the handle of her cup as she waited for him to continue. When he didn't she asked, "Has something happened with your family, Finn?"

The shake of his head was so negligible, she barely caught it.

"Not exactly. Dad called while I was out at the meadow working on the pump. I told him about buying the mustangs and he threw a little cussing fit."

Mariah's heart was suddenly aching for him. She

knew what it was like to feel unappreciated and misunderstood. And she didn't want that for Finn. She could see for herself that he was a hardworking, responsible man. He deserved his family's consideration.

"So what did you tell him?" Mariah asked.

She watched his jaw tighten and the corners of his mouth curve downward. Apparently, the conversation he'd had with his father was still making him angry. Which surprised her. Since Finn had come to the ranch, she hadn't ever seen him in this dark of a mood.

He said, "That I'd find some other place to put them. And wherever the mustangs go, that's where I'll go."

She drew in a sharp breath. "Oh, Finn. That was a pretty definitive thing to say, wasn't it?"

"Yeah. It was pretty final, all right. Especially considering that after I said it, I hung up the phone," he said flatly. "Now I have to decide what to do. About the horses and myself."

Leaning forward, she studied his profile in the waning twilight. "Finn, what is this going to mean? About Harry? And—"

"We're still waiting on the DNA," he interrupted.

"We both know that's just a formality."

He stared at her. "A formality? You insisted on it!"

Her gaze dropped sheepishly to her lap. "I know," she mumbled. "But I felt we both needed that certainty. And I guess a part of me was grasping at straws. Wanting a reason to keep Harry here longer. And wanting to keep you here longer, too."

"Oh, Mariah."

Suddenly he was on his feet, reaching for both her hands. With her heart beating wildly, she allowed him to draw her from the chair and fold her into his arms.

"I don't want you to worry about the test. About Harry or us. I just want you to touch me, love me and make me forget everything. Except this."

His mouth came down on hers and she melted against him as his lips promised a pleasure that only he could give her. And as her mouth accepted the thrust of his tongue, the doubts and fears that were racing through her mind only moments ago were suddenly wiped away with a sweeping flame of desire.

"Let's get Harry and go inside," he whispered.

She smiled against his lips. "It's pretty early to go to bed. Especially when I'm not a bit sleepy."

He chuckled. "It's going to be a long, long time before you get any sleep, my darling."

Chapter Ten

Nearly a week later, on late Thursday afternoon, Finn was in the mares' paddock, studying their condition and trying to determine how long it would be before the last three dropped their foals. Two days ago the brown mare had safely delivered a black colt, and Finn was thrilled to see he was thriving and already running and bucking alongside his mother.

To help him get an idea of their due dates, Mariah had searched through some of the last notes Aimee had recorded regarding the ranch's breeding schedule. The dates had given him a fairly close idea of when the mares would deliver, but sometimes they were as unpredictable as women. The last thing he wanted to do was put them on a horse van to travel several hours. But time was winding down and sooner rather than later, he was going to have to decide what to do with the mustangs.

You have a hell of a lot more than the mustangs to

worry about, Finn. Mariah has built herself a home smack in the middle of your heart. So what are you going to do about her?

The nagging voice in his head prompted Finn to walk over to the wooden fence and stare thoughtfully toward the house. Tomorrow was Mariah's last day at school. And they both expected Harry's DNA test to arrive at any time now. Once that happened there would be no reason for him to continue to stay here on Stallion Canyon. Unless Mariah asked him to. And so far that hadn't happened. But then Stallion Canyon wasn't going to be hers for much longer. She might feel it was pointless to ask him.

During the past week their relationship had grown even deeper. At least, it had felt that way to Finn. Each night she'd made love to him as though a lifetime of kissing him, holding him, would never be enough. Yet she'd never whispered a word to him about love, or forever, or the future. And now, as time was closing in, he was beginning to wonder if she'd become his bed partner only to ease her loneliness, not because she was falling in love with him.

Was that what he wanted? To hear Mariah say she loved him? Because he'd already fallen in love with her? For the past few days Finn had been in a perpetual wrestling match with those questions. Now he was beginning to realize it had been wrong of him to expect Mariah to open her heart to him first. Especially when he'd not said a word to her about love or marriage, something he should've done days ago. But he'd hesitated because he'd wanted to make sure what he was feeling was more than infatuation or lust.

Finn had never been in love before. As a very young

man, he'd thought the attachment he'd felt to Janelle was love, but now he could see his relationship with her had been little more than a childhood crush that had lasted longer than it should have. What he felt for Mariah was much, much deeper. He wanted the connection they'd built between them to go on forever. If that was love, then he needed to decide what it meant for both of their futures.

Thoughts about Mariah were continuing to roll through his head when he suddenly spotted a man and woman he'd never seen before step out the back door of the house. Dressed in dark office-type clothing, the woman had short gray hair and was carrying some sort of briefcase beneath one arm. The man was tall and wearing traditional ranch clothing. From this distance, Finn guessed him to be somewhere in his fifties.

The two paused on the edge of the patio, then the woman pointed toward the barn. At that moment, Finn realized the woman had to be the real estate agent Mariah had hired to sell Stallion Canyon. Obviously, the man with her was a serious buyer. Otherwise, the woman would've never bothered to bring him all the way out here to view the property.

With a sick feeling swimming in the pit of his stomach, Finn let himself out of the paddock and walked over to the shed row. By then the man and woman were fast approaching, and not wanting to appear evasive or rude, he forced himself to stand there and wait for them to arrive.

The woman introduced herself to Finn as Ella Clark, a real estate agent from Alturas. The man with her was Don Larson, a rancher looking for a larger spread to run cattle. After a short exchange of small talk, Finn decided

Larson appeared friendly enough. But all the while the other man was talking, Finn was trying to picture him working around these barns and arena, of him living in the house and perhaps even sleeping in the same room where he and Mariah made love. The idea sickened Finn more than he'd ever imagined it would. It also made him realize just how much he'd come to think of Stallion Canyon as his home.

Smiling at Finn, Ella said, "Mr. Larson is looking for good grazing land. I've been telling him how the Montgomery family has raised horses on this land for years, so it's bound to have a good supply of grass."

"It's like any place else. It has to rain to have grass," Finn said bluntly.

The woman's brows shot up, while Larson asked, "And how often does it rain around here?"

"I'm not the one to ask. I'm just a temporary resident." The admission was worse than coughing up nails, Finn thought. But the truth just the same.

"Oh," the man said. "I thought you worked here."

Finn grimaced. "There are no hired hands here on Stallion Canyon. And pretty soon there won't be any horses."

Ella Clark awkwardly cleared her throat. "Things must've changed around here."

"Yeah. You could say that," Finn replied. "Now if you'll excuse me, I'll let you show Mr. Larson the rest of the property."

Finn quickly left the two of them and headed to the house. When he let himself into the kitchen, he found Linda sitting at the breakfast bar, sniffing back tears. Across the room, Harry was sitting in his high chair working diligently to eat a graham cracker.

"What's the matter?" he asked Linda.

She used the corner of a paper towel to dab her eyes. "To have people traipsing through here like—this place already belongs to someone else." She sucked in a deep breath and looked at him. "When I think of Ray I can hardly bear it."

Since Finn had gotten to know Linda, he was beginning to understand more and more that the woman had been very close to Mariah's father. And that fact was even more apparent as he watched tears roll down her face.

"I met them out at the barn," was all he could say. "He's only looking. It's hardly a done deal."

"If he doesn't buy, the next one will," she said bitterly, then turned her back to him.

There wasn't much Finn could say to that. Instead of trying, he walked over and plucked Harry out of the high chair. Holding the boy in his arms always comforted him. But this evening he could only think of how much his son was about to lose.

A short while later, at the end of the long gravel drive leading to the ranch house, Mariah stopped her car at a rural mailbox fastened to a fat fence post. She'd lowered the window on the driver's side and was plucking a stack of envelopes from the metal box when the sound of an approaching vehicle had her peering through the windshield.

She recognized Linda's old red Ford heading toward her, and from the wake of dust billowing behind it, the woman was in a hurry. Apparently she'd gotten Finn to watch Harry so she could leave early.

By the time Mariah closed the mailbox and tossed the correspondence in the passenger seat, Linda's vehicle was drawing near. Mariah lowered the passenger window and waited for Linda to stop alongside the car to give her some sort of explanation as to why she was leaving early. Instead, the truck sped on, even as Mariah waved at the woman.

Puzzled by Linda's unusual behavior, Mariah started to drive on, but a piece of mail suddenly caught her eye. With her foot back on the brake, she twisted her head to read the return address.

The word *Laboratory* was all she needed to see. The results of Harry and Finn's DNA test had finally arrived. One way or the other, they were about to find out whether Finn had a legal right to the boy, or if the search for Harry's real father was just now beginning.

With Linda's unusual behavior momentarily pushed to the back of her mind, Mariah finished the short drive to the ranch house and hurried inside through the back entrance.

Immediately she spotted Finn standing in front of the microwave. Harry was propped against his shoulder and at the moment was emitting hungry wails around the tiny fist crammed in his mouth.

"Hi, darlin'," he greeted. "I'm heating Harry a bottle. Linda's already gone. Maybe you saw her."

Mariah walked to the breakfast bar and placed the stack of mail on one end. "All I saw was a blur. She was flooring that old Ford. She must've been running late to an appointment in town."

The microwave dinged and Finn pulled out the warmed bottle. "No appointment. She was upset. I suggested she go on home and let me handle Harry."

"Upset?" Mariah frowned. "Linda is always a rock. Did she get bad news or something?"

Finn carried Harry over to the bar, and after he'd taken a seat on one of the stools, offered the baby his bottle. With Harry happily drinking, Finn looked up at Mariah and she couldn't help but notice that the usual sparkle in his blue eyes was definitely missing.

He said, "She considered it bad news. The real estate agent and a potential buyer just left the place a few minutes ago. Linda is pretty torn up that the ranch might be selling soon."

A heavy weight of doom fell on Mariah's shoulders and sank to the bottom of her stomach. "Ms. Clark called me earlier today and informed me she'd be showing the place today. I could hardly tell her that now wasn't a good time. No time would be a good time."

"Really?"

A month ago she would've been shouting hallelujah at the idea of the ranch being taken off her hands. Now the whole idea made her sick. Was that what being in love did to a woman? she wondered. Was that the reason she was looking at everything differently? This place had once seemed such a burden. Now it felt like a home again. And all because of Finn. But he would be going back to Nevada soon. It would be irresponsible of her to dream the foolish dream of keeping him and Harry here, wouldn't it?

Her throat suddenly aching, she said, "I've come to realize how much I still love this place, Finn. But I… Well, we'll talk about Stallion Canyon later. Right now, there's something more important."

She picked up the piece of mail and with a trembling hand, thrust it at him. "The results are here. I think you should be the one to open it. This is all about you and Harry."

His gaze gently probed hers. "It's all about you, too," he said quietly.

Tears stung the back of her eyes and in a hoarse voice, she said, "Please open the damned thing before I decide to set a match to it."

With one hand occupied with holding Harry's bottle, he used the other to lift the envelope to his mouth. Using his teeth, he tore off the end, then fished out the contents.

As he began to read, Mariah suddenly found herself standing next to his shoulder. And in spite of all the certainty she'd felt about Finn being Harry's father, her heart was pounding and her mouth had gone dry with fear. What if the DNA didn't match? Finn would be crushed. And so would she.

Eons seemed to drag by before he finally spoke, and by then Mariah's emotions had run the gamut from panic to joy and everything in between.

"I am Harry's father," he said simply.

Mariah began to tremble all over and she wasn't sure if the reaction was from relief or the realization that everything was suddenly coming to an end. Harry was truly Finn's child. And even though he'd asked her to travel with him to his family ranch in Nevada, the short stay there to help get Harry accustomed to new surroundings would be only a temporary bandage on the gaping wound in her heart.

Her hand came to rest on Finn's shoulder and as she looked down at Harry's cheek pressed against his father's strong chest, she could only feel a sense of rightness. Harry would always be loved. And dear God, that was the thing she wanted most for him.

"Are you happy?"

He looked up at her and she was relieved to see that the sparkle had returned to his eyes.

"In my heart Harry was already mine. But it's great to see it verified. How do you feel about the news?"

Her fingers squeezed his shoulder. "I wouldn't have wanted anyone but you to be Harry's father. That's the way I feel."

A slow grin lifted the corner of his mouth. "When Harry gets finished with this bottle, I'm going to kiss you."

Chuckling now, she bent and kissed him gently on the cheek. "I'm going to remind you of that."

That night after dinner, as Finn helped Mariah clear away the remnants of their meal, she had little to say and he could see that her thoughts were preoccupied with something. Now that the matter of the DNA test was resolved and her job was finished for the summer, she had to be wondering what was next for the three of them.

Finn realized she deserved to know his feelings and what his plans included. But how could he explain to her that everything inside him was scattered and racing in all different directions? The plans he'd had when he'd first arrived on Stallion Canyon no longer appealed to him. Now when he thought of his and Harry's future, Mariah had to be in it. But was that what she wanted too?

"Have you called your family to let them know about the DNA?"

Her question interrupted his thoughts and he glanced over to see her scraping scraps of leftover food into the garbage container.

Running a hand through his hair, he said, "No. What with feeding the horses and having dinner, I haven't had a quiet moment yet."

"Then go on and make your call," she urged him. "I'll finish things here."

He hesitated. "There's no hurry about it."

Placing the plate in the bottom of the sink, she turned to him. A puzzled frown creased her forehead. "Finn, if I didn't know better, I'd think you're putting off talking to your family."

Realizing he looked more than sheepish, he wiped a hand over his face. "To tell you the truth, I'm not looking forward to it."

Her brows pulled together. "But why? I thought you were thrilled about the test results."

"I am. But they'll be asking me questions that— Well, after the awful conversation I had with Dad, I'm not sure what I want to tell them—about anything."

"If you feel awkward about calling your father, then talk to one of your brothers," she suggested.

Yes, he could speak with Rafe. Of all his brothers he was closest to him. But even Rafe would want to know his plans, and Finn wasn't ready to give him, or anyone, answers. Not until he knew exactly how Mariah felt about him.

"I will, Mariah. Just give me time."

Her expression full of concern, she stepped closer and rested her palms against his chest. "Tell me what's bothering you, Finn. And don't give me the old 'everything is fine' routine. I can see you're troubled."

He let out a heavy breath. "I'm not troubled. I'm thinking." Forcing a smile on his face, he looped his arms around her in a loose embrace. "I haven't even congratulated you for finishing the school year. Are you excited about summer vacation?"

She smiled gently up at him and Finn desperately

wanted to crush his mouth down on hers and carry her to the bedroom. To feel the need in her lips and the urgency of her hands moving over him would send all the anguish and worry from his mind. But Harry was still awake. And once Finn started making love to her, he didn't want anything to interrupt them.

"I always enjoy my time off in the summer. But come next fall I'll be anxious to get back in the classroom. Teaching is a part of me, I guess."

And her teaching job was here. She couldn't have made that any plainer, Finn thought.

"Hmm. Well, I never was a teacher's pet. But maybe there's hope for me yet." He kissed her gently in the middle of her forehead, then dropped his hold on her. "If you don't mind, Mariah, I think I'll go out to the barn for a while and check on the mares."

"I don't mind. Take your time."

He planted another kiss on the top of her head, then left the house with Mariah staring worriedly after him.

It was nearly dark by the time she heard Finn return to the house. As his boots echoed on the tiled floor of the breezeway, she carefully tucked a blanket around Harry's shoulders. The baby was growing every day. Before long he would be sitting alone and crawling. And then he would be walking and racing all over the place. But she wouldn't be chasing after him. Not unless some sort of miracle happened. And so far in her life, she hadn't experienced any of those.

She turned away from the crib and was stepping through the open doorway when she crashed head-on into Finn. His big hands grabbed her shoulders and steadied her.

"Mariah! I was just coming to see if you were here in the nursery. Did I hurt you?"

"No," she quickly assured him. "I heard you crossing the breezeway, but I thought you'd gone to your bedroom. Sorry I wasn't watching where I was walking."

His hands began to knead her shoulders. "Don't be sorry. I like being whammed in the belly by a beautiful brunette."

Beautiful. Not until Finn had come into her life had she ever felt truly beautiful. Oh, she'd been told in so many words by other men that she was attractive, but none of the compliments had come across as sincere. But something about the way Finn looked at her, touched her, made her feel special and womanly.

Laughing softly, she splayed her hands against his midsection. "I won't wham you again, but maybe I can think of doing something else you might like."

He pulled her close and whispered against her lips, "Is Harry asleep?"

"Yes." She slipped her arms around his waist. "How was everything at the barn? Did you have a good visit with the mares?"

"I'll tell you about it later," he said, then with a heady groan he closed the tiny space between their lips.

Minutes later, in the dusky dark interior of the bedroom, Mariah pushed everything from her mind except Finn. With his mouth fastened over hers and the thrusts of his hips driving into hers, thinking became impossible. Tiny bolts of lightning were exploding, creating a glorious network against the stormy swell of her emotions. Inside and out, from her head to her feet, every feminine cell in her body was glowing and aching for the man in her arms.

Pleasure was pouring through her and she wanted to give it all back to him. She wanted to thrill him more and more. She wanted to love him until their hearts had merged so tightly together that years of time could never untangle them.

Suddenly his mouth lifted from hers and his hoarse voice whispered against her cheek. "Oh, Mariah, Mariah—my sweet darling. I can't get enough of you."

"Love me, Finn," she breathlessly pleaded. "Keep on loving me."

With a needy groan, he rolled them over until his back was against the mattress and Mariah was riding the urgent thrusts of his hips. Gripping his shoulders, she hung on, matching his rhythm even though her lungs were burning, her heart pounding out of control. Like tangled threads, her body grew tighter and tighter until she was wrapped in captive knots.

She was crying his name, searching for relief, when he suddenly crushed her to him and buried his face in the side of her neck. In the next instant his warmth began to spill into her and suddenly she felt everything at once as sensations rocketed through her, blinding her with an ecstasy so great it momentarily stopped her breathing. And like a cornflower beneath a hot, hot sun, she bowed, then wilted completely.

It was long moments later before Mariah realized her cheek was resting against the sheet rather than the cool, grassy ground and the heat of the sun was actually the warmth of Finn's chest pressed against her back.

Turning into all that delicious warmth, she wrapped her arm around his waist and rested her head in the hollow of his shoulder.

With a contented groan, he lifted a hand to her hair and slowly stroked the thick strands lying against her back.

"Do you know how it makes me feel to have you here in my arms like this?" he asked.

His voice was still husky with desire, and the sound touched her as much as the calloused tips of his fingers. Both sent shivers of pleasure through her that knew no bounds.

"No," she whispered. "How does it make you feel?"

"Perfect. Absolutely perfect."

"Nothing is perfect," she said drowsily.

He chuckled softly. "You're wrong. I'm holding perfection in my arms."

Tilting her head back, she studied his face in the growing darkness. "You must have a bottle of wine or something hidden out at the horse barn. You're thinking is a little cockeyed."

Groaning, he pressed a kiss to her forehead. "My thinking has never been better."

"Really? This evening during dinner you seemed pretty mixed up about something."

His expression softened as his hand gently cupped the side of her face. "Hmm, I think I've been mixed up ever since I came to Stallion Canyon and laid eyes on you for the first time."

Her heart slowed as she anxiously tried to read the emotions on his face. There was a serious intensity in his eyes that she hadn't seen before. And she was suddenly afraid to guess what it might mean.

"That's understandable," she said. "Learning about Harry—that he was most likely your son, then coming up here to meet us—that had to be traumatic for you."

"I'm not talking about Harry now. I'm talking about you. And what you've done to me."

Lifting her hand, she pushed her fingers through the crisp burnished waves above his ear. "And what is that?" she asked softly.

Bending his head, he rubbed his cheek against her. "You've made me fall in love with you, my darling."

Mariah desperately needed to breathe, but her lungs seemed to have suddenly quit working.

"In love?" she whispered. "Is that what you just said?"

Drawing her closer, his hand made wide, sweeping circles across back. "That's exactly what I said. Why do you sound so surprised? Haven't I pretty much been saying that to you every night this past week or so?"

She'd wanted to believe the eagerness in his kisses and the urgency of his fiery touches were born from love. She'd even let herself imagine him saying those words to her. Yet she wasn't that same naive girl who'd once been duped by promises and pretty words. Once Aimee and Kris had betrayed her, she'd closed her heart to believing and hoping she would ever be truly loved.

Her throat suddenly tight, she said, "What you've been saying to me these past several nights is that you enjoy having sex with me. That's something very different than love."

He pulled back far enough to study her face. "I understand the difference, Mariah. And I can assure you that what I feel for you isn't just—raw desire. Yes, I want you. Yes, it's thrilling to have sex with you. But what I'm feeling goes way beyond that."

Not daring to believe the conviction in his voice, she sat up in the bed and drew the sheet over her breasts. "I don't know what to say, Finn. I wasn't expecting anything like this from you."

He scooted to a sitting position and once he was facing her, reached for her hand. As he wrapped his fingers around hers, she tried to still her racing mind, but it was impossible. What was the matter with her? Why couldn't she listen to her heart, wrap her arms around him and tell him that she loved him with every fiber of her being?

"Mariah, I've thought about this over and over. What I feel for you isn't going to end. And I—well, I don't want us to ever be apart. I realize that the first day I was here I asked you to go back to Nevada with me. But I don't want that now."

Trembling now, she stared at him. "You don't? But why? What—"

Before she could finish, he reached for her other hand and drew her closer. "I want us to be married, Mariah. I want the three of us to make our home here."

Her mouth fell open as she forced herself to breathe. Him and her and Harry together as a family. It would be a dream come true. If she could only believe that weeks and months from now, he'd still be wanting her. That she'd be enough woman to keep him happy.

"I think—you're getting way ahead of yourself. You haven't thought this through, Finn. Not completely."

"What have I not thought through? Marrying you?" he asked wryly. "Or making my home here?"

"Both. We haven't known each other that long and—"

"Long enough," he interrupted. "I've had plenty of time to realize how much I love you. And this evening, after I read the DNA letter, it dawned on me that everything was coming together. That I couldn't wait to tell you how I feel."

Her heart was aching to believe every word he was saying. For days now she'd been wondering how she could possibly go on living once he and Harry moved to Nevada. But she'd been too cautious for too long to simply let herself fall into his arms and promise to marry him. She'd done that once before and ended up getting her heart stomped. But this time there was more than the risk of breaking her heart. Harry's welfare had to be considered, too.

"Finn, you're suffering a memory lapse. This ranch is up for sale. You just saw Mr. Larson looking things over this afternoon. He could decide at any moment to put money down and—"

"I want you to contact Ella Clark in the morning and tell her that you've changed your mind and you're not going to sell Stallion Canyon."

The shock of his words actually caused her to rear back. "Not sell? Finn, the ranch is going under!"

A patient smile curved the corners of his mouth. "Only because it needs someone with money and the experience to run it. I certainly fall into both those categories."

"But why? You already have a prestigious job—a fancy home back in Nevada. Your family and friends are there and—"

"But I want you to be my family, Mariah. You and Harry. The three of us here on Stallion Canyon. You've already said that Harry should eventually inherit this ranch. I can make that possible. Even though willing it to Harry might prove to be a problem later on," he added with a sly grin.

"What do you mean?"

"Our other children might feel like they deserve a part of the ranch, too."

Other children? Oh God, he was going too fast for her. She couldn't think beyond this moment. She hadn't yet been able to completely grasp the notion that he could possibly love her and want to marry her.

"So what about your family? Your work on the Silver Horn? You can just turn your back on all that and stay here? That would be a huge change for you, Finn."

His hands closed firmly over her shoulders. "For a long time I've been thinking I could never be truly happy unless I branched out on my own. This argument I've had with my father and grandfather about the mustangs has been going on for a long while. Now I actually own some of them. And this is the perfect place to raise them, to do the kind of work I've always dreamed about doing. Can't you see, Mariah? Everything is just perfect. All you have to do is tell me that you love me. That you want to marry me."

Perfect. Yes, she thought sickly. It was all too perfect. He couldn't take his mustangs home to the Silver Horn, so he'd decided that keeping them here and using this ranch for his personal plans would be far more convenient.

"I'm sorry, Finn. I can't."

Tears were already gathering at the back of her eyes as she quickly scooted away from him and swung her legs over the side of the bed.

She was pulling on her robe when she heard Finn leave the bed, then the faint rustle of clothing. The next instant, he was standing in front of her, wearing nothing but jeans and a deep frown on his face. And as Mariah's gaze wandered over his perfectly carved torso and the thick hank of hair falling over his blue eye, she wondered if she'd lost her mind.

To have this man as her husband, under any circumstances, would be enough to make most any woman happy. But for as long as she could remember, she'd settled for less. Aimee had been the one who'd been loved and adored by every male who'd gotten within speaking distance of the two sisters. While Mariah had been grateful for any crumbs of affection that were left over. But she was finished with being grateful. Of selling herself short.

"Can you give me one good reason?" he asked gruffly.

Lifting her chin, her gaze defiantly met his. "I want a man to marry me because he loves me. Not because it's convenient. Or gives him everything he wants in one neat little package. No thanks, Finn."

"Then you're turning me down flat?"

He sounded incredulous, and anger spurted through her. No doubt he'd figured she was so weak-minded and besotted with him that the idea of her refusing his proposal had never entered his mind.

"Not only am I turning you down, but I think you need to start making plans to leave here. The sooner, the better!"

A muscle jumped in his jaw and for a split second, Mariah would've sworn she saw pain shadow his eyes. But as he silently turned and left the room, she couldn't be sure about anything, except that her heart had just splintered into a pile of painful pieces.

Chapter Eleven

The next morning Finn made sure he was out of the house before Mariah appeared in the kitchen for coffee. It would've been unbearable to sit across from her at the breakfast table, sharing a morning meal as though they were still a couple.

A couple. Had they ever been truly that? he wondered dismally. He'd thought so. Ever since that night the filly had been born and the two of them had first made love, he'd believed something rich and real had happened between them. And last night, before he'd proposed to her, he'd been sure he felt love in her kisses, heard it in her sighs.

But now she wanted him gone. She wanted nothing to do with marrying him. She refused to consider the three of them making a home on this beautiful ranch. Why had she twisted his hopes and dreams? His plans for their future together?

I want a man to marry me because he loves me. Not because it's convenient. Or gives him everything he wants in one neat little package.

In spite of the long, miserable hours that had passed since she'd said those words to him, they were still echoing through him, tormenting him with frustration.

Oh God, why would she think he was using her just to get a ranch? Hell, all it took to get a piece of land was money. And he had plenty of that. He'd have no problem acquiring land for his mustangs. But he couldn't come up with another woman. Not one that he loved to distraction. Not one that he wanted to be with until his life on this earth was over.

So what are you going to do now, Finn? She's ordered you to leave. Maybe you ought to head back to the house and put up a persuasive argument.

The cynical voice in his head had him groaning as he paused beneath the shed row. If he had to argue and plead to get a woman to marry him, then she clearly wasn't the wife he needed.

A black rubber feed bucket was sitting at the gate to one of the stalls. Finn flipped it over and once he'd taken a seat, pulled out his cell phone. At this hour of the morning, Sassy had more than likely fed the kids and headed out to the barn.

His sister answered on the second ring, and the sound of her cheerful voice caused his heart to wince. She was the one person who seemed to truly understand him.

"Finn, how did you guess I was just about to call you?"

"I have telepathy with my sister. But I can't guess what you were going to call me about. You sound happy about something."

"Oh, I am! And you're going to be the first to hear. After Jett, that is. I'm pregnant!"

Her announcement almost had him forgetting his own problems. But not quite. Just the mention of the word had him envisioning Mariah carrying his child.

"Pregnant? Again? Are you kidding me?"

Sassy laughed. "Why, no. Why do you sound so amazed? You knew that Jett and I wanted a big family. This one will only be number three."

"Well, yes, I was aware that you two wanted more kids, but little Skyler was only born a few months ago! Don't you need a rest?"

His question brought another crow of laughter from her. "Me rest? Finn, I'll do that when I get old. Besides, Gypsy is a wonderful nanny. When I'm out working with the cattle or horses, I don't have to worry one second about the kids. I know she's taking care of everything."

Yes, Sassy had been lucky in finding the young Shoshone woman to care for her children. If only he could be that lucky in finding a nanny for Harry, Finn thought. Because it was quite obvious that Mariah wasn't going to be around to make sure his son had the care he needed.

"Well, if you and Jett are happy about the coming baby, then I'm thrilled, too."

"Awww, thanks, dear brother, I knew you'd be happy for me," she said with affection, then swiftly changed the subject. "So what were you calling about? You got news about the DNA?"

Oh Lord, it seemed like it had been days ago since he'd opened that letter, instead of last night. So much had happened that his head was still spinning. And his heart—well, the pain it was causing him was so excruciating it was indescribable.

"Last evening. I'm Harry's father, all right."

"Oh, Finn. That's wonderful. Are you happy about it?"

"I'm happy and relieved. I think I loved him from the moment I held him in my arms." He took a deep breath and let it out. "So we'll be coming home—probably tomorrow. That's why I'm calling. I need your help."

"Sure. Anything."

He looked over at the mares milling about in the paddock. The two that had already foaled were now out to pasture with their babies. The other three he'd kept confined so that he could keep a close watch on their progress.

"I've bought ten mustangs plus two new babies and I need to find a place to put them for a while. Until I can come up with a permanent spot to keep them. I thought—maybe you had a few acres I could use. That land on the north edge of your ranch is still empty, isn't it?"

"Yes, but there's no water there yet. Unless it rains. And God only knows when that might happen. But forget about that. You can use the section on the west side of the ranch. We don't have any cattle on it right now. And the windmill is in good working order. You might have to feed them a bit, but I think they'll find a little to graze on."

"But you might need that pasture soon, Sassy. Jett might not like the idea of me using it."

She laughed as though his suggestion was ludicrous. "I run the ranch. Jett runs his law office. Whatever decisions I make about the livestock or land are fine with him. Besides, he loves you. He'll be glad we could help."

Finn swallowed at the lump that had suddenly formed

in his throat. "Thanks, Sassy. I really appreciate it. What with Dad and Gramps—"

"You don't have to explain, Finn. You and I have talked about this before. Frankly, I'm really happy that you've taken this step. It's something you've always wanted to do. And you're going to do great with the mustangs. I just know it."

"Hearing you say that means a lot to me. Especially—"

He broke off as his gaze strayed toward the house. Now wasn't the time to explain his broken relationship with Mariah. Maybe later after he'd gotten back to Nevada, he could talk to Sassy about it.

"Especially, what?" she prompted when he didn't go on. "Is anything wrong, Finn? You don't exactly sound like yourself."

"I'm fine. What with getting Harry ready to go and making arrangements for the horses to be shipped, I have a lot to deal with."

"Dealing with a thousand things at once has always been easy for you, Finn. And you do it with a happy grin. But you don't sound exactly happy to me right now. Having a new son without any time to prepare to become a dad would be pretty overwhelming. If you need me to help, Finn, just tell me. Gypsy can handle one more baby…if you'd like to come stay with us for a while."

"Thanks, but no. I— My job is waiting on me at the ranch. And the sooner I get Harry settled in there, the better off we'll both be," he said flatly. "But there is something else you can do for me."

"Name it."

"Call Rafe and tell him I'll be heading home tomorrow. He can let the others know."

"Oh, you don't want to speak with your brother?" she asked thoughtfully.

"No."

There was a long pause and then she said, "Okay. I love you, Finn. See you when you get home."

"I love you, too, sis," he told her, then ended the call before she could guess the gruffness in his voice was actually the sound of his broken heart.

Later that morning, Mariah was in her father's old room, sitting at a desk where she kept all the ranch's paperwork. The bills stacked in front of her were enough to make her sick to her stomach. But her worry over the unpaid bills was minor compared to the misery she felt over Finn.

You brought it all on yourself. Instead of telling him you love him and want to marry him, you had to get all indignant and start accusing him of wanting this ranch more than he wants you. I hope your pride is worth this, Mariah.

Bending her head, she pressed fingertips to her closed eyelids and willed the mocking voice in her head to go away. She felt bad enough without it constantly reminding her that she'd ruined everything between them. As if anyone could ruin a fairy tale, she thought bitterly. Because that's all it had been. Just wishful dreaming on her part.

A light knock on the door brought her head up and she glanced around to see Finn standing in the open doorway. The sight of him caused everything inside her to go rigid with pain.

"Sorry to interrupt," he said flatly. "But there are a few things I need to discuss with you."

She rose to her feet. "We had our discussion last night," she said hoarsely. "There's nothing more to be said."

He walked into the room. "I'm not here to discuss any of that. We both said enough on the subject last night. I'm here to talk about Harry. I've informed my family that I'll be heading home tomorrow. Can you have his things ready to go by midmorning?"

If she hadn't been holding on to the back of her chair, Mariah felt sure she would have wilted to the floor. Her knees felt like wet sponges and her heart was beating a loud protest against her ribs.

"Yes. I'll have everything packed."

"Good. A livestock transporter will be here early in the morning to pick up the mustangs. So I plan to leave shortly after the horses do."

Tomorrow. He and Harry would be leaving tomorrow. She'd told him that the quicker he left, the better. He was giving her just what she'd asked for. The reality of it left her numb.

"What about the mares? Aren't you worried one of them might go into labor during the trip?"

His expression turned harder than granite. "You're not worried. Why should I be?"

She supposed she deserved that. But he ought to understand that the longer he remained here, the more difficult it would be for everyone.

"I wouldn't mind if you left them," she offered stiffly. "At least until they've foaled."

"No thanks. I want them with me."

So he'd already found a place to put the mustangs, she thought. She wanted to ask him where they'd be going, but if he'd wanted her to know that, he would have told her. Besides, the mustangs were no longer her worry. After tomorrow horses would never be a part of her life. Neither would Finn. As for Harry, an occasional visit with her little nephew would be the most she could hope for.

"I see. Well, I'll start getting Harry's things collected and packed. Do you think—uh, you can make the trip okay with him? I mean, traveling with a baby isn't easy."

He stared at her, his expression unflinching. "We'll make it fine," he said flatly. "Without you."

Tears burned her throat as she walked over to stand in front of him. "I'm sorry, Finn. That—things didn't work out."

"I'm sorry, too, Mariah. Damned sorry."

He turned and left the room and as Mariah watched him go, she had to fight the urge to run after him. He and Harry were everything to her. She didn't want them to go. But on the other hand, she wanted to be loved just for being her. Not because she owned a ranch or was a ready-made mother.

Maybe that kind of love would never come to her. But she had to hope and believe that someday it would.

An hour later, Mariah was in the nursery, packing Harry's toys into a cardboard box while on the other side of the room, Linda sat rocking Harry.

"Have you lost your mind, Mariah?"

Mariah frowned at the woman. "I feel very sane at the moment, thank you."

"Yeah, but how will you feel tomorrow? How will you feel when you see Harry and Finn drive away?"

Mariah's jaw tightened as she tried to steel herself against that heartbreaking image. "I'll feel like my life is taking on a new beginning."

"Like hell," Linda muttered. "You're going to be

crushed. You're going to realize what a mistake you're making."

The only mistake she'd made was in thinking Finn had taken her to bed because he really loved her. When all along, his main thoughts had been on this ranch and making it a home for a herd of mustangs.

Dear Lord, he'd turned out to be more like her father than she could've ever imagined. Her daddy had been a man who'd worn spurs and now Harry's daddy wore them, too. She supposed that was fitting. At least Aimee would've been happy about it. But for the past few days, Mariah had felt as though she'd truly become important to Finn. Much more important than a herd of mustangs and a piece of land.

"Linda, when Finn told me he loved me, I would have believed him—if he'd stopped right there. But in the next breath, he was saying he wanted this ranch and how perfect it would be for his mustangs. What am I supposed to think—feel?"

Linda's short laugh was mocking. "Mariah, listen to yourself. What do you think this ranch has been for the past twenty years? Your father put his heart and soul into this land to make it a great place to raise horses. You should be proud and happy that Finn can appreciate that."

Mariah picked up a little brown teddy bear with intentions of placing it in the box, but somehow it found its way to her chest, where she pressed it tight against her aching heart. "I don't have to tell you what it was like for me...with Dad. And Aimee. Stallion Canyon was their life, their love. I was just around. And then when things went wrong with Kris..." As her words trailed away, she shook her head. "It doesn't matter anymore. None of it matters."

Harry let out another fussy cry and Linda rose from the rocker and began to bounce the baby in her arms. "Is that why you don't care whether Finn takes Harry out of your life? Because he's actually Aimee's baby? Because Finn made love to Aimee before he made love to you?"

Whirling around, Mariah glared at her. "That's a low blow."

"I meant for it to be," she said sharply, then started toward the door. "I'll be in the kitchen putting some ice on Harry's gums."

Once Linda and Harry had disappeared, Mariah covered her face with both hands and sucked in several long breaths in an attempt to collect herself. But her effort did little to compose her ragged emotions. With a watery wall of tears blurring her vision, she finished packing Harry's things.

Two weeks later, Finn was sitting in his office, a small square room located inside the main horse barn on the Silver Horn Ranch. For the past hour he'd been staring at a catalog for an upcoming horse auction, trying to determine if any of the offered horses were something the Horn could use, but his heart wasn't in the effort.

Finally, he tossed aside the catalog and was scanning through the newspaper when his father knocked on the open door and stepped into the room.

At sixty-three, Orin Calhoun was still an imposing figure of a man. Tall and broad-shouldered, with thick iron-gray hair that waved away from his face, he was in top physical shape. He could outride and out-rope most of the hands on the Silver Horn, and he didn't let them forget it, either.

"Am I interrupting?" Orin asked.

Finn folded the newspaper and placed it to one side of the desktop. "Not at all. Just catching up on the news."

Orin sank into one of the straight-backed chairs sitting at an angle to Finn's messy desk. He cocked a brow at the newspaper, then looked directly at his son. "I didn't realize they printed news articles in the classifieds. I'll have to start reading that section of the paper, too. Just to make sure I don't miss anything," he said pointedly.

Finn bit back a sigh. Even though Orin had happily welcomed Finn back home, the strained words they'd exchanged over the mustangs were still standing between them. Once he'd informed his father that Sassy had given the horses a temporary home, Orin had dropped the subject completely. Even so, Finn wasn't fooled by the silence. Orin and his grandfather Bart were silently keeping an eye on anything and everything Finn had been doing since he returned from Stallion Canyon. And the notion irked him greatly.

"Actually, I was going through the real estate ads to see if there was any land I might be interested in buying."

Orin grimaced. "We have all the land we need here on the Silver Horn."

"It's not mine. It belongs to the family."

"And you're a part of this family, Finn. For a while there I was thinking you'd forgotten that. But now you're home and hopefully getting settled back in your old routine."

Two weeks. That's how much time had actually passed since Finn had driven away from Stallion Canyon. But it felt more like two hundred weeks since he'd last seen Mariah's lovely face.

There'd been a flood of tears in her eyes when she'd said good-bye to Harry that morning on the front porch of the ranch house. But she'd said nothing to Finn. In fact, she hadn't even looked at him. She'd walked back into the house and left him standing there like a hopeful fool.

Since then, Harry was slowly getting accustomed to his new surroundings, but he was clearly still missing Mariah. There'd been times these past couple of weeks when he'd cried for no reason and nothing seemed to make him happy. During those times the women of the house had tried their best to pacify him, but Harry wanted Mariah. He wanted his mother—the one thing Finn couldn't give him.

So far he hadn't attempted to hire a nanny. What with Lilly already being in the house watching over her two children, and Tessa, the young ranch-house maid, to help with Harry, the two women kept insisting he didn't need a nanny. And frankly, Finn was loath to start interviewing women for the position.

All along, he'd planned on Mariah being with him and the two of them caring for their son together. Now that those plans had been crushed, he didn't know where to begin or how to start feeling like a human being again, instead of a miserable fool.

"Things with the horses are slow now that foaling season is over," Finn replied.

"There's plenty of training for you to oversee," Orin told him. "And Dad and I have been talking about purchasing a new stallion for the ranch's working remuda. Blue Cat is getting on in years. We need to bring another stallion in before his fertility drops. And we'd like to hear your input on the bloodlines you think would fit."

Rimrock. He was the sturdy stallion this ranch needed. But Finn would be wasting his breath to make such a suggestion. Instead, he bit back a weary sigh and said, "Sure. I'll think on the matter."

He felt his father's gaze boring into him.

"I've never heard you sound so enthusiastic."

"Sorry. I guess I haven't had time to get back into the swing of things yet."

"You don't need time to do a job you normally could manage with both eyes closed. Is this about Harry? Are you thinking that having a baby son has cramped your style?"

Incensed, Finn stared at his father. "My style! You make it sound like I'm some sort of playboy or something. Hell, just because I had one brief fling with a woman! Even before I met Aimee, I rarely left this ranch for any reason. And that includes spending time with the opposite sex. So, no! Harry hasn't cramped anything. I love him dearly."

"Then it's something else. You're moping about those damned mustangs, aren't you? You're still angry with me and your grandfather because we don't want any part of them. Well, if it means that much to you, then bring the things over here and put them out on the far west range. Just make sure the fence is bull strong."

Finn rose from his chair and walked over to the doorway. As he stared down the alleyway of the huge horse barn, he realized that he could look in any direction and see the best of everything. Horses, equipment, facilities, and competent ranch hands. Here Finn didn't have to want for anything. But as thankful as he was, it wasn't quite enough. And that realization only served to make him feel worse.

"Thanks, but that's not what I want."

Finn heard his father stir from the chair and then his strong hand closed over his shoulder.

"I'm sorry, Finn. That didn't sound very sincere. And I—well, I didn't come out here to fight with you about the mustangs. Far from it. I can see how miserable you've been and I don't want that. I want my son to be happy. To hell with what your grandfather wants. Bring the mustangs home. It'll be fine with me and him—once I set him straight."

But that was just it, Finn thought. Home didn't feel the same to him anymore. Home was back on Stallion Canyon with Mariah. Holding her, kissing her and making love to her. He'd thought it would never end. Their meals together and the precious playtime they'd shared with Harry. Those hours and days had been burned into his memory. He couldn't shake them. And today he'd reached the decision that he didn't want to shake them. He wanted them back. But how to manage that miracle was still something he hadn't figured out.

"I don't want that, Dad."

"Finn, I—"

"I'm not angry," Finn gently interrupted. "And I do appreciate the offer. But I want a place of my own." He turned to look at his father and was surprised to see a wry acceptance on his face. "You've told me that when my great-grandfather started the Silver Horn he didn't own much and this place was just a ragged piece of desert. But he had a dream, a plan. And he went for it. I don't think it's wrong for me to want the same things he wanted."

Orin patted his shoulder with understanding. "No, son. It's not wrong. I'd hoped the Horn would be your lifelong calling. But ever since you returned from California, it's become obvious to me that you need more to make you completely happy. And that's what I want for you, Finn, to be happy. Even if it means I have to give you a loose rein. Whatever it takes, I want you to go for it."

"Yeah," Finn said softly. "Whatever it takes."

The following week Mariah was sitting cross-legged in the middle of the floor of Aimee's old bedroom. Boxes of clothes, photos, horsemanship ribbons and trophies, and other souvenirs were scattered here and there, while a few books and stuffed animals were piled directly in front of her.

At the moment, Mariah's thoughts were lost in the past as she held a tiny gold locket in her palm. It was one of the last pieces of jewelry she'd seen her sister wear. At the time Mariah hadn't taken much notice of the necklace. Aimee had always had piles of inexpensive fashion jewelry lying around. But now as she opened up the little locket and found a tiny picture of Finn inside, an overwhelming sense of loss and bitterness swept over her. Maybe her sister had actually cared about Finn, she thought. In any case, he'd deeply affected both of their lives.

"Mariah? Are you home?"

The sudden sound of Linda's voice calling out to her had Mariah snapping the locket shut and dropping the piece into her shirt pocket. "In here, Linda. In Aimee's old room."

Moments later, the woman appeared in the open

doorway. "What a mess!" she exclaimed. "What are you doing dragging out all this stuff? Haven't you had enough to cry over here lately without getting into Aimee's things?"

Mariah sighed. "I've been putting off sorting through my sister's things, but I decided I can't keep doing that. Whenever I leave here and start living in an apartment I won't have room to keep Aimee's stuff. I'm going to pick out a few pieces to keep and give the rest to charity."

Linda entered the room and sank onto the edge of the queen-size bed. Mariah rose to her feet and dusted off the backside of her jeans.

"Sorry about the mess," Mariah told her. "Want to go to the kitchen for coffee?"

"In a bit." Gesturing toward the things on the floor, Linda asked, "So other than this project have you been keeping yourself occupied?"

Since Harry and Finn had left, she'd only seen her friend a couple of times. Once when Linda had attended graduation ceremonies at the high school where Mariah was employed. The second time had been about a week ago when the two women had inadvertently spotted each other in the produce section of a local supermarket.

"As best as I can now that school is out. And the house is—well, like a tomb with Harry not around. I can't even bear to walk into the nursery. It's still the same as it was the day that Finn and Harry left," she finished woefully. "What about you? How does it feel not to be a nanny to Harry anymore?"

Linda grimaced. "I hate it. Just like I hate the thought of you moving away from here. Have you heard more from that Clark woman? Is anyone getting closer to buying?"

Mariah shook her head. "No. As far as I know the man who came out for a look at the place has momentarily cooled his heels about buying. Ms. Clark keeps reminding me that the lending rules on mortgages are much stricter than they used to be. And the real estate market is still a little slow in our area. She tells me I need to be patient."

Linda let out a breath of relief. "Thank God! Maybe you'll come to your senses before a buyer shows up."

Groaning, Mariah picked up one of the boxes of clothing and sat it on the end of the bed. "Get real, Linda. Right now there's a stack of bills on the end of the bar just waiting to be mailed. But I can't do anything with them until my paycheck goes into the bank. And then hopefully there will be enough left over to buy groceries and gasoline for the car."

"Everyone has a sob story, Mariah. You think you have a corner on hard times?"

Linda's cutting remarks were so unlike her that Mariah was momentarily stunned. She dropped the sweater she'd plucked out of the box. "What in heck is wrong with you?"

Linda raised back up to a sitting position. "It disgusts me to see you losing everything that was ever important in your life, while you just stand around doing nothing about it."

Mariah walked around to the side of the bed and took a seat a short space from Linda. "What am I supposed to do about it? Harry is Finn's child, not mine. I had no right to keep him here."

"I wasn't just talking about Harry. But now that you've mentioned him, how is he? Has anyone been keeping you informed?"

"Not Finn, if that's what you're getting at," she said glumly. "His sister-in-law, Lilly, has been seeing after Harry and she's called me a few times. She says he's getting adjusted. And his tooth finally broke through. The first one. I kept hoping that would happen before he left. But—"

Her throat too choked to go on, she bent her head and tried to swallow away the burning pain.

"Here. None of that," Linda gently scolded. "Let's go to the kitchen. I'll make some coffee while you pull yourself together."

Out in the kitchen, Mariah took a seat at the bar and waited for Linda to brew the coffee. By the time the other woman joined her, Mariah was able to accept the cup of coffee and give her friend a lopsided smile.

"Thanks. And sorry about all the whining. I've been telling myself I'm not going to be doing any more of it, but—I'm still having my moments. And going through Aimee's things hasn't made matters any easier."

Linda sighed. "Aimee was irresponsible and most of the time I wanted to smack her and tell her to wake up. But I loved her. With everything inside me I wish she was still alive."

"I wish that same thing, too," Mariah murmured thoughtfully. "Except that—well, it would be hard for me to see her and Finn married and raising Harry together. That's awful of me, isn't it?"

Linda shook her head. "Trust me, Mariah, if your sister was still living she and Finn wouldn't be married. She was hardly his type."

"She must've been his type," Mariah argued. "They had a child together."

"It hardly takes a long-term relationship to make a

child. No, he would've figured Aimee out very quickly. Now you, Mariah, are a different matter. I saw the way Finn looked at you. I've never seen so much adoration in any man's eyes."

"I don't want to talk about Finn. It—hurts too much."

"Maybe you need to hurt. Long and hard. Maybe then you'll realize how wrong you were to send him away."

Confused, Mariah look at the older woman. "Why are you being so mean to me today?"

"I'm not being mean. I'm trying to wake you up— before it's too late."

Mariah stared at the brown liquid in her cup. "Oh, Linda, don't you think I've been asking myself over and over if I was wrong? If I should've trusted Finn completely? There are moments when I think I must have been crazy to send him away. And then others when I realize I was right to stand up for myself, my feelings. But even that doesn't make me feel any better now. Having Finn and Harry gone is making me ache all the way to my bones."

Linda placed her coffee cup on the bar, then turned to Mariah. "I think it's time I told you something. About your dad. And me."

Mariah's head came up. "What could Dad have to do with me and Finn? He's been gone for more than four years now."

"And I've grieved for the man every day of those years," Linda said bluntly.

Mariah continued to study the rueful expression on Linda's face. "I realize you loved him, too. Like a friend."

"No. That's where you're confused. I loved him like a woman loves a man. And Ray loved me. But all those years we could've been together—really together—were wasted. Because he wouldn't consider marriage. You see, your mother had crushed him in that aspect. He was afraid to try to be a husband again. Afraid to reach for the happiness he so deserved. I don't want that to happen to you, Mariah. I don't want the best years of your life to be wasted because of fear or pride or doubts."

Amazed at Linda's revelation, Mariah reached over and placed her hand on the woman's forearm. "I feel like a fool. It never dawned on me that you loved Dad in that way. I never realized that Dad loved you. I always thought you two were just very good friends. Now, I only wish—oh, Linda, you would've made him the perfect wife. And Aimee and I needed you—as a mother." She shook her head with regret. "You're right. Dad wasted so many years."

Leaning forward, Linda gently touched her hand to Mariah's cheeks. "You love Finn. Go to him. Tell him that, if nothing else. Then if it's meant for you to be together, it will happen."

Could Linda be right? Could there be a chance that Finn really loved her?

"Me go to him?" she asked dazedly.

Linda gave her a wry smile. "You're the one who sent him away."

Go to Nevada and face Finn? What would she tell him? How could she make him understand that all she'd ever wanted was his love? She didn't know. She only knew she had to try.

Rising to her feet, she wrapped her arms around the other woman. "I love you," she said thickly.

Linda patted her back. "Ray would be proud of you. And so am I."

Chapter Twelve

Two days later, Finn stood next to his sister as they gazed across an open section of the J Bar J. A few yards away, his herd of mustangs was grazing on the summer grasses that were currently flourishing after a flurry of unexpected rain showers had hit the area.

"The babies are sturdy little things," Sassy said as one paint colt kicked up his heels and began to run circles around his mother. "Look at that. He thinks he belongs on the racetrack."

Finn grunted with amusement. The sight of the babies was bittersweet. They were all safely born now. And all growing like weeds. He was proud of his expanding herd. And at one time, he'd believed Mariah had been proud, too. But he'd been wrong about her feelings for the horses. And her feelings for him.

"That guy won't be going to a track. But he might

turn into a nice roping horse." He glanced at Sassy. "Just bear with me, sis. I promise you'll have your pasture back soon. Tomorrow I'm going to look at some land east of here. Actually, it's not far from Grandma and Grandpa Reeves. It might not be exactly what I need, but I'll know when I see it."

Sassy wrapped her hands around his upper arm and gave it a hard yank. "I've told you over and over, Finn. There's no hurry. In fact, I'm loving having them here. You wouldn't want to sell them to me, would you?"

He rolled his eyes at her. "Not hardly. Maybe when I get a big herd I'll give you a few. How's that?"

She pressed her cheek against his arm. "I might just take you up on that, brother. But in the meantime, what is Dad saying about this step you're taking to get a place of your own?"

"He's coming around. Gramps isn't happy about it. But he won't say much. What can he say? I'm thirty-two years old."

Sassy stepped back and gave him a long, searching look. "Well, I'm glad you're going on with your plans. But to be honest, you look awful, Finn. In fact, I've never seen you looking so drawn and—well, sad. I'm worried about you. And so is Jett."

Finn grimaced. Since he'd come home from California he'd tried his best to return to normal, to be the same happy-go-lucky guy he'd been before he'd met Mariah and his son. But nothing felt the same. He was a different man now. And though he wanted to believe he'd changed for the better, he actually felt like a gullible fool. He'd let one Montgomery sister seduce him, then he'd turned right around and let the second sister snag a hold of his heart.

"Guess my acting ability needs work. I thought I was putting on a pretty good show of being happy. Not convincing enough, huh?"

Sassy shook her head. "Not even a little."

Taking her by the arm, he urged her in the direction of the truck. "We'd better get back to the house. Gypsy is going to be pulling her hair out trying to see after three kids."

Sassy walked a few steps with him, then stopped. "Gypsy could handle five kids if need be. And we're going to stand right here in the middle of the pasture until you tell me what's going on. Is it Harry's aunt? Are you feeling guilty or something about taking Harry from her?"

With a painful groan, Finn looked toward the sky. There wasn't a cloud to be seen and the sun was hot on his face. Normally this was the kind of day that made him want to jump a fence or sing at the top of his lungs. Instead, he felt as though the heavy weight in his heart would never lift.

"Or something," he muttered. "I don't want to talk about her. Or California. Or anything about it. I have Harry now. It's over and done with."

His pretty redheaded sister folded her arms against her chest in a stance of defiance. "Too bad if you don't want to talk. There was a time a few years ago when I didn't want to talk, either. I was pregnant and afraid—especially afraid that no one in the Calhoun family really wanted me around. And Jett—I couldn't believe that a man like him might really love me. You forced me to talk about those things, and if you hadn't—well, I shudder to think that I might have turned my back on this wonderful life I have now."

His expression softened as he studied her face. Several years ago, no one in the Calhoun family had known Sassy existed. But she'd come here from New Mexico on a hunch. Someone had told her that she looked like Finn and she'd wondered if there was some sort of connection between her and the Calhoun family. The moment he'd first laid eyes on her, Finn had been certain she was his sister, and he'd fought to get the truth revealed.

In doing so, he and Sassy had opened up a dark family secret. Not only had the Calhoun brothers learned that Orin had been unfaithful to their mother, they'd also learned their grandfather Bart had schemed to keep the affair and Sassy's birth a secret. But time had a way of sweeping things into the past. Orin and Bart had been forgiven and Sassy had become a cherished member of the family.

"That's true," Finn admitted. "I did force you to open up and face things that I'm not sure I would've been brave enough to face. I even talked you into the DNA test. And if I bullied you a bit, I'm not sorry. I have my sister now."

"And your sister wants you to be happy. So talk. What is the problem with Mariah?"

Frowning, he turned and stared hollowly at the herd of horses. "She isn't the problem. I guess I am. I made a fool of myself. I proposed to her—believing that she loved me. She turned me down. And—well, after that she wanted me to leave Stallion Canyon as soon as I could. So I did. I got Harry and my horses and came home."

"But now this doesn't feel like home to you anymore. Right?"

Finn turned back to his sister. "How did you know that?"

She smiled slyly. "Because once I met Jett, New Mexico didn't feel like home anymore to me."

"You're too smart, sis," he said glumly.

Stepping forward, she grabbed up his hand and squeezed it between both of hers. "I'm just a good guesser," she told him. "And I'm guessing that Mariah does love you. Otherwise, she wouldn't have made an issue of you leaving. Did she give you a reason for turning you down?"

Finn grimaced. "She believes I was after her ranch," he muttered, then shook his head with frustration. "And maybe I did botch the way I proposed to her. Maybe it was insensitive of me to mention the ranch at all. But it's where I wanted us to make our home. Was that so wrong?"

Sassy gave his hand a hard tug. "Finn, a woman wants to know that she's loved just for herself. You need to convince Mariah that you'd be happy to live with her anywhere. You would be, wouldn't you?"

He nodded soberly. "Nowhere on this earth would make me happy unless she was with me."

With a big smile, Sassy urged him into a walk. "Then you need to tell her that. And I don't mean pick up the phone and call her. You need to take her into your arms and show her."

He cast her a doubtful glance. "Do you think she'll listen?"

Sassy chuckled softly. "I'd be willing to bet twelve of my new calves against your mustangs that she'll listen."

Finn suddenly urged her into a faster walk back to the truck. "Come on, slowpoke. I've got to get to the Horn and start making arrangements to drive back to Alturas."

Laughing, Sassy turned loose of his hand and started

trotting the last few yards to the waiting pickup truck. "Thank God I have my brother back!"

Back on the Silver Horn, after Finn turned Harry over to Tessa, he hurried down to the horse barn to discuss his schedule with Colley, the Horn's head horse trainer and Finn's right-hand man.

As the two men stood outside the open doorway of Finn's office, Finn informed the rugged cowboy of his plans. "I'm not certain how long I'll be gone. Maybe just a day. Or it might be several. Either way I'll make sure Rafe and Dad keep in close touch with you."

"Don't worry about anything, Finn. We'll be working on the yearlings for the next few days. And Rafe wants us to rotate the remuda to another pasture. So we'll be doing that, too."

"Sounds good," Finn told him. "I'll see you when—"

Finn broke off as a flash of movement at the opposite end of the barn caught the corner of his eye. Glancing down the wide alleyway, he peered through the dim, dusty light. Beyond a stable hand pushing a wheelbarrow full of dirty shavings, a woman was walking in their direction. And she looked incredibly like Mariah.

"What's the matter?" Colley turned his head to follow Finn's stare. "Oh. Is she here to buy horses?"

For a moment, Finn wasn't sure he was going to be able to answer Colley's question. His throat had gone so tight he could scarcely breathe.

"Uh, no. That's Harry's aunt." He jerked his gaze back to the cowboy. "Would you excuse me, Colley? I'll talk to you later."

The man gave Mariah one last curious glance. "Sure, Finn. I'll be out with the yearlings."

Colley walked away while Finn stood where he was, watching in disbelief as Mariah came to a stop a few feet in front of him. She was wearing a white cotton sundress with pink and yellow flowers splashed over the full skirt. A pink silk scarf had been twisted into a tight cord and wrapped around her black hair to keep it off her face. She was the loveliest thing he'd ever seen in his life, and he suddenly prayed for the right words to come to him.

"Hello, Finn. I just came from the house. Tessa told me I could probably find you here at the barn. Am I interrupting anything?"

Only his whole life, he thought.

"No. That was my assistant. I'll finish my conversation with him later." He stepped toward her and his heart was suddenly pounding so hard he could hear a whooshing noise in his ears. "You must be here to see Harry. He's going to be happy to see you."

She moved closer and Finn folded his hands into fists to keep from reaching out and grabbing her. She looked so incredibly soft and womanly. And the sweet scent drifting from her called up all sorts of evocative memories.

"I do want to see Harry. But that's not why I came here today," she said.

Doubts and uncertainties were practically paralyzing him. His brain felt frozen, and even if the barn suddenly caught fire, he doubted he could move a muscle.

"Why are you here?" he finally managed to ask.

"You."

She'd spoken the word so lowly that he barely heard it. But it was enough to send a thrill of hope rushing through him. Or was he getting way ahead of himself?

Maybe she was here to tell him she wanted partial custody of Harry? But that didn't make sense. Not when she'd always insisted Harry needed to be with his father.

He gestured toward the open doorway behind him, all the while aware that two young grooms leading a pair of yearlings down the alleyway had stopped to stare at Mariah. It wasn't unusual for women to visit the horse barn. The Silver Horn probably sold more horses to women than men. But Mariah was different from those women. Seeing her in this dusty barn was like spotting a violet in the middle of a prickly pear patch.

"My office is right here," he told her. "We can talk in private."

She moved past him and stepped into the room. Finn followed right behind her and was amazed to find that his legs were trembling as though he'd just run several miles at a torrid pace.

"How did you get here? Drive?" he asked.

"Yes. I left early this morning," she said as he carefully shut the door behind him. "I'm sorry about showing up without warning. I started to call. But I was afraid you might tell me not to come."

He walked over to his desk and rested a hip on one corner. She continued to stand awkwardly in the middle of the room and Finn could only wonder how she would react if he closed the short distance between them and pulled her into his arms. Would she remind him that their lovemaking had ended back at Stallion Canyon?

"Why would you think I'd do that?" he asked.

She made a helpless gesture with her hands. "We—uh—didn't exactly part on pleasant terms."

He swallowed as his mind was suddenly consumed with the pain he'd endured these past weeks. Losing her had turned his skies gray. He wanted to see the sun again. He wanted to believe that the magic they'd shared on Stallion Canyon had never died.

"No. There was nothing pleasant about leaving you or Stallion Canyon," he confessed. "So what are you going to say now? That I'm still after your ranch?"

"If I truly believed that I wouldn't be here."

His gaze locked with hers and before he knew it, he was crossing the small space between them and wrapping his hands around her shoulders.

"I don't know why you're here, Mariah," he said hoarsely. "But I have to tell you—"

"Wait, Finn!" She touched her fingertips to his cheek. "Before you say anything, I have to tell you—I'm here because I love you. I should've told you that from the very beginning. But I was mixed up and so afraid."

"Afraid? Oh, Mariah, there wasn't any reason for you to be afraid. Not of me."

Her head moved back and forth as tears began to fill her eyes. "It wasn't you, Finn. I was doubting myself. When you told me you loved me—that you wanted for us to get married—I couldn't believe it. You see, I've always thought of myself as the forgotten daughter—the second-best sister. Compared to Aimee I was the quiet wallflower who rarely got noticed."

He gave her shoulders a gentle shake. "That's ridiculous, Mariah. You're a beautiful, intelligent woman with so much to offer. I'm sure there have been plenty of guys who'd give their eyeteeth to date you."

Her gaze slipped to the middle of his chest and Finn could suddenly see the raw vulnerability on her features. The sight made his heart ache, made him want to wrap her in a tight hold and shield her from every hurtful thing in the world.

"A few," she said quietly. "But once they met Aimee I was usually forgotten."

"That's hard for me to believe."

"I imagined it would be. That's why I never said anything. But now I have to tell you how things were back then. So that maybe you'll understand."

"Tell me what?" he urged.

She sighed. "The reason why my engagement ended all those years ago. You see, when I met Kris during my college studies, I thought he was different. When he proposed and gave me a beautiful engagement ring, I thought finally someone loved me just for being me."

"But something happened."

Nodding, she said, "We were about to set the date for the wedding when Aimee started insisting she couldn't let me make a mistake. She kept telling me Kris was no good. Which didn't make sense. When we'd first gotten engaged, she'd thought he was a great catch for me. I finally demanded that she explain herself and that's when she admitted that she'd been sleeping with Kris. That she'd seduced him as a test to determine whether he was going to be faithful to me and he'd failed."

Finn felt sick. "Oh God, Mariah, I can't imagine what that must've done to you. But I'm guessing that you forgave your sister. You have that kind of heart. It's why I fell in love with you."

She let out a long breath and lifted her gaze back to him. Tears were still in her eyes and as she tried to blink them away, they dropped like wet diamonds onto her cheeks. "Yes, I forgave her. But I couldn't forget. After that, I couldn't trust her. And I especially couldn't trust another man. So when you started talking about love and marriage—it all came crashing at me."

He nodded glumly. "And I'd already had a brief affair with Aimee. And had a baby with her. You must've been feeling like you were my second choice."

Hope suddenly lit her gray eyes. "Then—you do understand?"

Groaning, he pulled her into his arms and pressed his cheek against the top of her head. "I do now," he murmured.

"Oh, Finn, I've been so miserable without you. I've been moping about, wondering how I could go on without you and Harry."

"What made you finally decide to drive down here?"

"You can give Linda the credit for opening my eyes. She convinced me I'd be making a huge mistake if I let you get away from me."

The joy surging through Finn couldn't be contained, and for the first time since they'd parted, he was able to put a genuine smile on his face. "I wasn't going to get away from you, my darling. When you walked up a few minutes ago, I was explaining to Colley that I was leaving for California in the morning."

Her head reared back as she stared wondrously up at him. "For California! To see me?"

He laughed at her dismay. "Yes. To see you. Sassy did some convincing with me, too. She told me I'd be a fool if I didn't do something to win you back." Pressing his lips to her forehead, he said, "I'm so sorry, Mariah. I made such a mess of things that night when I proposed. Nothing about it was right. I shouldn't have mentioned the ranch. I shouldn't have said anything—except that I love you and want you to be my wife. It doesn't matter where we live. As long as we're together."

With a rueful shake of her head, she reached up and tenderly cradled his face with both hands. "No, Finn. You didn't make a mess of things," she said huskily. "Everything you said was right—and beautiful. I was just too blinded with self-doubt to let myself see the love on your face. Can you forgive me?"

"I already have. Now, tell me, are you going to marry me?"

Smiling, she slipped her arms around his waist and pressed herself tight against him. "Yes. As soon as you'd like."

"How about tomorrow?" he asked excitedly. "We can drive down to Vegas, get married, and catch a plane to anywhere you'd like for our honeymoon."

"Tomorrow? I don't have a dress with me. Except the one I have on."

"As far as I'm concerned you look perfect in it. But I'll buy you a dress for the wedding. I'll buy you a dozen dresses and whatever else you'll need while we're away."

"Hmm. That's quite an offer," she said slyly, her eyes gleaming. "And I can choose where we go on our honeymoon?"

"That's right. Hawaii, Europe, Australia, anywhere. Just name it."

"All right, since you're letting me choose, what would you say about us going back to Stallion Canyon?"

Uncertain, he stared at her. "Are you serious?"

She nodded. "I'm very serious. Now that the three of us are going to be living there as a family, Stallion Canyon is going to be a new and exciting place for us.

Can you think of a better place for us to go for a honeymoon?"

For a moment Finn was so overwhelmed with emotion he couldn't speak. All he could do was press her head against his chest, stroke her hair and savor the amazing joy filling his heart.

"I don't deserve you, my darling," he finally managed to whisper. "But I promise that you will always come first in my life. You and our children. The horses, the land, the ranch, they'll be a distant second. You do believe that, don't you?"

"I do," she said, then tilting her head back, she smiled impishly up at him. "But I won't mind you proving it from time to time."

"Mmm. What a pleasure that will be."

Bending his head, he kissed her. A kiss that bound their future together. A future that spread before them like a bright, beautiful sunrise.

"Finn, what—"

Finn's head jerked up, and over Mariah's head, he saw his father standing in the doorway. From Orin's expression, he was clearly shocked to find his son with a woman in his arms.

"Sorry for the interruption," Orin said awkwardly. "I'll come back later."

"Don't go," Finn said quickly. "You've actually shown up at a great time."

His expression full of questions, Orin entered the room and Mariah stepped out of Finn's arms to face her future father-in-law.

"Dad, this is Mariah," Finn explained. "She's just agreed to marry me."

Mariah quickly walked over and extended her hand to Orin. "It's nice to finally meet you, Mr. Calhoun."

Pressing her hand between his, he gave Finn a crooked grin. "I can see what you've been pining for now." He turned his attention back to Mariah. "Welcome to the family, Mariah. I've no doubts that you and Finn will be very happy."

"Very happy," Mariah agreed, then glanced coyly at Finn. "Raising mustangs."

Moving up behind her, Finn wrapped his arm around Mariah's shoulder and drew her close to his side. "And babies," Finn added. "Let's not forget those."

"I doubt you'll let me forget that part of our bargain," she teased.

Orin shot Finn a perceptive look. "Besides giving me more grandchildren, I have a feeling my new daughter-in-law is going to change my mind about those damned wild horses."

Laughing softly, she said, "I'll be disappointed if you don't come visit us often, Mr. Calhoun."

"I'm not Mr. Calhoun," he told her. "Call me Dad. We're going to be family."

She smiled at Orin, then looked up at Finn. Her eyes were glittering with happy tears.

"Yes," she murmured. "One big family. For always."

Epilogue

Six months later, on a cold November night, Finn and Mariah were in the kitchen of Stallion Canyon's ranch house, preparing for tomorrow and the big Thanksgiving meal they planned to share with some of Finn's family. The smell of baking pumpkin pies filled the room, and holiday music played softly on the radio. While Mariah stood at the cabinet counter peeling boiled eggs to put into the dressing, Finn washed a sink full of pots and pans. Across the room, Harry, who'd been walking for the past two weeks, was squealing with delight as he tried to keep up with a collie pup.

Mariah placed the last egg into an airtight container before she glanced over her shoulder at Harry. The toddler had managed to catch the collie, or the pup had simply tired of the game of tag. Presently, boy and dog were now cuddled together on a braided rug near the breakfast bar.

"You made our son one happy little boy when you brought that puppy home to him," she told Finn. "Look, he's stroking Samson's head exactly how you showed him."

"Naturally," Finn said proudly. "He's a smart little boy. And our next son will probably be brilliant, too."

Smiling, Mariah's hand slipped to the growing mound of her waistline. A month after she and Finn were married, she'd gotten pregnant. Now that she was five months along, Finn was already making plans to turn one of the larger bedrooms in the house into a nursery big enough to hold Harry and the new baby.

"You don't know if this one is a boy," she reminded her husband. "Remember, we didn't want the doctor to tell us. It's going to be a surprise."

"I confess. I called him a few days ago without you knowing and asked him to spill the beans," Finn teased. "The baby is going to be a boy."

Mariah chuckled as she placed a stalk of celery on a chopping board. "You're telling a whopper. And what are you going to say when the baby turns out to be a girl?"

He gave her a broad grin. "Yippee! That's what I'll say. And right now I say you've been on your feet for too long. You need to sit."

"I have a few more things to do here first," she protested. "And I feel fine."

He stepped over and took her by the arm. "Don't argue. You can finish things here in the kitchen after you rest a few minutes."

With Harry and the puppy leading the way, they made their way to the living room, where Finn guided Mariah over to a big stuffed armchair. Once she'd sunk into the soft leather, he propped her feet on a matching footstool.

"There. Comfy now?" he asked.

She patted the wide armrest of the chair. "I'll be even more comfy if you sit down here beside me."

"Okay. For a minute. And then I'm going to go make you a cup of hot chocolate. You need the extra milk."

She let out a good-natured groan. "Finn, you fuss over me more than you do your pregnant mares."

Leaning over her, he slid his forefinger beneath her chin. "You're number one to me. Didn't I promise that you'd always be number one?"

Tilting her head back, she smiled dreamily up at him. "Yes. And you've kept your promise."

She reached for his hand and drew it to her lips. The past six months of being Finn's wife had changed her life in the most wonderful way. Harry was happy and healthy. Their new baby was coming soon and Finn was slowly and surely building Stallion Canyon into the ranch he'd always wanted. He'd made several profitable sales in the past couple of months, but he'd used most of that to purchase more of the wild horses in order to keep building the herd.

Seeing the ranch return to a thriving business had lifted Mariah's spirits more than she could've ever guessed, and she thanked God every day that a buyer hadn't come along before she and Finn had married. As for her teaching job, she was still enjoying being in the classroom on a daily basis. And with Linda more than glad to help her with Harry and the coming baby, she didn't see any reason to give up a job that was an important part of her life.

She let out a contented sigh. "We haven't had a big Thanksgiving dinner in this house for several years. It's wonderful to be celebrating again. And I'm so excited about Dad and Rafe and his family coming tomorrow to spend a few days with us. I only wish Sassy and Jett could come with them."

"With Sassy's baby due any day now it wouldn't be safe for her to travel. But she promises to come soon and bring the whole brood with her. I'll have to erect bunk beds in the big bedroom to sleep them all," he joked. "Or maybe I should forget the bunk beds and send them all out to the barn to sleep on the hay."

They both laughed before Finn looked over to make sure Harry and Samson weren't getting into trouble.

"Look at those two," Finn said softly. "I think they're going to be the best of buddies."

Mariah glanced over to see Harry and the puppy curled up together, asleep on the rug in front of the fireplace. The precious sight put a smile in her heart. "I'll get a blanket and cover them," she said. "It's warm there in front of the fire, but just in case there's a draft on the floor."

Before she could rise, Finn put a hand on her arm and rose to his feet. "I'll do it. I'm going after the hot chocolate anyway."

Minutes later he returned from the kitchen to find Mariah staring out the window at the frosty night.

"What are you thinking?" he asked softly as he knelt next to her chair and handed her the mug of hot chocolate.

A wistful smile touched the corners of her lips. "Actually, I was thinking of Aimee."

"Oh. I hope you're not about to get sad on me. Thanksgiving is supposed to be a joyful time. A time to appreciate all our blessings."

"I'm not getting sad. I was remembering some of the nice times we had together as sisters growing up.

Dad gave us a puppy once, too. She looked almost like Samson. We adored her." She sipped the hot drink, then glanced gratefully at Finn. "Aimee was a troubled young woman. But I loved her in spite of everything."

He gave her shoulder a loving squeeze. "I made a big mistake by getting involved with her. But on the other hand I can't regret it. If not for Aimee, I wouldn't have Harry. I would've never met you, my darling wife. And our new baby wouldn't be on the way. Strange as it seems, we owe her for bringing us together."

"That's true," Mariah said. "And tomorrow I think we should light a special candle for Aimee. She might just be able to see it. After all, it is a time for giving thanks."

Finn leaned over and softly kissed her lips. "And I'm thankful every day that I have you and our son, my love."

* * * * *

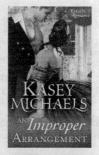

Don't miss Sarah Morgan's
next Puffin Island story

Some Kind of Wonderful

Brittany Forrest has stayed away from Puffin Island
since her relationship with Zach Flynn went bad.
They were married for ten days and only just
managed not to kill each other by the
end of the honeymoon.

But, when a broken arm means she must return,
Brittany moves back to her Puffin Island home.
Only to discover that Zac is there as well.

Will a summer together help two lovers reunite or
will their stormy relationship crash on to the
rocks of Puffin Island?

Some Kind of Wonderful
COMING JULY 2015
Pre-order your copy today

MILLS & BOON®

Cherish™

EXPERIENCE THE ULTIMATE RUSH OF FALLING IN LOVE

A sneak peek at next month's titles...

In stores from 17th July 2015:

- **The Texas Ranger's Bride** – Rebecca Winters *and*
  His Unforgettable Fiancée – Teresa Carpenter

- **The Boss, the Bride & the Baby** – Judy Duarte *and*
  Return of the Italian Tycoon – Jennifer Faye

In stores from 7th August 2015:

- **Do You Take This Maverick?** – Marie Ferrarella *and*
  Hired by the Brooding Billionaire – Kandy Shepherd

- **A Will, a Wish...a Proposal** – Jessica Gilmore *and*
  A Reunion and a Ring – Gina Wilkins

Available at WHSmith, Tesco, Asda, Eason, Amazon and Apple

Just can't wait?
Buy our books online a month before they hit the shops!
visit www.millsandboon.co.uk

These books are also available in eBook format!